VOLUME 02

USAGI YOJIMBO™ ORIGINS

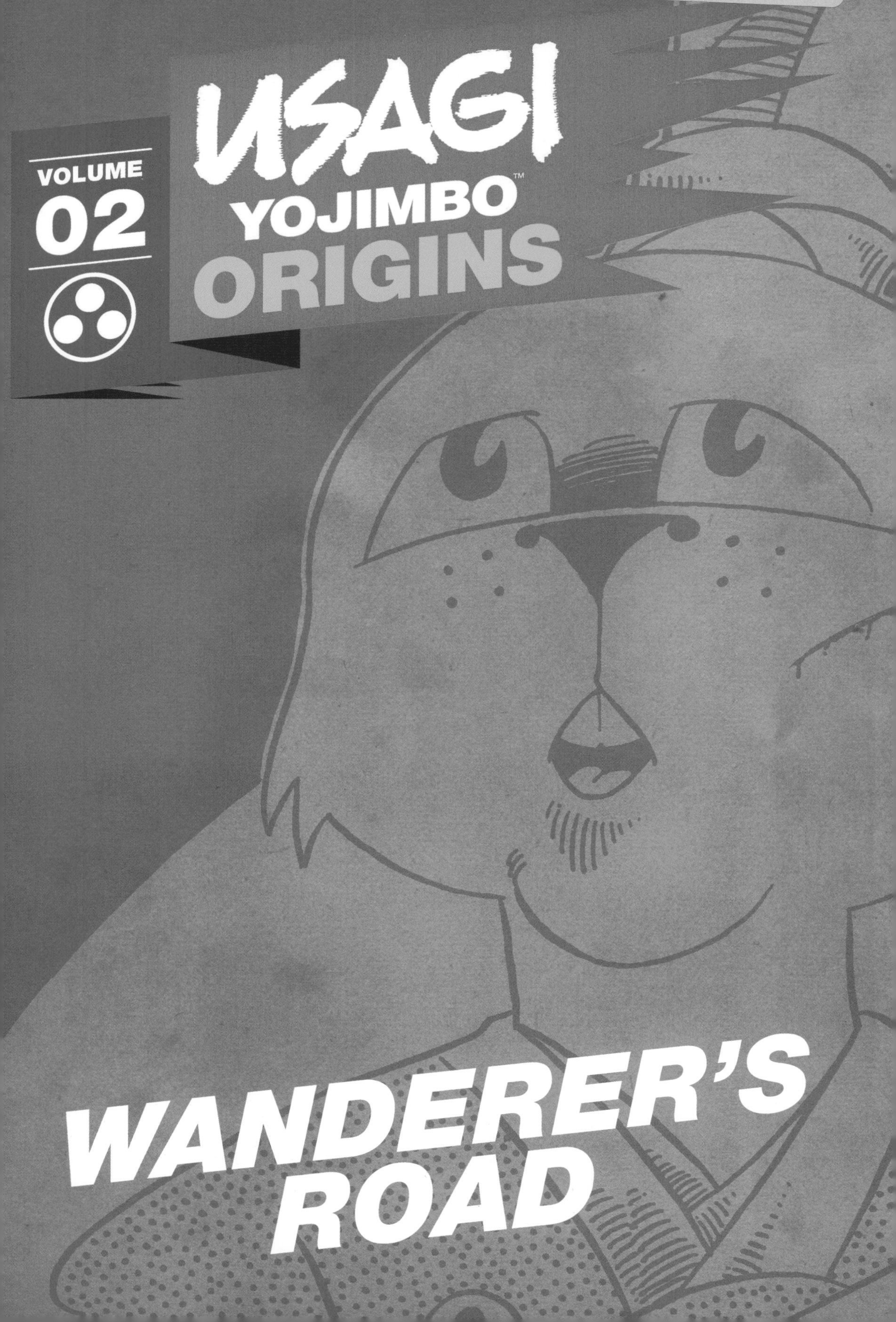

WANDERER'S ROAD

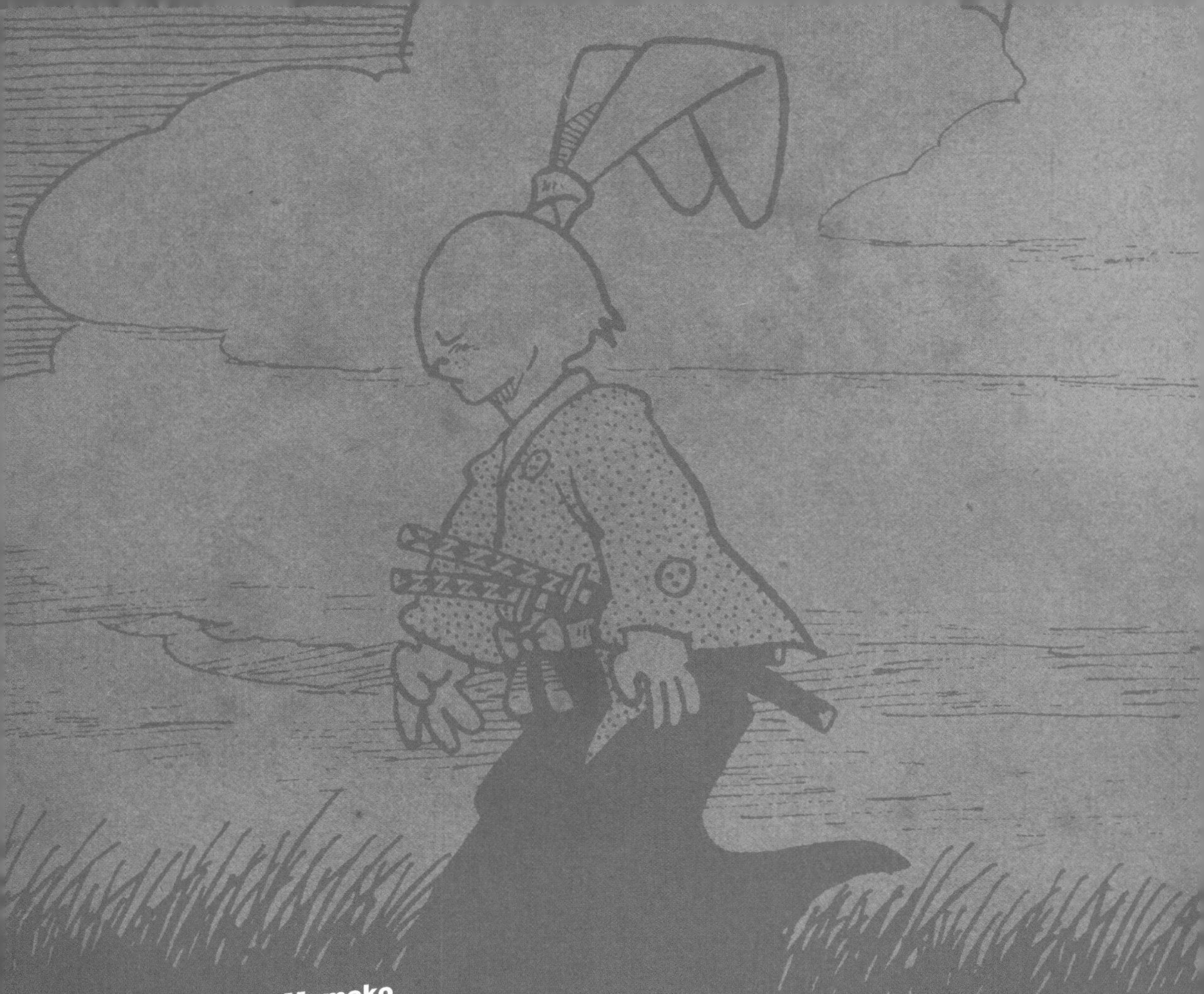

Cover Artist: **Peach Momoko**
Series Editor: **Bobby Curnow**
Collection Editors: **Alonzo Simon** and **Zac Boone**
Collection Designer: **Shawn Lee**

Nachie Marsham, Publisher | Blake Kobashigawa, VP of Sales
Tara McCrillis, VP Publishing Operations | John Barber, Editor-in-Chief
Mark Doyle, Editorial Director, Originals | Erika Turner, Executive Editor
Scott Dunbier, Director, Special Projects | Mark Irwin, Editorial Director, Consumer Products Manager
Joe Hughes, Director, Talent Relations | Anna Morrow, Sr. Marketing Director
Alexandra Hargett, Book & Mass Market Sales Director | Keith Davidsen, Senior Manager, PR
Topher Alford, Sr Digital Marketing Manager | Shauna Monteforte, Sr. Director of Manufacturing Operations
Jamie Miller, Sr. Operations Manager | Nathan Widick, Sr. Art Director, Head of Design | Neil Uyetake, Sr. Art Director Design & Production | Shawn Lee, Art Director Design & Production | Jack Rivera, Art Director, Marketing

Ted Adams and Robbie Robbins, IDW Founders

ISBN: 978-1-68405-843-3 | 24 23 22 21 1 2 3 4

Originally published by IDW as USAGI YOJIMBO: WANDERER'S ROAD issues #1–6.

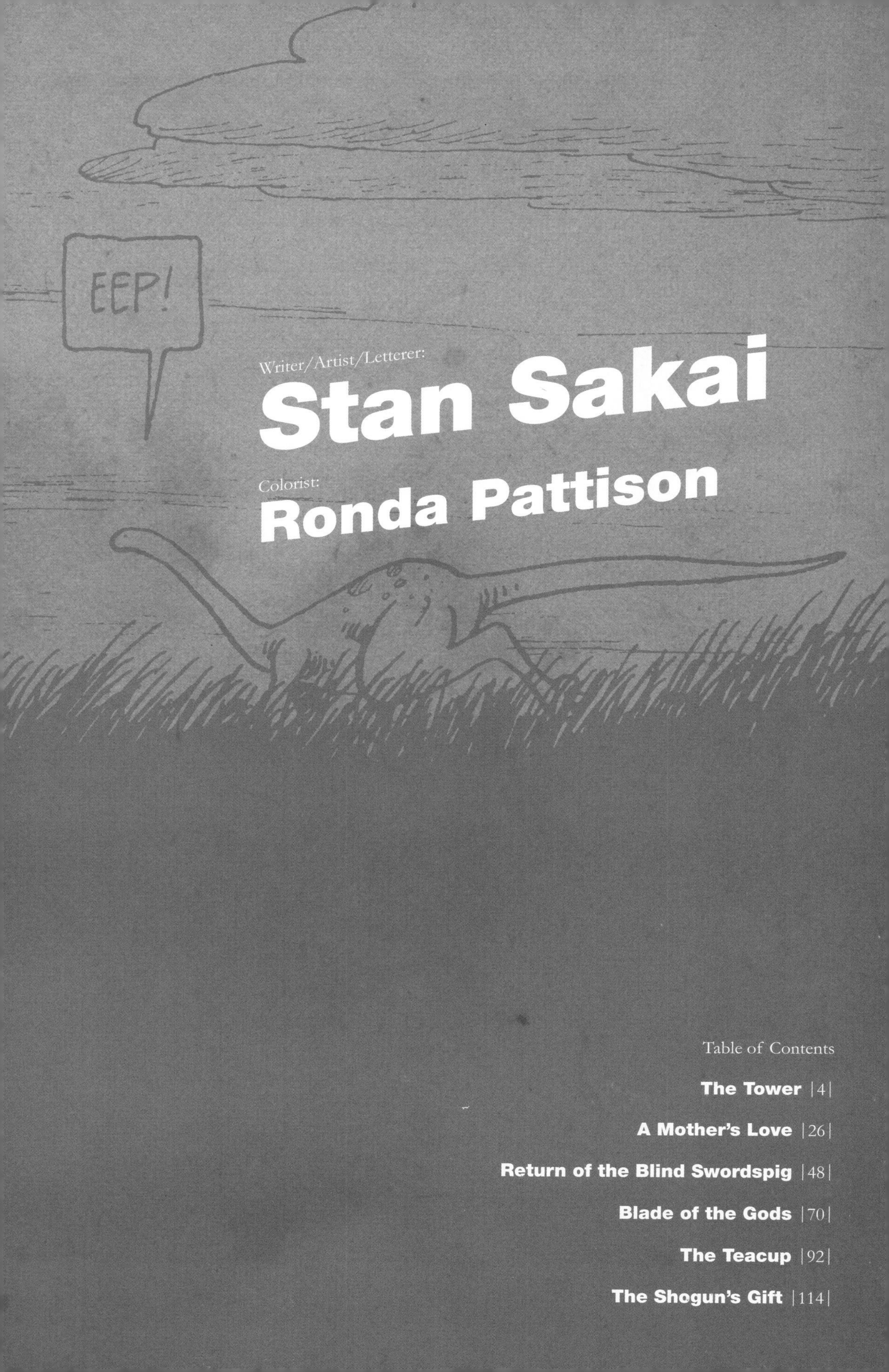
EEP!

Writer/Artist/Letterer:

Stan Sakai

Colorist:

Ronda Pattison

Table of Contents

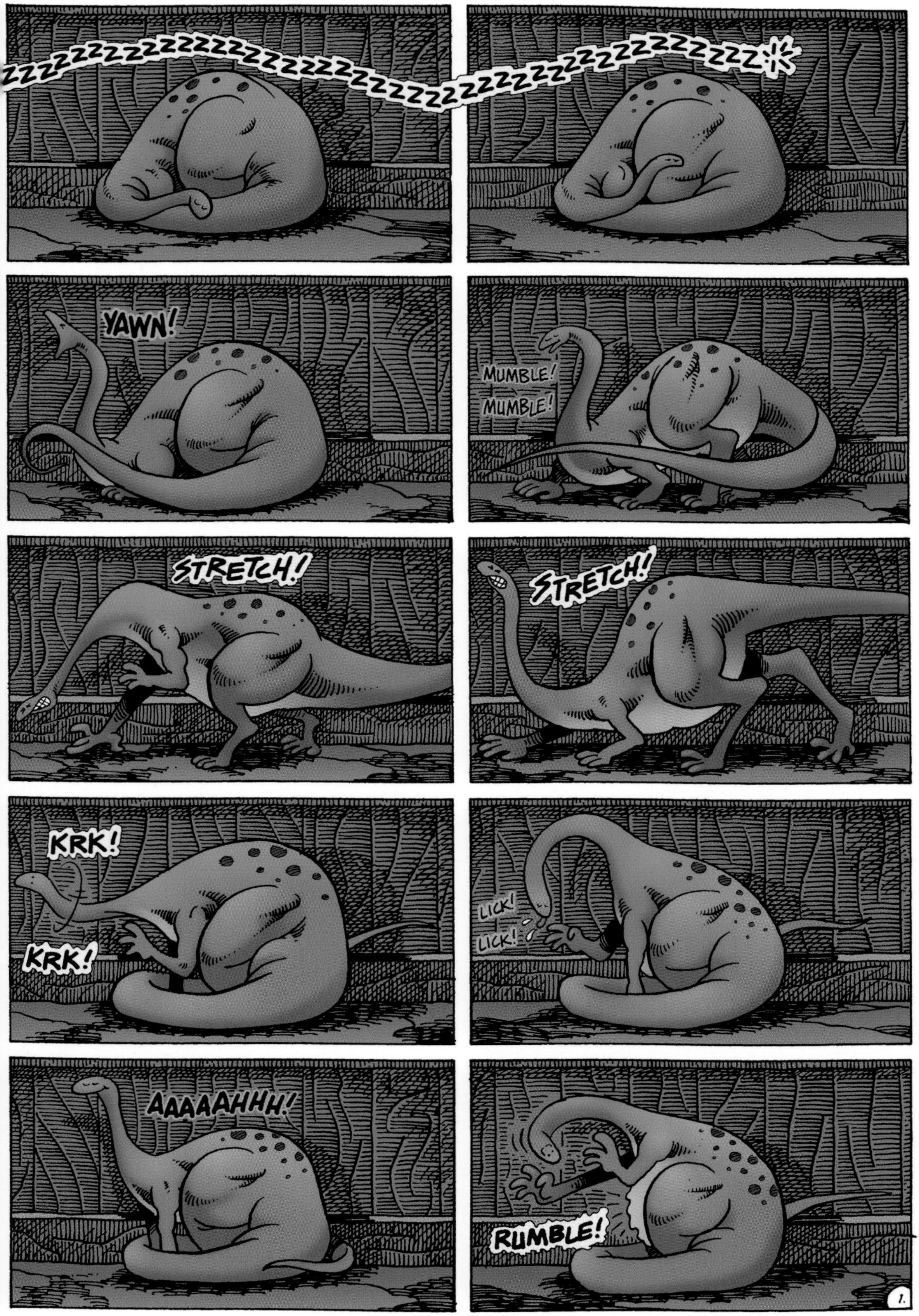
ZZZZZZZZZZZZZZZZZZZZZZZZZZZZZZZZZZZZZZZZZZZZZZZZZZZZZZZ
YAWN!
MUMBLE!
MUMBLE!
STRETCH!
STRETCH!
KRK!
KRK!
LICK!
LICK!
AAAAAHHH!
RUMBLE!
1.

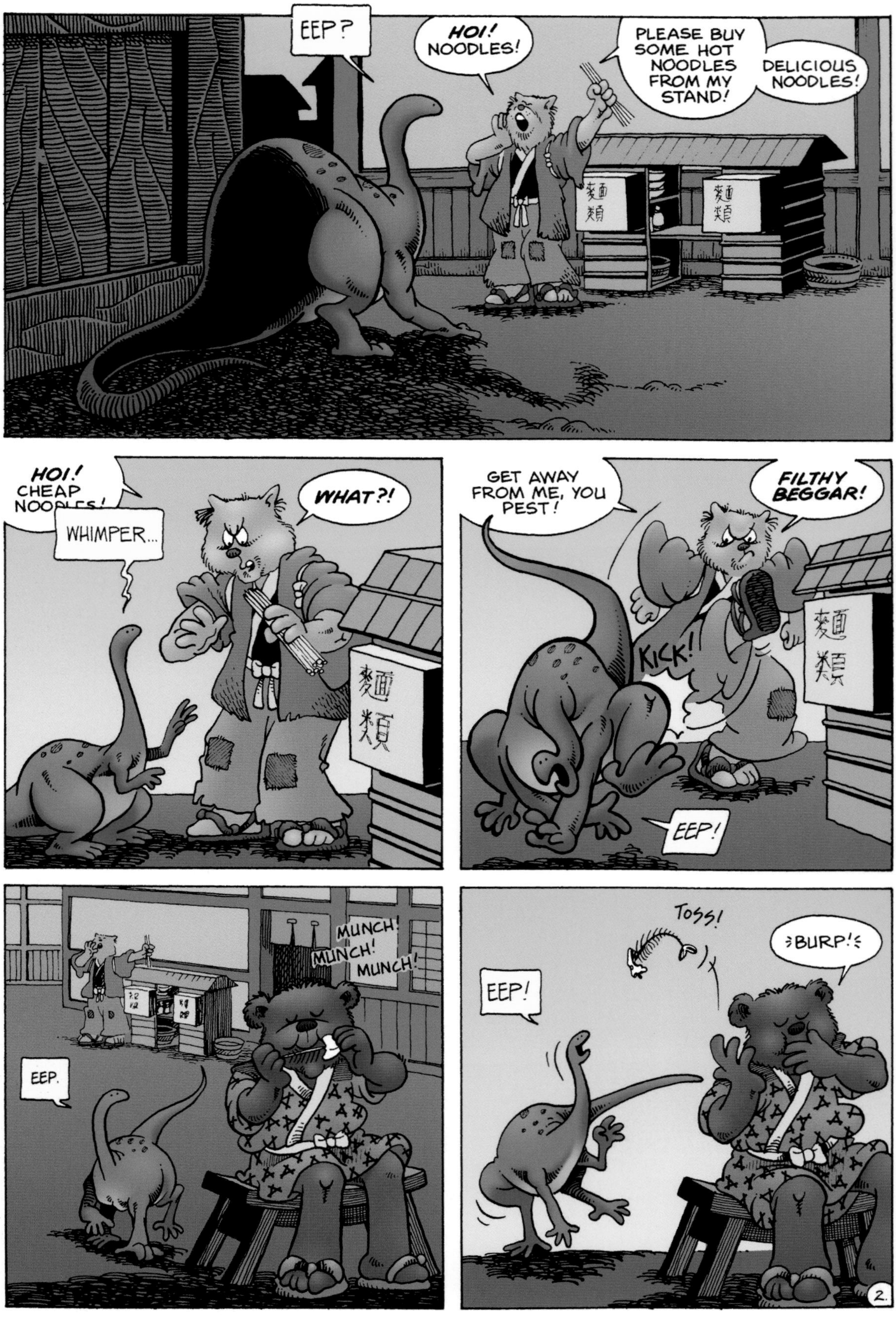

EEP?
HOI! NOODLES!
PLEASE BUY SOME HOT NOODLES FROM MY STAND!
DELICIOUS NOODLES!
HOI! CHEAP NOODLES!
WHIMPER...
WHAT?!
GET AWAY FROM ME, YOU PEST!
FILTHY BEGGAR!
KICK!
EEP!
MUNCH! MUNCH! MUNCH!
EEP.
TOSS!
BURP!
EEP!
2.

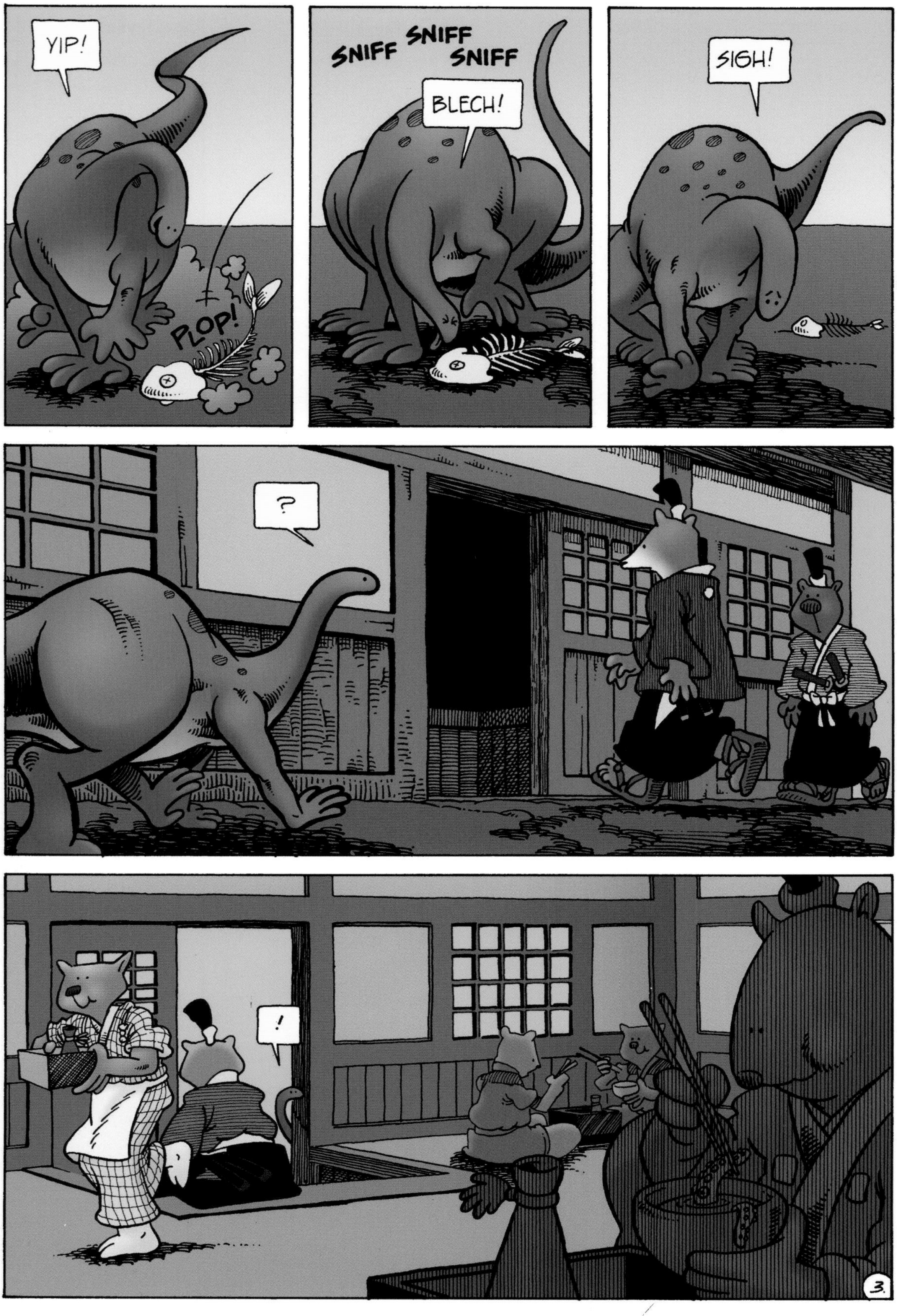
YIP!
PLOP!
SNIFF SNIFF SNIFF
BLECH!
SIGH!
?
!
3.

EEP?
HEY!
YIPE!
SO YOU AGAIN, EH? ALWAYS COMING IN AND STEALING MY CUSTOMERS' FOOD!
WELL, THIS IS THE LAST TIME IT'S GOING TO HAPPEN!
ULP!
I'M GOING TO GET RID OF YOU IF IT'S THE LAST THING I DO!
COME BACK HERE, YOU!
EEK!
4

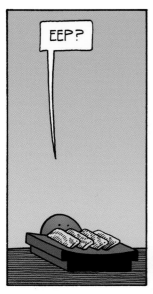

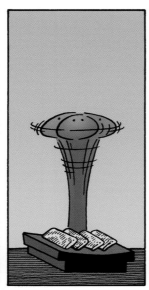

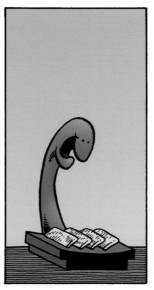

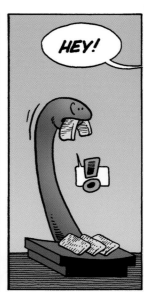

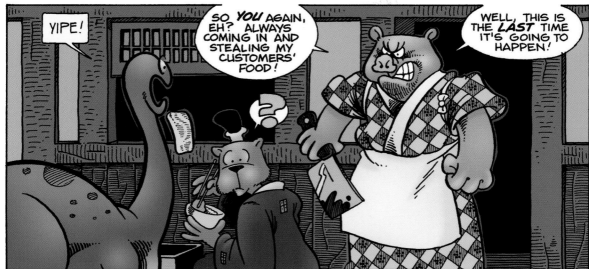

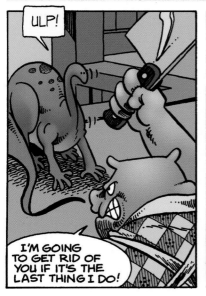

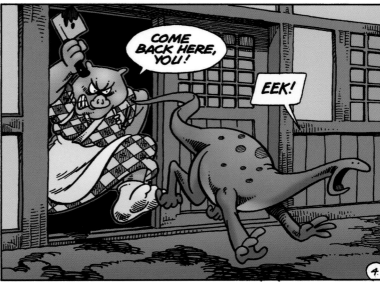

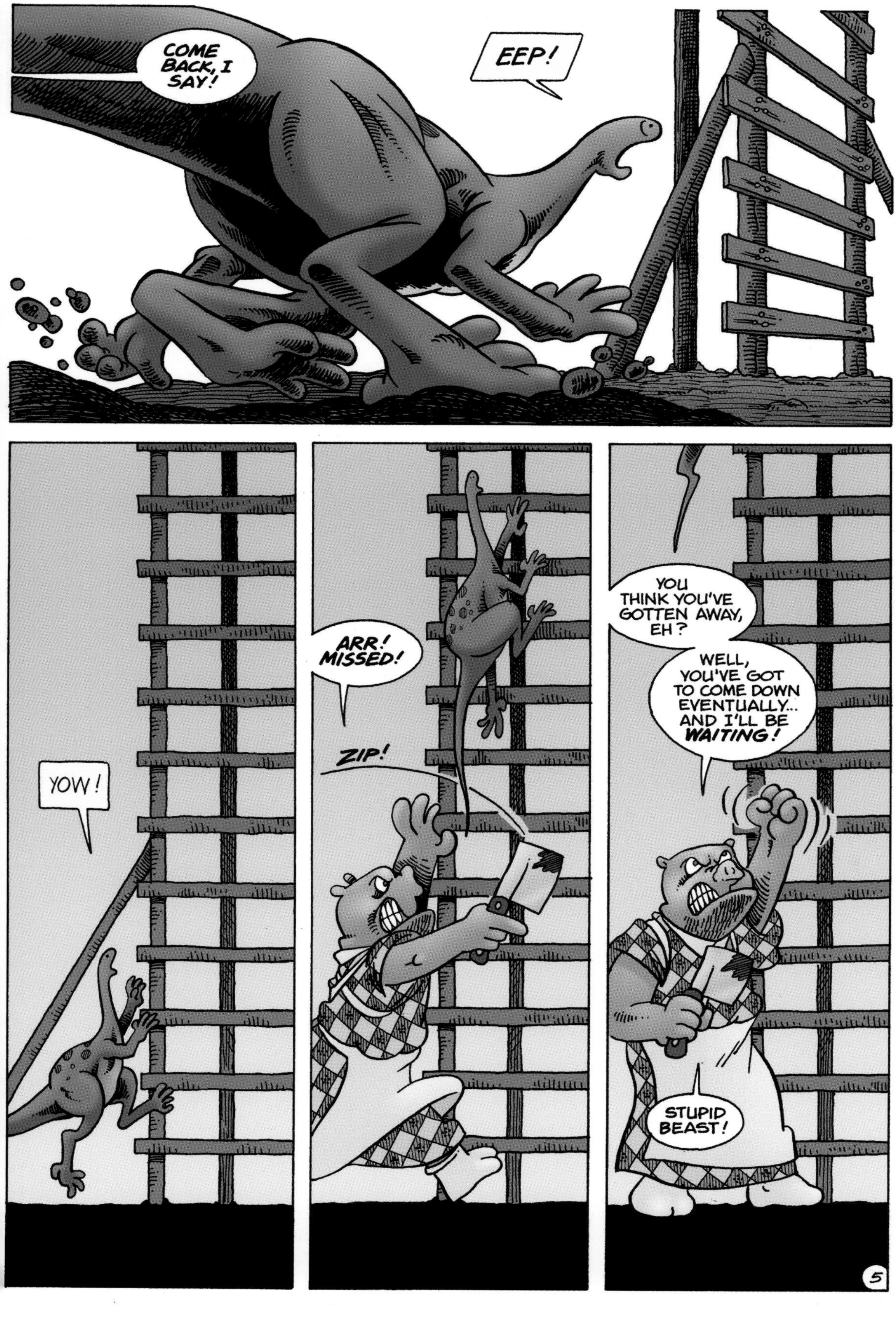
COME BACK, I SAY!
EEP!
YOW!
ARR! MISSED!
ZIP!
YOU THINK YOU'VE GOTTEN AWAY, EH?
WELL, YOU'VE GOT TO COME DOWN EVENTUALLY... AND I'LL BE WAITING!
STUPID BEAST!
5

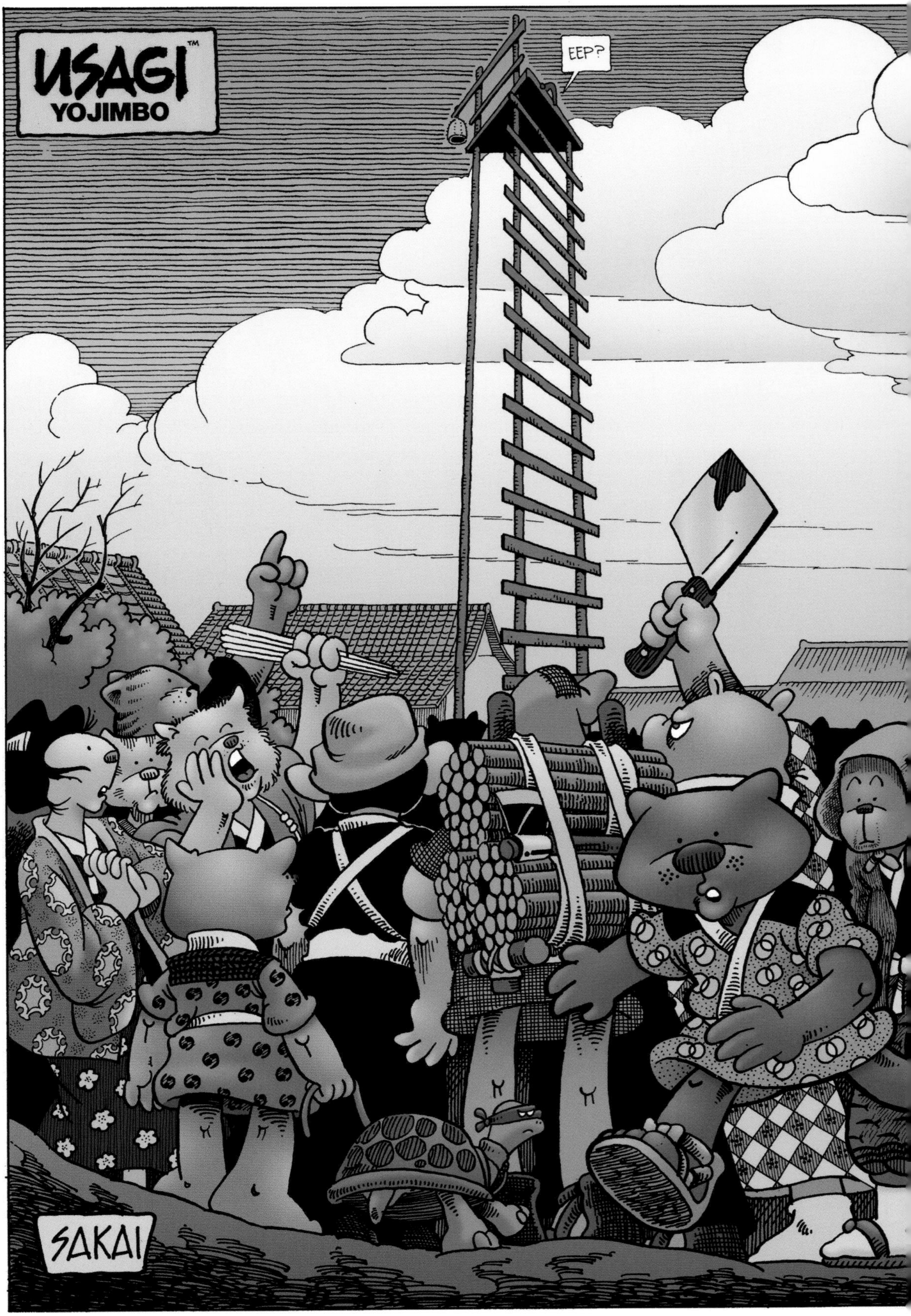
USAGI™
YOJIMBO
EEP?
SAKAI

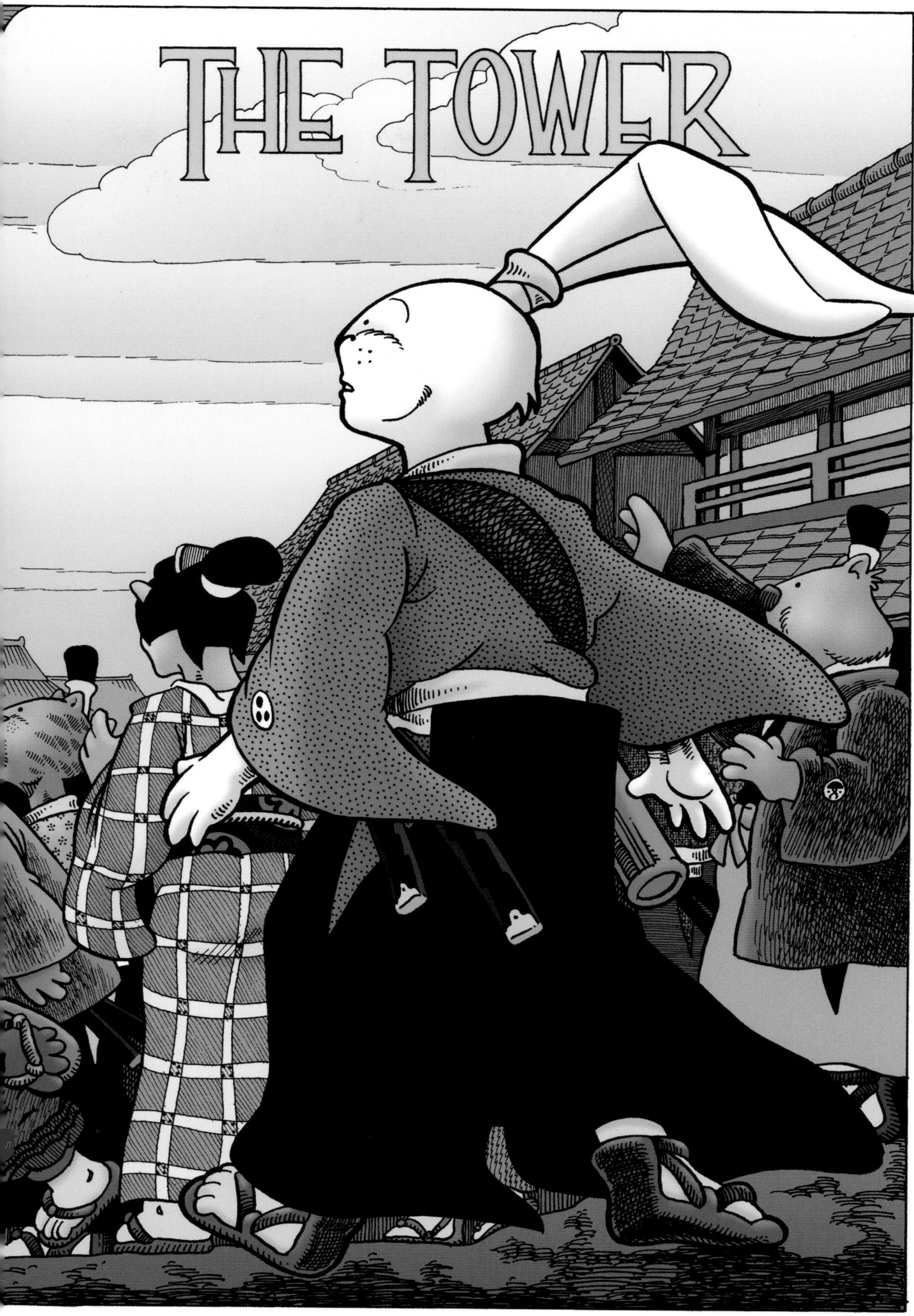
THE TOWER

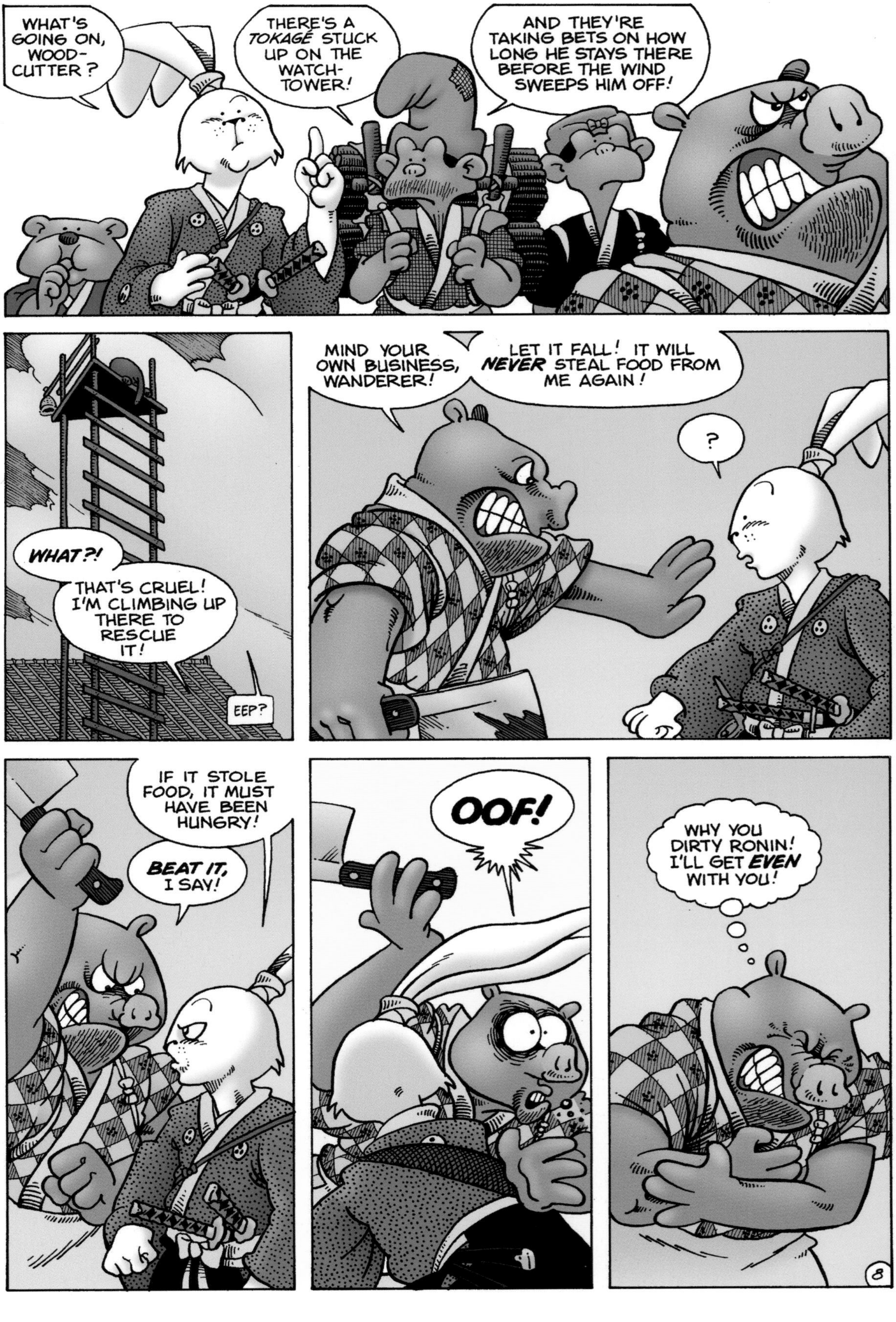
WHAT'S GOING ON, WOOD-CUTTER?
THERE'S A *TOKAGÉ* STUCK UP ON THE WATCH-TOWER!
AND THEY'RE TAKING BETS ON HOW LONG HE STAYS THERE BEFORE THE WIND SWEEPS HIM OFF!
WHAT?!
THAT'S CRUEL! I'M CLIMBING UP THERE TO RESCUE IT!
EEP?
MIND YOUR OWN BUSINESS, WANDERER!
LET IT FALL! IT WILL ***NEVER*** STEAL FOOD FROM ME AGAIN!
?
IF IT STOLE FOOD, IT MUST HAVE BEEN HUNGRY!
BEAT IT, I SAY!
OOF!
WHY YOU DIRTY RONIN! I'LL GET ***EVEN*** WITH YOU!
8

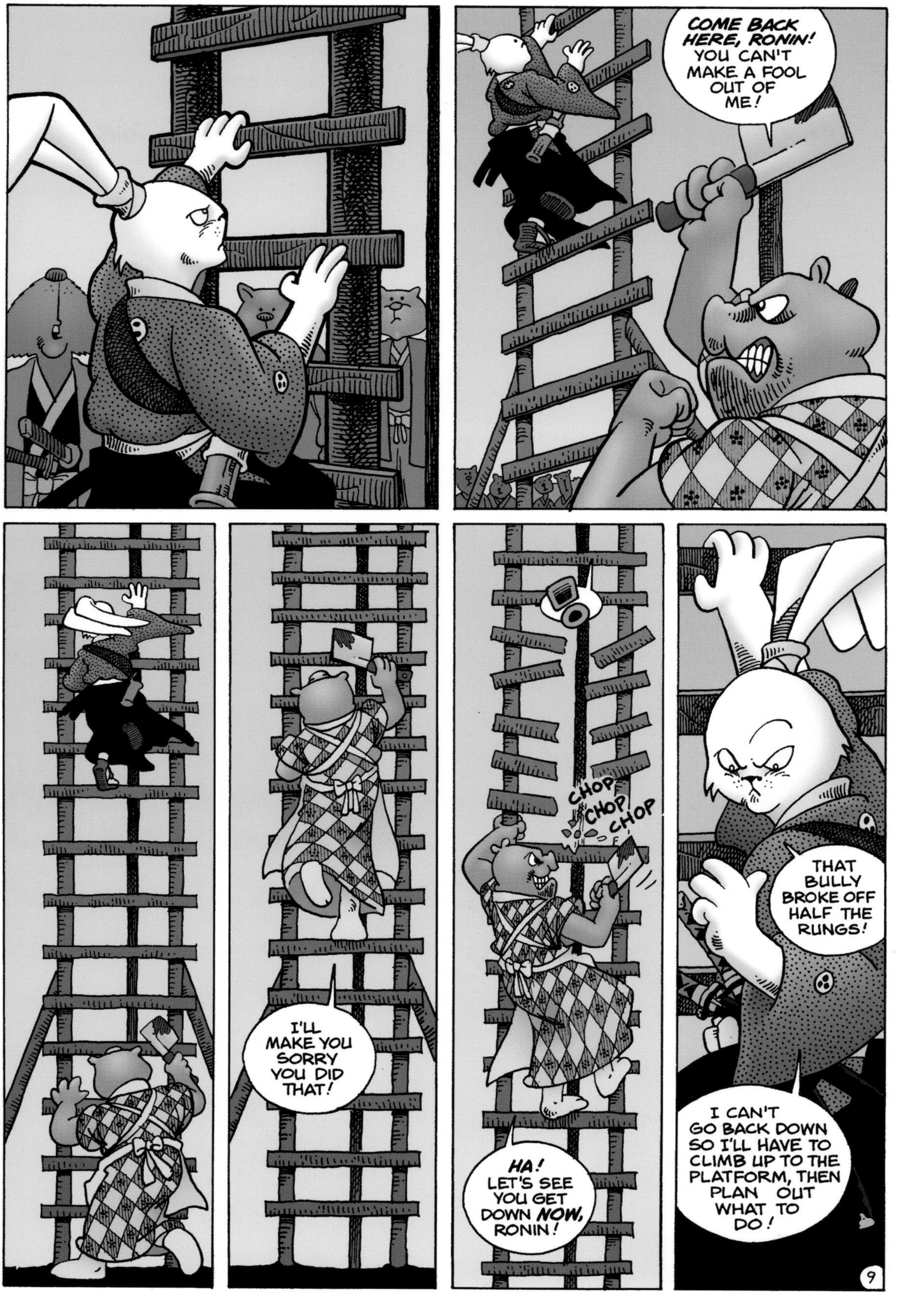

COME BACK HERE, RONIN! YOU CAN'T MAKE A FOOL OUT OF ME!
I'LL MAKE YOU SORRY YOU DID THAT!
CHOP CHOP CHOP
HA! LET'S SEE YOU GET DOWN NOW, RONIN!
THAT BULLY BROKE OFF HALF THE RUNGS!
I CAN'T GO BACK DOWN SO I'LL HAVE TO CLIMB UP TO THE PLATFORM, THEN PLAN OUT WHAT TO DO!
9

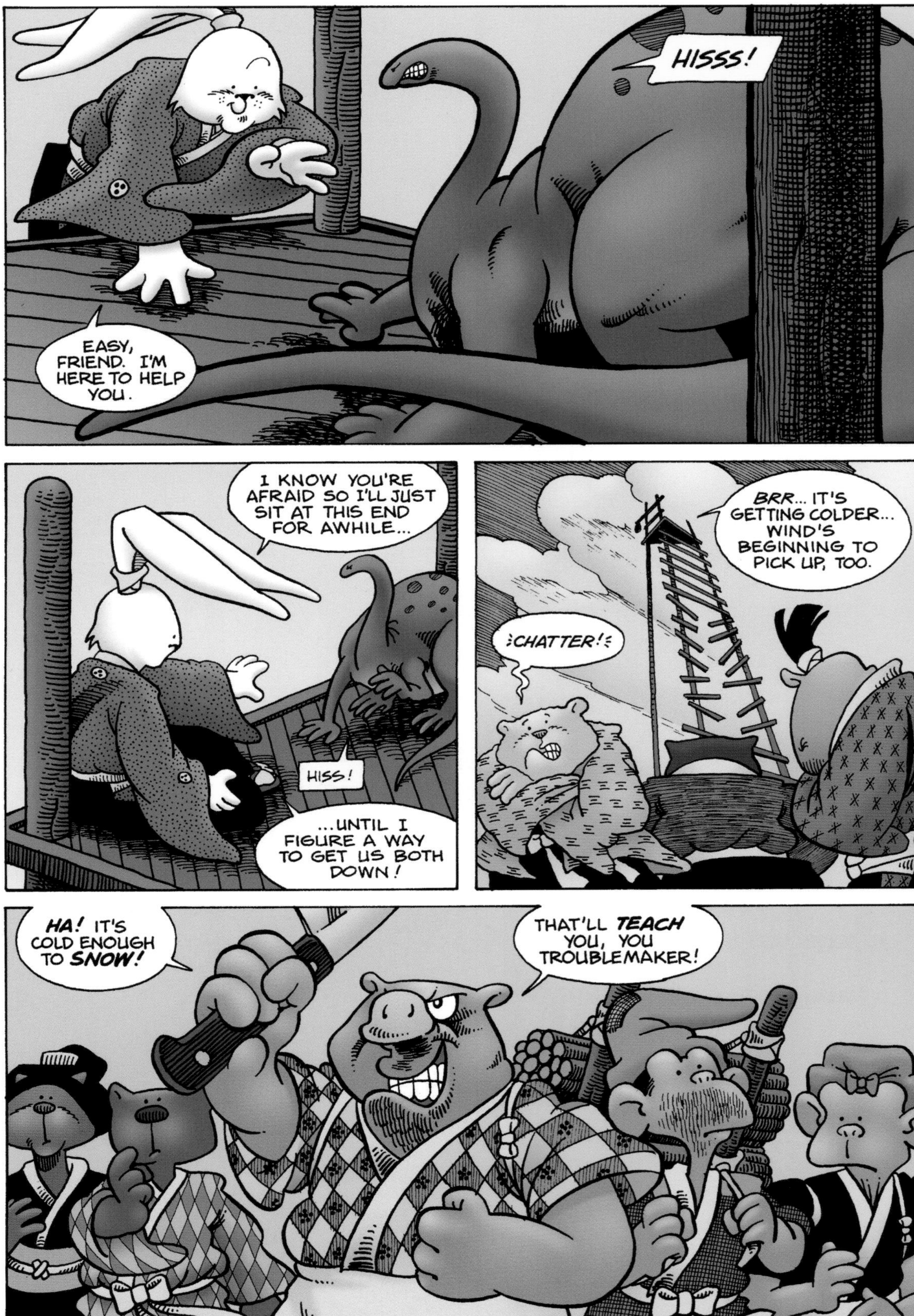
HISSS!
EASY, FRIEND. I'M HERE TO HELP YOU.
I KNOW YOU'RE AFRAID SO I'LL JUST SIT AT THIS END FOR AWHILE...
HISS!
...UNTIL I FIGURE A WAY TO GET US BOTH DOWN!
BRR... IT'S GETTING COLDER... WIND'S BEGINNING TO PICK UP, TOO.
CHATTER!
HA! IT'S COLD ENOUGH TO SNOW!
THAT'LL TEACH YOU, YOU TROUBLEMAKER!
10

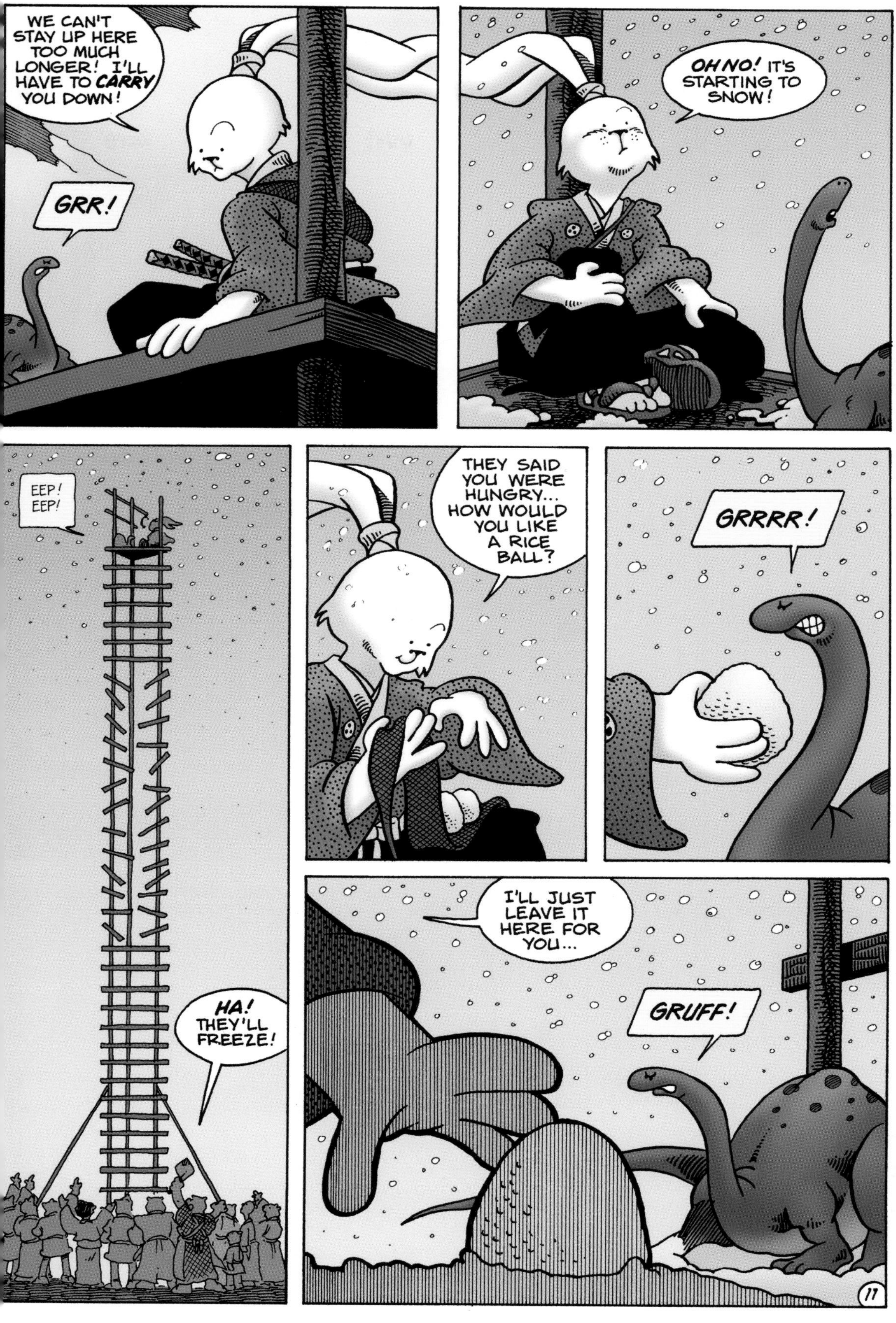

WE CAN'T STAY UP HERE TOO MUCH LONGER! I'LL HAVE TO CARRY YOU DOWN!
GRR!
OH NO! IT'S STARTING TO SNOW!
EEP! EEP!
HA! THEY'LL FREEZE!
THEY SAID YOU WERE HUNGRY... HOW WOULD YOU LIKE A RICE BALL?
GRRRR!
I'LL JUST LEAVE IT HERE FOR YOU...
GRUFF!
17

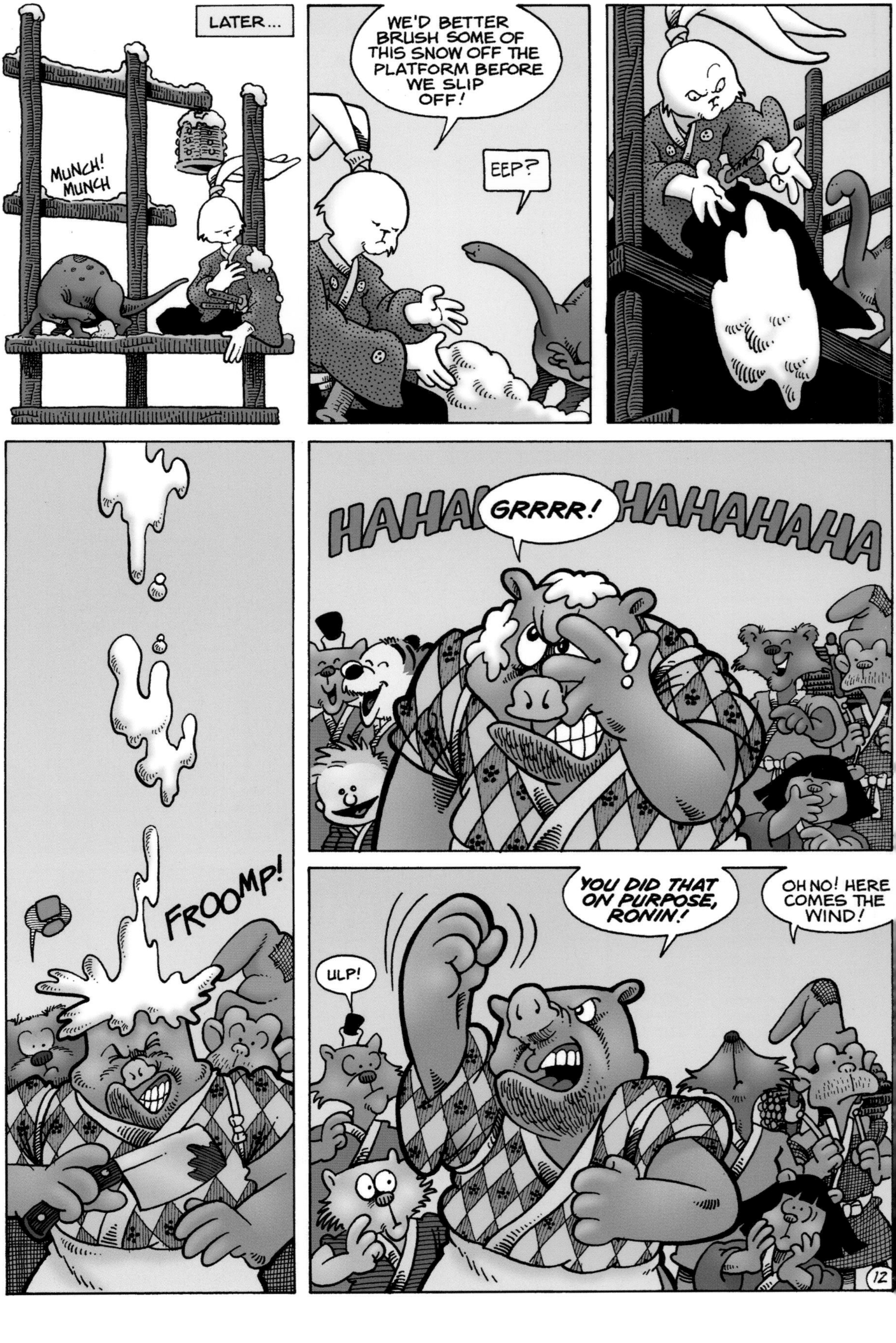
LATER...
MUNCH! MUNCH
WE'D BETTER BRUSH SOME OF THIS SNOW OFF THE PLATFORM BEFORE WE SLIP OFF!
EEP?
FROOMP!
HAHAHA
GRRRR!
HAHAHAHA
YOU DID THAT ON PURPOSE, RONIN!
OH NO! HERE COMES THE WIND!
ULP!
12

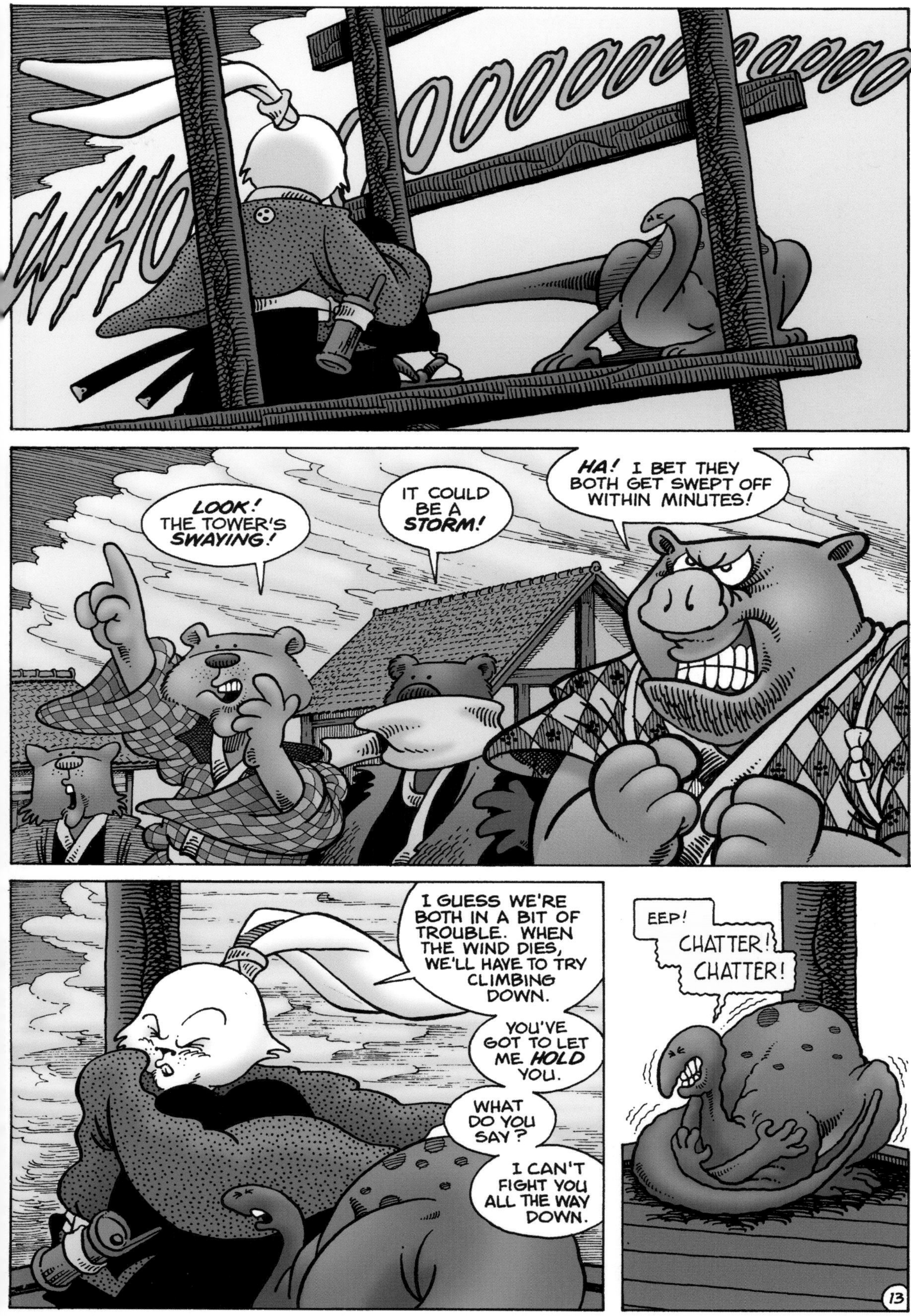
WHOOOOOOOOOOOOoooo
LOOK! THE TOWER'S SWAYING!
IT COULD BE A STORM!
HA! I BET THEY BOTH GET SWEPT OFF WITHIN MINUTES!
I GUESS WE'RE BOTH IN A BIT OF TROUBLE. WHEN THE WIND DIES, WE'LL HAVE TO TRY CLIMBING DOWN.
YOU'VE GOT TO LET ME HOLD YOU.
WHAT DO YOU SAY?
I CAN'T FIGHT YOU ALL THE WAY DOWN.
EEP!
CHATTER! CHATTER!
13

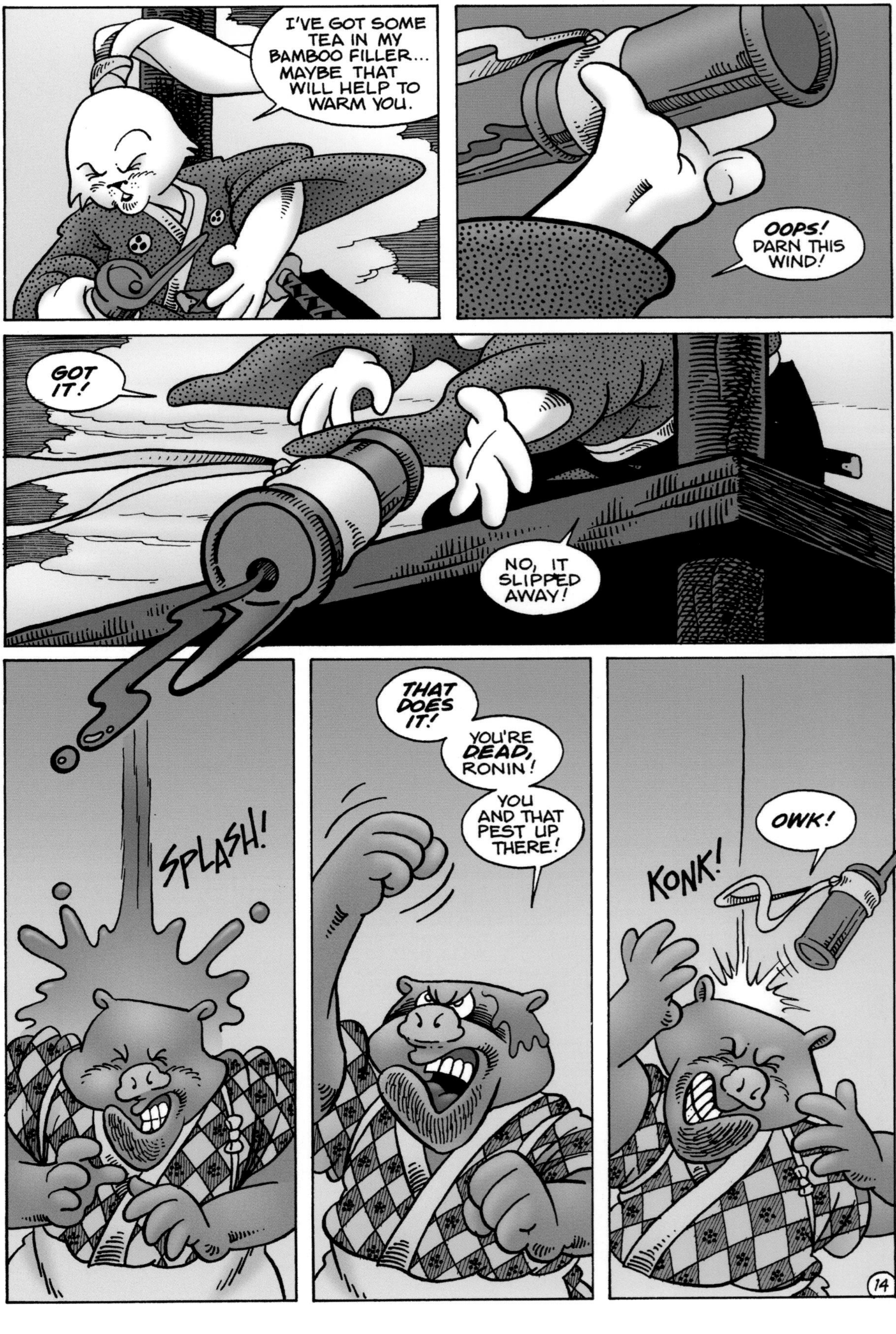
I'VE GOT SOME TEA IN MY BAMBOO FILLER... MAYBE THAT WILL HELP TO WARM YOU.
OOPS! DARN THIS WIND!
GOT IT!
NO, IT SLIPPED AWAY!
SPLASH!
THAT DOES IT!
YOU'RE DEAD, RONIN!
YOU AND THAT PEST UP THERE!
KONK!
OWK!
14

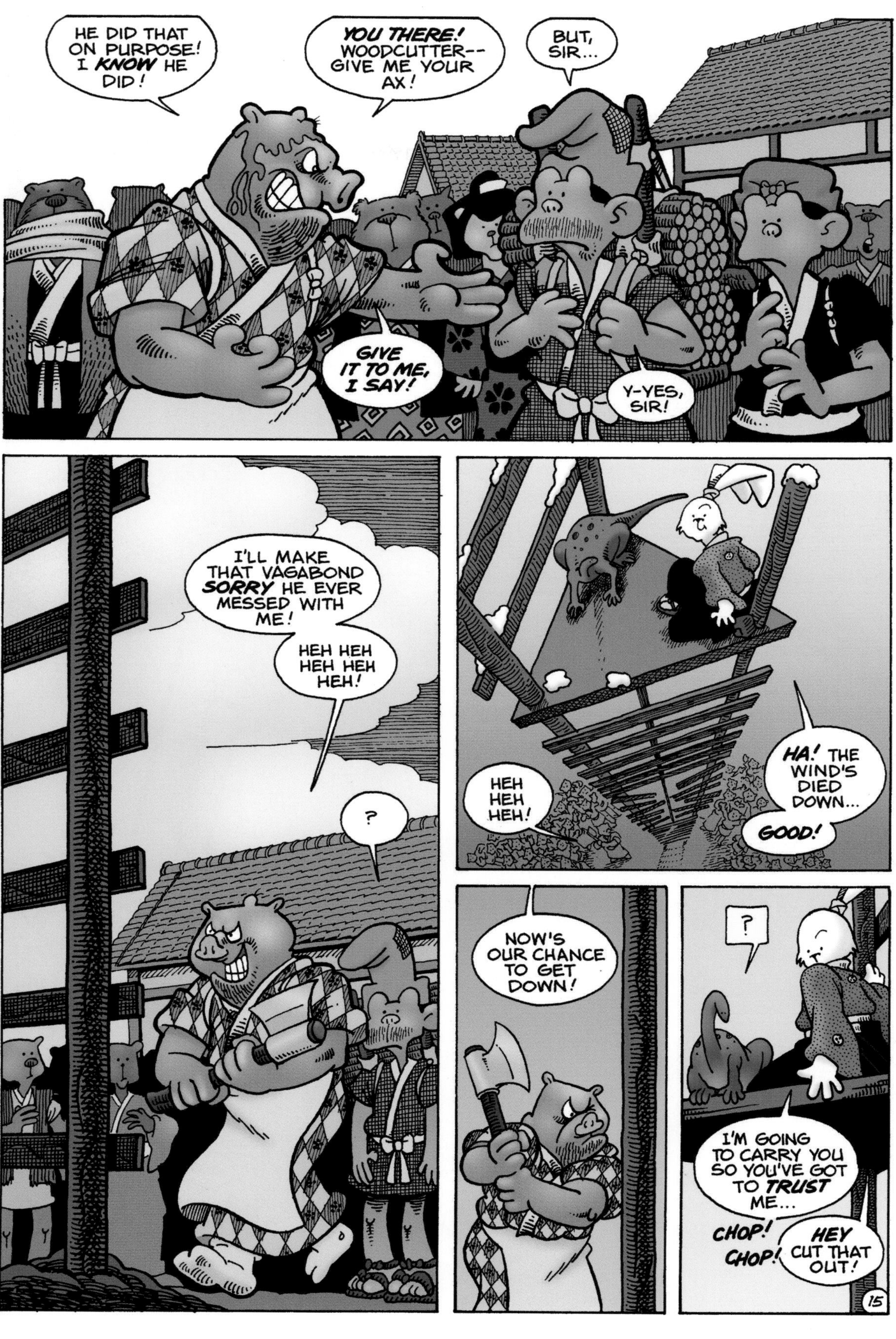
HE DID THAT ON PURPOSE! I KNOW HE DID!
YOU THERE! WOODCUTTER-- GIVE ME YOUR AX!
BUT, SIR...
GIVE IT TO ME, I SAY!
Y-YES, SIR!
I'LL MAKE THAT VAGABOND SORRY HE EVER MESSED WITH ME!
HEH HEH HEH HEH HEH!
?
HA! THE WIND'S DIED DOWN...
GOOD!
HEH HEH HEH!
NOW'S OUR CHANCE TO GET DOWN!
?
I'M GOING TO CARRY YOU SO YOU'VE GOT TO TRUST ME...
CHOP! CHOP!
HEY CUT THAT OUT!
15

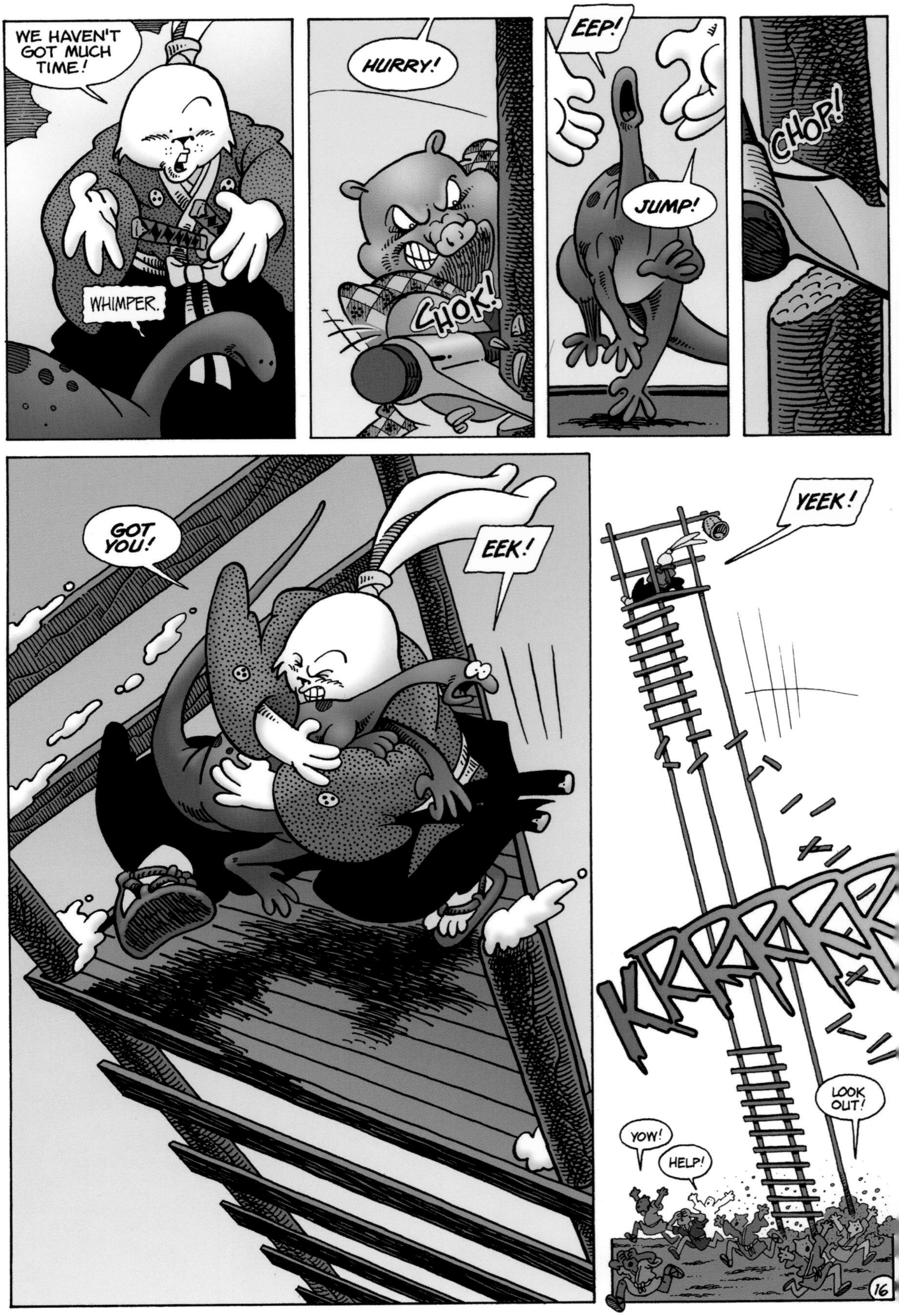
WE HAVEN'T GOT MUCH TIME!
WHIMPER.
HURRY!
CHOK!
EEP!
JUMP!
CHOP!
GOT YOU!
EEK!
YEEK!
KRRRRRR
YOW!
HELP!
LOOK OUT!
16

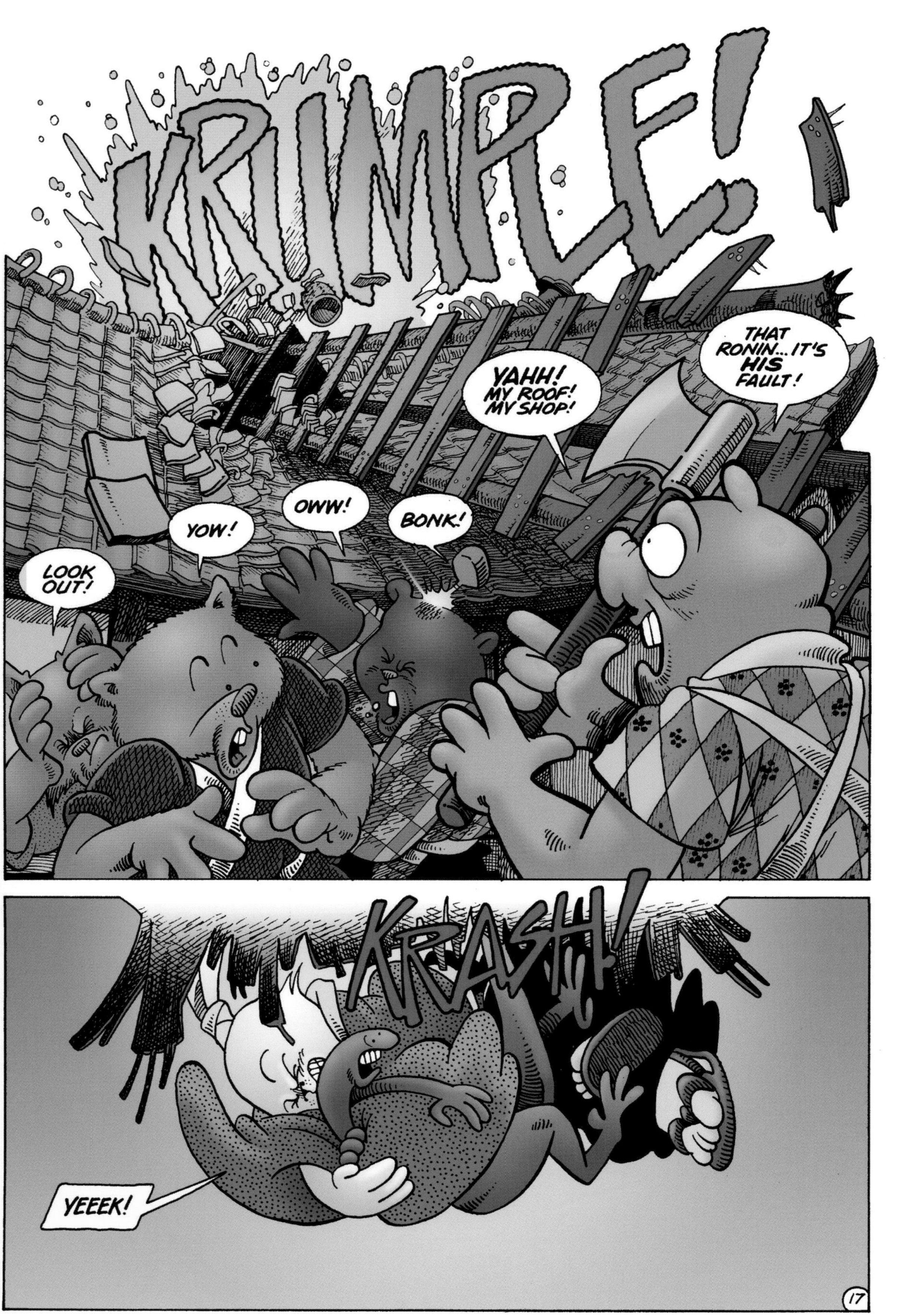
KRUMPLE!
LOOK OUT!
YOW!
OWW!
BONK!
YAHH! MY ROOF! MY SHOP!
THAT RONIN... IT'S HIS FAULT!
KRASH!
YEEEK!
17

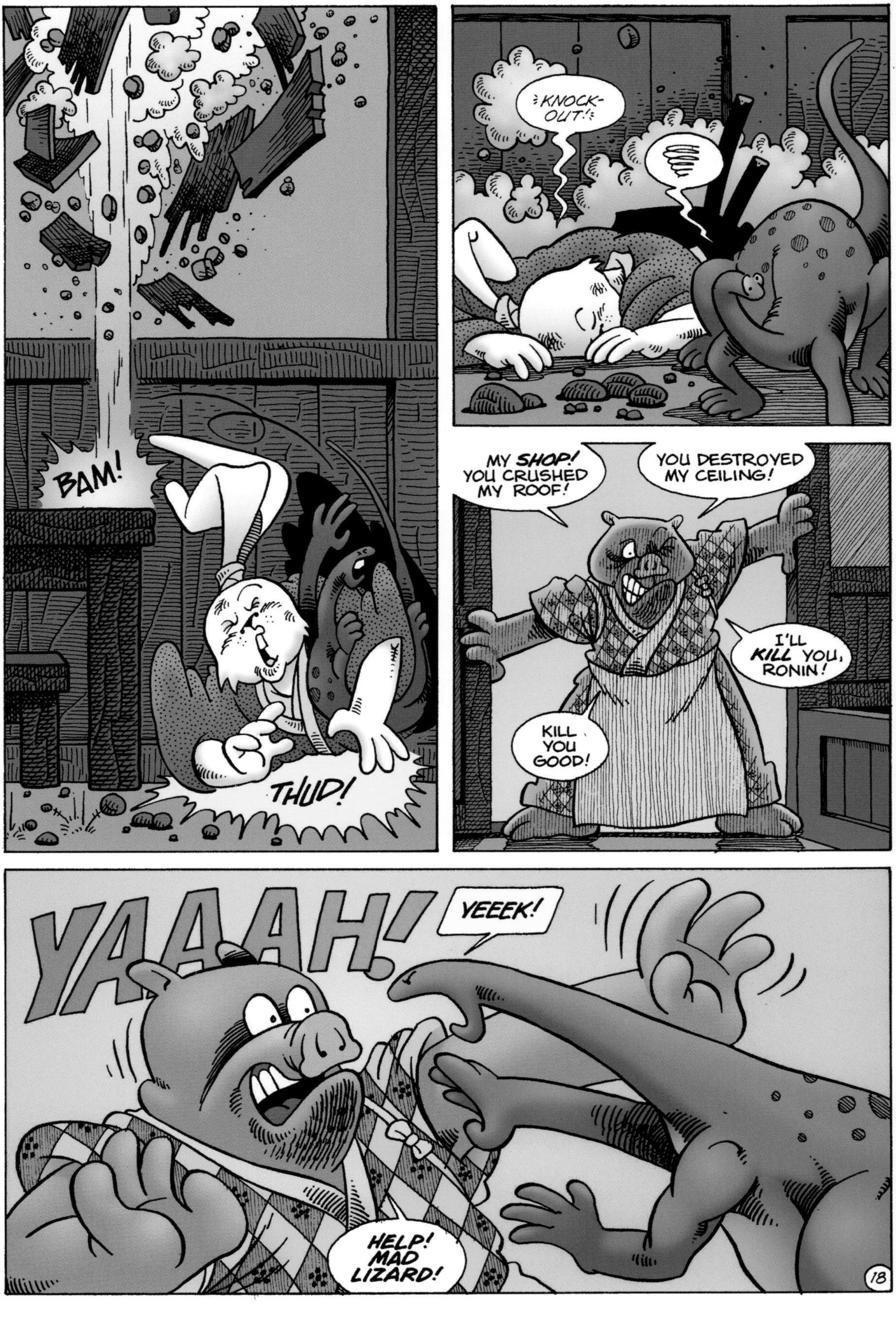
BAM!
THUD!
KNOCK-OUT!
MY SHOP! YOU CRUSHED MY ROOF!
YOU DESTROYED MY CEILING!
I'LL KILL YOU, RONIN!
KILL YOU GOOD!
YAAAH!
YEEEK!
HELP! MAD LIZARD!
18

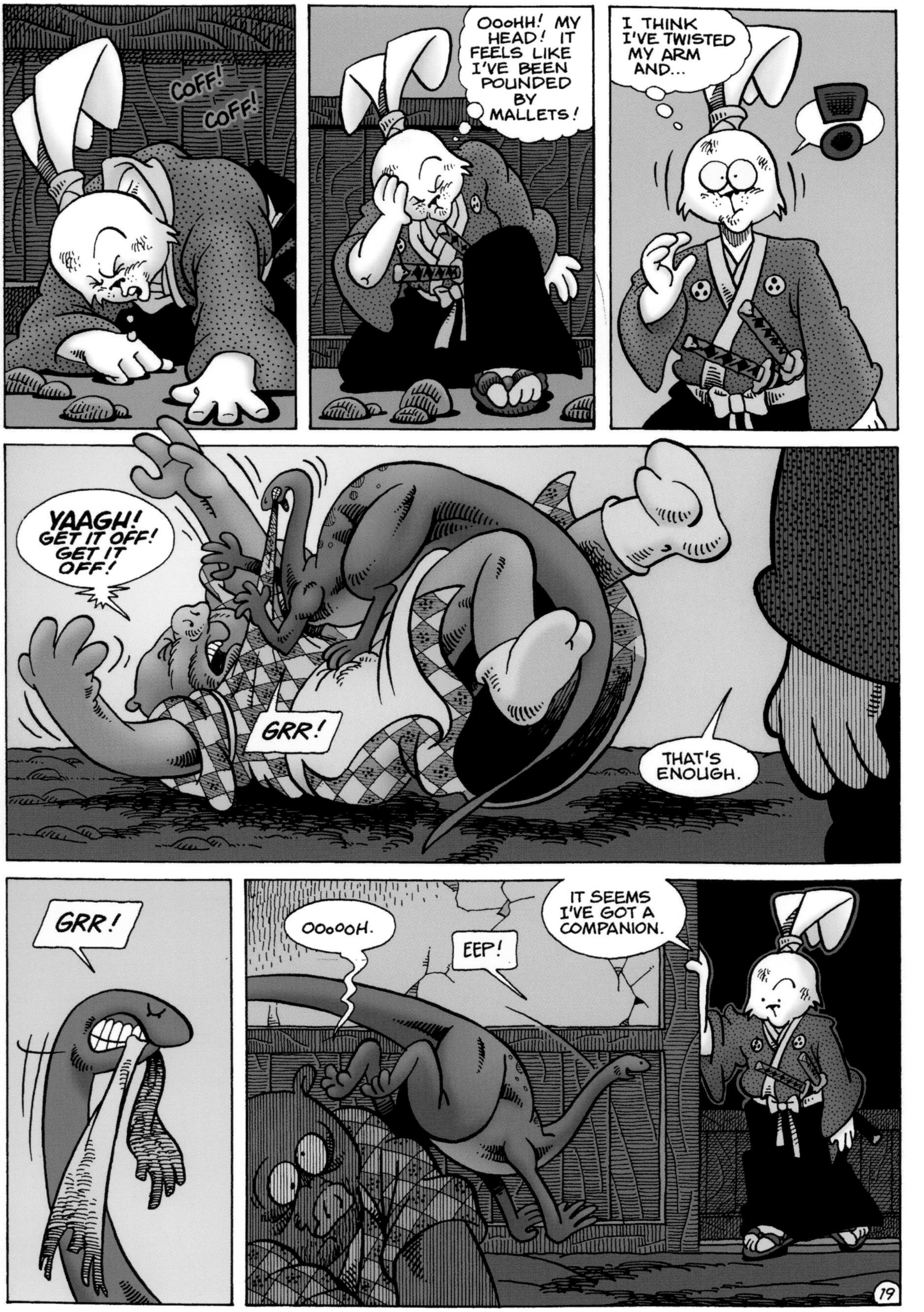
COFF!
COFF!
OooHH! MY HEAD! IT FEELS LIKE I'VE BEEN POUNDED BY MALLETS!
I THINK I'VE TWISTED MY ARM AND...
YAAGH! GET IT OFF! GET IT OFF!
GRR!
THAT'S ENOUGH.
GRR!
OOoooH.
EEP!
IT SEEMS I'VE GOT A COMPANION.
19

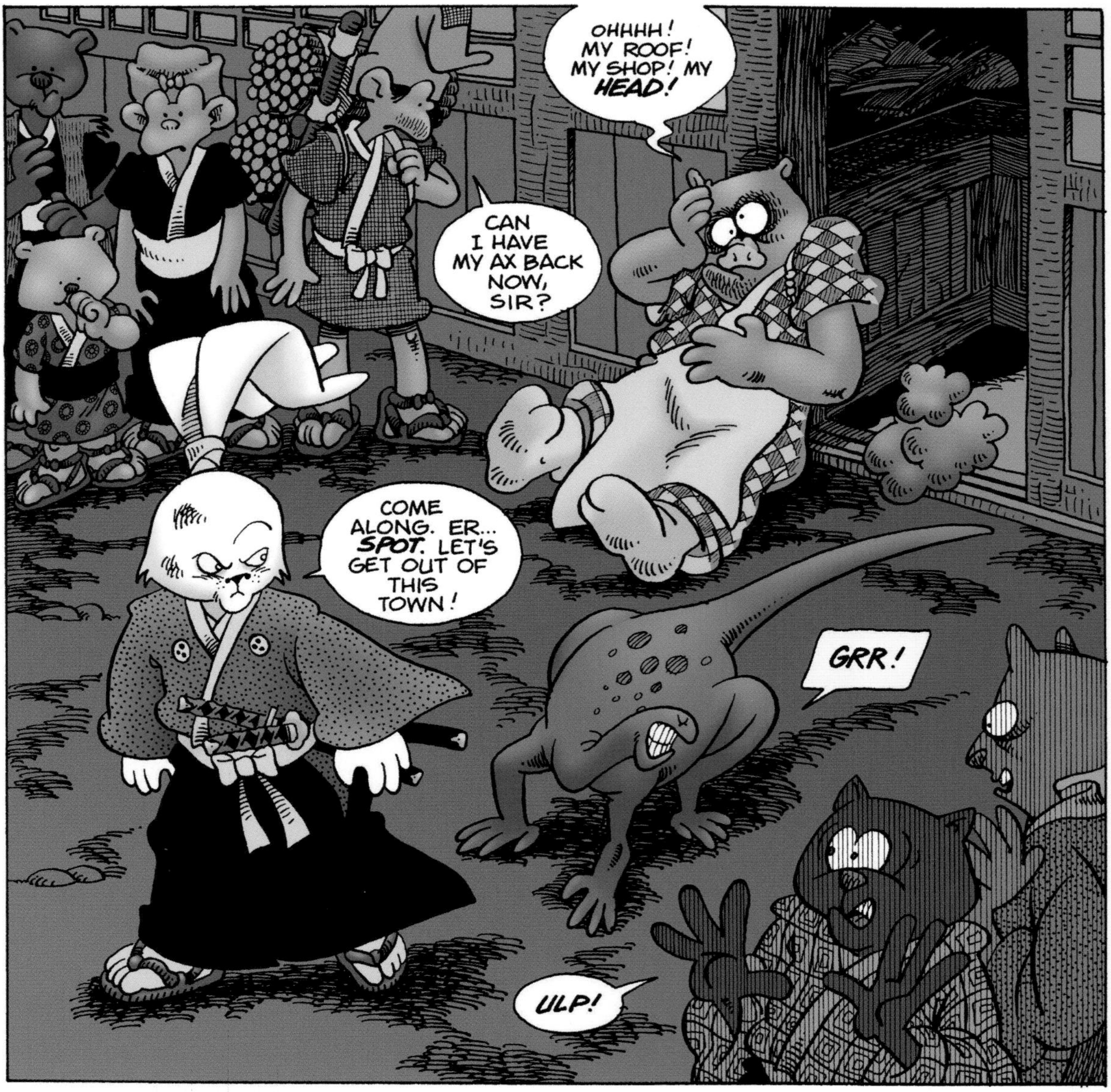
OHHHH! MY ROOF! MY SHOP! MY HEAD!
CAN I HAVE MY AX BACK NOW, SIR?
COME ALONG. ER... SPOT. LET'S GET OUT OF THIS TOWN!
GRR!
ULP!
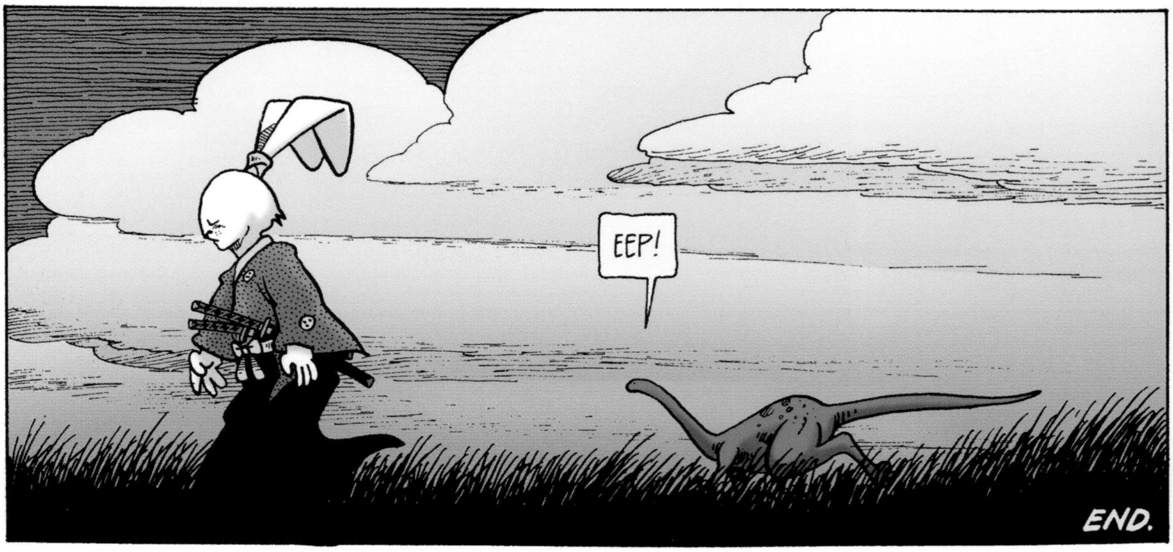
EEP!
END.

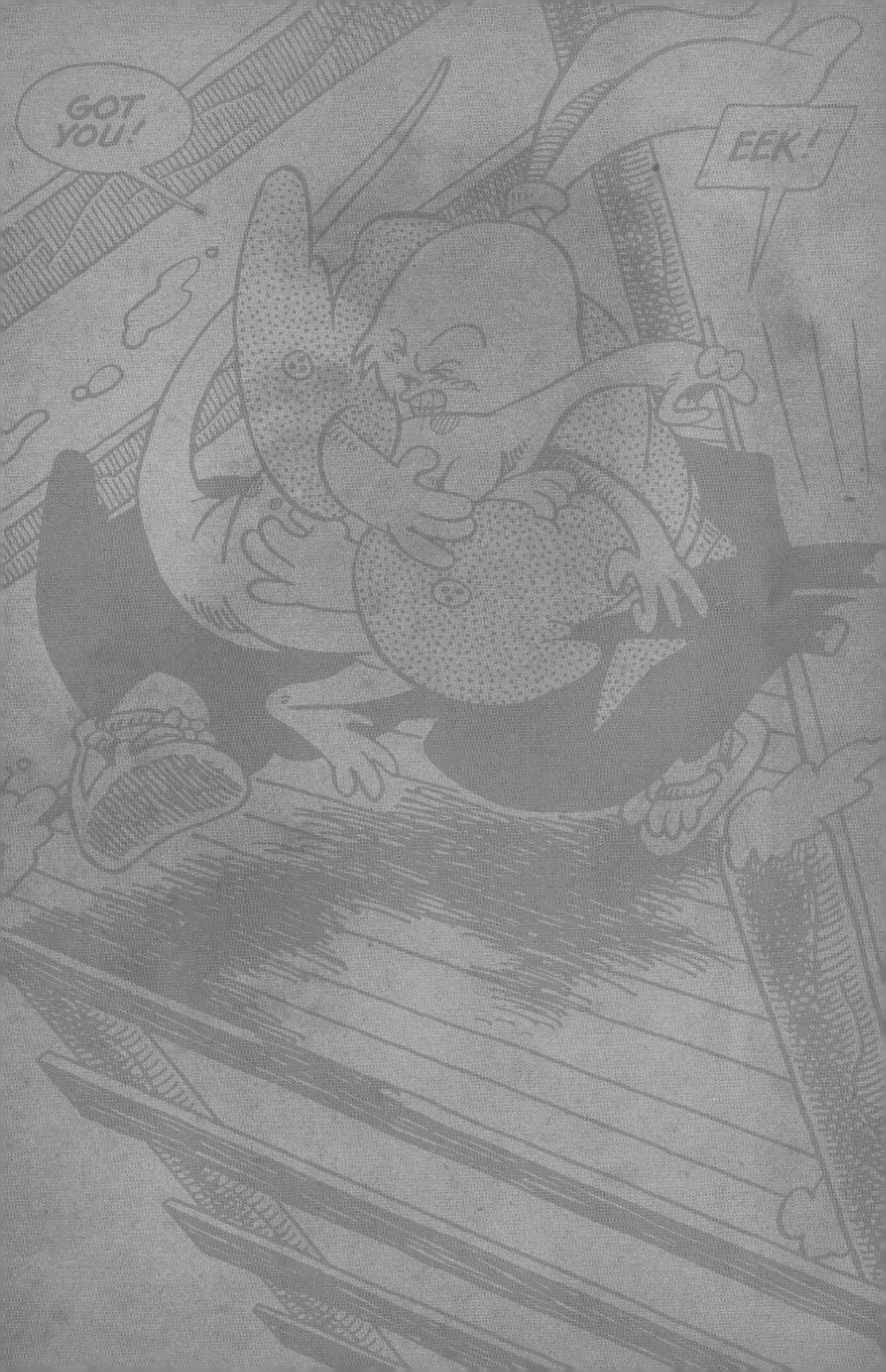
GOT YOU!
EEK!

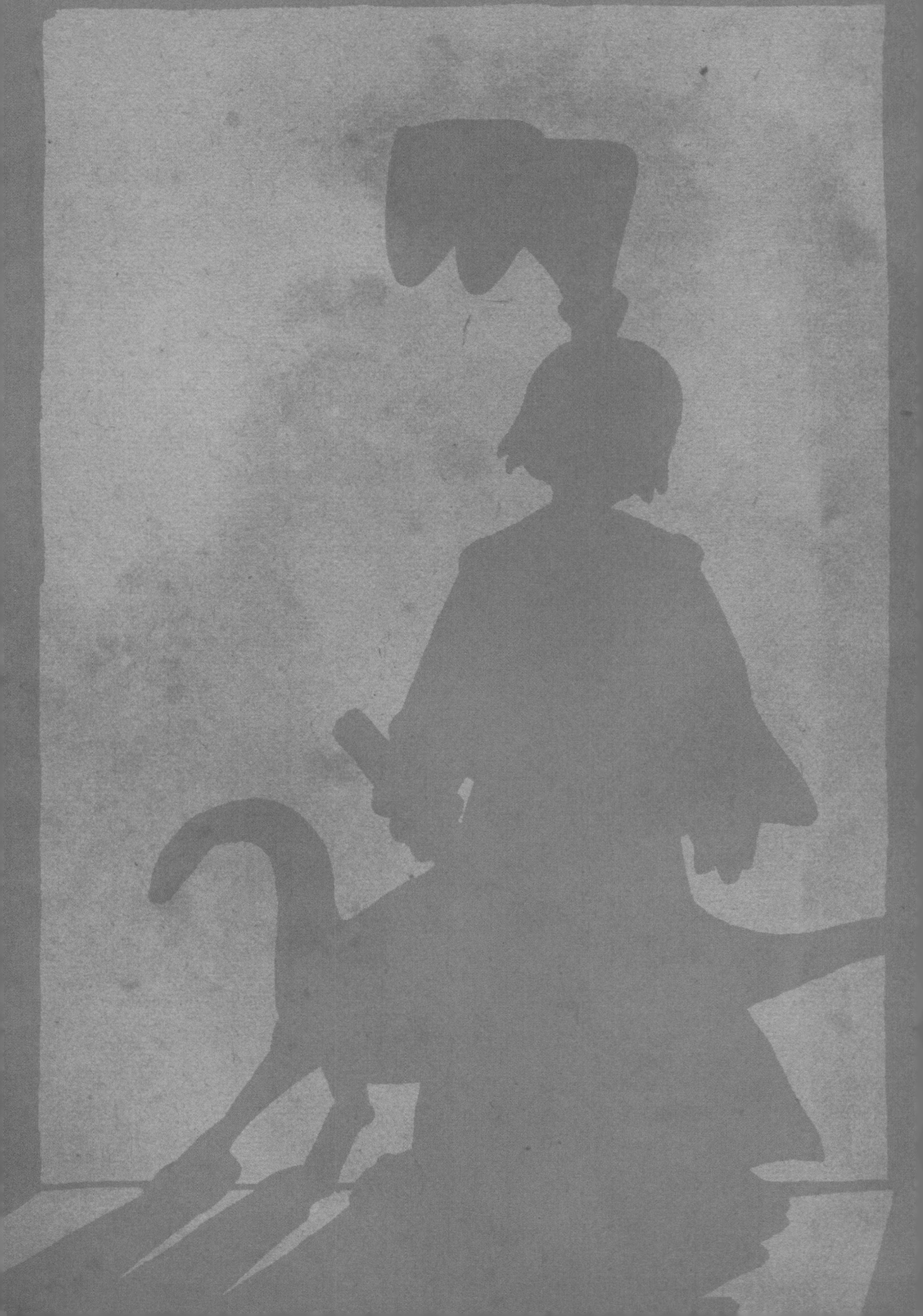

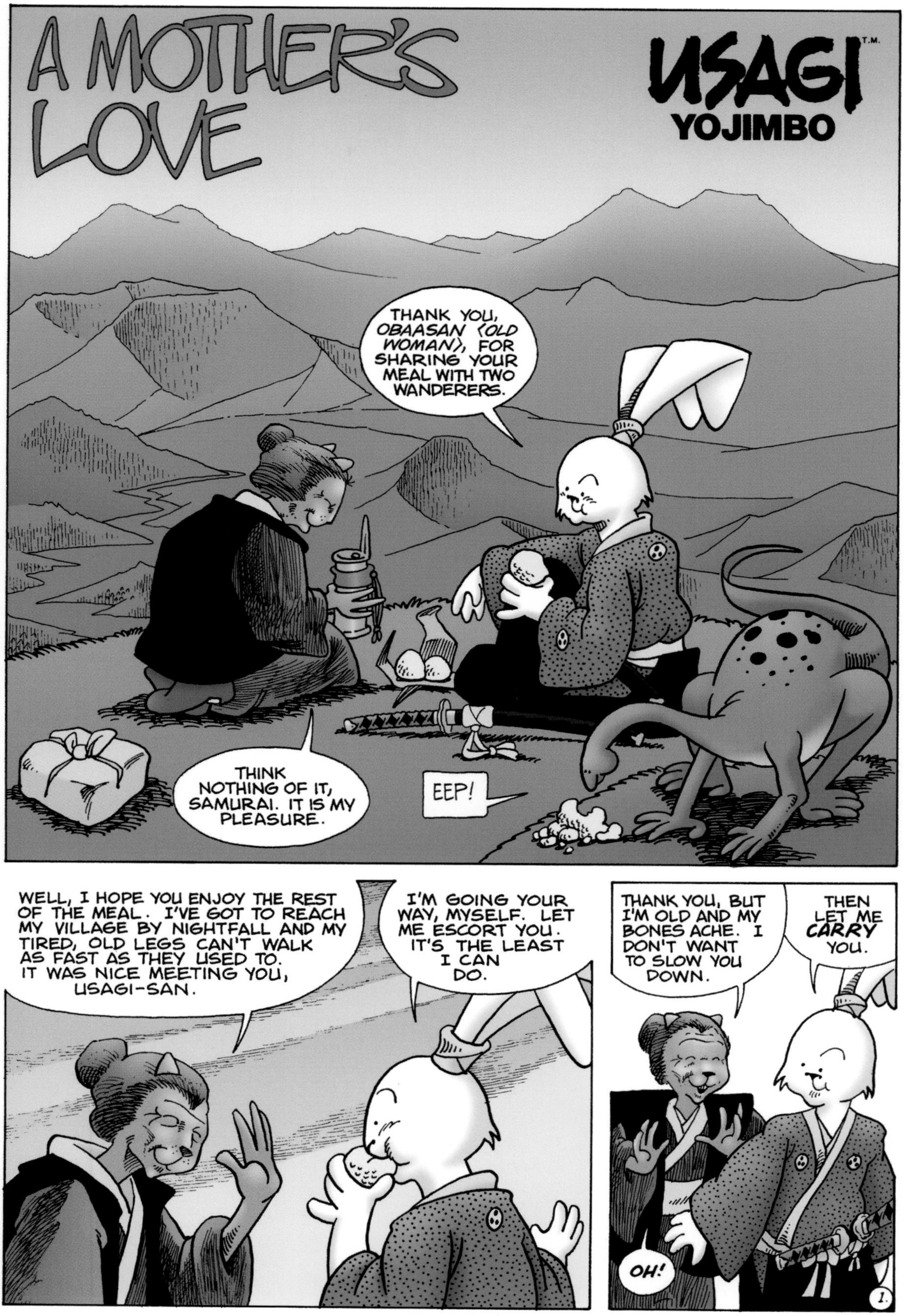
A MOTHER'S LOVE
USAGI YOJIMBO
THANK YOU, *OBAASAN* <*OLD WOMAN*>, FOR SHARING YOUR MEAL WITH TWO WANDERERS.
THINK NOTHING OF IT, SAMURAI. IT IS MY PLEASURE.
EEP!
WELL, I HOPE YOU ENJOY THE REST OF THE MEAL. I'VE GOT TO REACH MY VILLAGE BY NIGHTFALL AND MY TIRED, OLD LEGS CAN'T WALK AS FAST AS THEY USED TO. IT WAS NICE MEETING YOU, USAGI-SAN.
I'M GOING YOUR WAY, MYSELF. LET ME ESCORT YOU. IT'S THE LEAST I CAN DO.
THANK YOU, BUT I'M OLD AND MY BONES ACHE. I DON'T WANT TO SLOW YOU DOWN.
THEN LET ME **CARRY** YOU.
OH!
1.

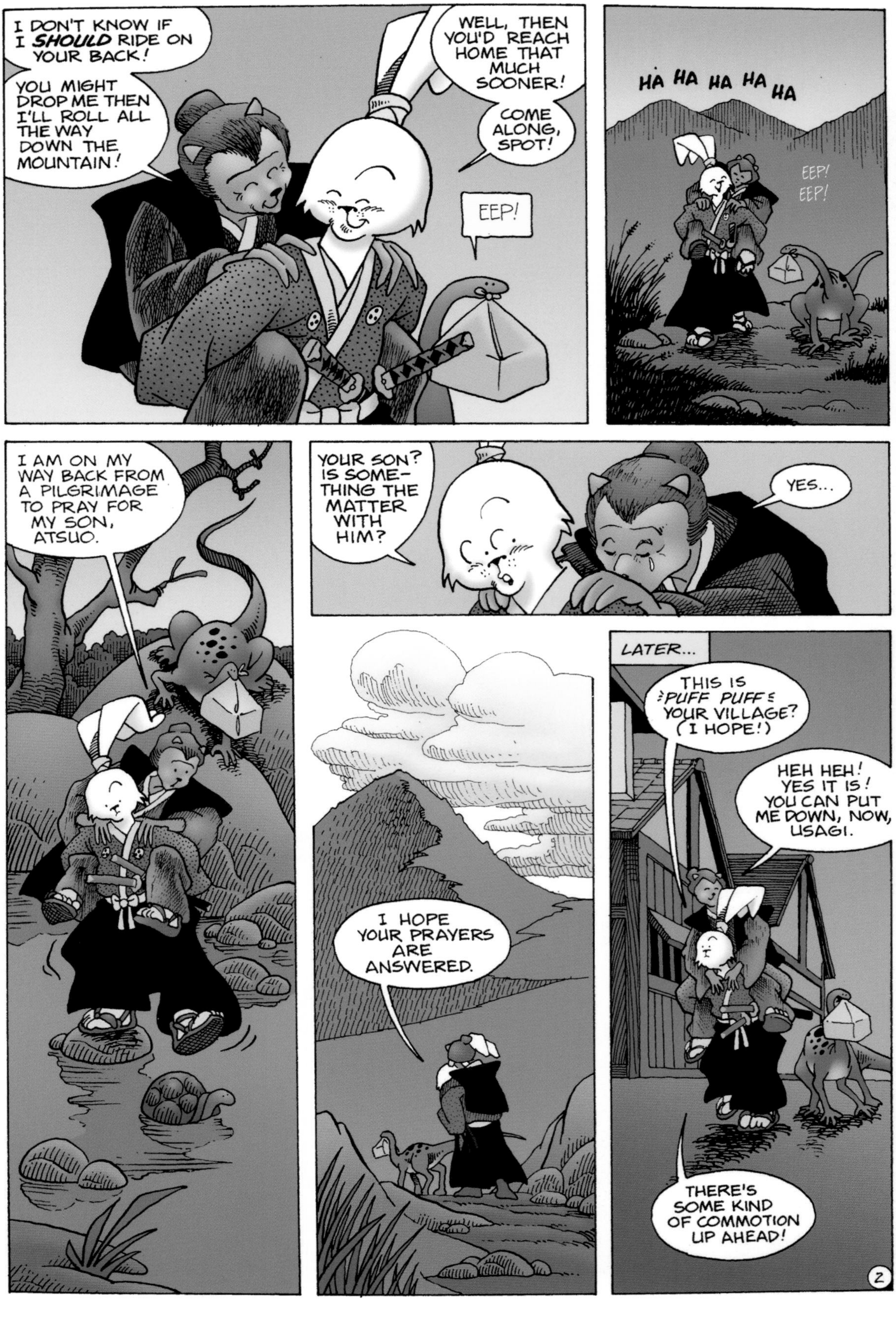
I DON'T KNOW IF I SHOULD RIDE ON YOUR BACK!
YOU MIGHT DROP ME THEN I'LL ROLL ALL THE WAY DOWN THE MOUNTAIN!
WELL, THEN YOU'D REACH HOME THAT MUCH SOONER!
COME ALONG, SPOT!
EEP!
HA HA HA HA HA
EEP! EEP!
I AM ON MY WAY BACK FROM A PILGRIMAGE TO PRAY FOR MY SON, ATSUO.
YOUR SON? IS SOMETHING THE MATTER WITH HIM?
YES...
I HOPE YOUR PRAYERS ARE ANSWERED.
LATER...
THIS IS PUFF PUFF YOUR VILLAGE? (I HOPE!)
HEH HEH! YES IT IS! YOU CAN PUT ME DOWN, NOW, USAGI.
THERE'S SOME KIND OF COMMOTION UP AHEAD!
2

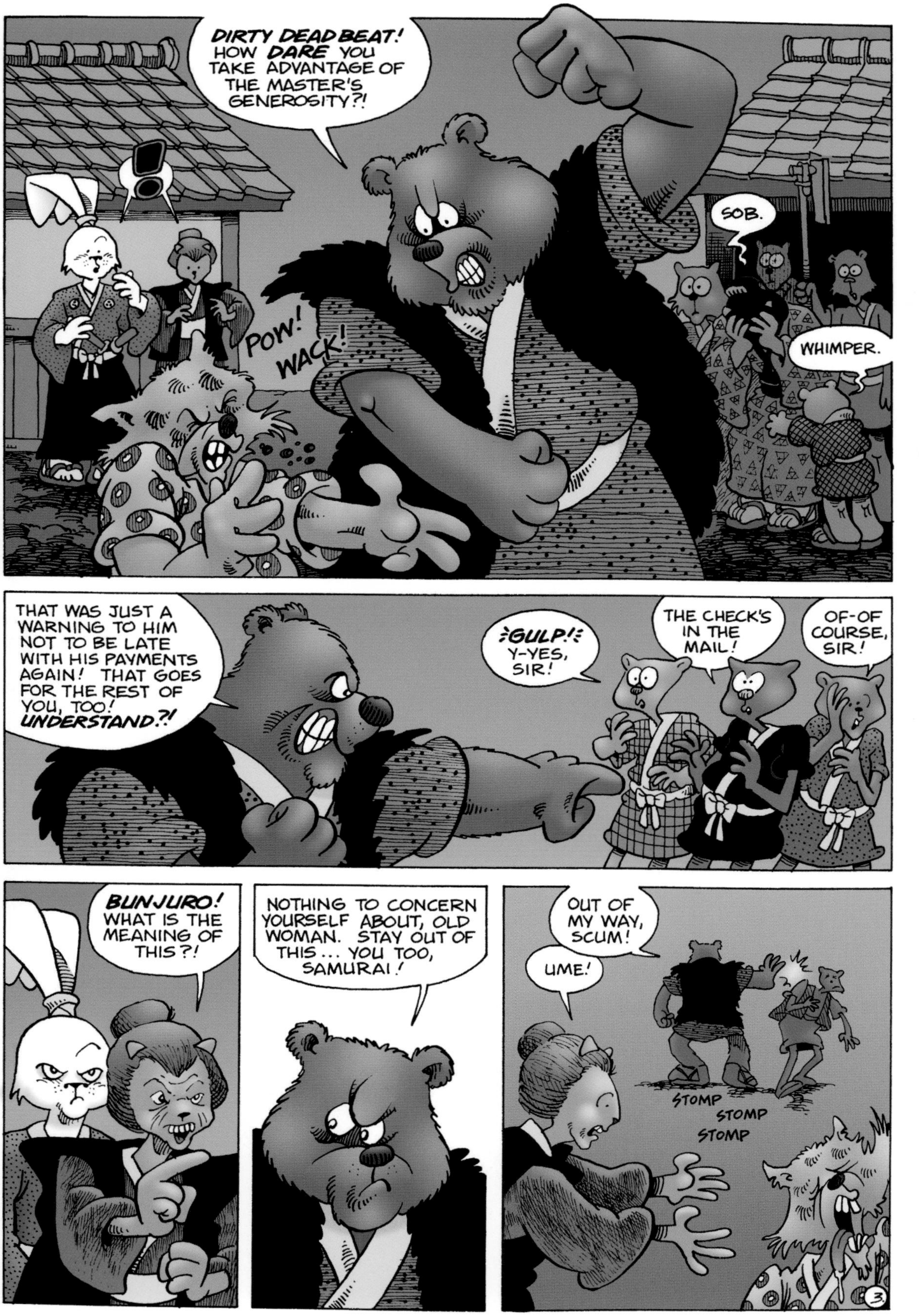
DIRTY DEADBEAT! HOW DARE YOU TAKE ADVANTAGE OF THE MASTER'S GENEROSITY?!
SOB.
POW! WACK!
WHIMPER.
THAT WAS JUST A WARNING TO HIM NOT TO BE LATE WITH HIS PAYMENTS AGAIN! THAT GOES FOR THE REST OF YOU, TOO! UNDERSTAND?!
GULP! Y-YES, SIR!
THE CHECK'S IN THE MAIL!
OF-OF COURSE, SIR!
BUNJURO! WHAT IS THE MEANING OF THIS?!
NOTHING TO CONCERN YOURSELF ABOUT, OLD WOMAN. STAY OUT OF THIS... YOU TOO, SAMURAI!
OUT OF MY WAY, SCUM!
UME!
STOMP
STOMP
STOMP
3

YOU... YOU **KNOW** THAT ROGUE?

HE WORKS FOR MY SON.

OH, I'M SO SORRY! ARE YOU ALL RIGHT?

DON'T TOUCH MY HUSBAND, YOU WITCH! **GET AWAY FROM HIM!**

≶GROAN≶

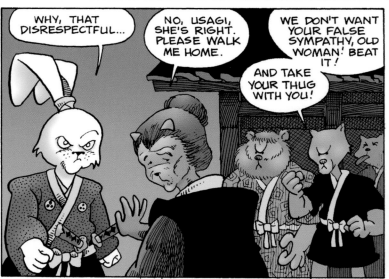

WHY, THAT DISRESPECTFUL...

NO, USAGI, SHE'S RIGHT. PLEASE WALK ME HOME.

WE DON'T WANT YOUR FALSE SYMPATHY, OLD WOMAN! BEAT IT!

AND TAKE YOUR THUG WITH YOU!

MY SON IS A MONEY LENDER. HE PRACTICALLY **OWNS** THE WHOLE TOWN!

THIS IS OUR HOME, USAGI-SAN. YOU AND SPOT MUST SPEND THE NIGHT WITH US!

EEP?

WHAT ARE **YOU** DOING HERE, SAMURAI?

4.

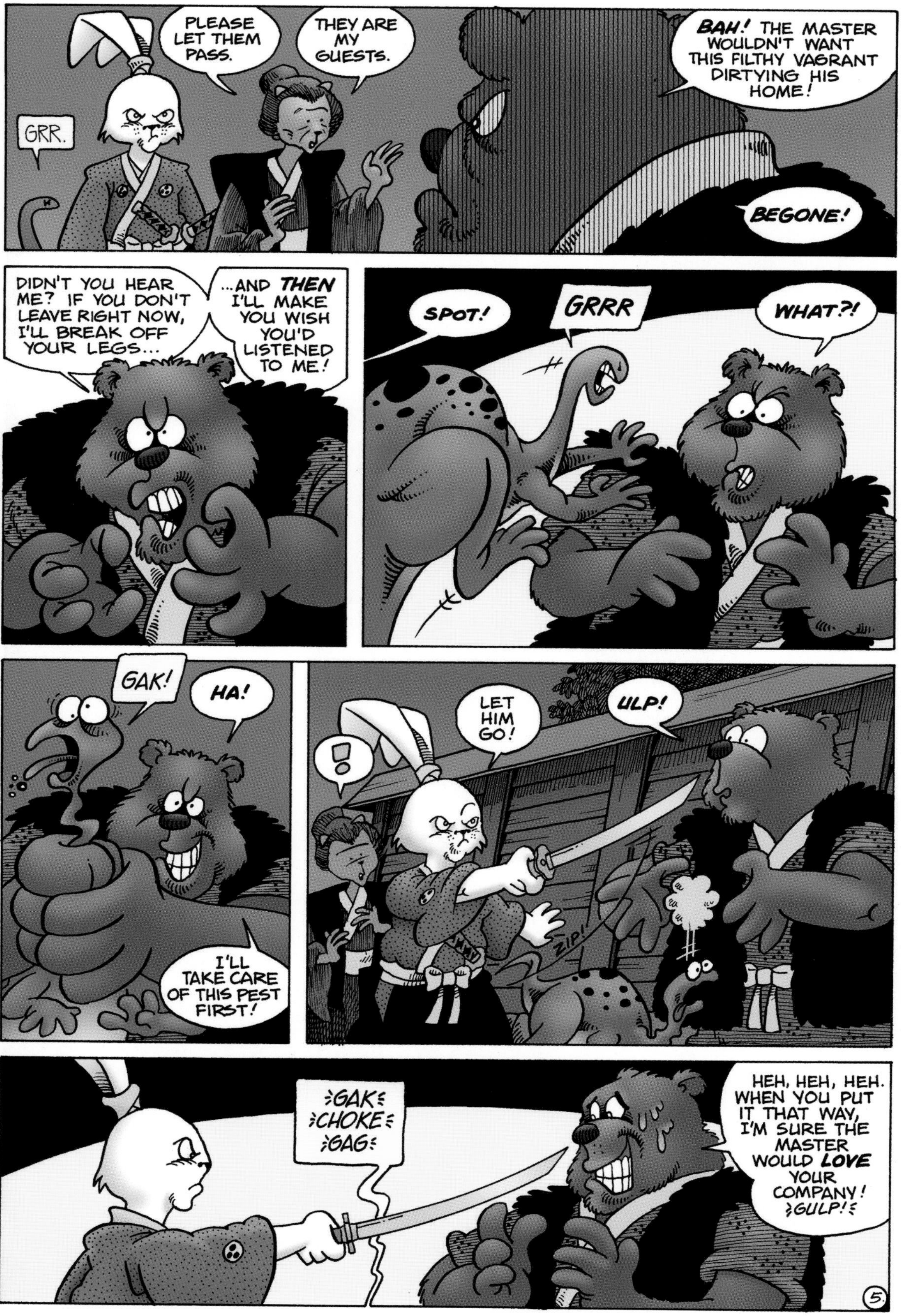
PLEASE LET THEM PASS.
THEY ARE MY GUESTS.
GRR.
BAH! THE MASTER WOULDN'T WANT THIS FILTHY VAGRANT DIRTYING HIS HOME!
BEGONE!
DIDN'T YOU HEAR ME? IF YOU DON'T LEAVE RIGHT NOW, I'LL BREAK OFF YOUR LEGS...
...AND THEN I'LL MAKE YOU WISH YOU'D LISTENED TO ME!
SPOT!
GRRR
WHAT?!
GAK!
HA!
I'LL TAKE CARE OF THIS PEST FIRST!
!
LET HIM GO!
ULP!
ZIP!
GAK
CHOKE
GAG
HEH, HEH, HEH. WHEN YOU PUT IT THAT WAY, I'M SURE THE MASTER WOULD LOVE YOUR COMPANY!
GULP!
5

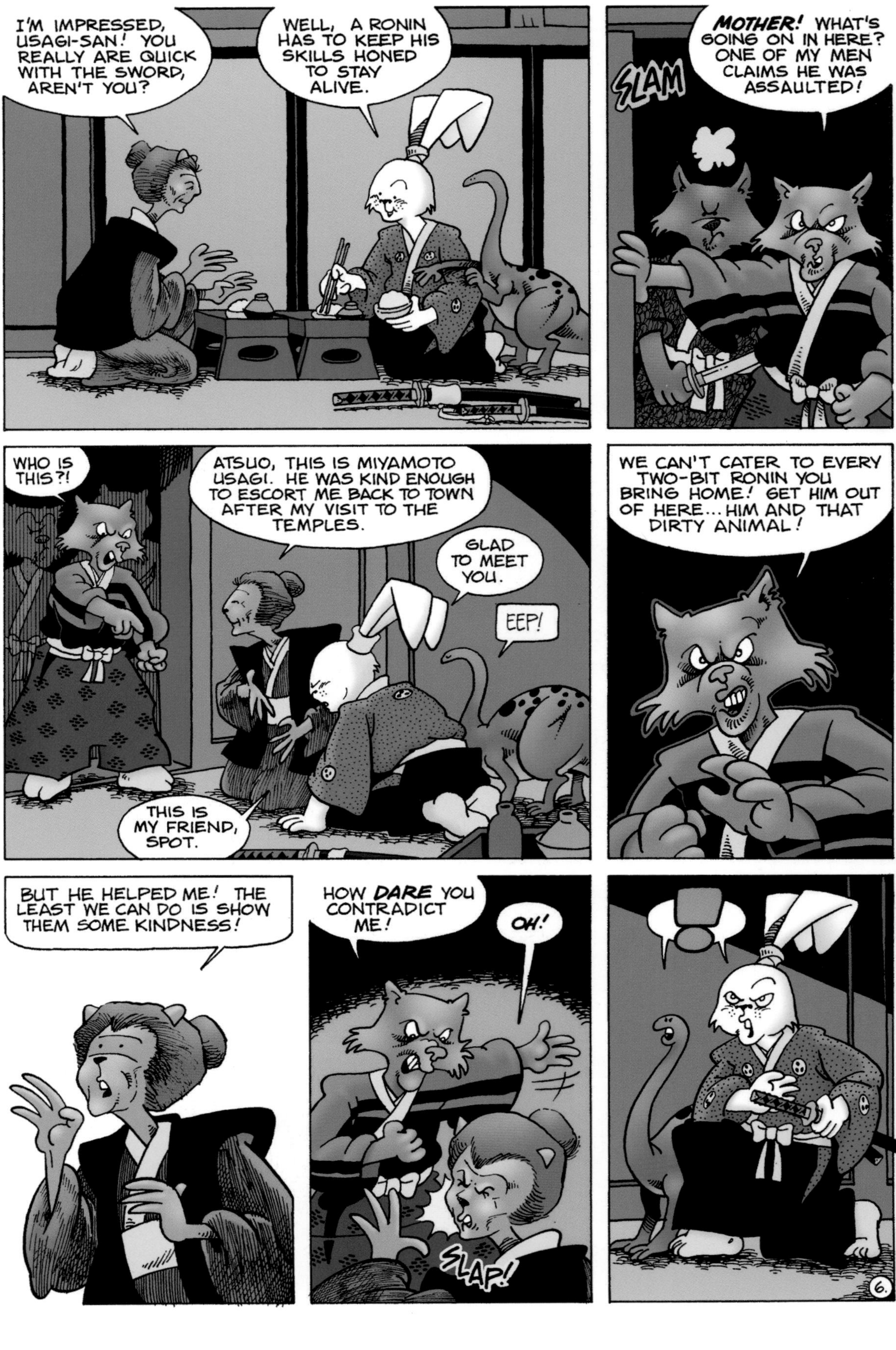

I'M IMPRESSED, USAGI-SAN! YOU REALLY ARE QUICK WITH THE SWORD, AREN'T YOU?
WELL, A RONIN HAS TO KEEP HIS SKILLS HONED TO STAY ALIVE.
SLAM
MOTHER! WHAT'S GOING ON IN HERE? ONE OF MY MEN CLAIMS HE WAS ASSAULTED!
WHO IS THIS?!
ATSUO, THIS IS MIYAMOTO USAGI. HE WAS KIND ENOUGH TO ESCORT ME BACK TO TOWN AFTER MY VISIT TO THE TEMPLES.
GLAD TO MEET YOU.
EEP!
THIS IS MY FRIEND, SPOT.
WE CAN'T CATER TO EVERY TWO-BIT RONIN YOU BRING HOME! GET HIM OUT OF HERE... HIM AND THAT DIRTY ANIMAL!
BUT HE HELPED ME! THE LEAST WE CAN DO IS SHOW THEM SOME KINDNESS!
HOW DARE YOU CONTRADICT ME!
OH!
SLAP!
6.

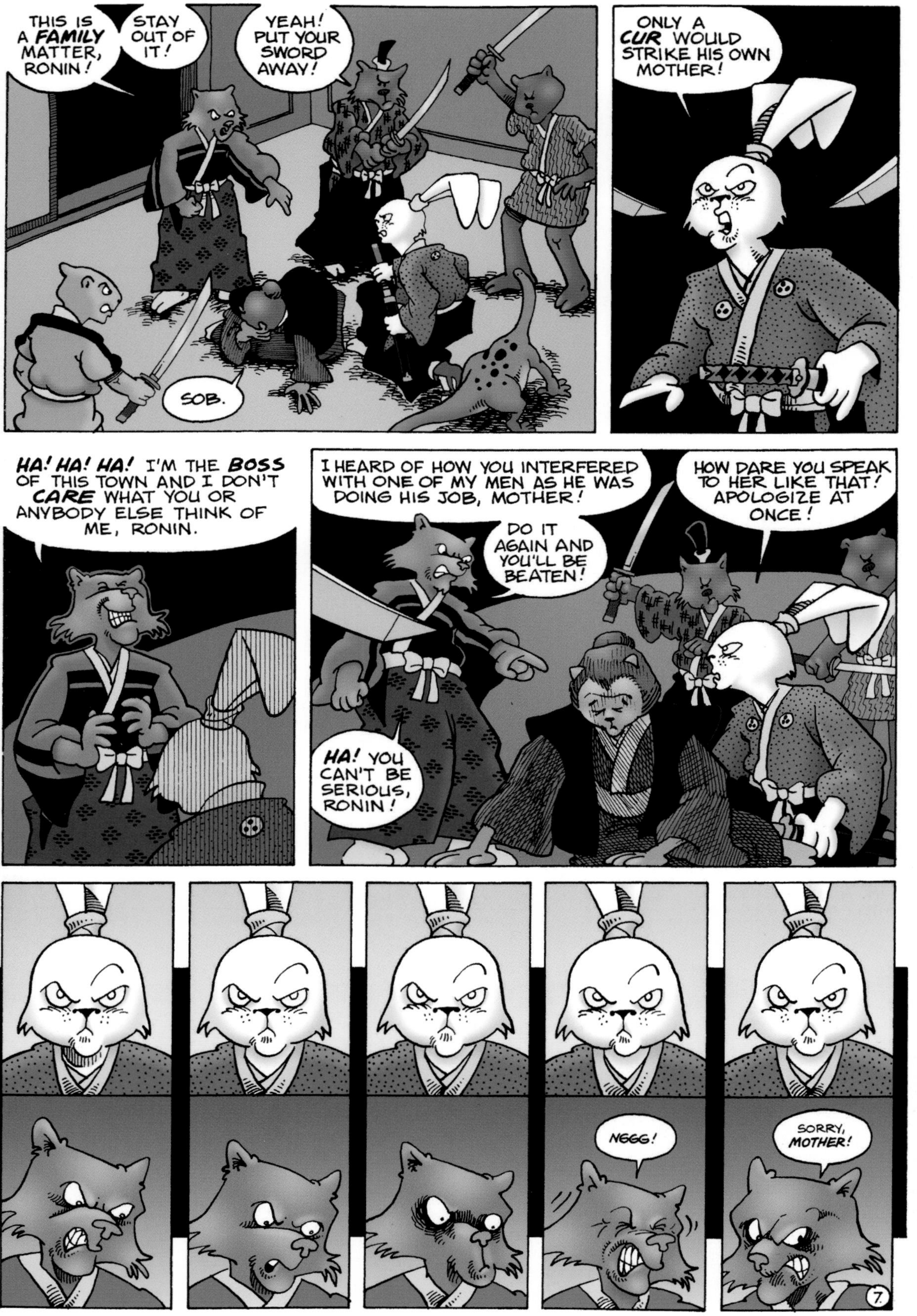
THIS IS A FAMILY MATTER, RONIN!
STAY OUT OF IT!
YEAH! PUT YOUR SWORD AWAY!
SOB.
ONLY A CUR WOULD STRIKE HIS OWN MOTHER!
HA! HA! HA! I'M THE BOSS OF THIS TOWN AND I DON'T CARE WHAT YOU OR ANYBODY ELSE THINK OF ME, RONIN.
I HEARD OF HOW YOU INTERFERED WITH ONE OF MY MEN AS HE WAS DOING HIS JOB, MOTHER!
DO IT AGAIN AND YOU'LL BE BEATEN!
HOW DARE YOU SPEAK TO HER LIKE THAT! APOLOGIZE AT ONCE!
HA! YOU CAN'T BE SERIOUS, RONIN!
NEGG!
SORRY, MOTHER!
7

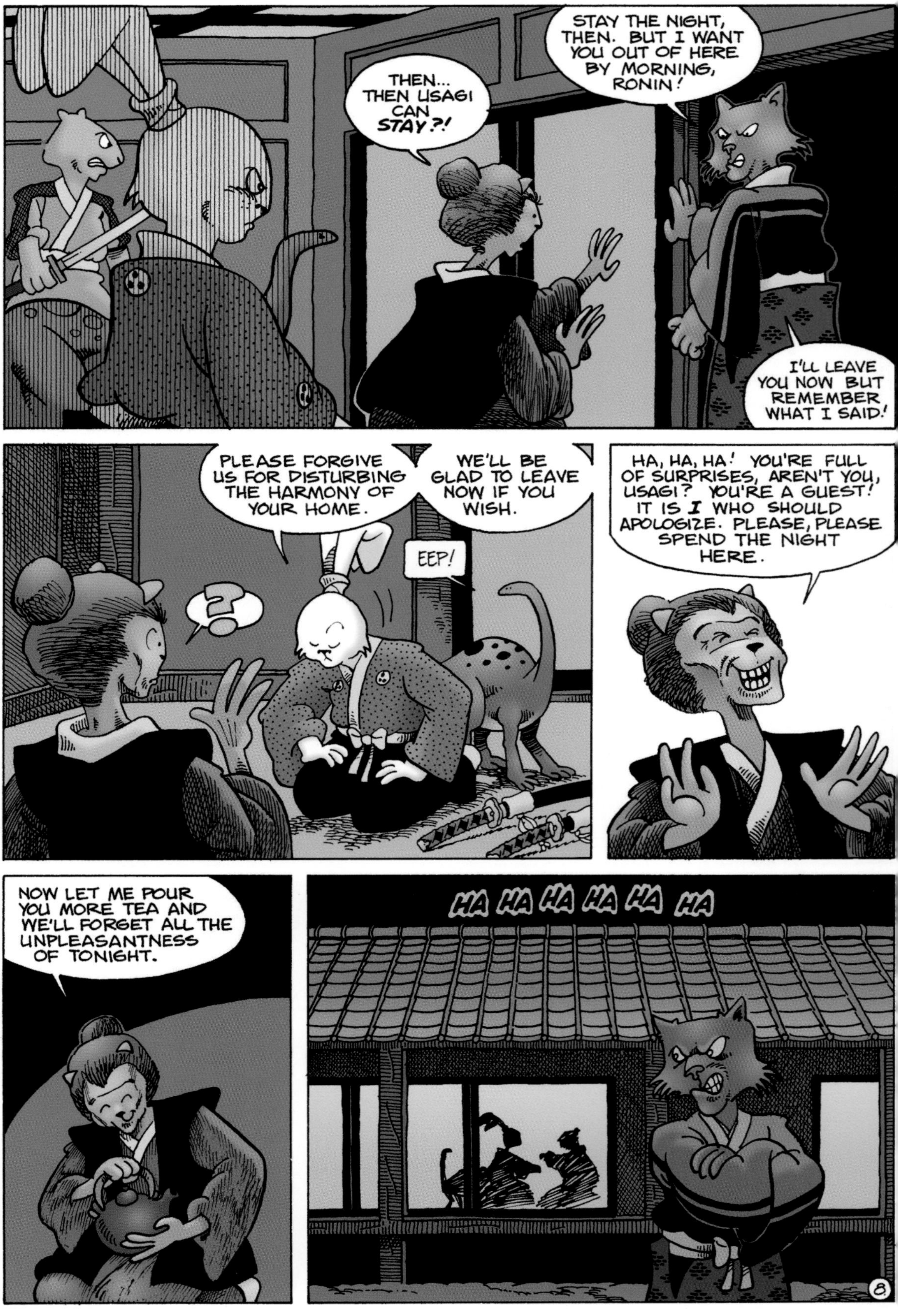
STAY THE NIGHT, THEN. BUT I WANT YOU OUT OF HERE BY MORNING, RONIN!
THEN... THEN USAGI CAN STAY?!
I'LL LEAVE YOU NOW BUT REMEMBER WHAT I SAID!
PLEASE FORGIVE US FOR DISTURBING THE HARMONY OF YOUR HOME.
WE'LL BE GLAD TO LEAVE NOW IF YOU WISH.
?
EEP!
HA, HA, HA! YOU'RE FULL OF SURPRISES, AREN'T YOU, USAGI? YOU'RE A GUEST! IT IS I WHO SHOULD APOLOGIZE. PLEASE, PLEASE SPEND THE NIGHT HERE.
NOW LET ME POUR YOU MORE TEA AND WE'LL FORGET ALL THE UNPLEASANTNESS OF TONIGHT.
HA HA HA HA HA HA
8

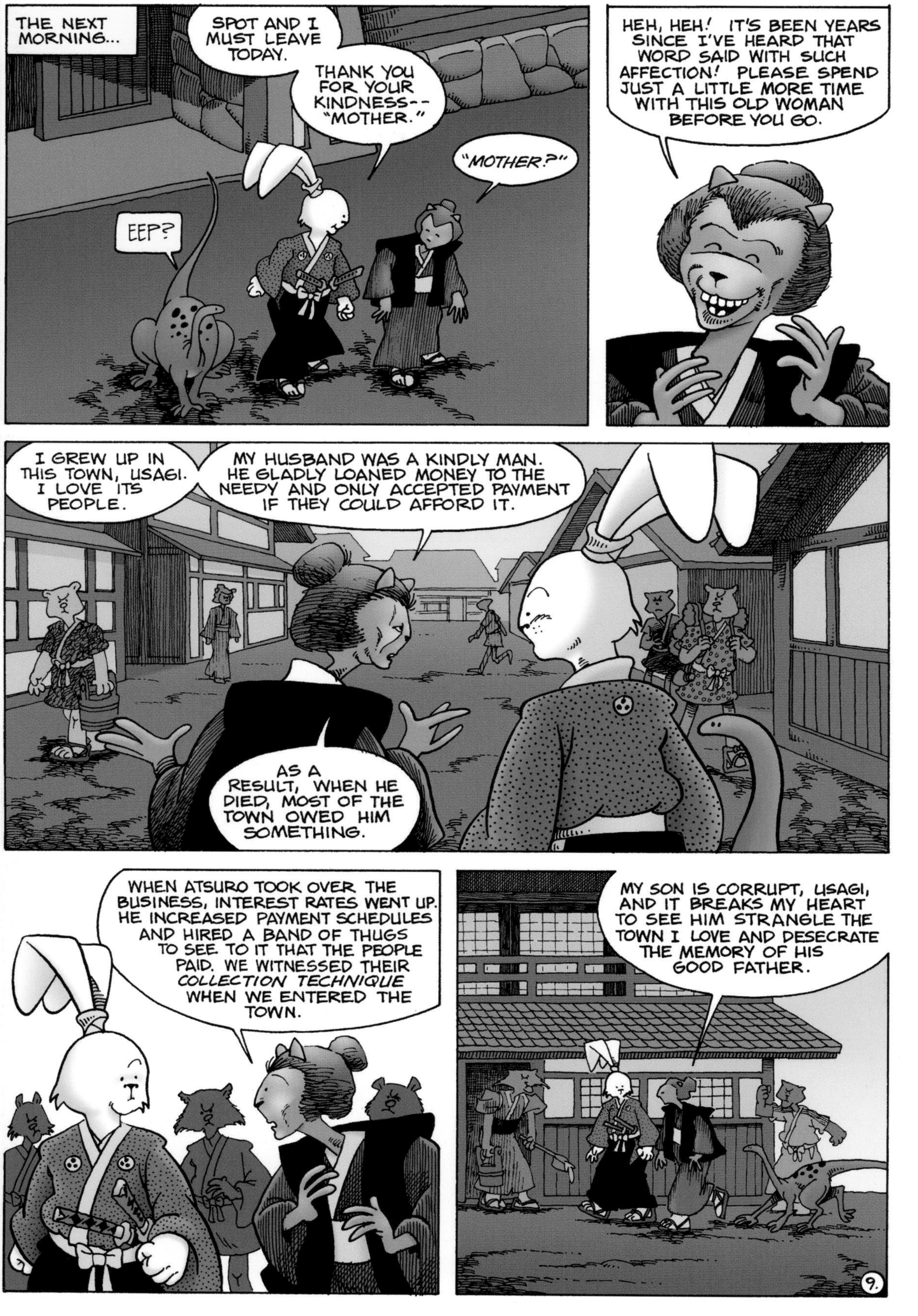
THE NEXT MORNING...
SPOT AND I MUST LEAVE TODAY.
THANK YOU FOR YOUR KINDNESS-- "MOTHER."
"MOTHER?"
EEP?
HEH, HEH! IT'S BEEN YEARS SINCE I'VE HEARD THAT WORD SAID WITH SUCH AFFECTION! PLEASE SPEND JUST A LITTLE MORE TIME WITH THIS OLD WOMAN BEFORE YOU GO.
I GREW UP IN THIS TOWN, USAGI. I LOVE ITS PEOPLE.
MY HUSBAND WAS A KINDLY MAN. HE GLADLY LOANED MONEY TO THE NEEDY AND ONLY ACCEPTED PAYMENT IF THEY COULD AFFORD IT.
AS A RESULT, WHEN HE DIED, MOST OF THE TOWN OWED HIM SOMETHING.
WHEN ATSURO TOOK OVER THE BUSINESS, INTEREST RATES WENT UP. HE INCREASED PAYMENT SCHEDULES AND HIRED A BAND OF THUGS TO SEE TO IT THAT THE PEOPLE PAID. WE WITNESSED THEIR *COLLECTION TECHNIQUE* WHEN WE ENTERED THE TOWN.
MY SON IS CORRUPT, USAGI, AND IT BREAKS MY HEART TO SEE HIM STRANGLE THE TOWN I LOVE AND DESECRATE THE MEMORY OF HIS GOOD FATHER.
9.

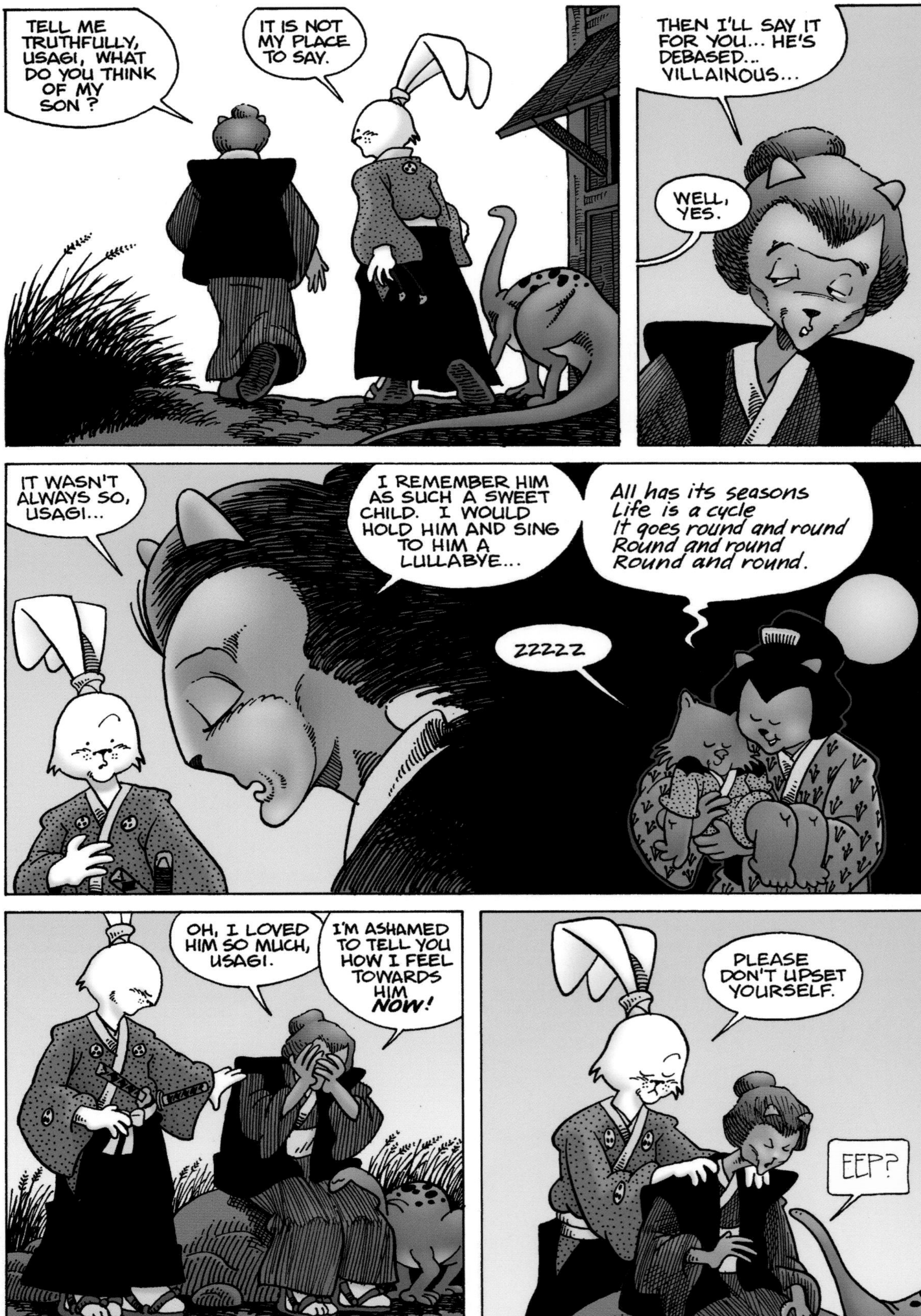
TELL ME TRUTHFULLY, USAGI, WHAT DO YOU THINK OF MY SON ?
IT IS NOT MY PLACE TO SAY.
THEN I'LL SAY IT FOR YOU... HE'S DEBASED... VILLAINOUS...
WELL, YES.
IT WASN'T ALWAYS SO, USAGI...
I REMEMBER HIM AS SUCH A SWEET CHILD. I WOULD HOLD HIM AND SING TO HIM A LULLABYE...
All has its seasons
Life is a cycle
It goes round and round
Round and round
Round and round.
ZZZZZ
OH, I LOVED HIM SO MUCH, USAGI.
I'M ASHAMED TO TELL YOU HOW I FEEL TOWARDS HIM NOW!
PLEASE DON'T UPSET YOURSELF.
EEP?
10.

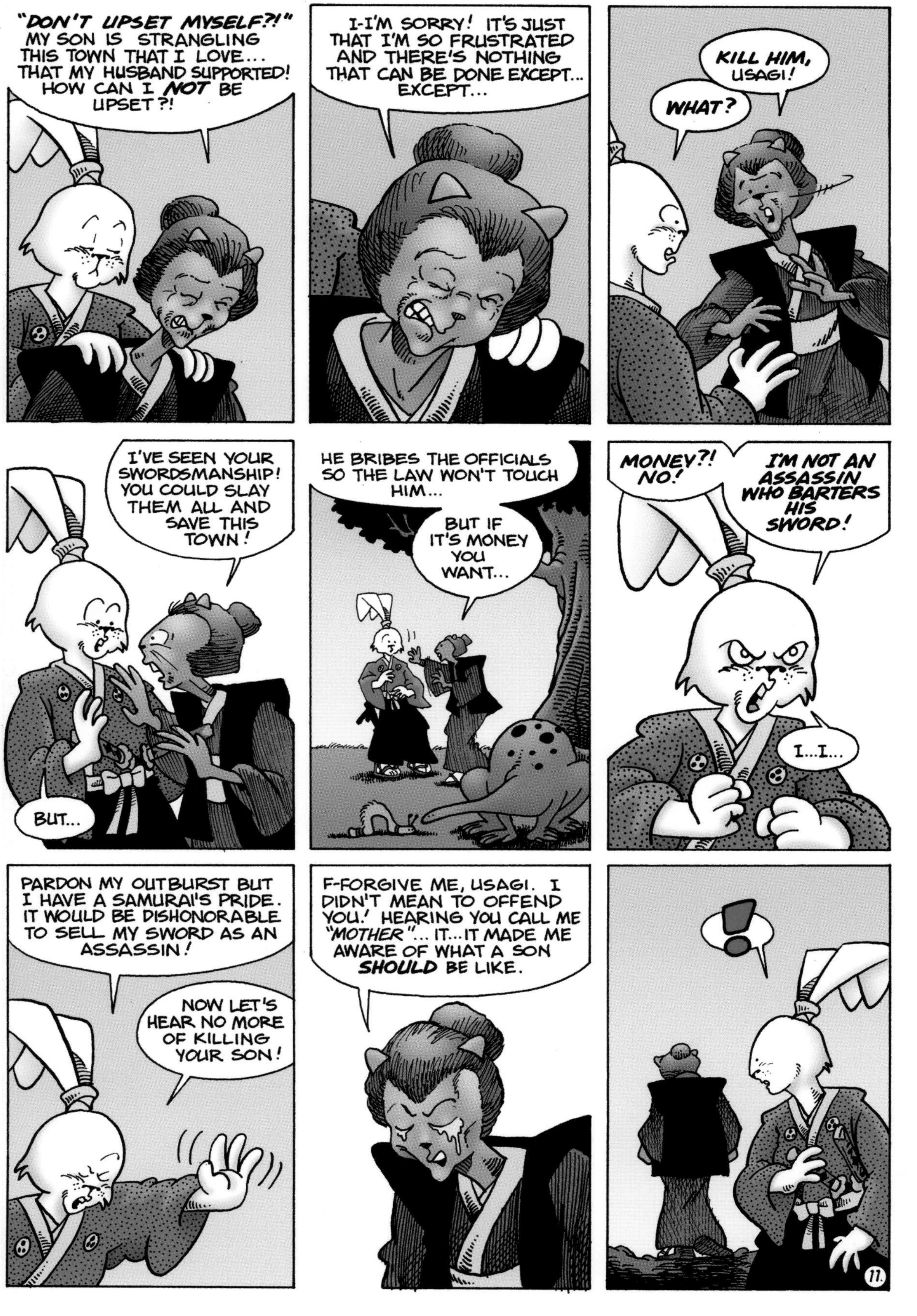
"DON'T UPSET MYSELF?!" MY SON IS STRANGLING THIS TOWN THAT I LOVE... THAT MY HUSBAND SUPPORTED! HOW CAN I NOT BE UPSET?!
I-I'M SORRY! IT'S JUST THAT I'M SO FRUSTRATED AND THERE'S NOTHING THAT CAN BE DONE EXCEPT... EXCEPT...
KILL HIM, USAGI!
WHAT?
I'VE SEEN YOUR SWORDSMANSHIP! YOU COULD SLAY THEM ALL AND SAVE THIS TOWN!
BUT...
HE BRIBES THE OFFICIALS SO THE LAW WON'T TOUCH HIM...
BUT IF IT'S MONEY YOU WANT...
MONEY?! NO!
I'M NOT AN ASSASSIN WHO BARTERS HIS SWORD!
I...I...
PARDON MY OUTBURST BUT I HAVE A SAMURAI'S PRIDE. IT WOULD BE DISHONORABLE TO SELL MY SWORD AS AN ASSASSIN!
NOW LET'S HEAR NO MORE OF KILLING YOUR SON!
F-FORGIVE ME, USAGI. I DIDN'T MEAN TO OFFEND YOU! HEARING YOU CALL ME "MOTHER"... IT...IT MADE ME AWARE OF WHAT A SON SHOULD BE LIKE.
!
11.

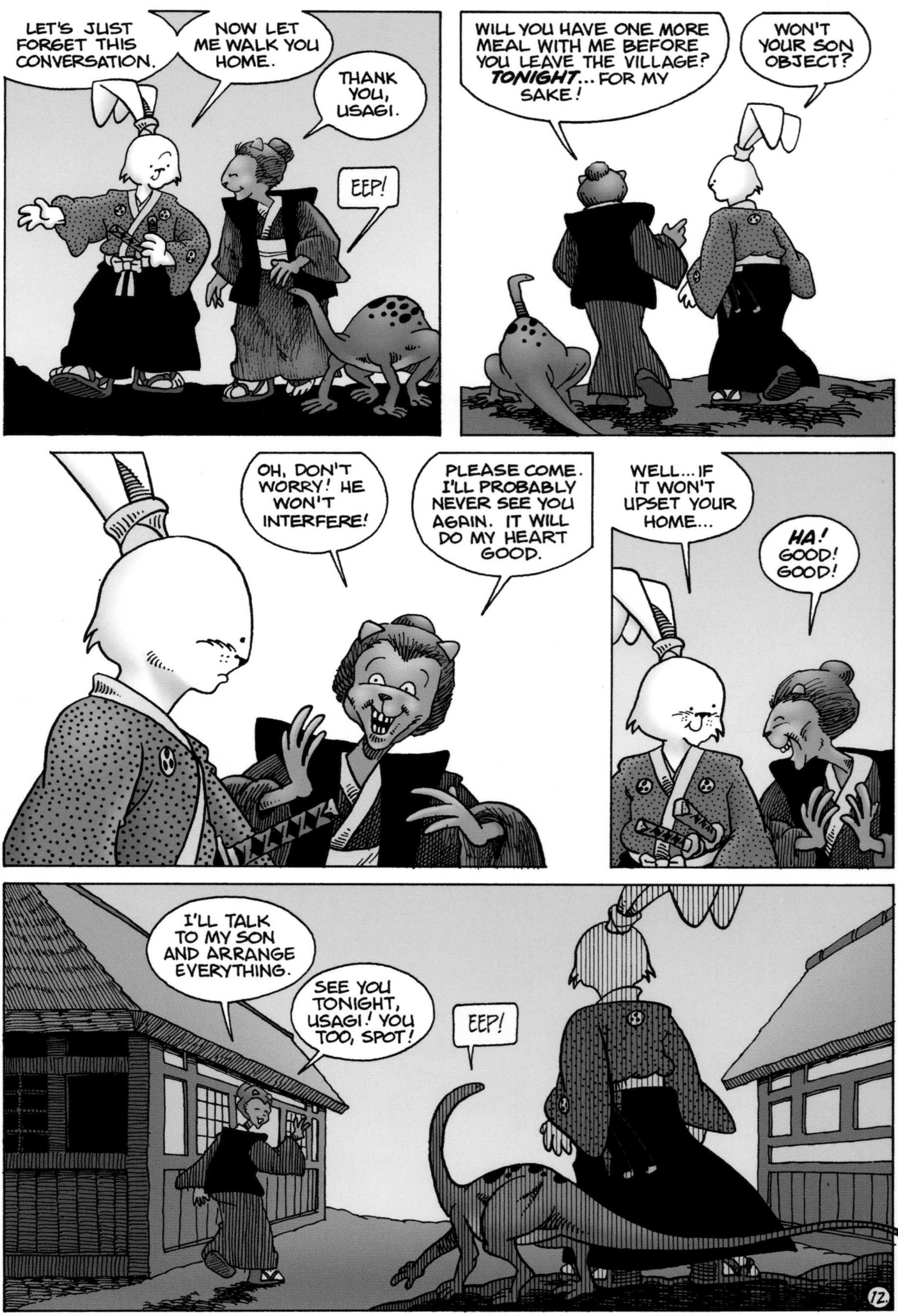
LET'S JUST FORGET THIS CONVERSATION.
NOW LET ME WALK YOU HOME.
THANK YOU, USAGI.
EEP!
WILL YOU HAVE ONE MORE MEAL WITH ME BEFORE YOU LEAVE THE VILLAGE? TONIGHT... FOR MY SAKE!
WON'T YOUR SON OBJECT?
OH, DON'T WORRY! HE WON'T INTERFERE!
PLEASE COME. I'LL PROBABLY NEVER SEE YOU AGAIN. IT WILL DO MY HEART GOOD.
WELL... IF IT WON'T UPSET YOUR HOME...
HA! GOOD! GOOD!
I'LL TALK TO MY SON AND ARRANGE EVERYTHING.
SEE YOU TONIGHT, USAGI! YOU TOO, SPOT!
EEP!
12.

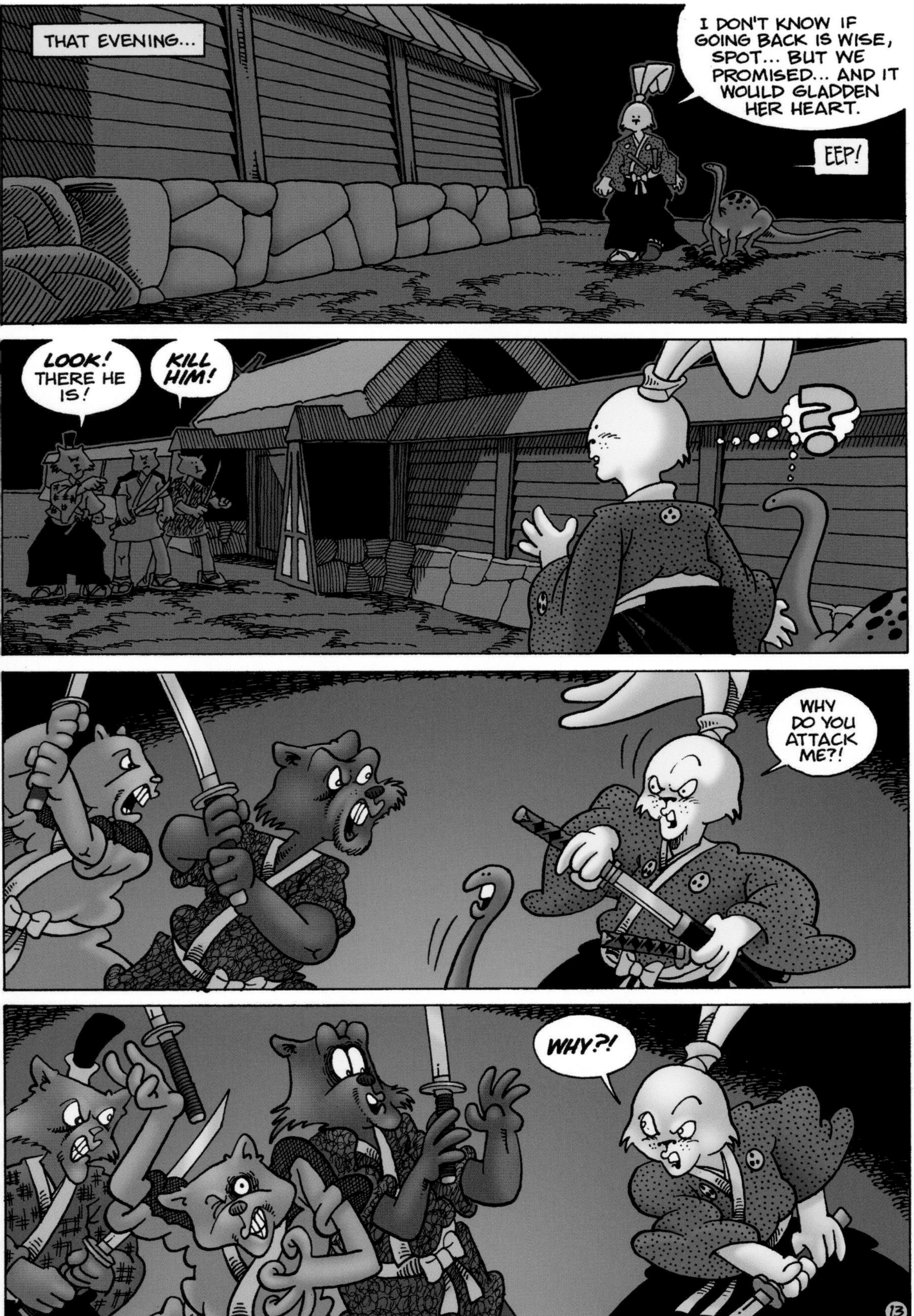
THAT EVENING...
I DON'T KNOW IF GOING BACK IS WISE, SPOT... BUT WE PROMISED... AND IT WOULD GLADDEN HER HEART.
EEP!
LOOK! THERE HE IS!
KILL HIM!
?
WHY DO YOU ATTACK ME?!
WHY?!
13

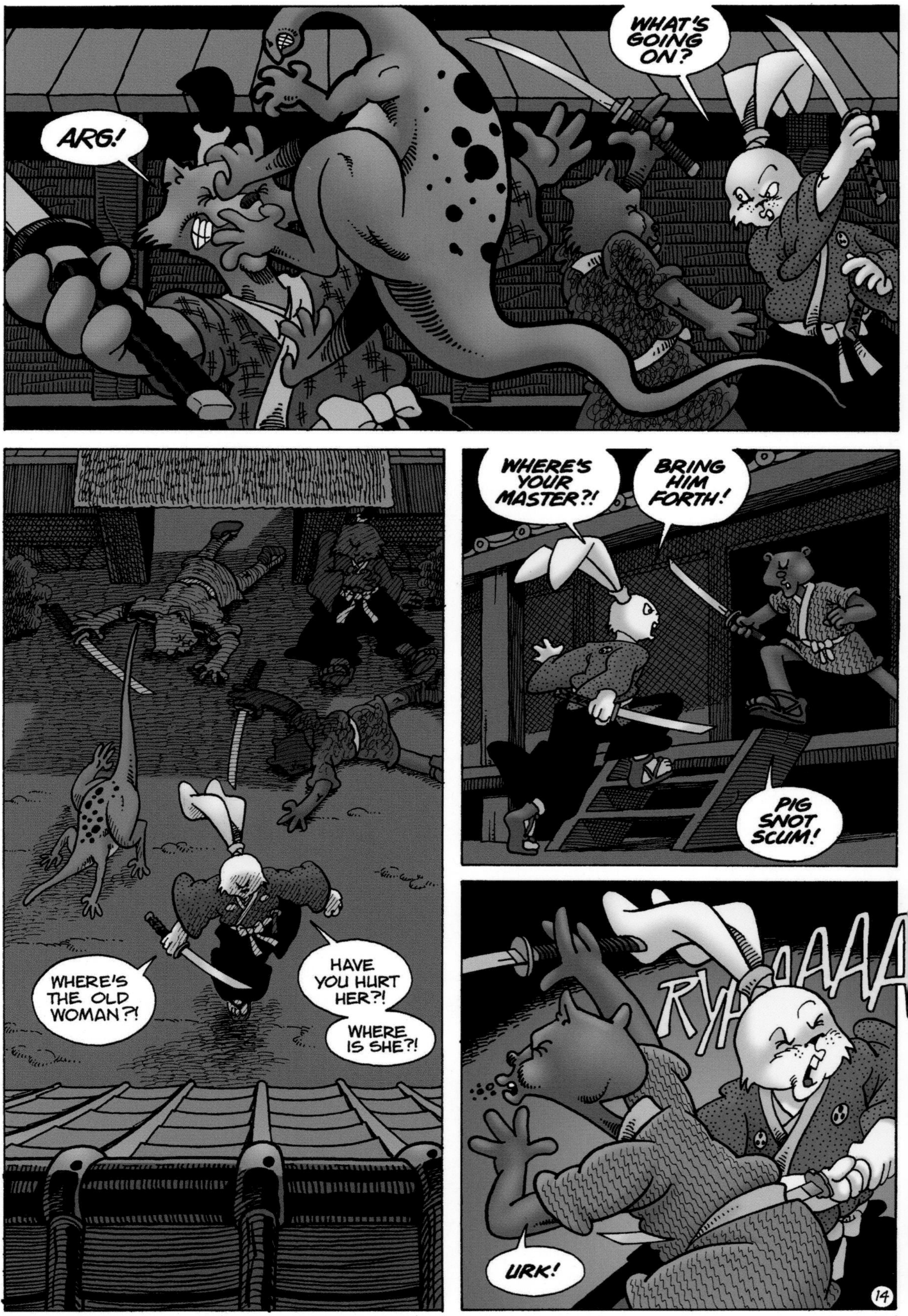
ARG!
WHAT'S GOING ON?
WHERE'S THE OLD WOMAN?!
HAVE YOU HURT HER?!
WHERE IS SHE?!
WHERE'S YOUR MASTER?!
BRING HIM FORTH!
PIG SNOT SCUM!
RYAAAAA
URK!
14

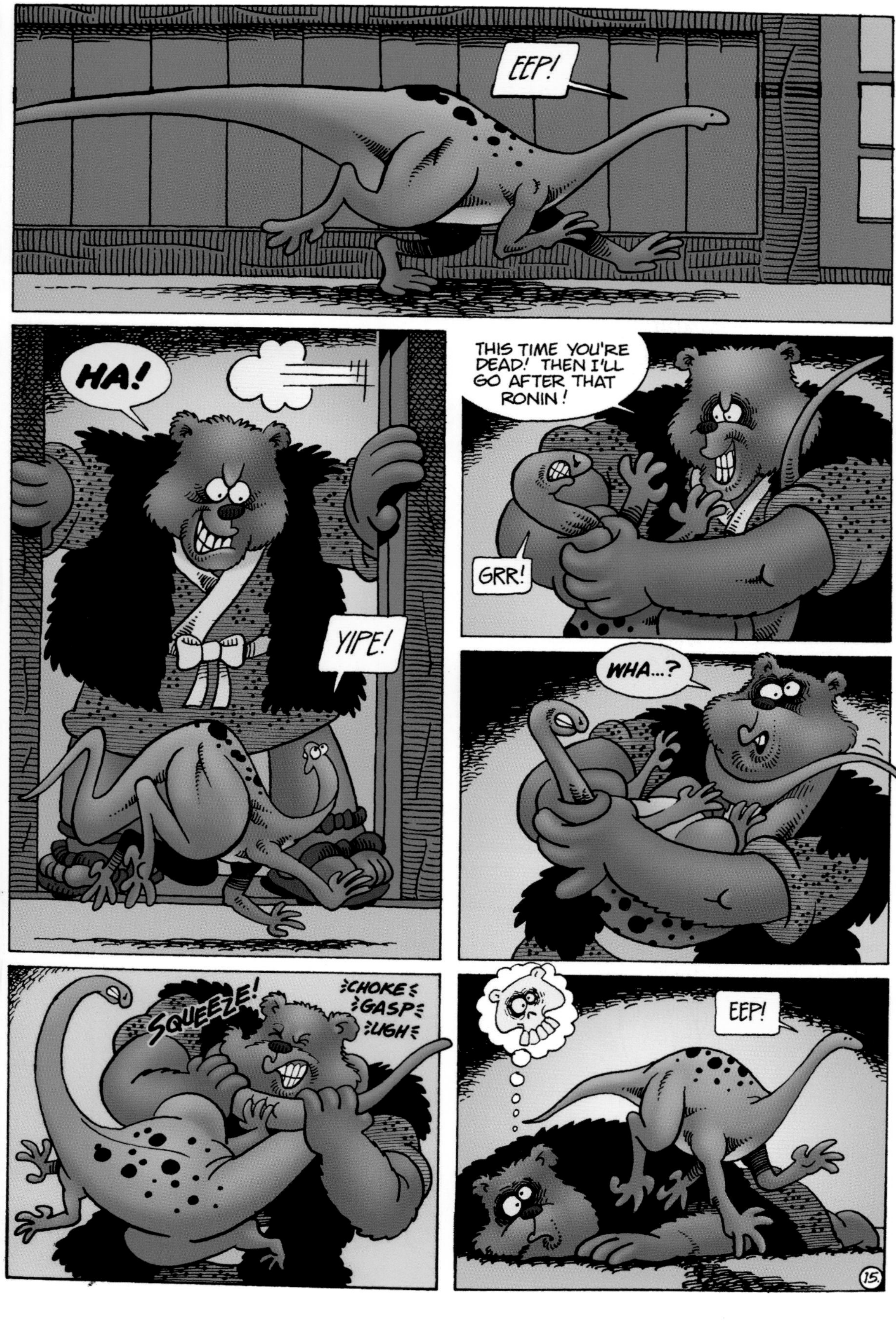
EEP!
HA!
YIPE!
THIS TIME YOU'RE DEAD! THEN I'LL GO AFTER THAT RONIN!
GRR!
WHA...?
SQUEEZE!
CHOKE
GASP
UGH
EEP!
15.

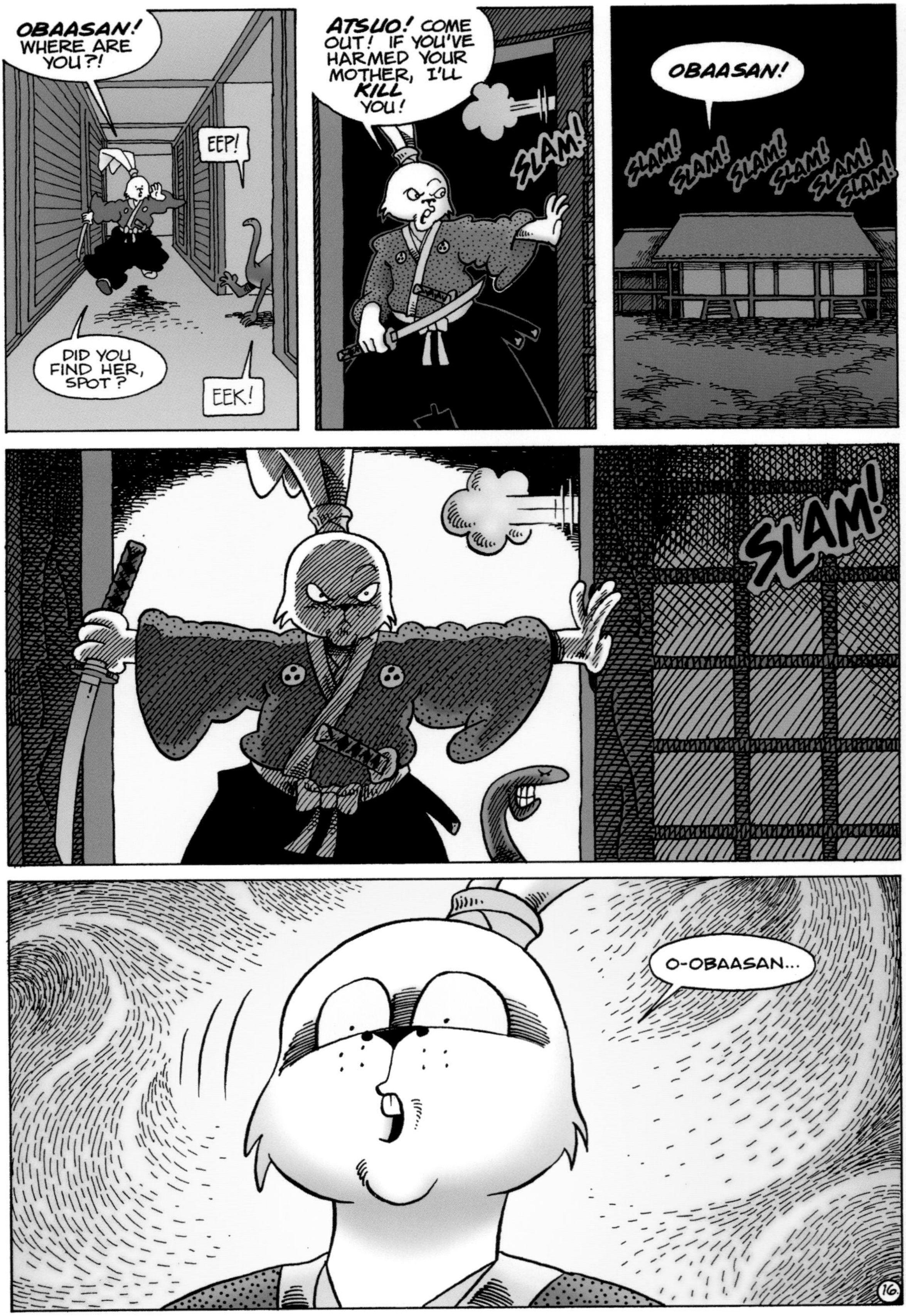
OBAASAN! WHERE ARE YOU?!
EEP!
DID YOU FIND HER, SPOT?
EEK!
ATSUO! COME OUT! IF YOU'VE HARMED YOUR MOTHER, I'LL KILL YOU!
SLAM!
OBAASAN!
SLAM! SLAM! SLAM! SLAM! SLAM! SLAM!
SLAM!
O-OBAASAN...
16.

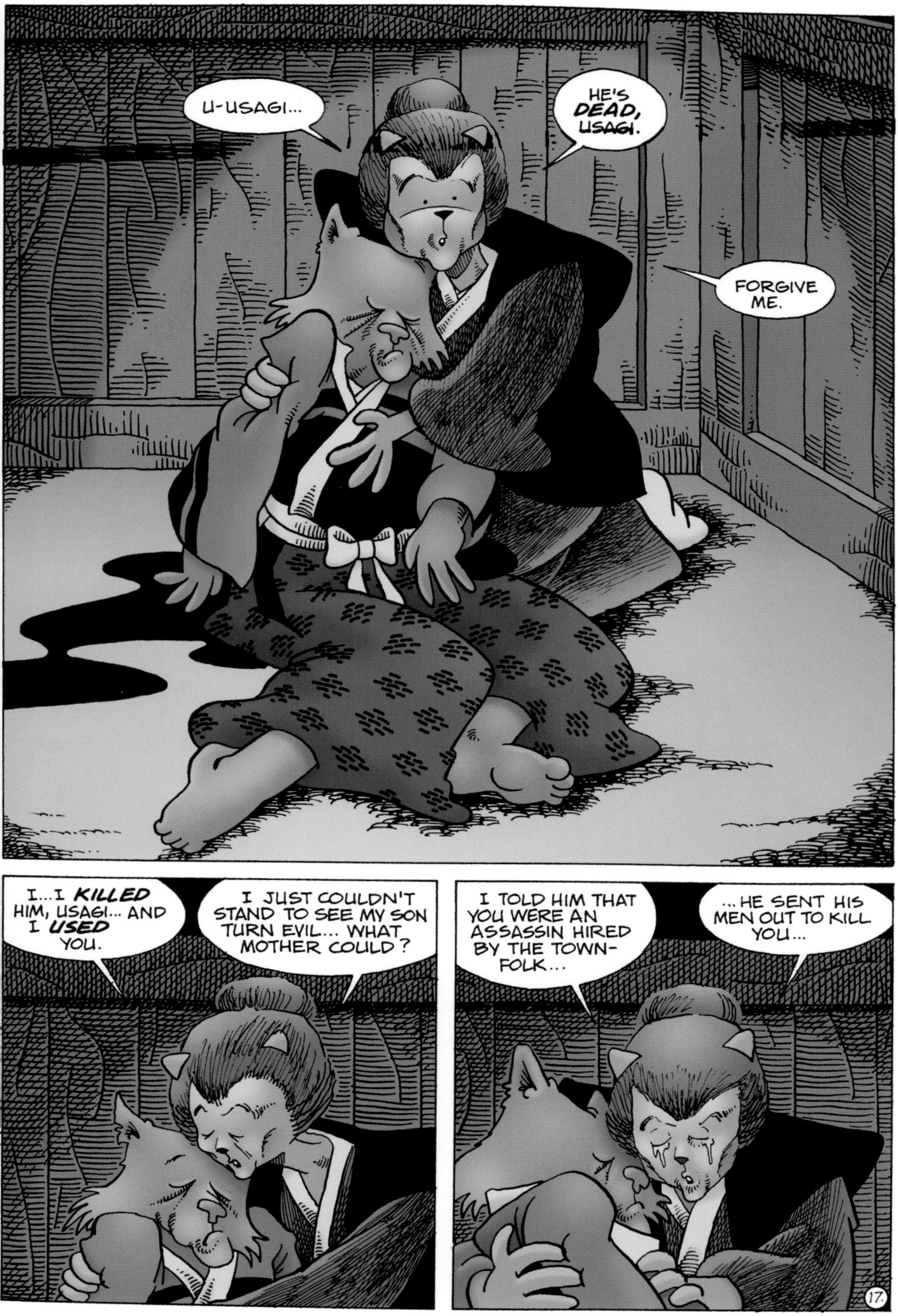
U-USAGI...
HE'S DEAD, USAGI.
FORGIVE ME.
I...I KILLED HIM, USAGI... AND I USED YOU.
I JUST COULDN'T STAND TO SEE MY SON TURN EVIL... WHAT MOTHER COULD?
I TOLD HIM THAT YOU WERE AN ASSASSIN HIRED BY THE TOWN-FOLK...
...HE SENT HIS MEN OUT TO KILL YOU...
17

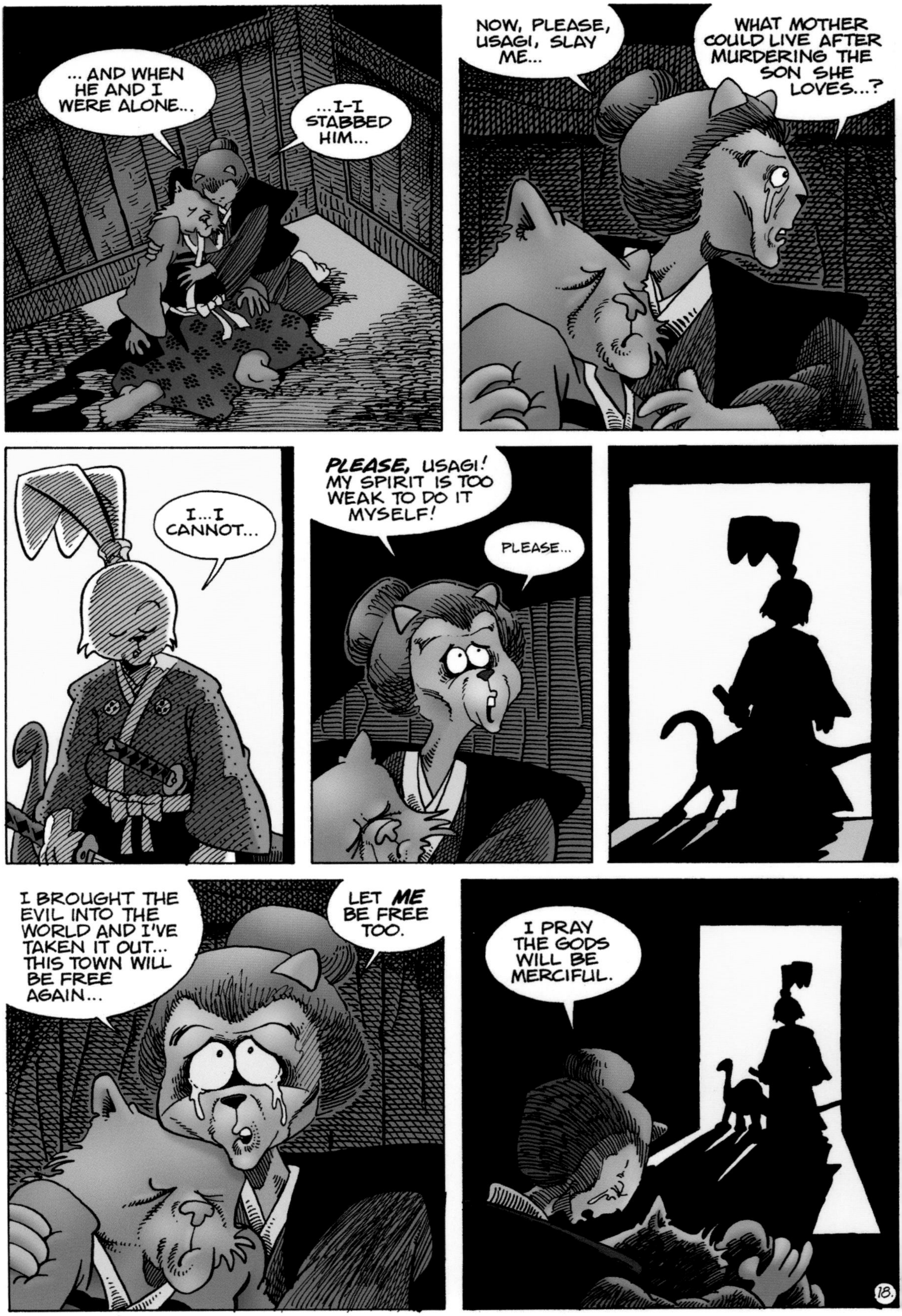
... AND WHEN HE AND I WERE ALONE...
...I-I STABBED HIM...
NOW, PLEASE, USAGI, SLAY ME...
WHAT MOTHER COULD LIVE AFTER MURDERING THE SON SHE LOVES...?
I...I CANNOT...
PLEASE, USAGI! MY SPIRIT IS TOO WEAK TO DO IT MYSELF!
PLEASE...
I BROUGHT THE EVIL INTO THE WORLD AND I'VE TAKEN IT OUT... THIS TOWN WILL BE FREE AGAIN...
LET ME BE FREE TOO.
I PRAY THE GODS WILL BE MERCIFUL.
18.

I'LL HOLD YOU TIGHT, MY SON... AND SING TO YOU-- JUST LIKE I USED TO...

The grass of summertime Grows long and green...

But it withers Before autumn's cold, harsh wind...

Winter covers all With a blanket of snow...

But lo how they reappear With the spring thaw...

All has its seasons Life is a cycle. It goes round and round Round and round Round and rou--※

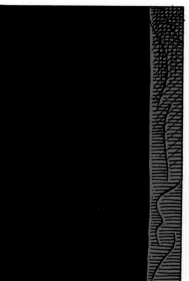

19.

45

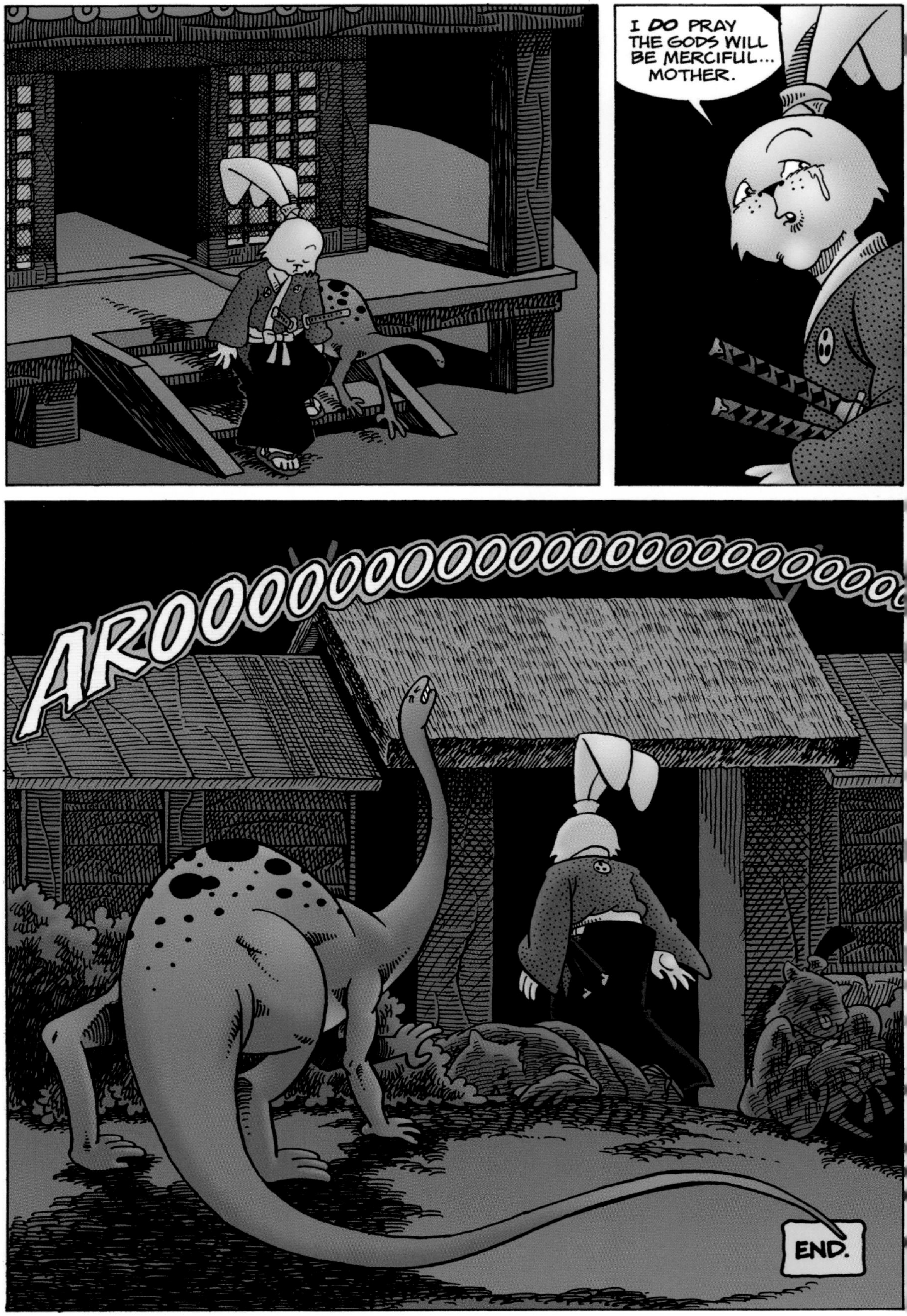

I DO PRAY THE GODS WILL BE MERCIFUL... MOTHER.
AROOOOOOOOOOOOOOOOOOOOOOOOOOOOOO
END.

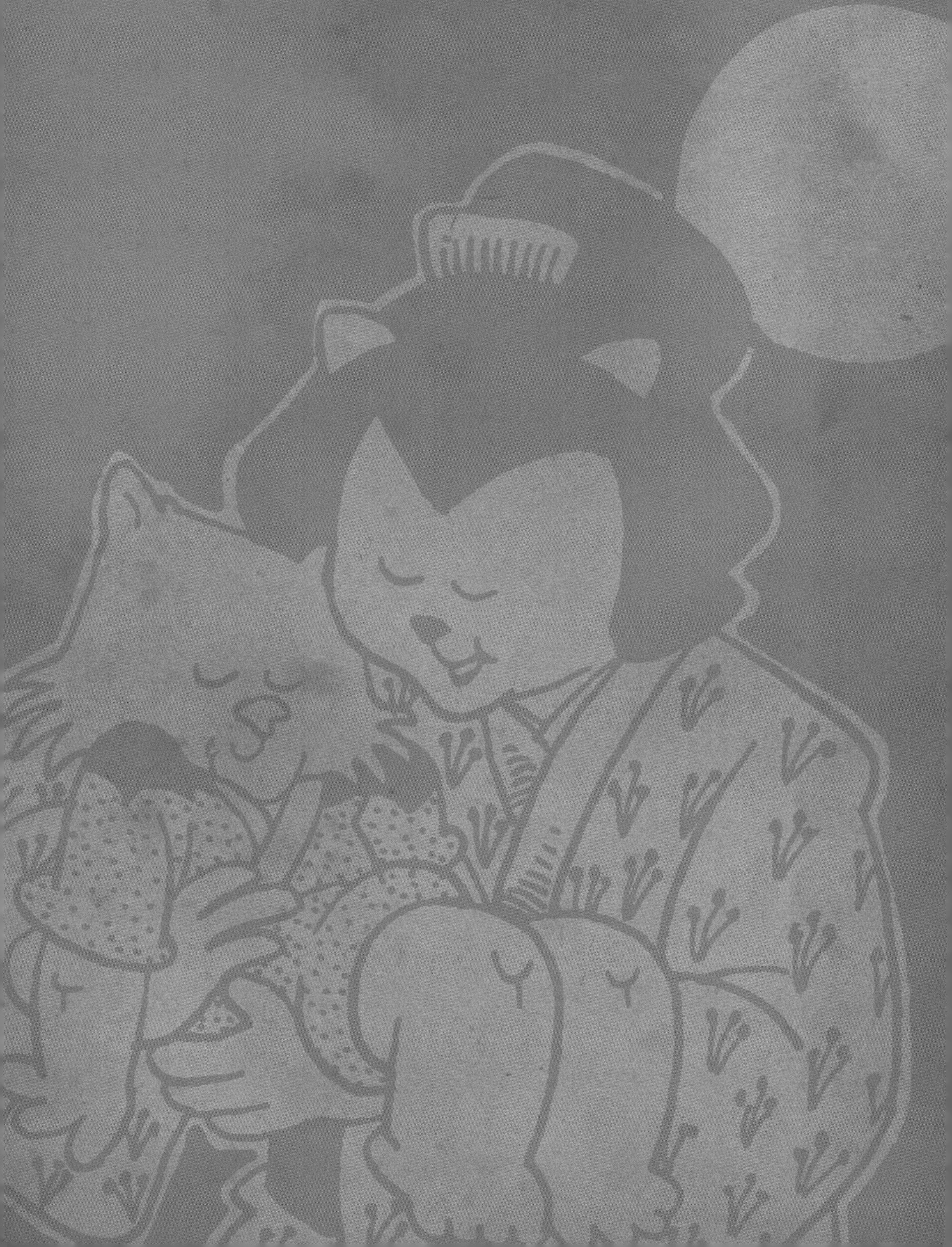

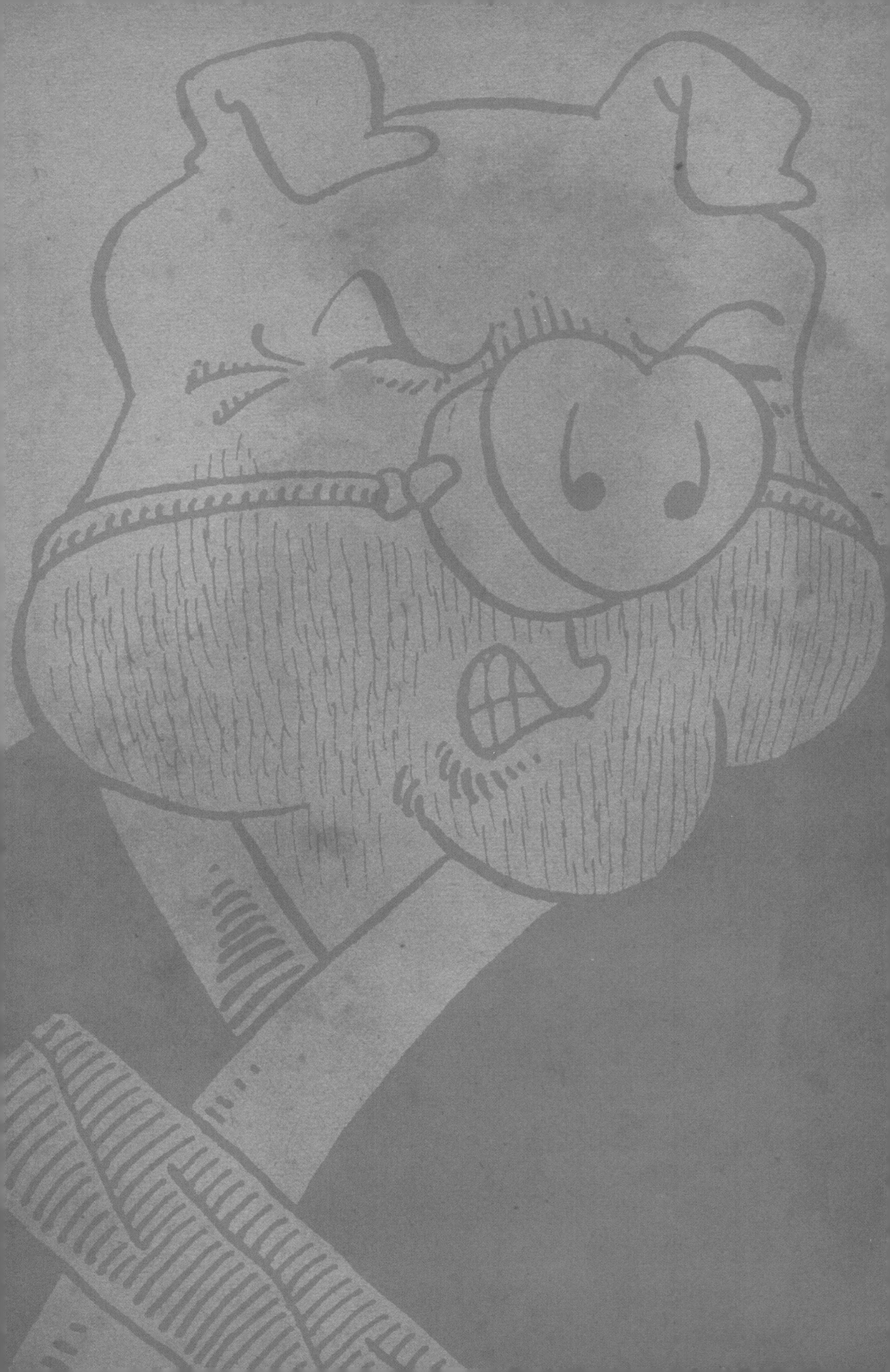

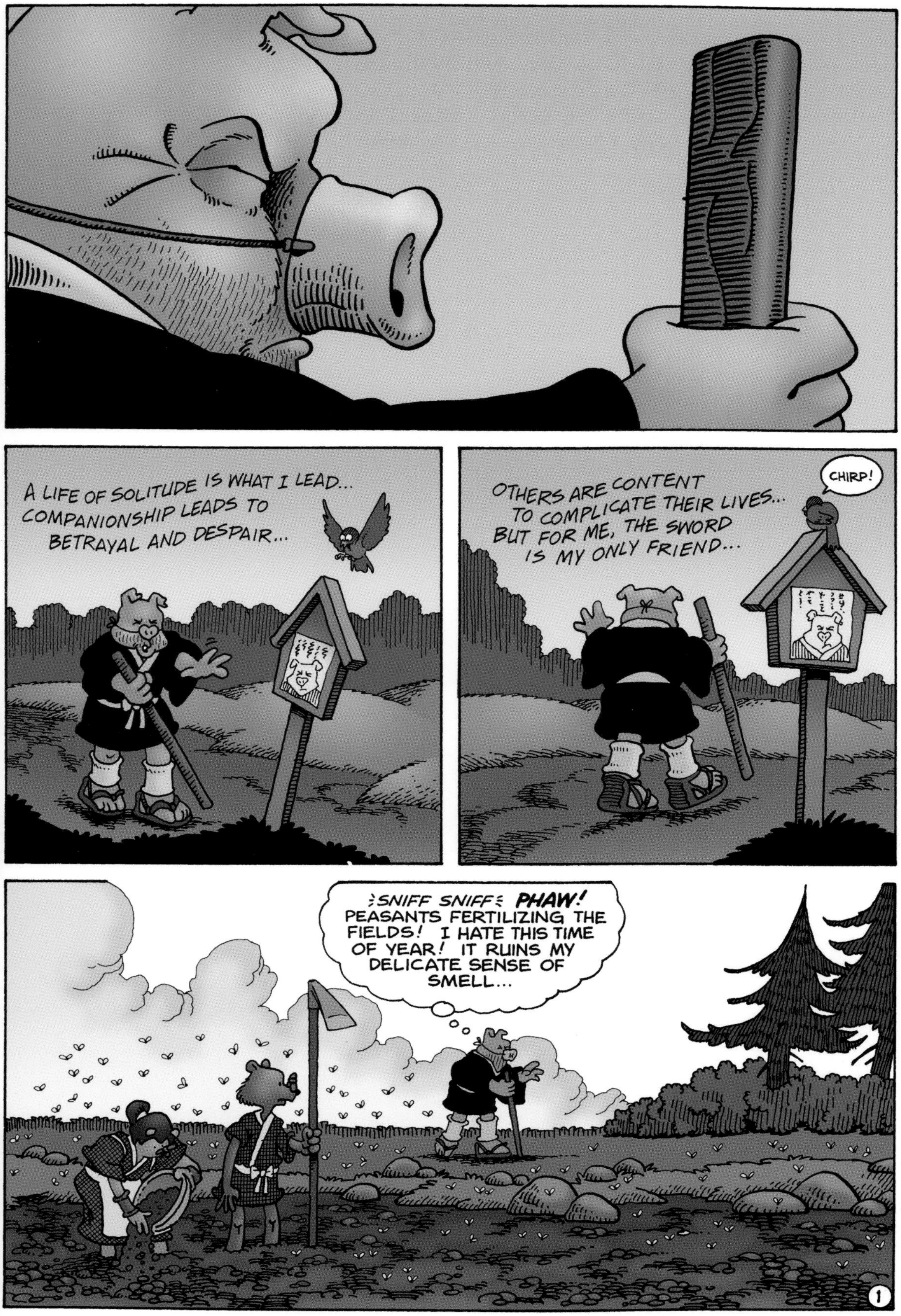
A LIFE OF SOLITUDE IS WHAT I LEAD... COMPANIONSHIP LEADS TO BETRAYAL AND DESPAIR...
OTHERS ARE CONTENT TO COMPLICATE THEIR LIVES... BUT FOR ME, THE SWORD IS MY ONLY FRIEND...
CHIRP!
SNIFF SNIFF PHAW! PEASANTS FERTILIZING THE FIELDS! I HATE THIS TIME OF YEAR! IT RUINS MY DELICATE SENSE OF SMELL...
1

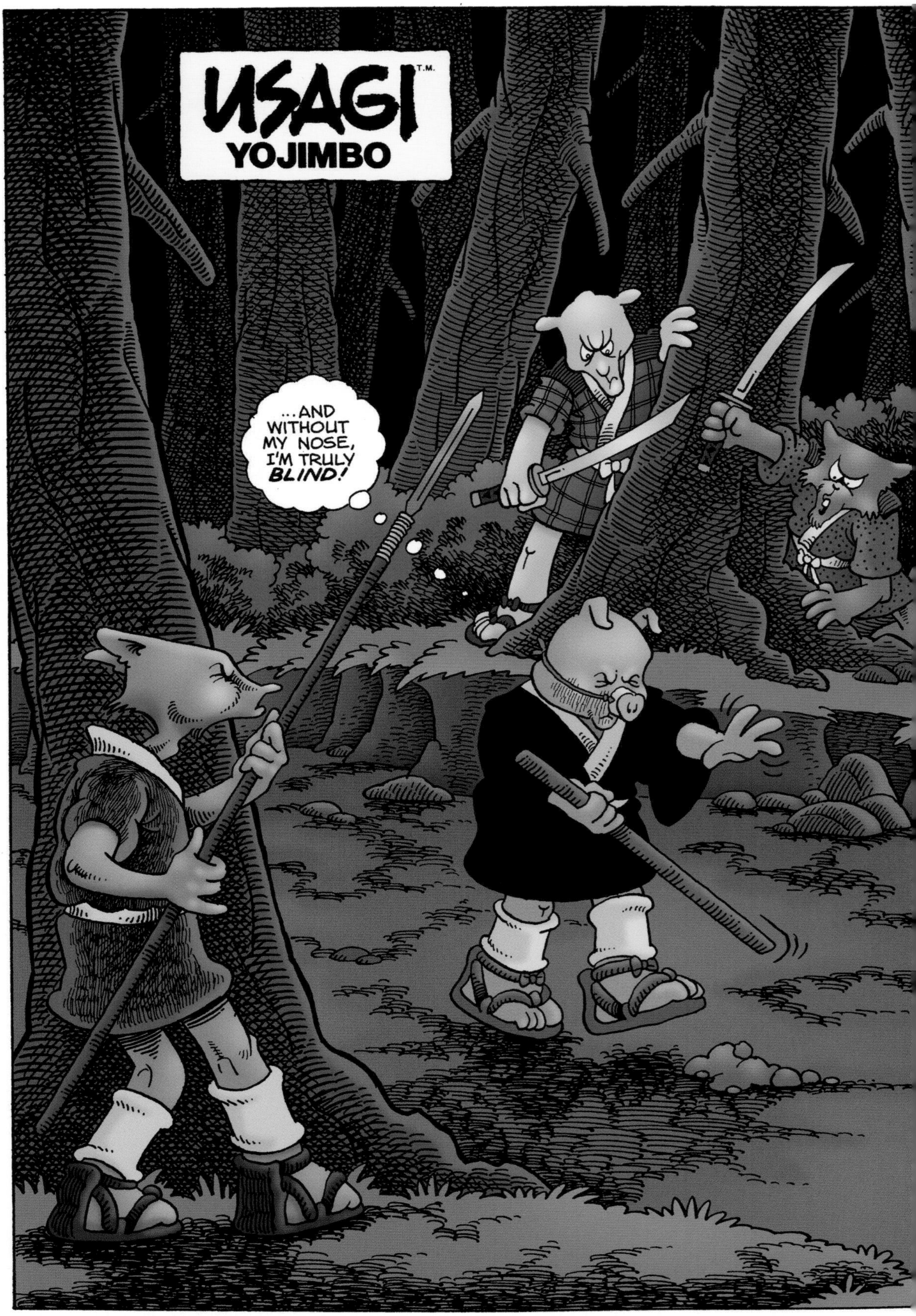
USAGI T.M.
YOJIMBO
...AND WITHOUT MY NOSE, I'M TRULY BLIND!

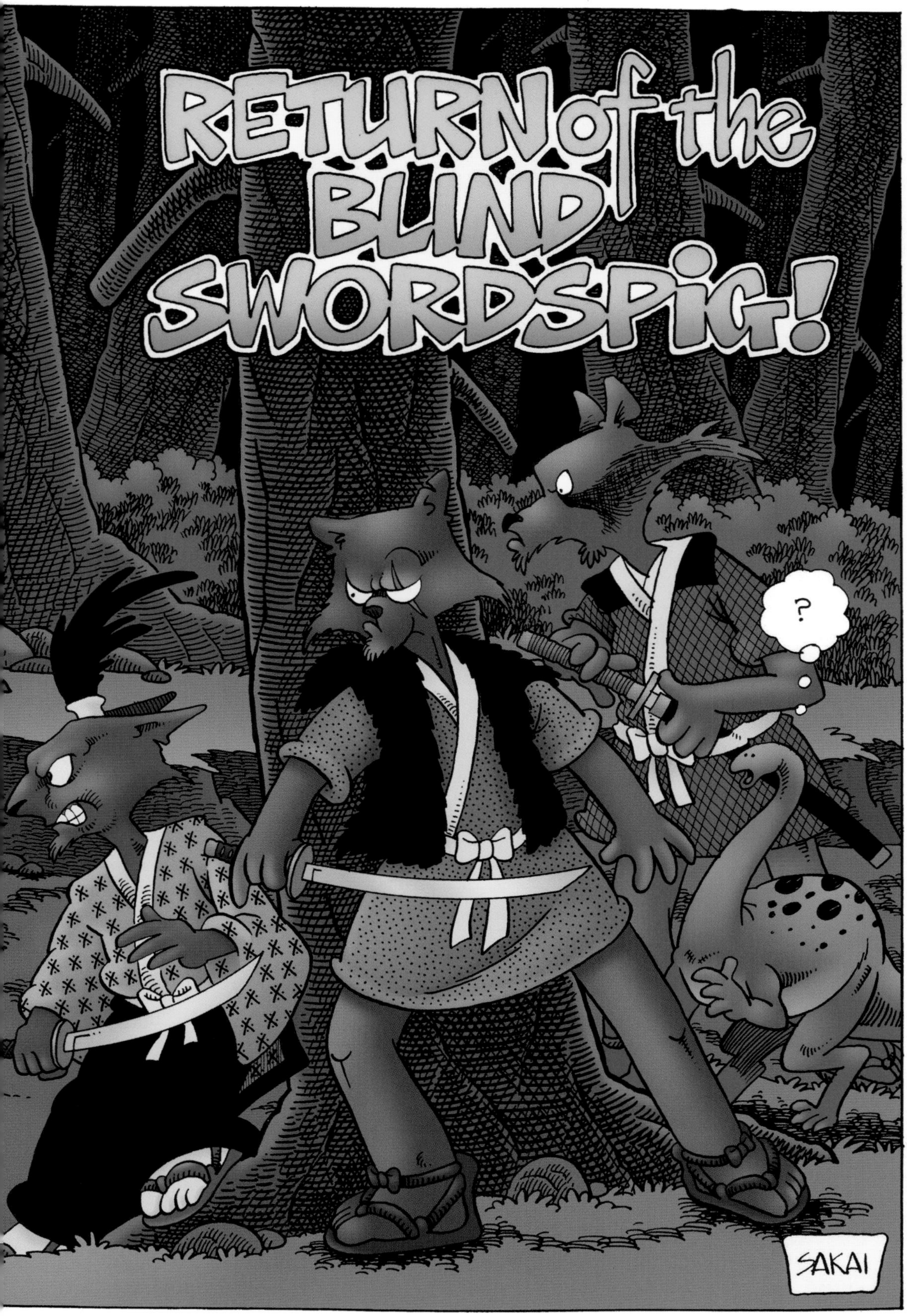
RETURN of the BLIND SWORDSPIG!
?
SAKAI

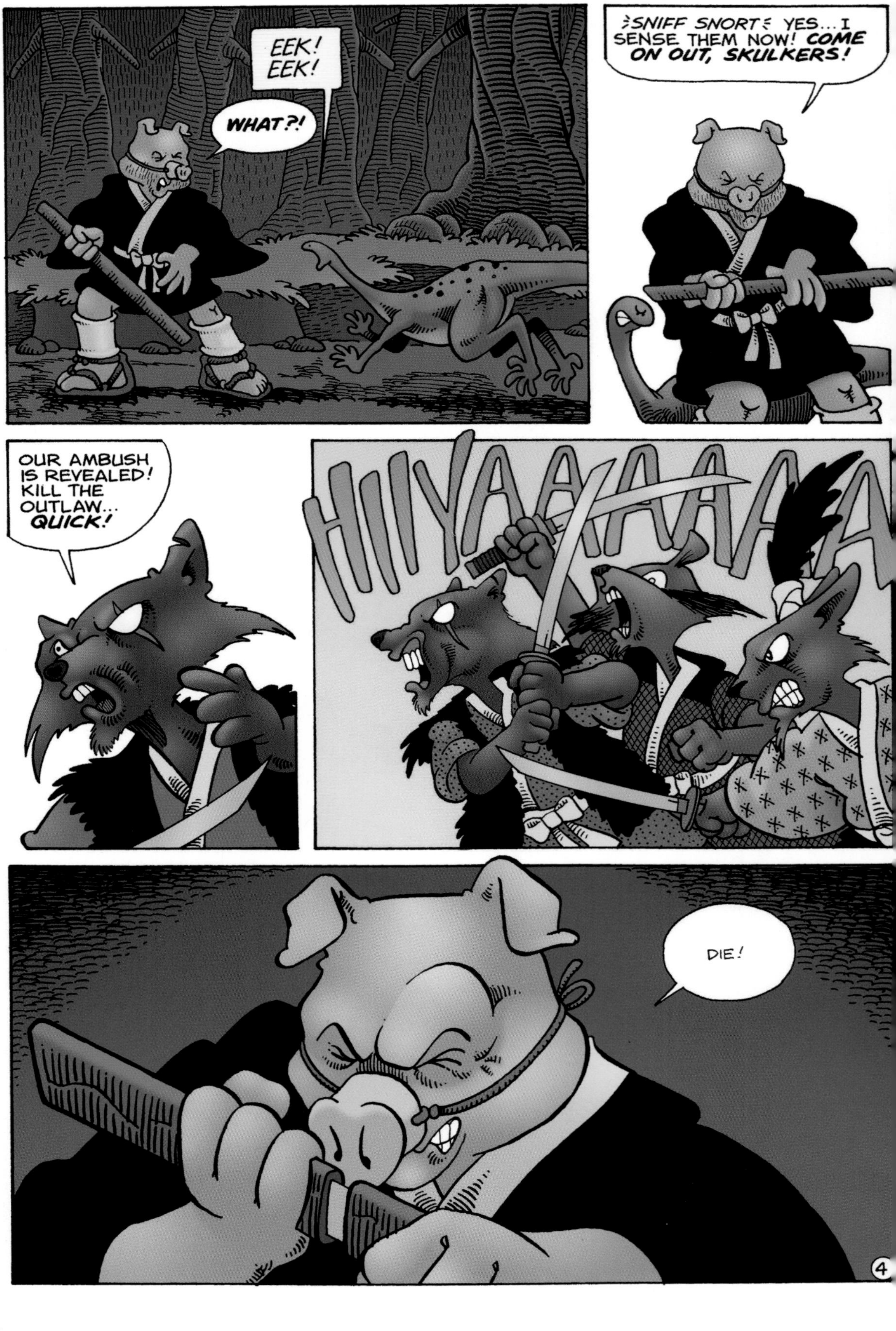
EEK! EEK!
WHAT?!
≥SNIFF SNORT≤ YES... I SENSE THEM NOW! COME ON OUT, SKULKERS!
OUR AMBUSH IS REVEALED! KILL THE OUTLAW... QUICK!
HIIYAAAAAA
DIE!
4

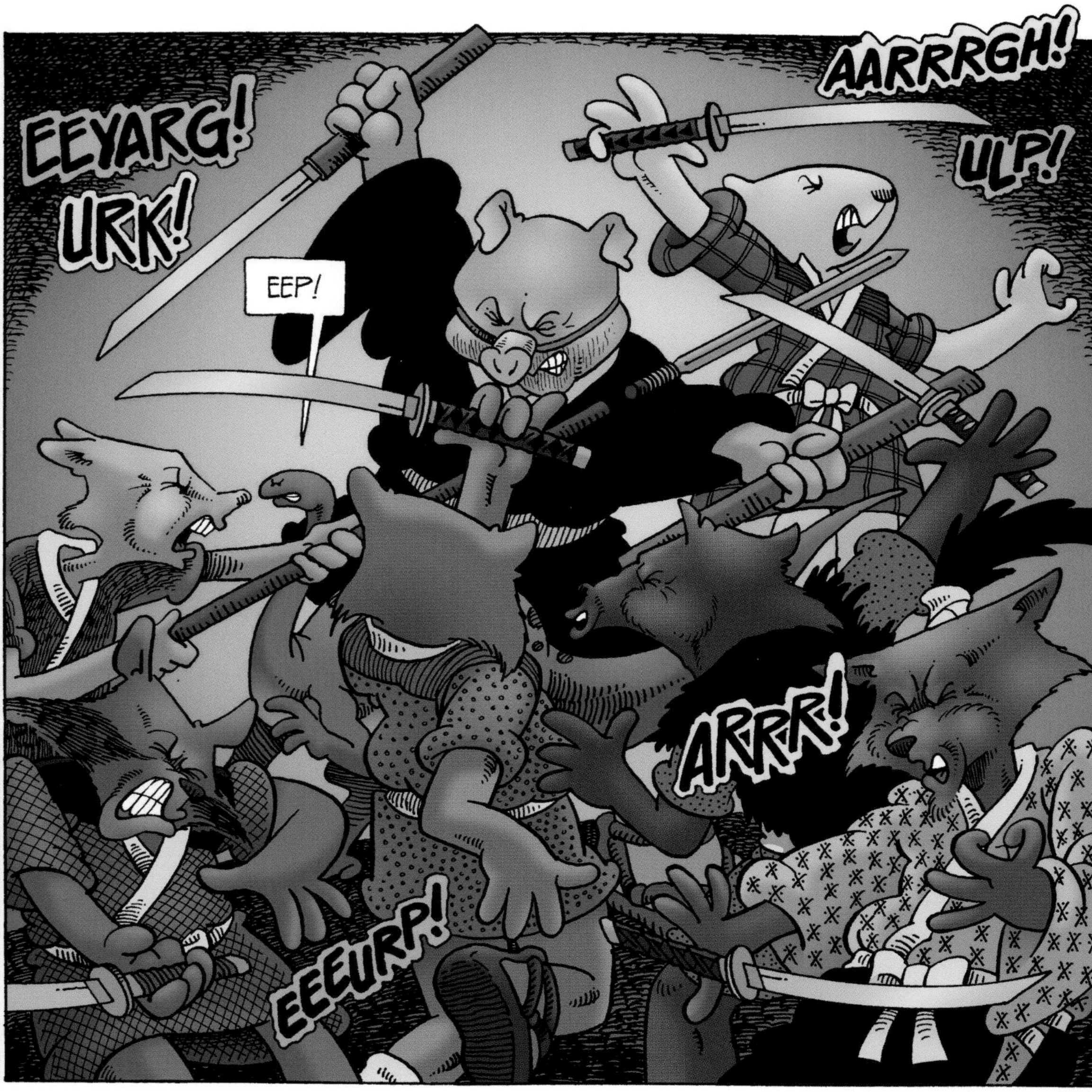
EEYARG!
URK!
AARRRGH!
ULP!
EEP!
ARRR!
EEEURP!

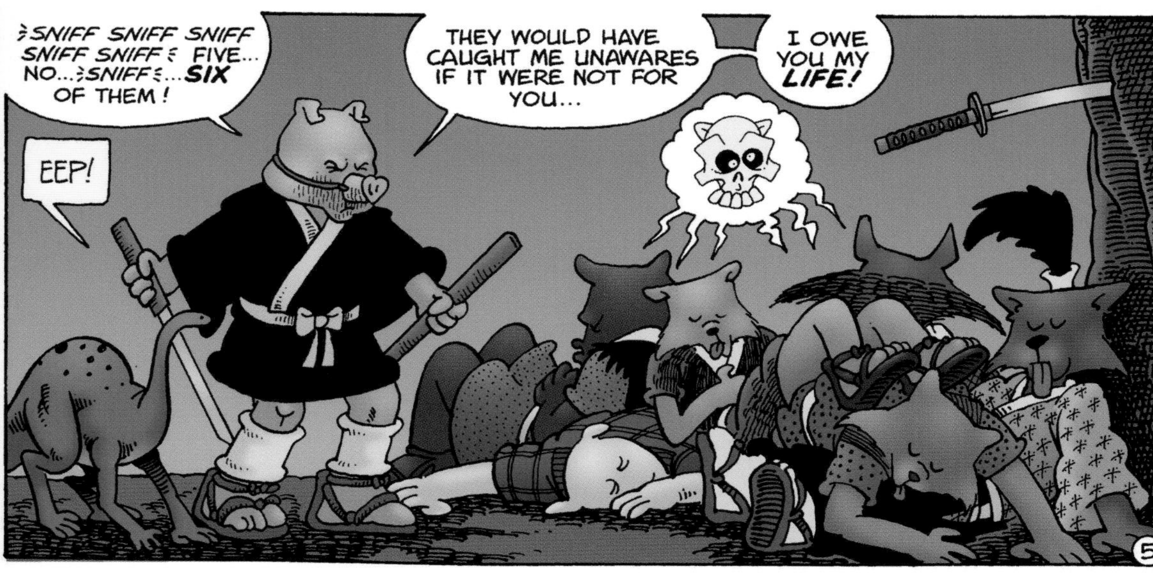
SNIFF SNIFF SNIFF SNIFF SNIFF FIVE... NO... *SNIFF*... SIX OF THEM!
THEY WOULD HAVE CAUGHT ME UNAWARES IF IT WERE NOT FOR YOU...
I OWE YOU MY LIFE!
EEP!
5

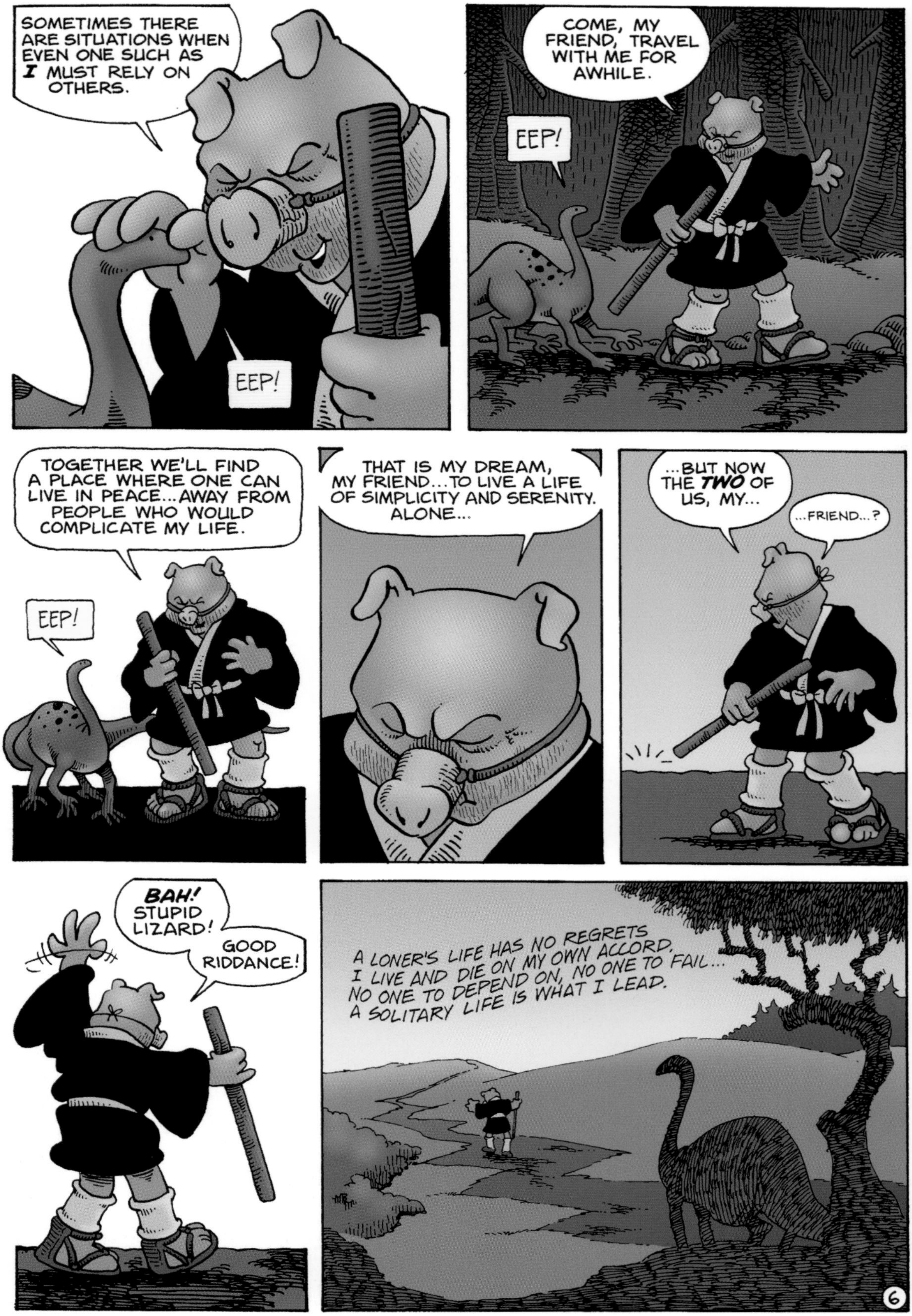
SOMETIMES THERE ARE SITUATIONS WHEN EVEN ONE SUCH AS ***I*** MUST RELY ON OTHERS.
EEP!
COME, MY FRIEND, TRAVEL WITH ME FOR AWHILE.
EEP!
TOGETHER WE'LL FIND A PLACE WHERE ONE CAN LIVE IN PEACE...AWAY FROM PEOPLE WHO WOULD COMPLICATE MY LIFE.
EEP!
THAT IS MY DREAM, MY FRIEND...TO LIVE A LIFE OF SIMPLICITY AND SERENITY. ALONE...
...BUT NOW THE ***TWO*** OF US, MY...
...FRIEND...?
BAH! STUPID LIZARD!
GOOD RIDDANCE!
A LONER'S LIFE HAS NO REGRETS
I LIVE AND DIE ON MY OWN ACCORD,
NO ONE TO DEPEND ON, NO ONE TO FAIL...
A SOLITARY LIFE IS WHAT I LEAD.
6

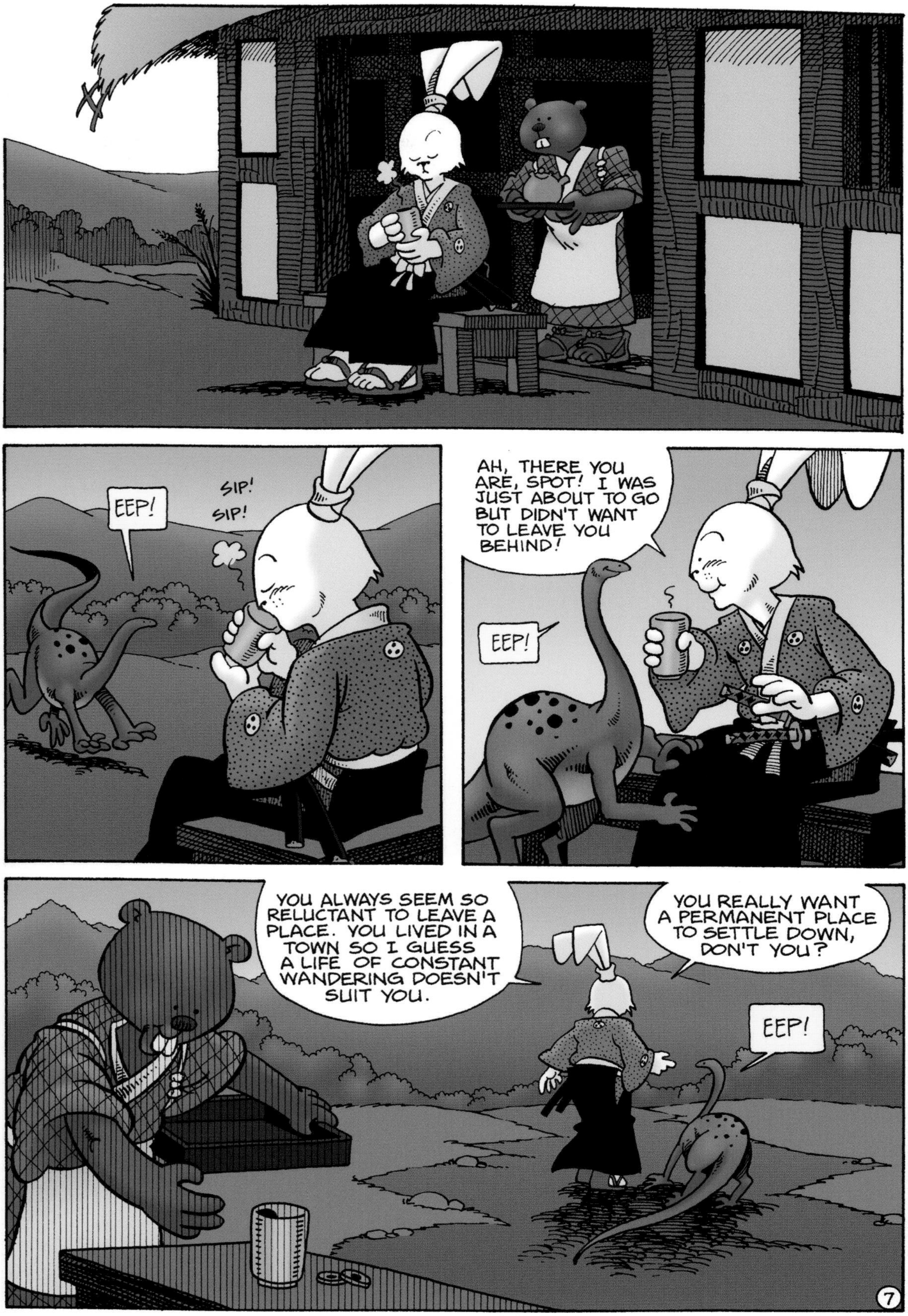
EEP!
SIP!
SIP!
AH, THERE YOU ARE, SPOT! I WAS JUST ABOUT TO GO BUT DIDN'T WANT TO LEAVE YOU BEHIND!
EEP!
YOU ALWAYS SEEM SO RELUCTANT TO LEAVE A PLACE. YOU LIVED IN A TOWN SO I GUESS A LIFE OF CONSTANT WANDERING DOESN'T SUIT YOU.
YOU REALLY WANT A PERMANENT PLACE TO SETTLE DOWN, DON'T YOU?
EEP!
7

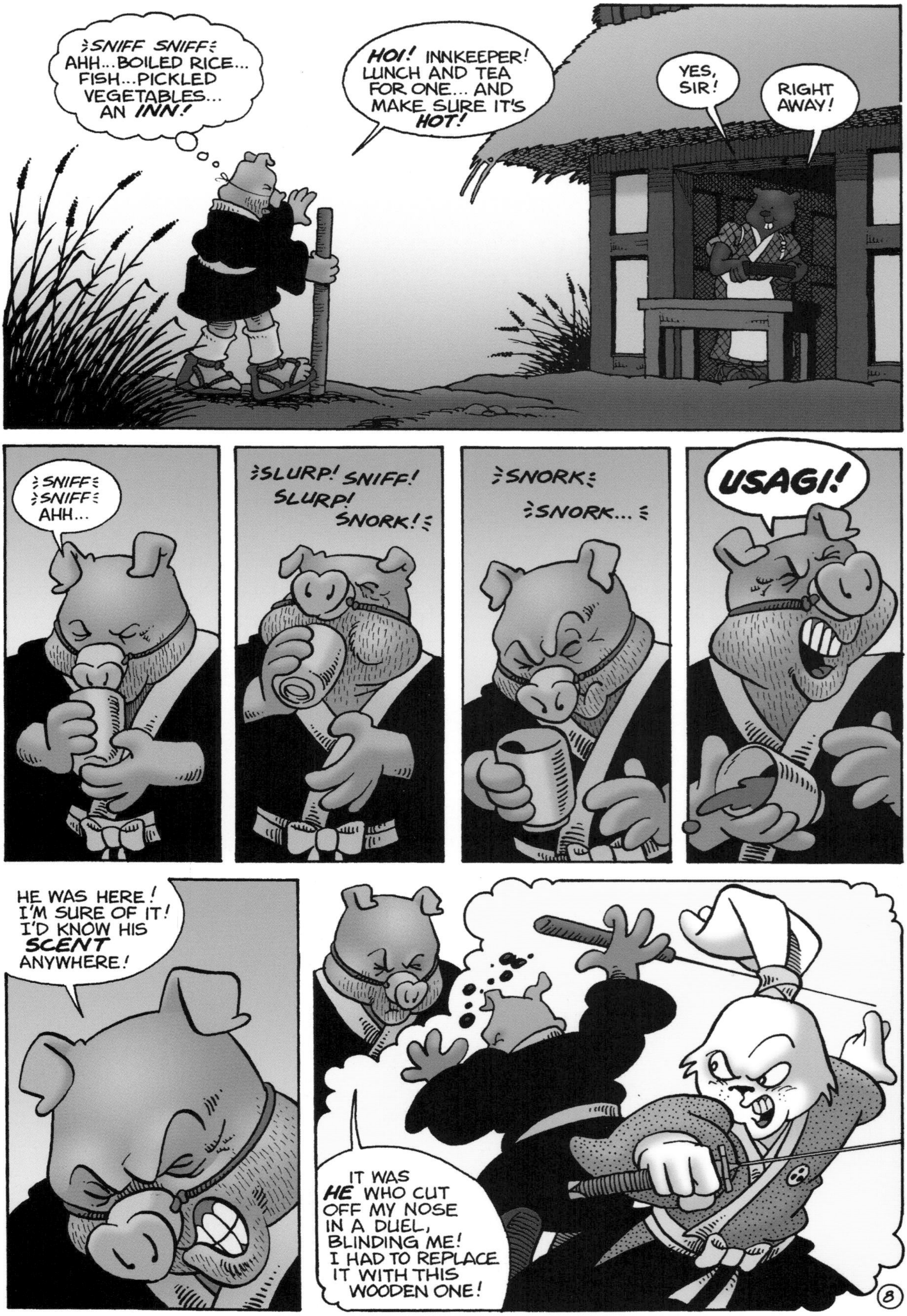

SNIFF SNIFF AHH... BOILED RICE... FISH... PICKLED VEGETABLES... AN INN!
HOI! INNKEEPER! LUNCH AND TEA FOR ONE... AND MAKE SURE IT'S HOT!
YES, SIR!
RIGHT AWAY!
SNIFF SNIFF AHH...
SLURP! SNIFF! SLURP! SNORK!
SNORK SNORK...
USAGI!
HE WAS HERE! I'M SURE OF IT! I'D KNOW HIS SCENT ANYWHERE!
IT WAS HE WHO CUT OFF MY NOSE IN A DUEL, BLINDING ME! I HAD TO REPLACE IT WITH THIS WOODEN ONE!
8

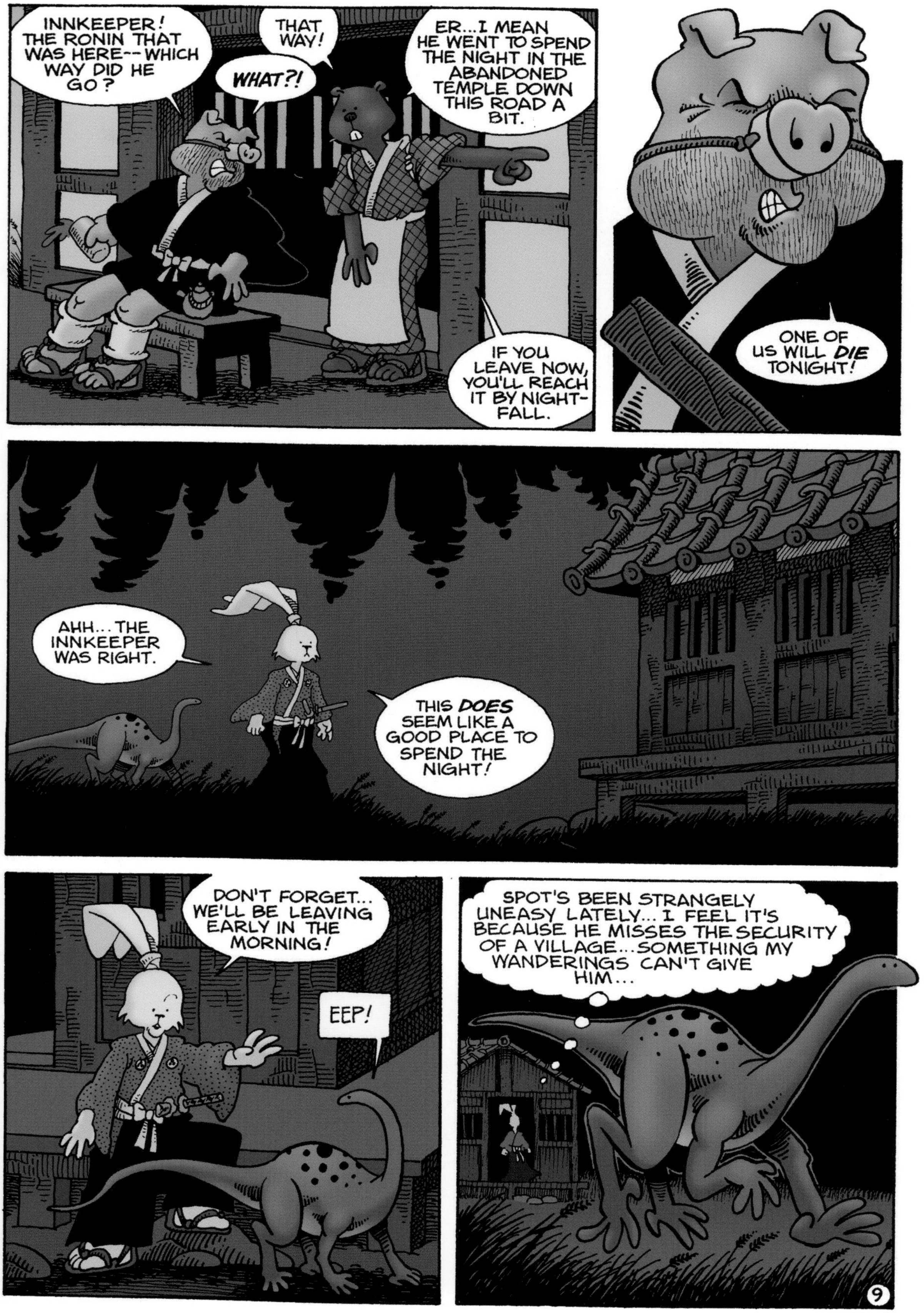
INNKEEPER! THE RONIN THAT WAS HERE-- WHICH WAY DID HE GO?
THAT WAY!
WHAT?!
ER...I MEAN HE WENT TO SPEND THE NIGHT IN THE ABANDONED TEMPLE DOWN THIS ROAD A BIT.
IF YOU LEAVE NOW, YOU'LL REACH IT BY NIGHT-FALL.
ONE OF US WILL DIE TONIGHT!
AHH... THE INNKEEPER WAS RIGHT.
THIS DOES SEEM LIKE A GOOD PLACE TO SPEND THE NIGHT!
DON'T FORGET... WE'LL BE LEAVING EARLY IN THE MORNING!
EEP!
SPOT'S BEEN STRANGELY UNEASY LATELY... I FEEL IT'S BECAUSE HE MISSES THE SECURITY OF A VILLAGE... SOMETHING MY WANDERINGS CAN'T GIVE HIM...
9

SPOT...?

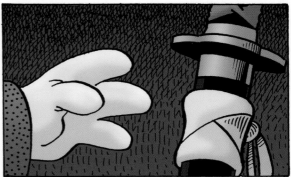

WHO'S OUT THERE?! SHOW YOUR- SELF!

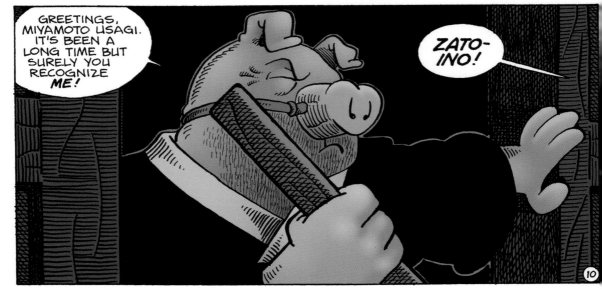
GREETINGS, MIYAMOTO USAGI. IT'S BEEN A LONG TIME BUT SURELY YOU RECOGNIZE ME!

ZATO- INO!

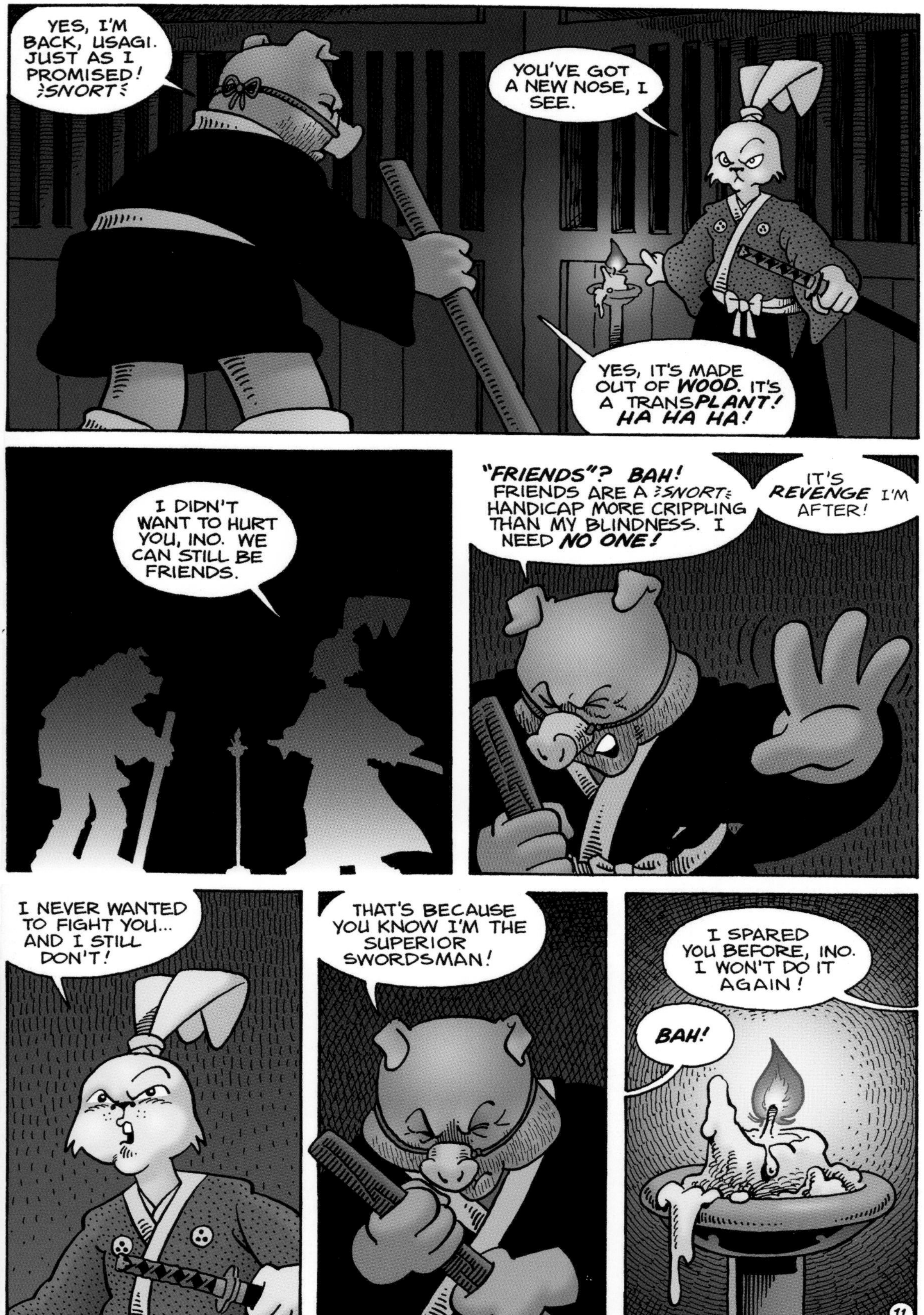
YES, I'M BACK, USAGI. JUST AS I PROMISED! SNORT
YOU'VE GOT A NEW NOSE, I SEE.
YES, IT'S MADE OUT OF WOOD. IT'S A TRANSPLANT! HA HA HA!
I DIDN'T WANT TO HURT YOU, INO. WE CAN STILL BE FRIENDS.
"FRIENDS"? BAH! FRIENDS ARE A SNORT HANDICAP MORE CRIPPLING THAN MY BLINDNESS. I NEED NO ONE!
IT'S REVENGE I'M AFTER!
I NEVER WANTED TO FIGHT YOU... AND I STILL DON'T!
THAT'S BECAUSE YOU KNOW I'M THE SUPERIOR SWORDSMAN!
I SPARED YOU BEFORE, INO. I WON'T DO IT AGAIN!
BAH!
11

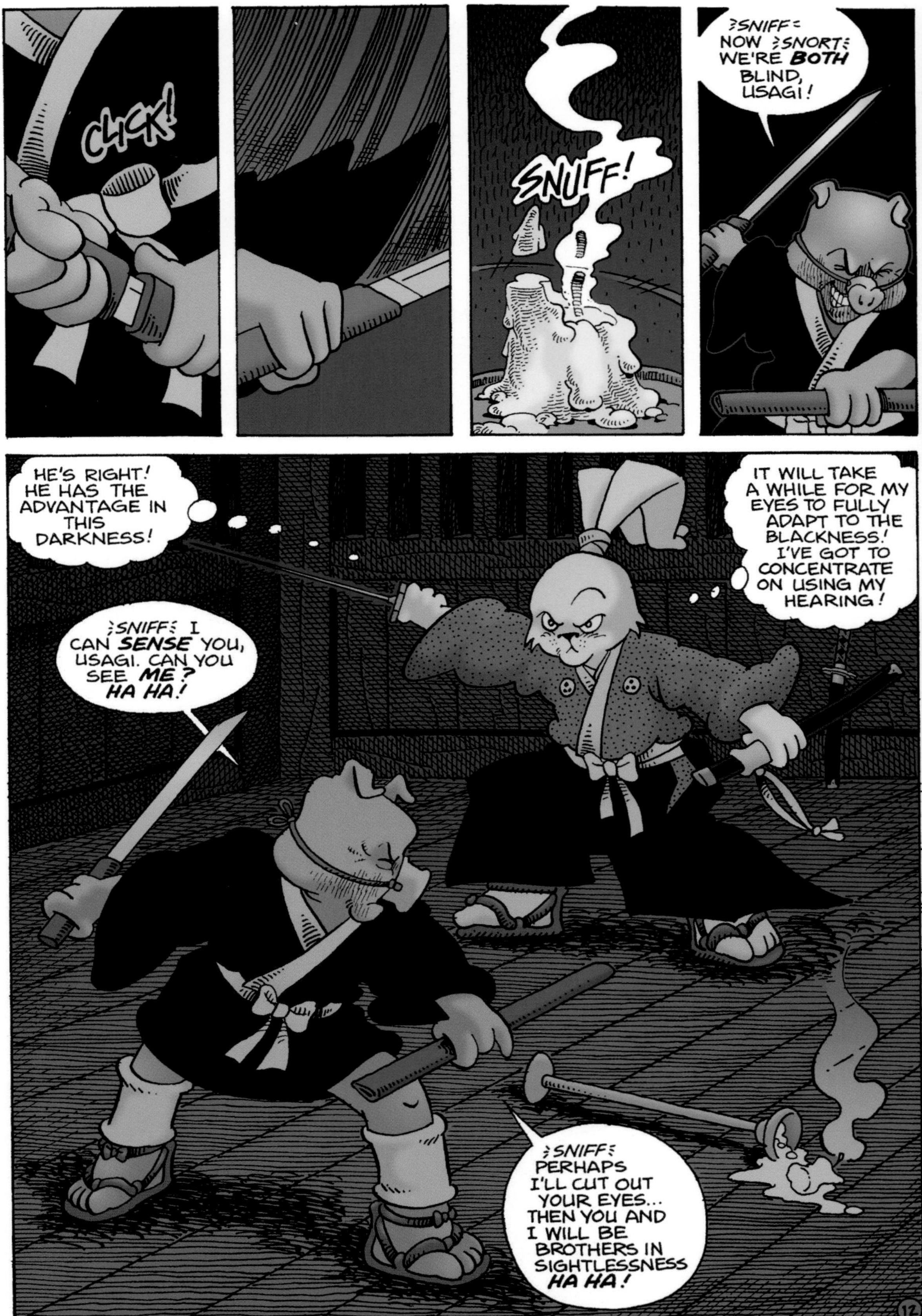
CLICK!
SNUFF!
SNIFF NOW SNORT WE'RE BOTH BLIND, USAGI!
HE'S RIGHT! HE HAS THE ADVANTAGE IN THIS DARKNESS!
IT WILL TAKE A WHILE FOR MY EYES TO FULLY ADAPT TO THE BLACKNESS! I'VE GOT TO CONCENTRATE ON USING MY HEARING!
SNIFF I CAN SENSE YOU, USAGI. CAN YOU SEE ME? HA HA!
SNIFF PERHAPS I'LL CUT OUT YOUR EYES... THEN YOU AND I WILL BE BROTHERS IN SIGHTLESSNESS HA HA!
12

CRIK

CRIK

HIIYAAAAAA

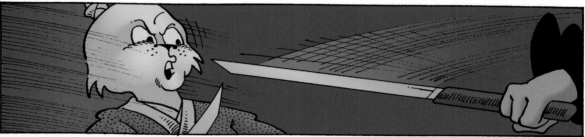

KA-TANG

KA-TANG

KA-TANG

KA-TANG

HEH, HEH, HEH... YOU *IMPRESS* ME, USAGI... ≷SNIFF≷

YOUR TALENTS ARE INDEED FORMIDABLE ≷SNORT≷ FOR YOU TO BE ABLE TO SENSE MY THRUSTS.

I'LL NOT UNDERESTIMATE YOU ≷SNIF≷ ANY LONGER! ≷SNORK≷

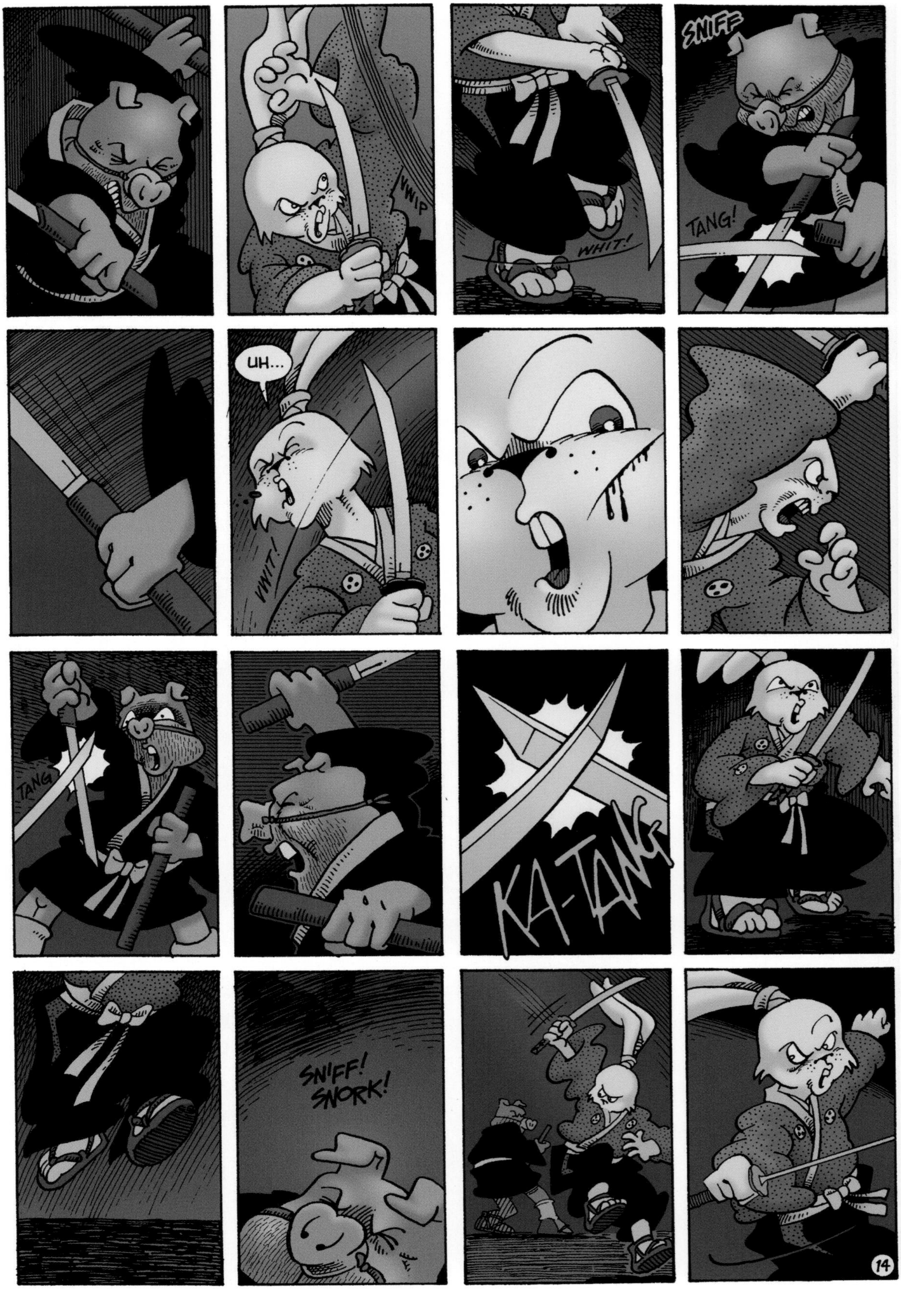

VWIP
WHIT!
SNIFF
TANG!
UH...
VWIT!
TANG
KA-TANG
SNIFF!
SNORK!
14

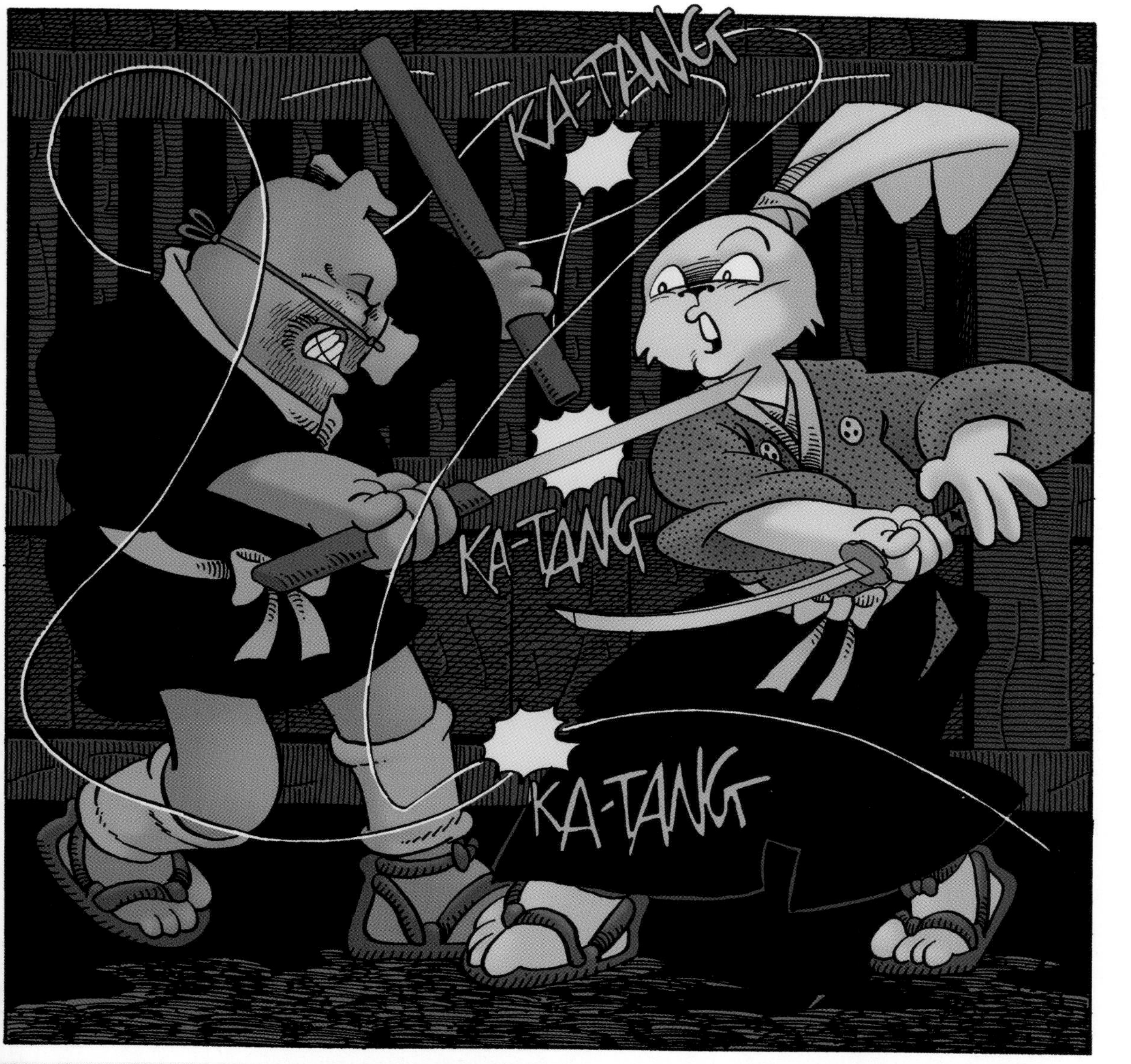
KA-TANG
KA-TANG
KA-TANG

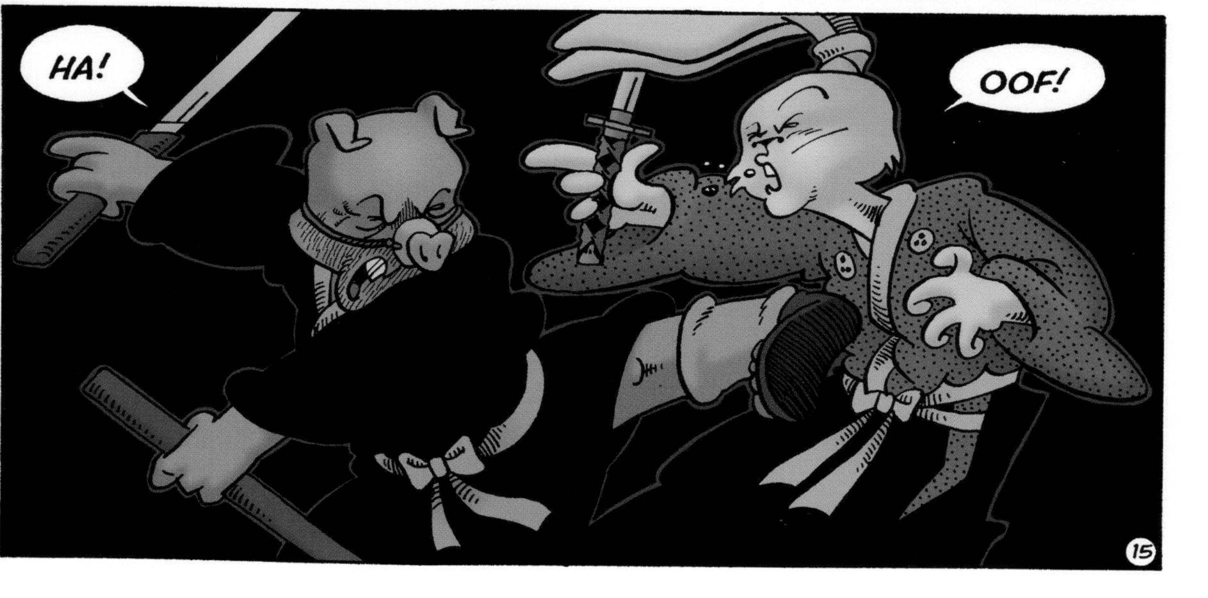
HA!
OOF!
15

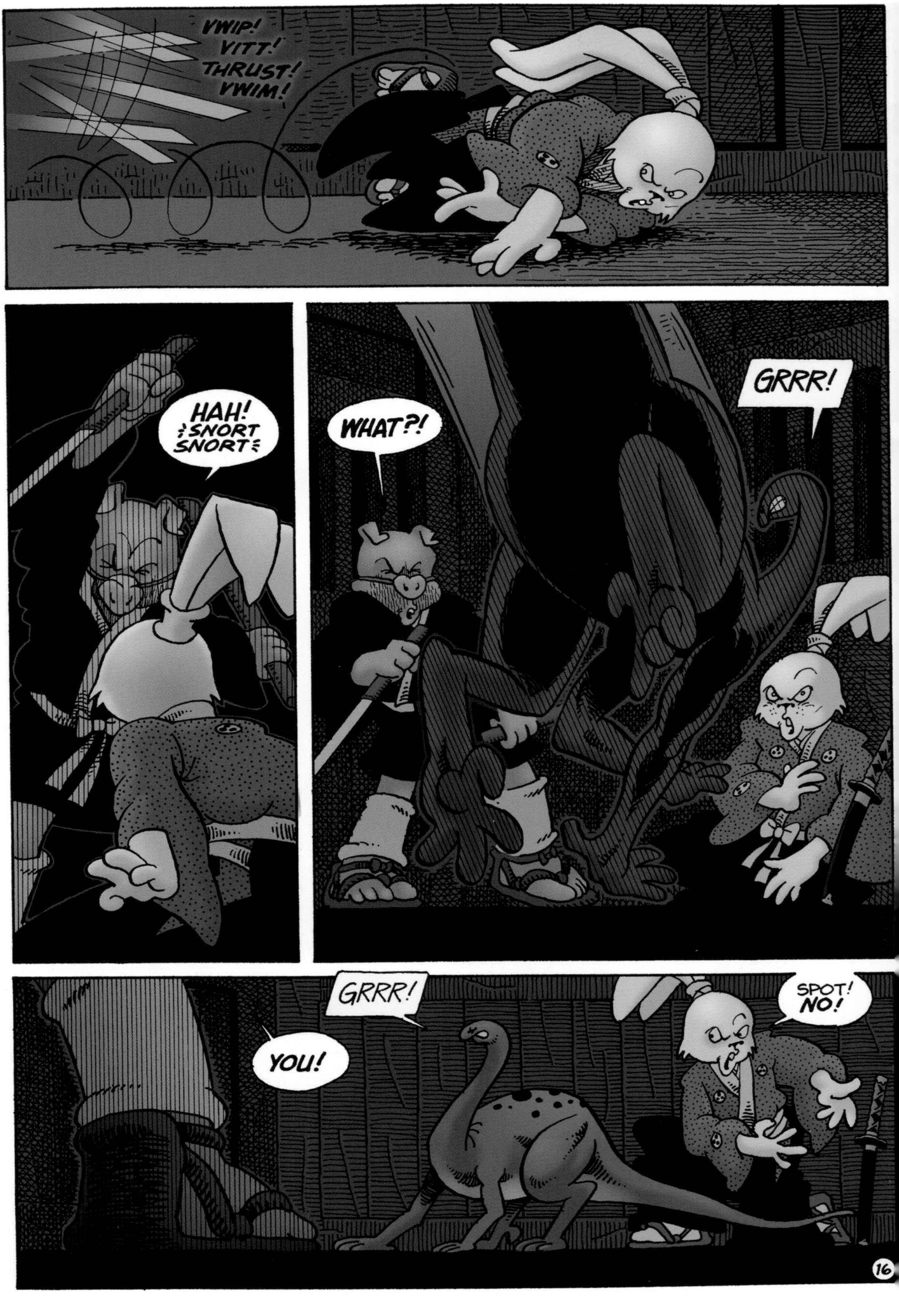
VWIP! VITT! THRUST! VWIM!
HAH! SNORT SNORT
WHAT?!
GRRR!
GRRR!
YOU!
SPOT! NO!
16

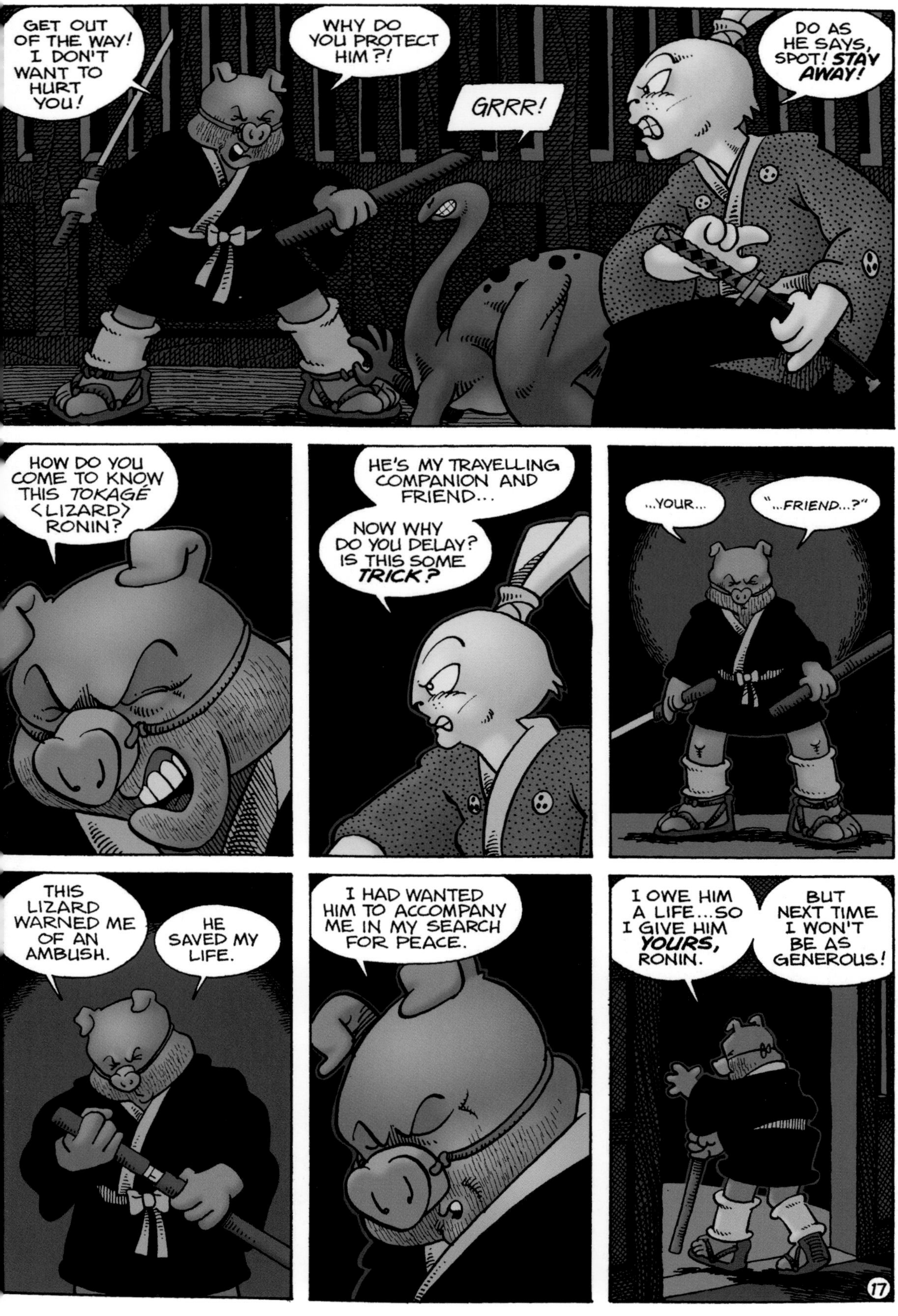
GET OUT OF THE WAY! I DON'T WANT TO HURT YOU!
WHY DO YOU PROTECT HIM?!
GRRR!
DO AS HE SAYS, SPOT! STAY AWAY!
HOW DO YOU COME TO KNOW THIS TOKAGÉ <LIZARD> RONIN?
HE'S MY TRAVELLING COMPANION AND FRIEND...
NOW WHY DO YOU DELAY? IS THIS SOME TRICK?
...YOUR...
"...FRIEND...?"
THIS LIZARD WARNED ME OF AN AMBUSH.
HE SAVED MY LIFE.
I HAD WANTED HIM TO ACCOMPANY ME IN MY SEARCH FOR PEACE.
I OWE HIM A LIFE...SO I GIVE HIM YOURS, RONIN.
BUT NEXT TIME I WON'T BE AS GENEROUS!
17

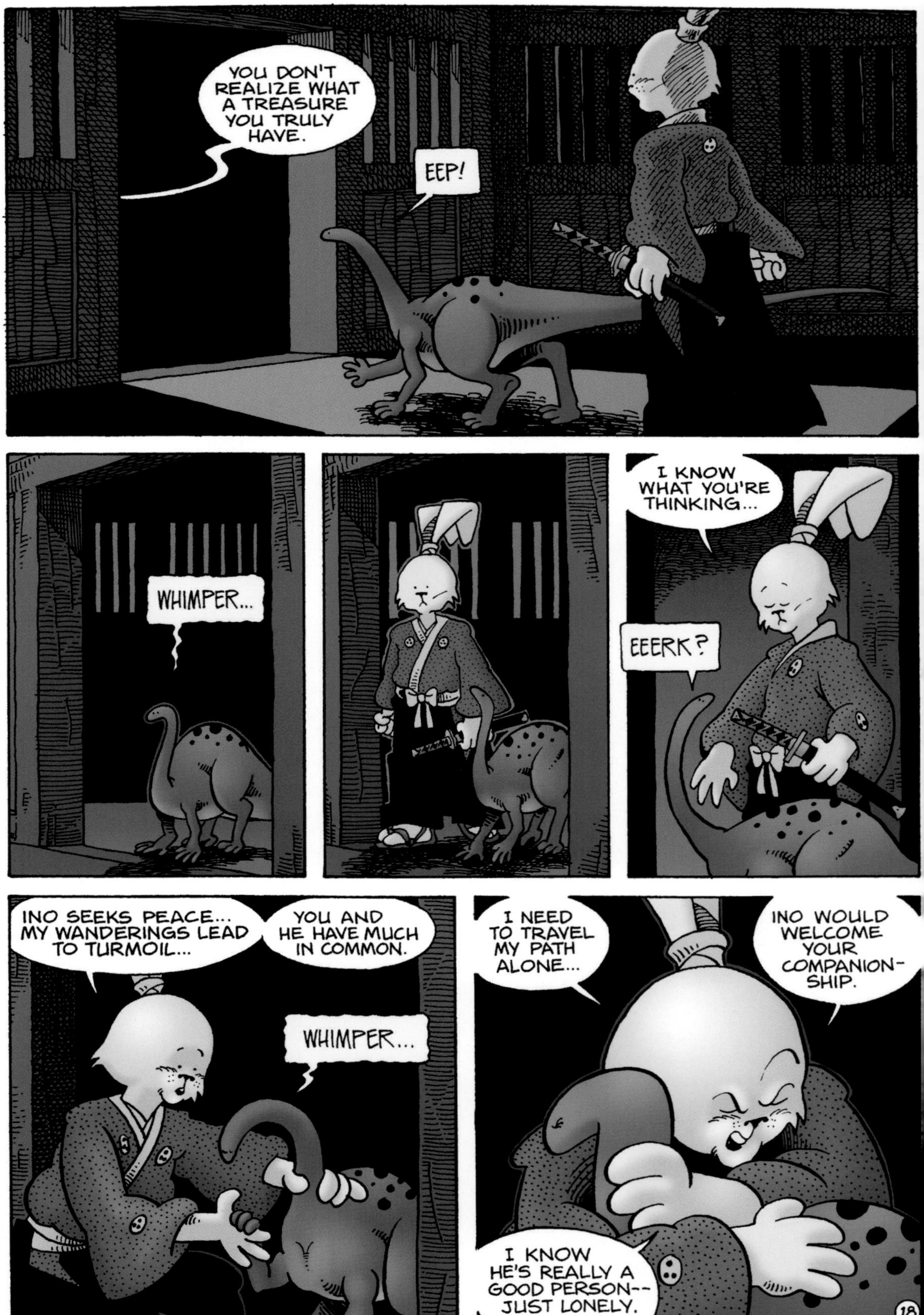
YOU DON'T REALIZE WHAT A TREASURE YOU TRULY HAVE.
EEP!
WHIMPER...
I KNOW WHAT YOU'RE THINKING...
EEERK?
INO SEEKS PEACE... MY WANDERINGS LEAD TO TURMOIL...
YOU AND HE HAVE MUCH IN COMMON.
WHIMPER...
I NEED TO TRAVEL MY PATH ALONE...
INO WOULD WELCOME YOUR COMPANION-SHIP.
I KNOW HE'S REALLY A GOOD PERSON-- JUST LONELY.
18

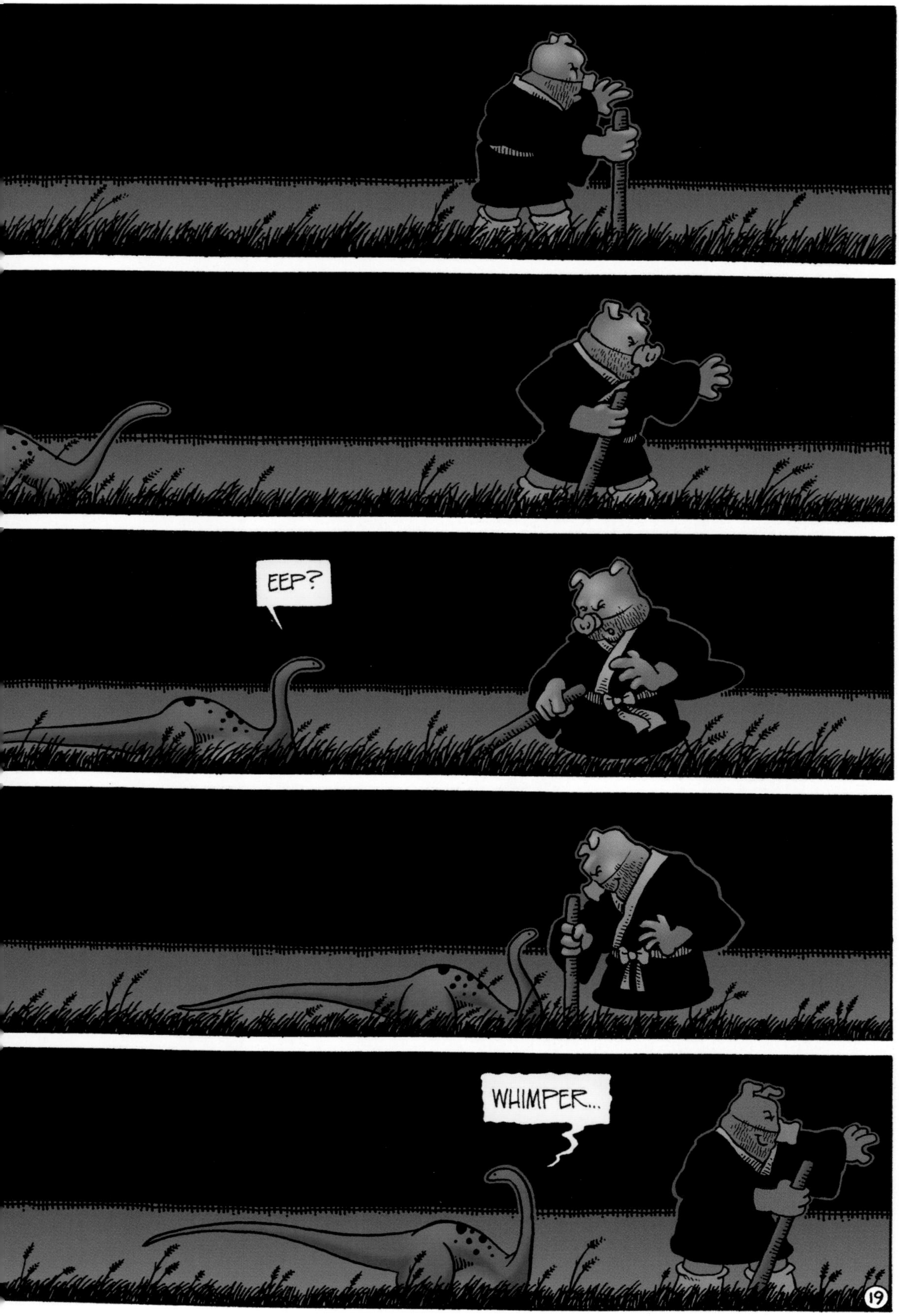
EEP?
WHIMPER...
19

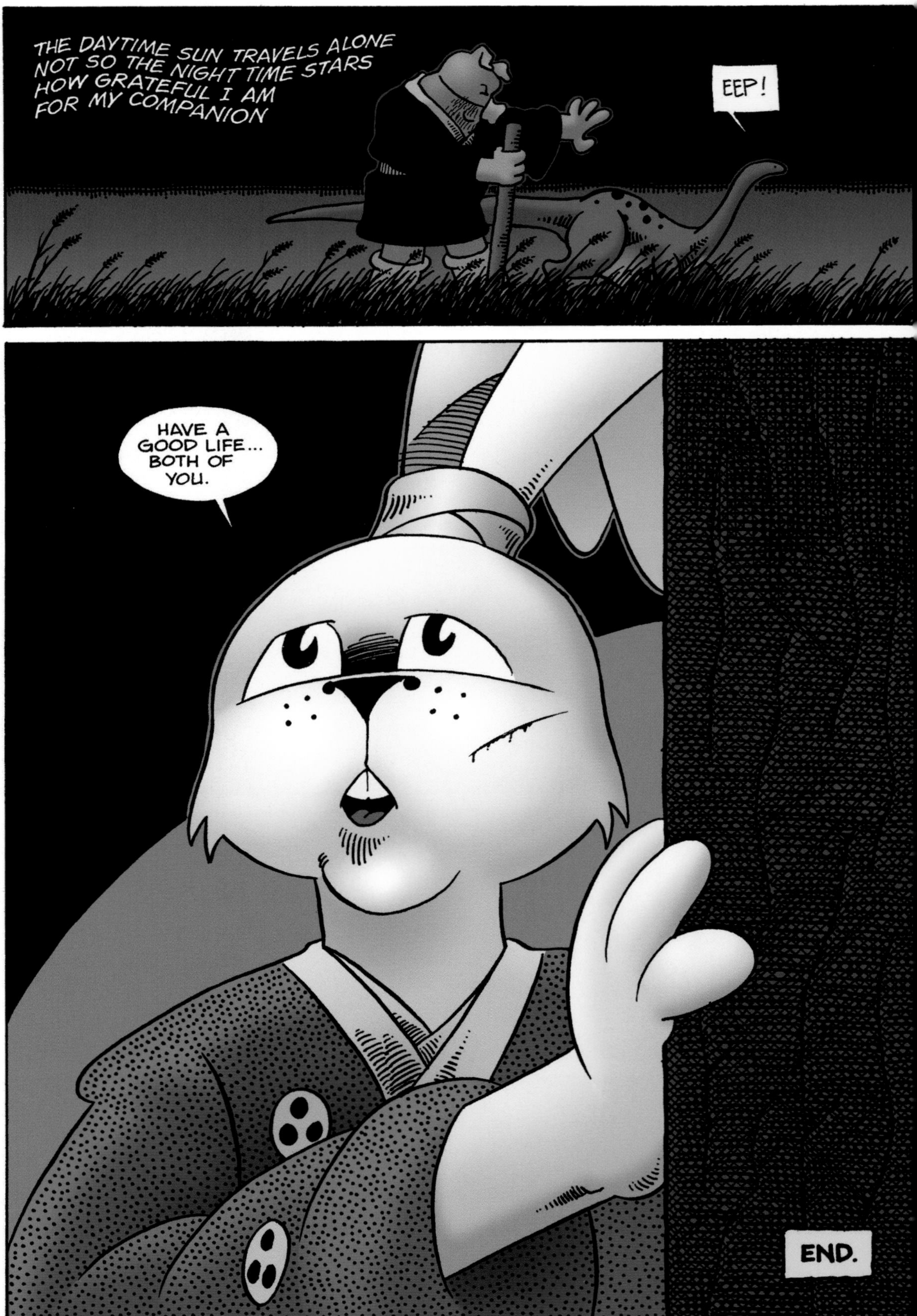
THE DAYTIME SUN TRAVELS ALONE
NOT SO THE NIGHT TIME STARS
HOW GRATEFUL I AM
FOR MY COMPANION
EEP!
HAVE A GOOD LIFE... BOTH OF YOU.
END.

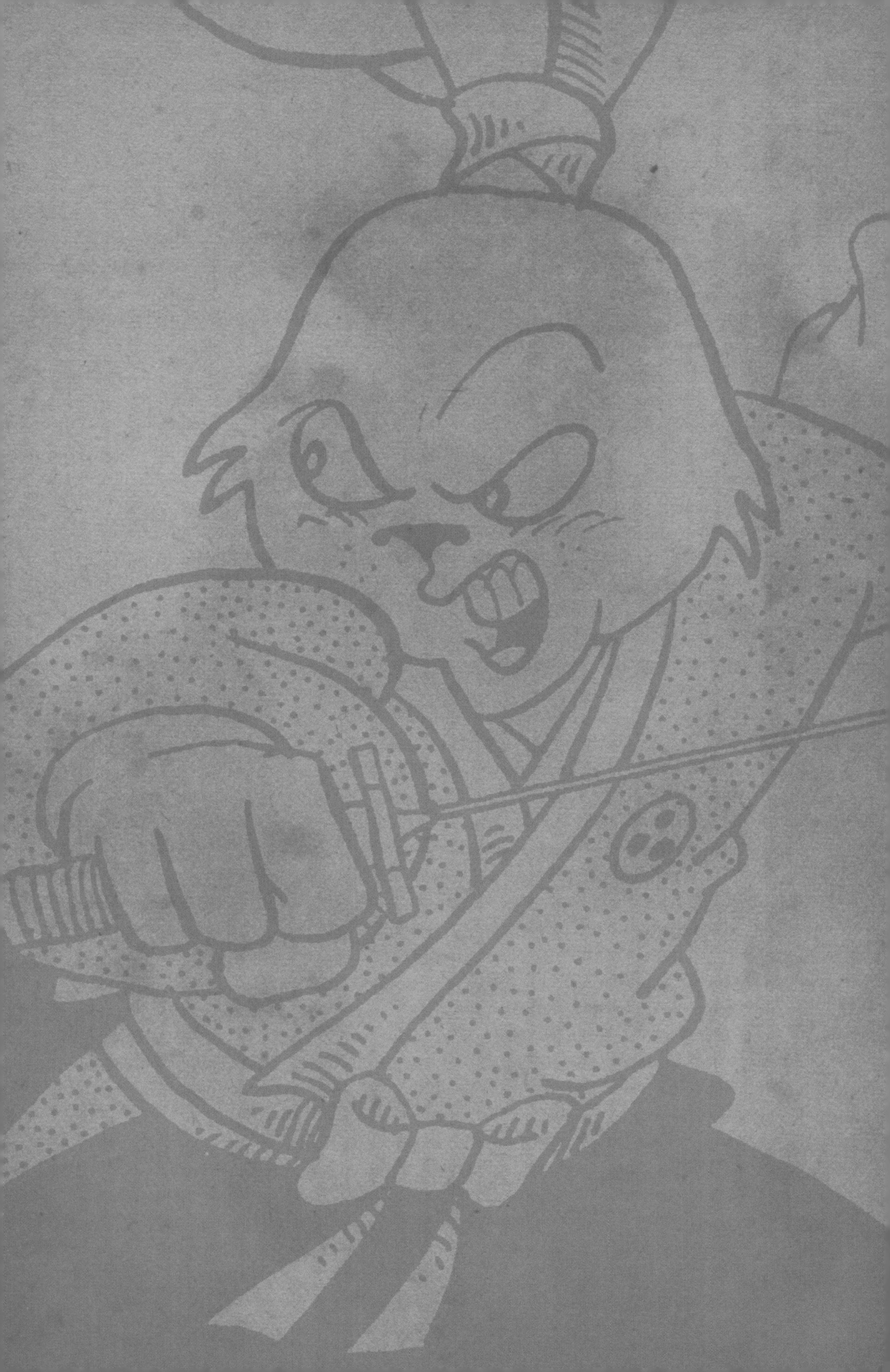

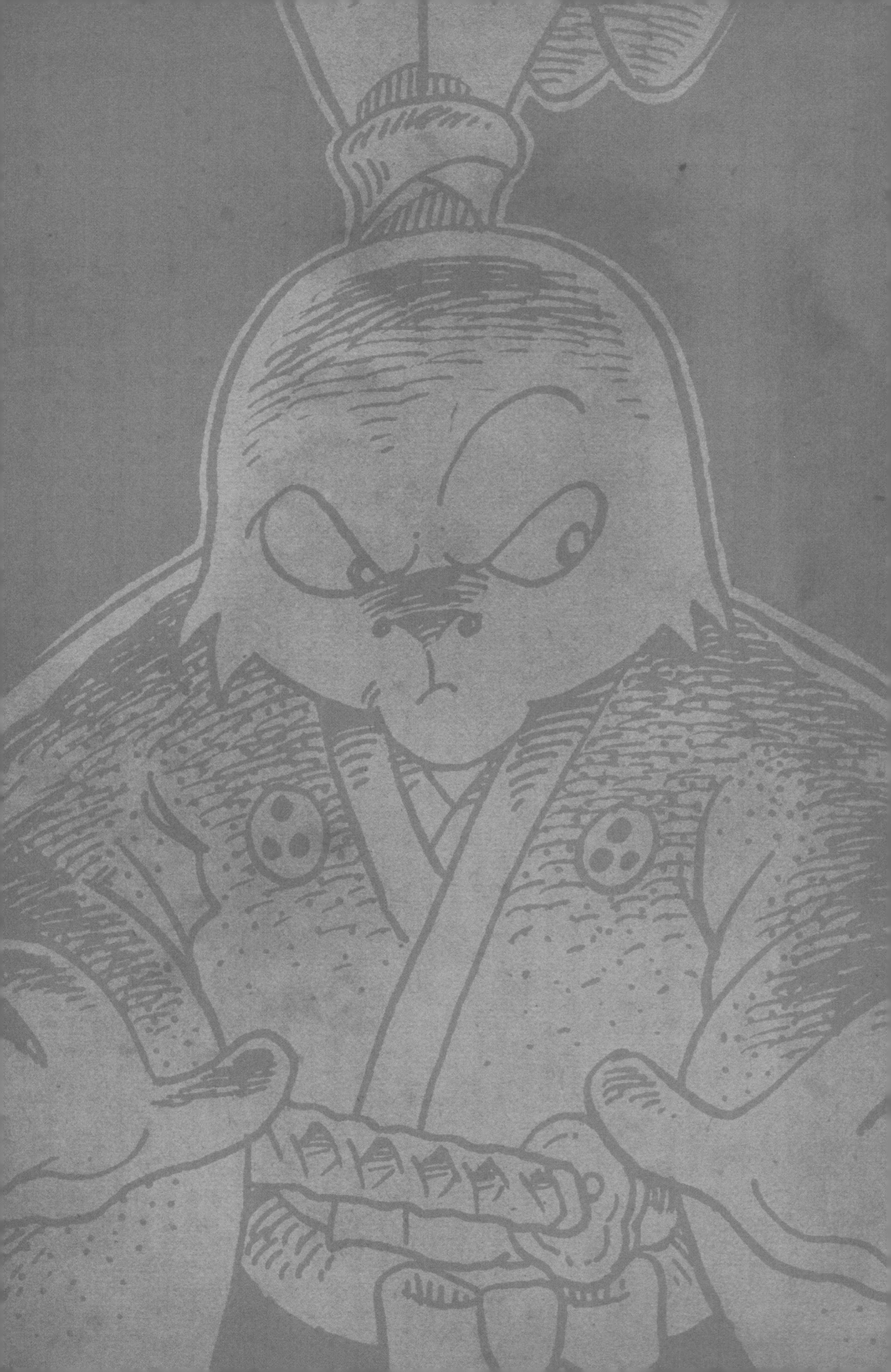

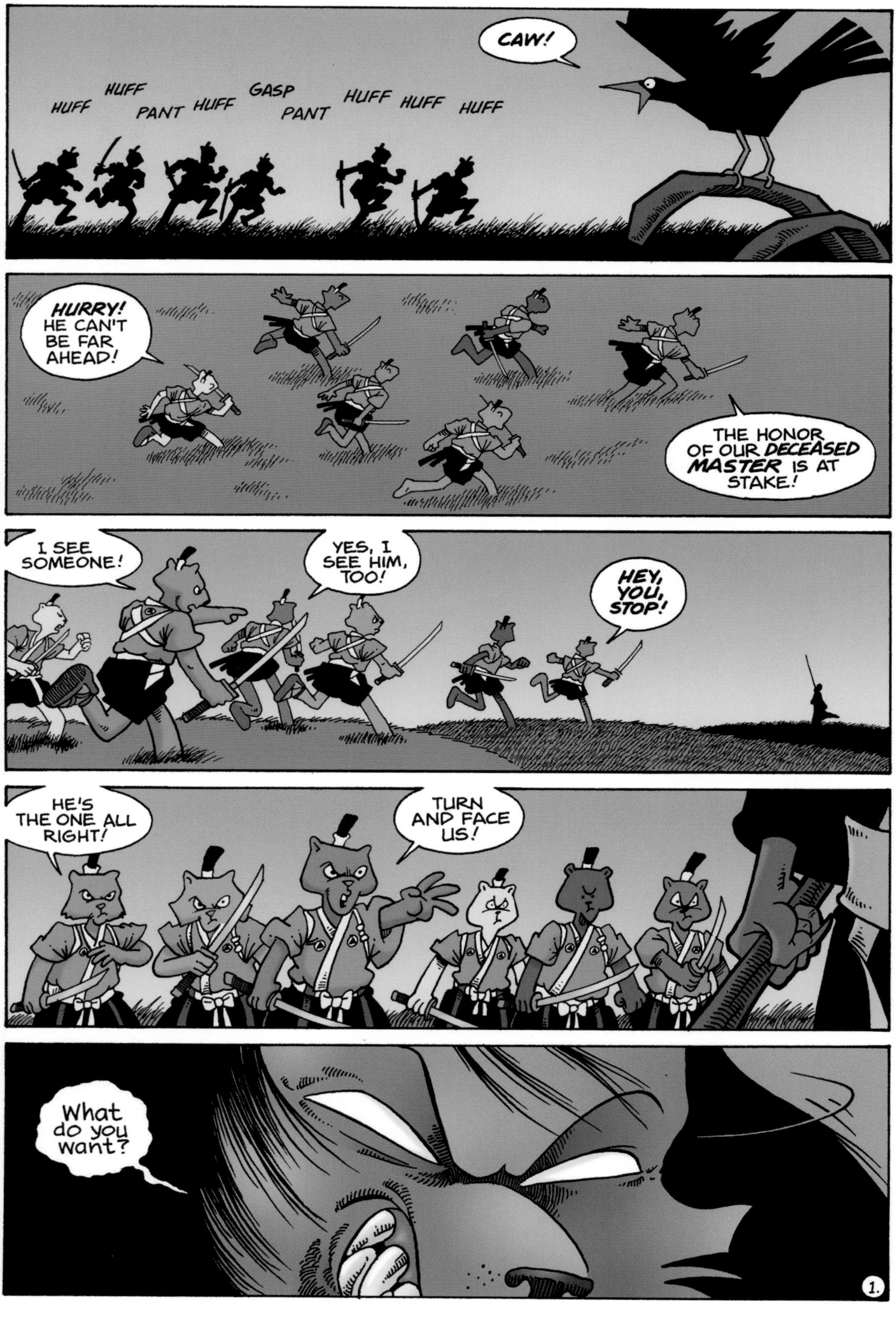
CAW!
HUFF
HUFF
PANT
HUFF
GASP
PANT
HUFF
HUFF
HUFF
HURRY! HE CAN'T BE FAR AHEAD!
THE HONOR OF OUR DECEASED MASTER IS AT STAKE!
I SEE SOMEONE!
YES, I SEE HIM, TOO!
HEY, YOU, STOP!
HE'S THE ONE ALL RIGHT!
TURN AND FACE US!
What do you want?
1.

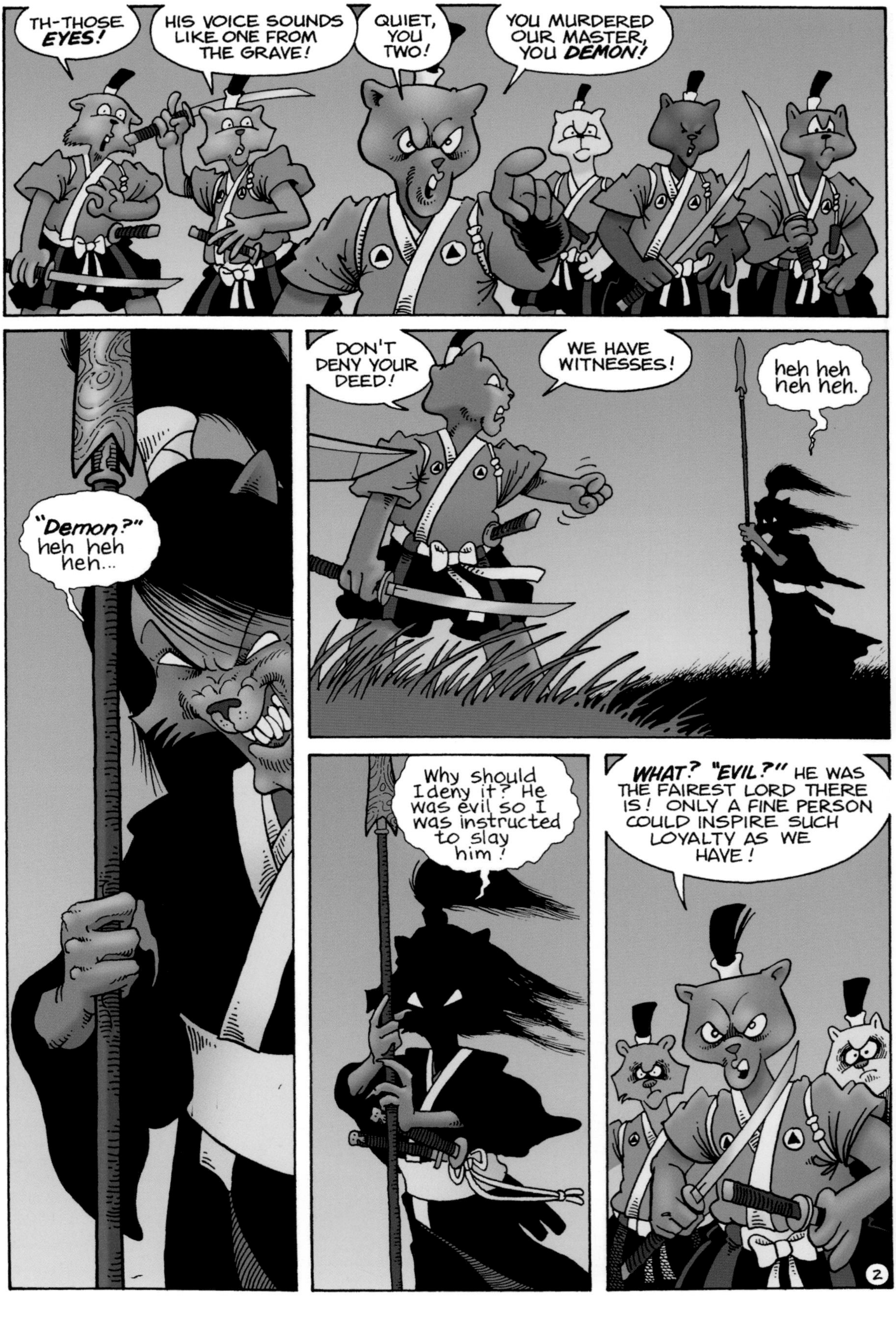
TH-THOSE EYES!
HIS VOICE SOUNDS LIKE ONE FROM THE GRAVE!
QUIET, YOU TWO!
YOU MURDERED OUR MASTER, YOU DEMON!
"Demon?" heh heh heh...
DON'T DENY YOUR DEED!
WE HAVE WITNESSES!
heh heh heh heh.
Why should I deny it? He was evil so I was instructed to slay him!
WHAT? "EVIL?" HE WAS THE FAIREST LORD THERE IS! ONLY A FINE PERSON COULD INSPIRE SUCH LOYALTY AS WE HAVE!
2

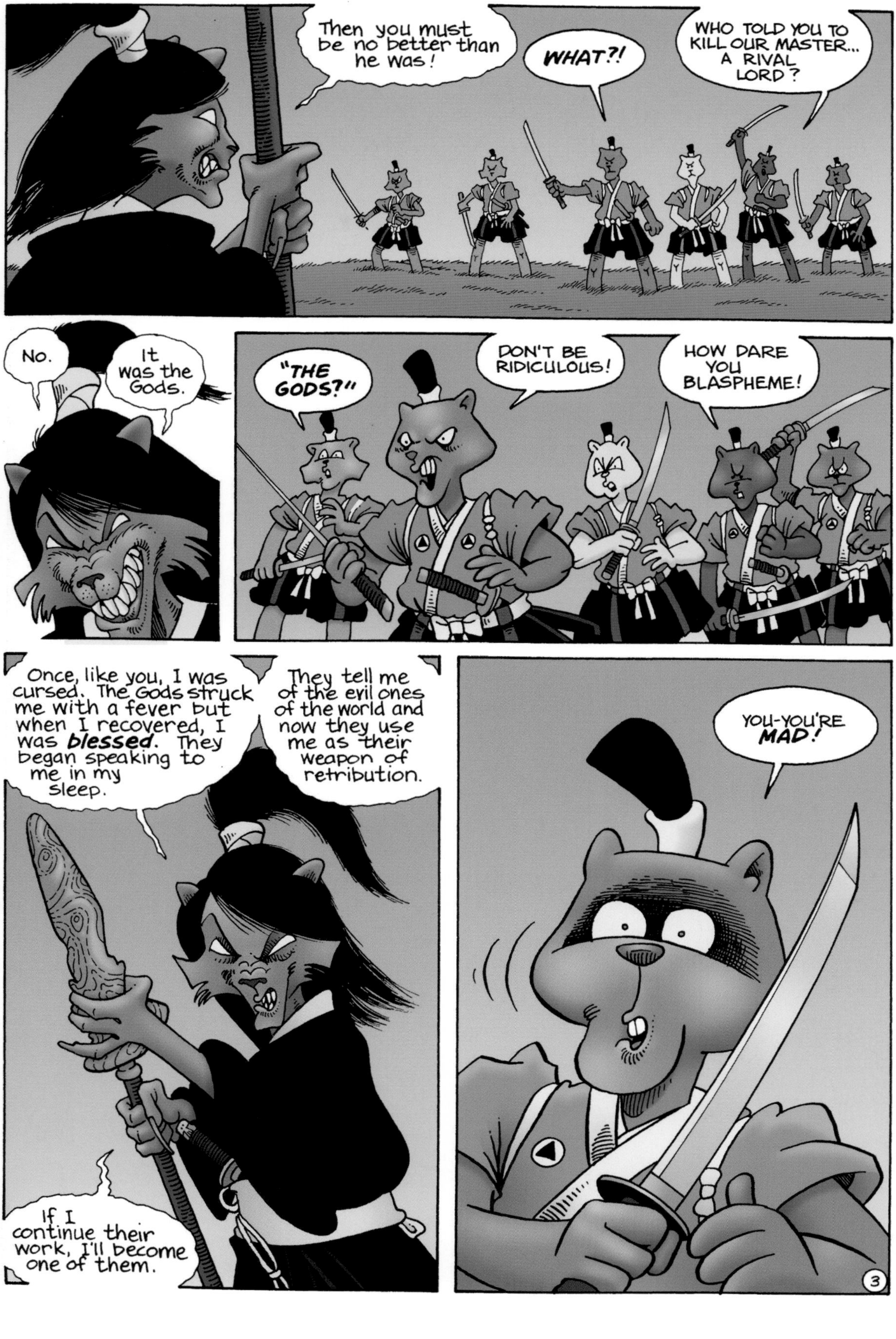
Then you must be no better than he was!
WHAT?!
WHO TOLD YOU TO KILL OUR MASTER... A RIVAL LORD?
No.
It was the Gods.
"THE GODS?"
DON'T BE RIDICULOUS!
HOW DARE YOU BLASPHEME!
Once, like you, I was cursed. The Gods struck me with a fever but when I recovered, I was blessed. They began speaking to me in my sleep.
They tell me of the evil ones of the world and now they use me as their weapon of retribution.
If I continue their work, I'll become one of them.
YOU-YOU'RE MAD!
3

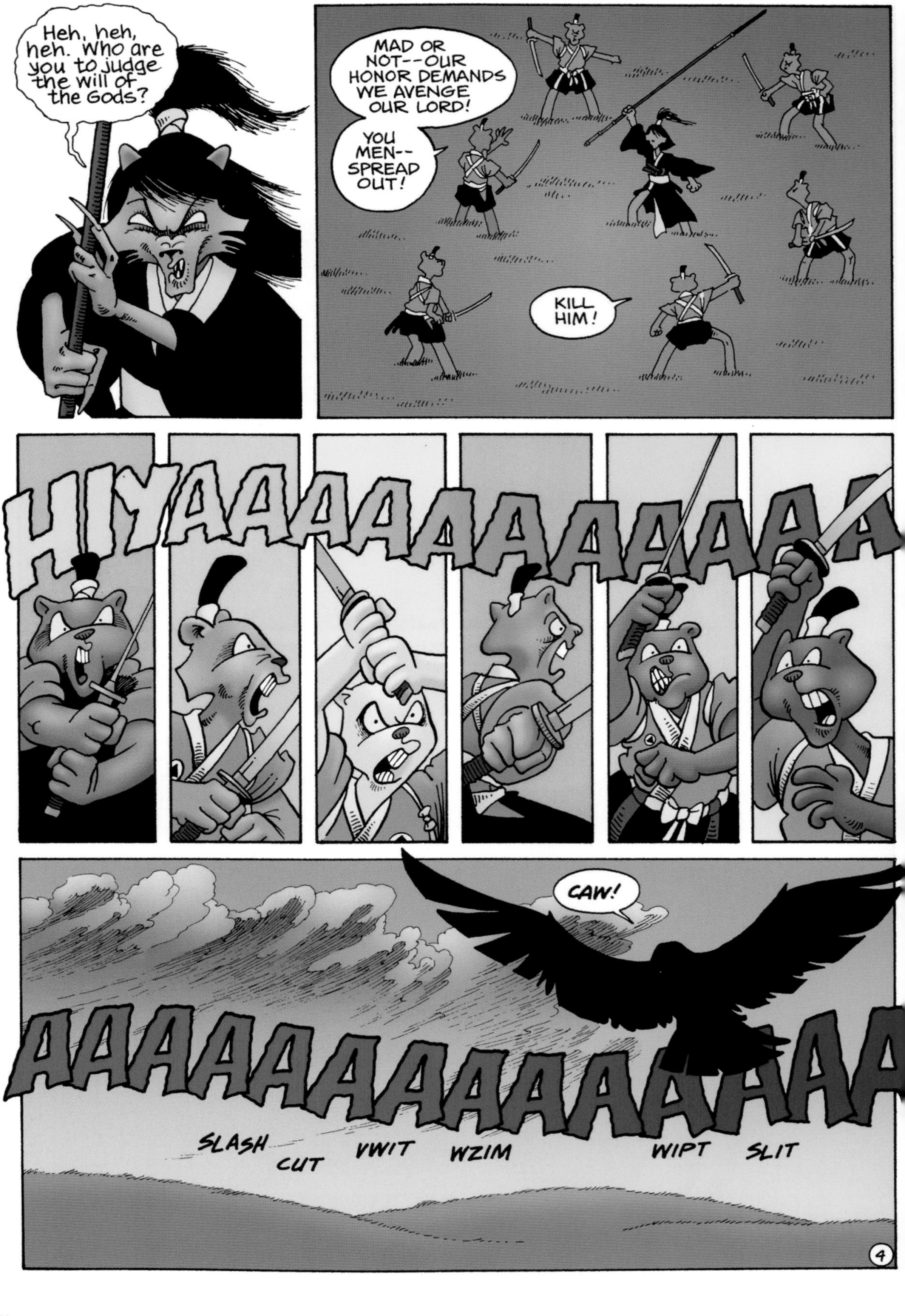

Heh, heh, heh. Who are you to judge the will of the Gods?
MAD OR NOT--OUR HONOR DEMANDS WE AVENGE OUR LORD!
YOU MEN--SPREAD OUT!
KILL HIM!
HIYAAAAAAAAAAA
CAW!
AAAAAAAAAAAAAAA
SLASH
CUT
VWIT
WZIM
WIPT
SLIT
4

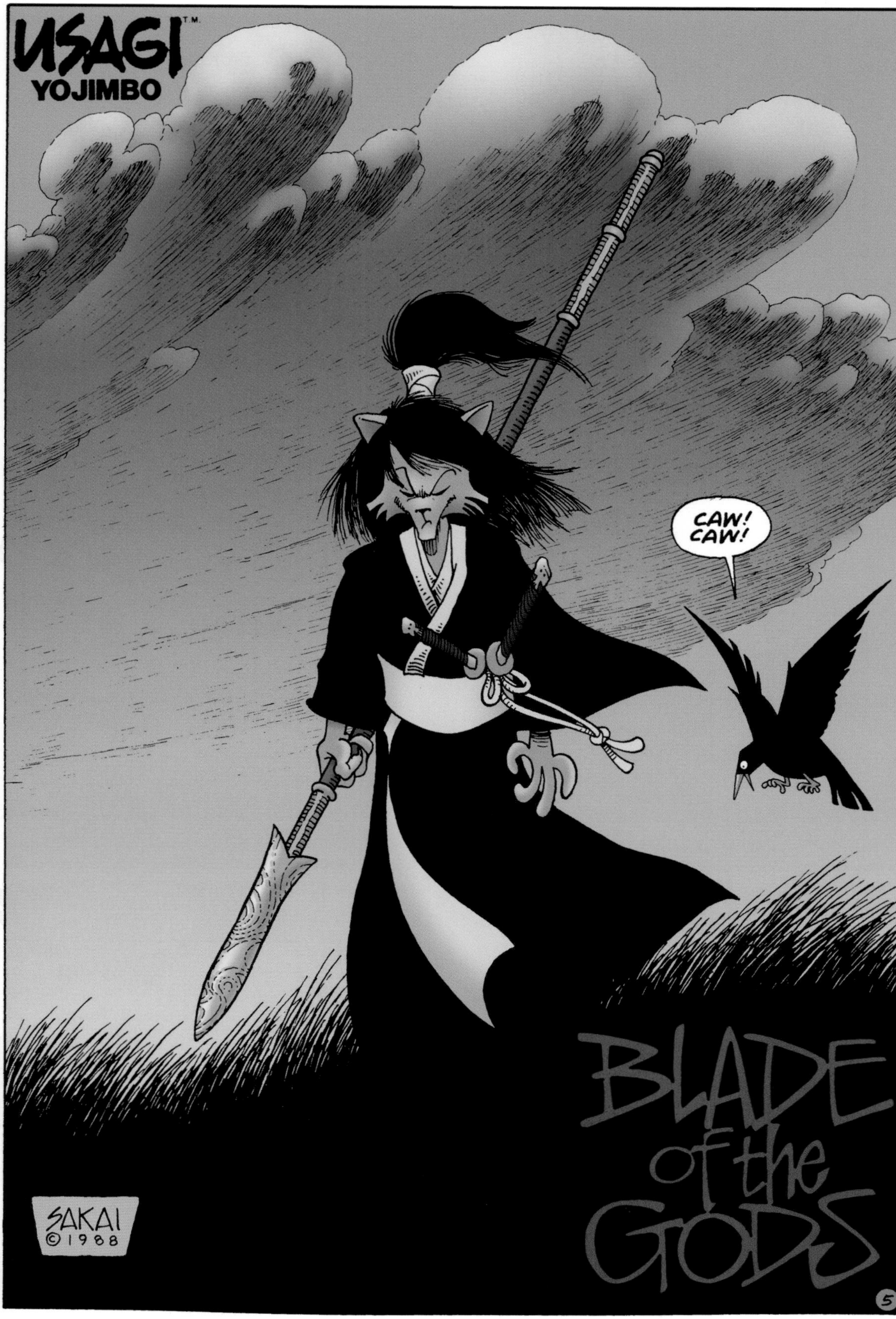
USAGI YOJIMBO
CAW! CAW!
BLADE of the GODS
SAKAI ©1988
5

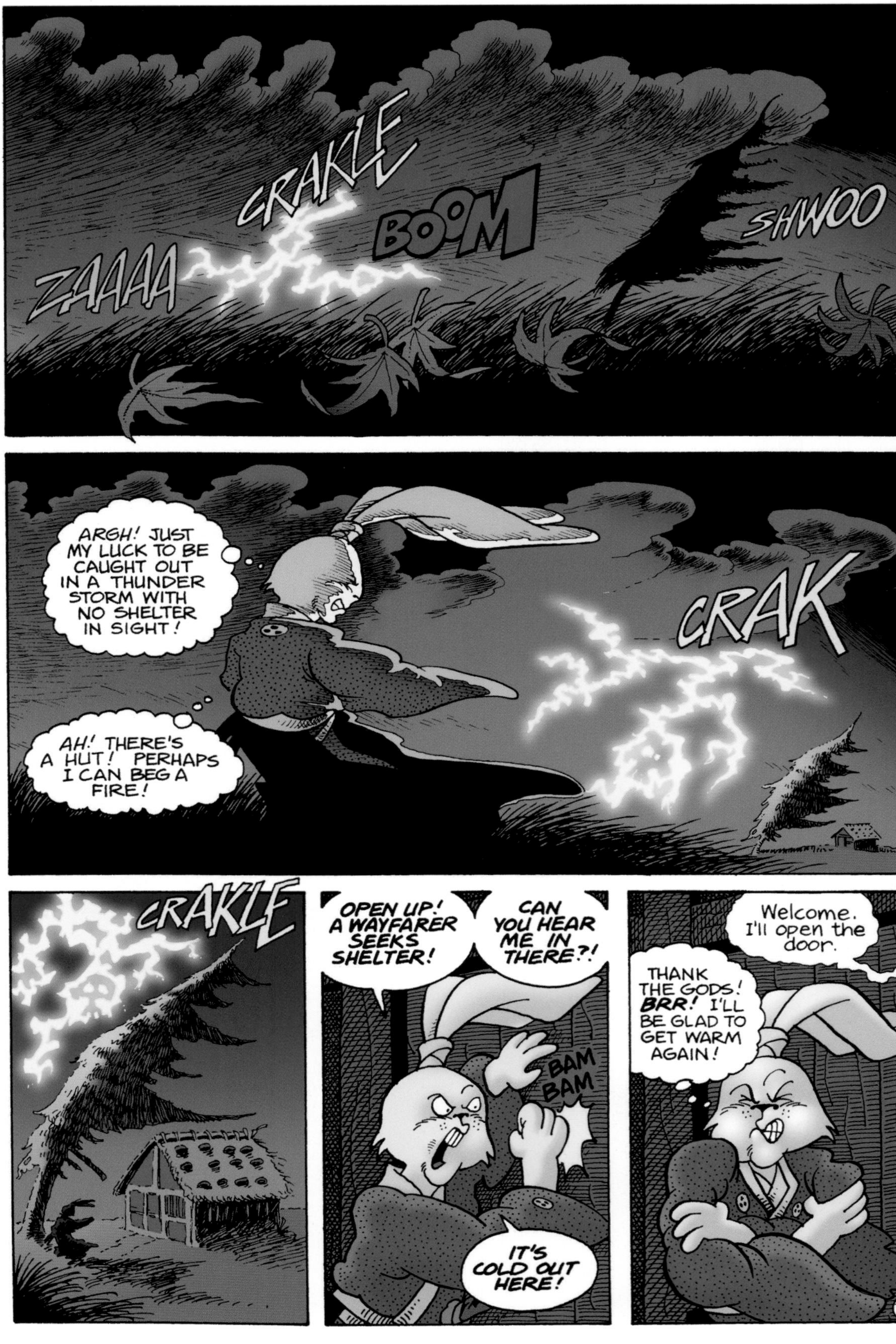

CRAKLE
BOOM
ZAAAA
SHWOO
ARGH! JUST MY LUCK TO BE CAUGHT OUT IN A THUNDER STORM WITH NO SHELTER IN SIGHT!
CRAK
AH! THERE'S A HUT! PERHAPS I CAN BEG A FIRE!
CRAKLE
OPEN UP! A WAYFARER SEEKS SHELTER!
CAN YOU HEAR ME IN THERE?!
BAM BAM
IT'S COLD OUT HERE!
Welcome. I'll open the door.
THANK THE GODS! BRR! I'LL BE GLAD TO GET WARM AGAIN!
6

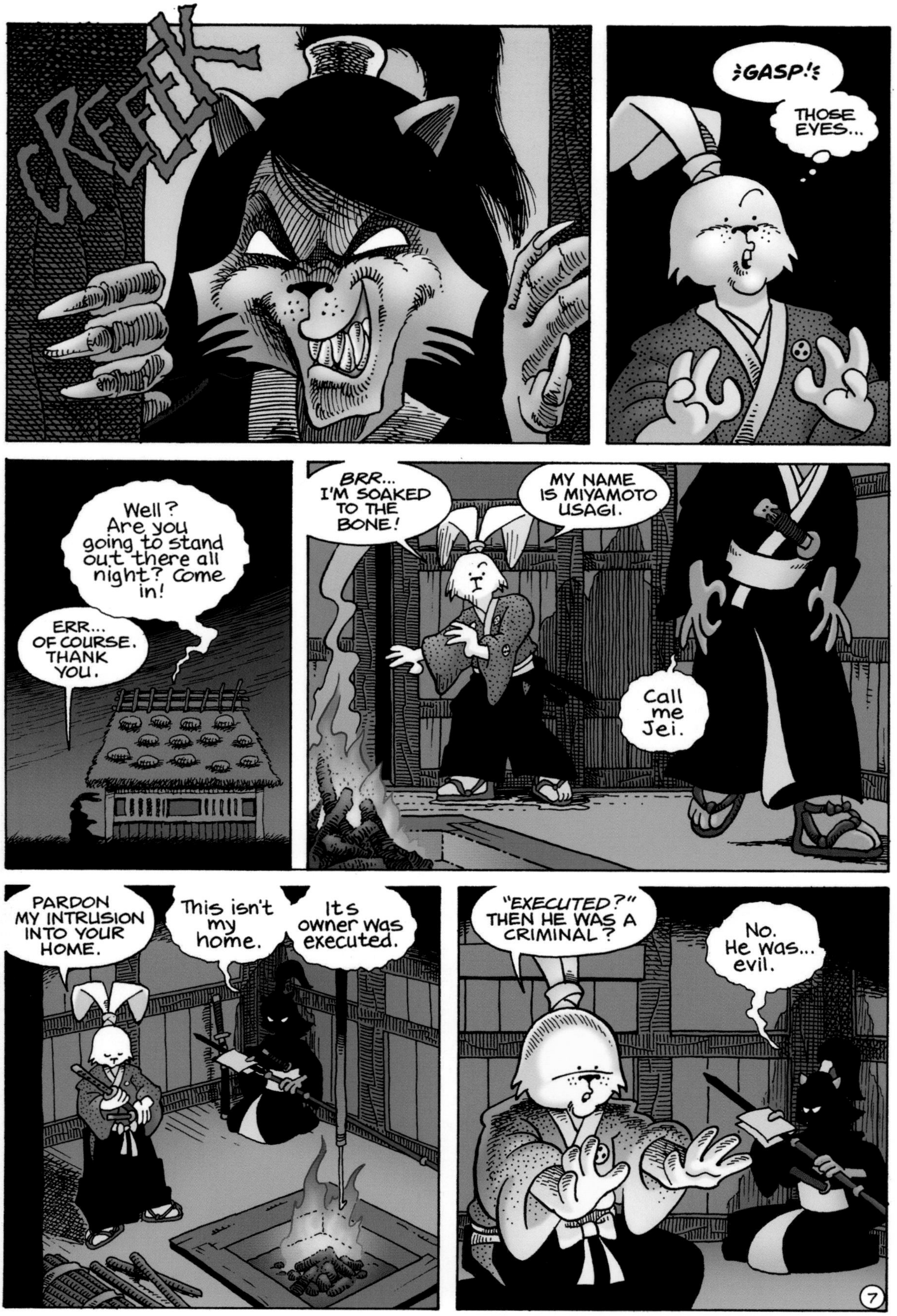
CREEEK
¡GASP!
THOSE EYES...
Well? Are you going to stand out there all night? Come in!
ERR... OF COURSE. THANK YOU.
BRR... I'M SOAKED TO THE BONE!
MY NAME IS MIYAMOTO USAGI.
Call me Jei.
PARDON MY INTRUSION INTO YOUR HOME.
This isn't my home.
It's owner was executed.
"EXECUTED?" THEN HE WAS A CRIMINAL?
No. He was... evil.
7

"EVIL?"
I DON'T
UNDER-
STAND.

Heh, heh.
Don't mind
me. I was
just making
conversation.

BLACK!
YOUR BLADE
IS BLACK!

What?!

ER...FORGIVE
ME. IT WAS A
TRICK OF THE
LIGHT AS YOU
CLEANED YOUR
SPEAR.

I KNOW THE
BLADE IS THE
SOUL OF THE
SAMURAI... I
MEANT NO
OFFENCE!

Well...

Forget it.
Let's blame it
on the flickering
fire.

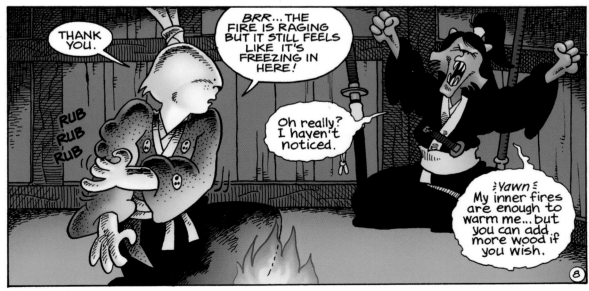

THANK
YOU.

RUB
RUB
RUB

BRR... THE
FIRE IS RAGING
BUT IT STILL FEELS
LIKE IT'S
FREEZING IN
HERE!

Oh really?
I haven't
noticed.

≶Yawn≶
My inner fires
are enough to
warm me...but
you can add
more wood if
you wish.

8

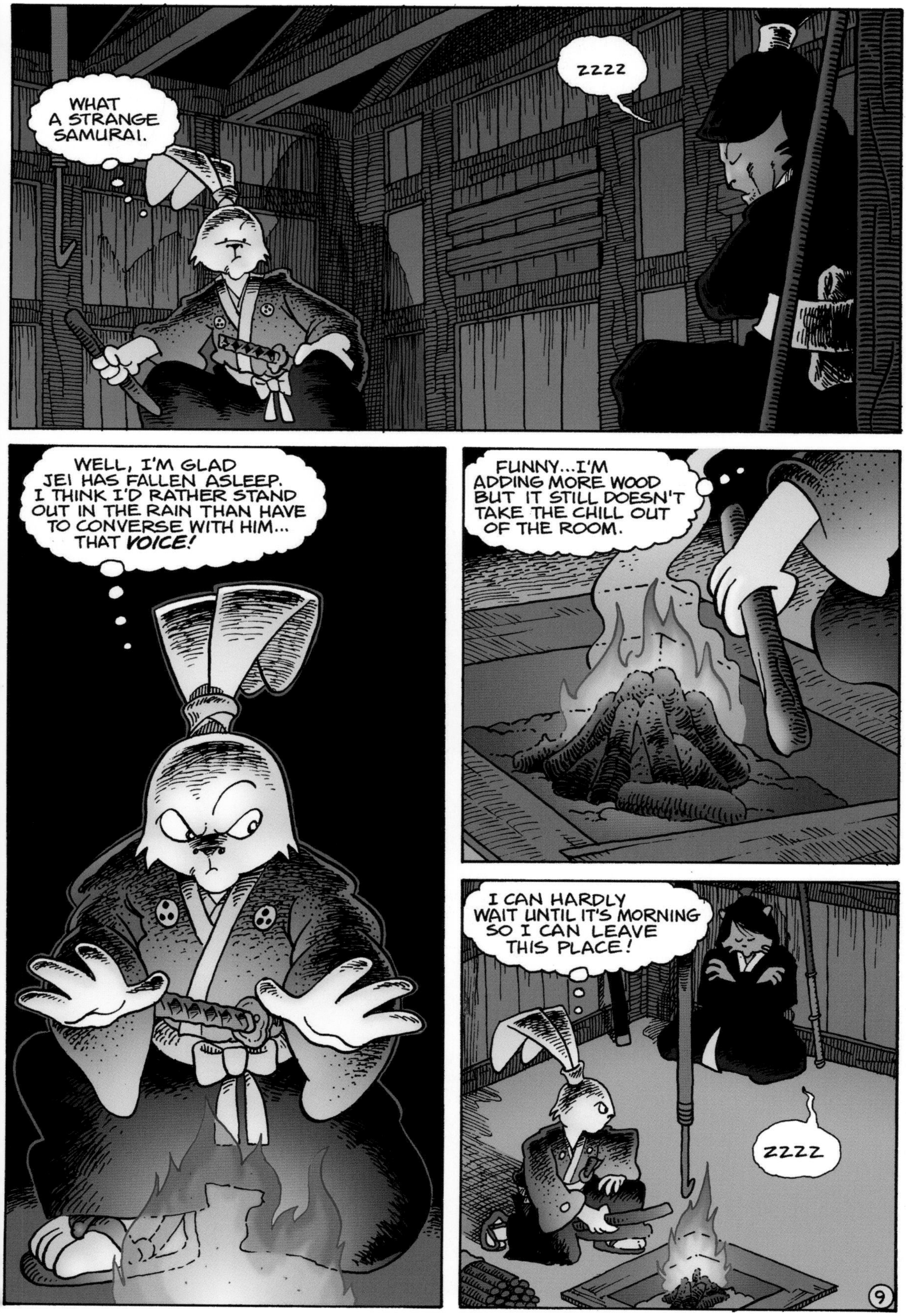
WHAT A STRANGE SAMURAI.
ZZZZ
WELL, I'M GLAD JEI HAS FALLEN ASLEEP. I THINK I'D RATHER STAND OUT IN THE RAIN THAN HAVE TO CONVERSE WITH HIM... THAT VOICE!
FUNNY...I'M ADDING MORE WOOD BUT IT STILL DOESN'T TAKE THE CHILL OUT OF THE ROOM.
I CAN HARDLY WAIT UNTIL IT'S MORNING SO I CAN LEAVE THIS PLACE!
ZZZZ
9

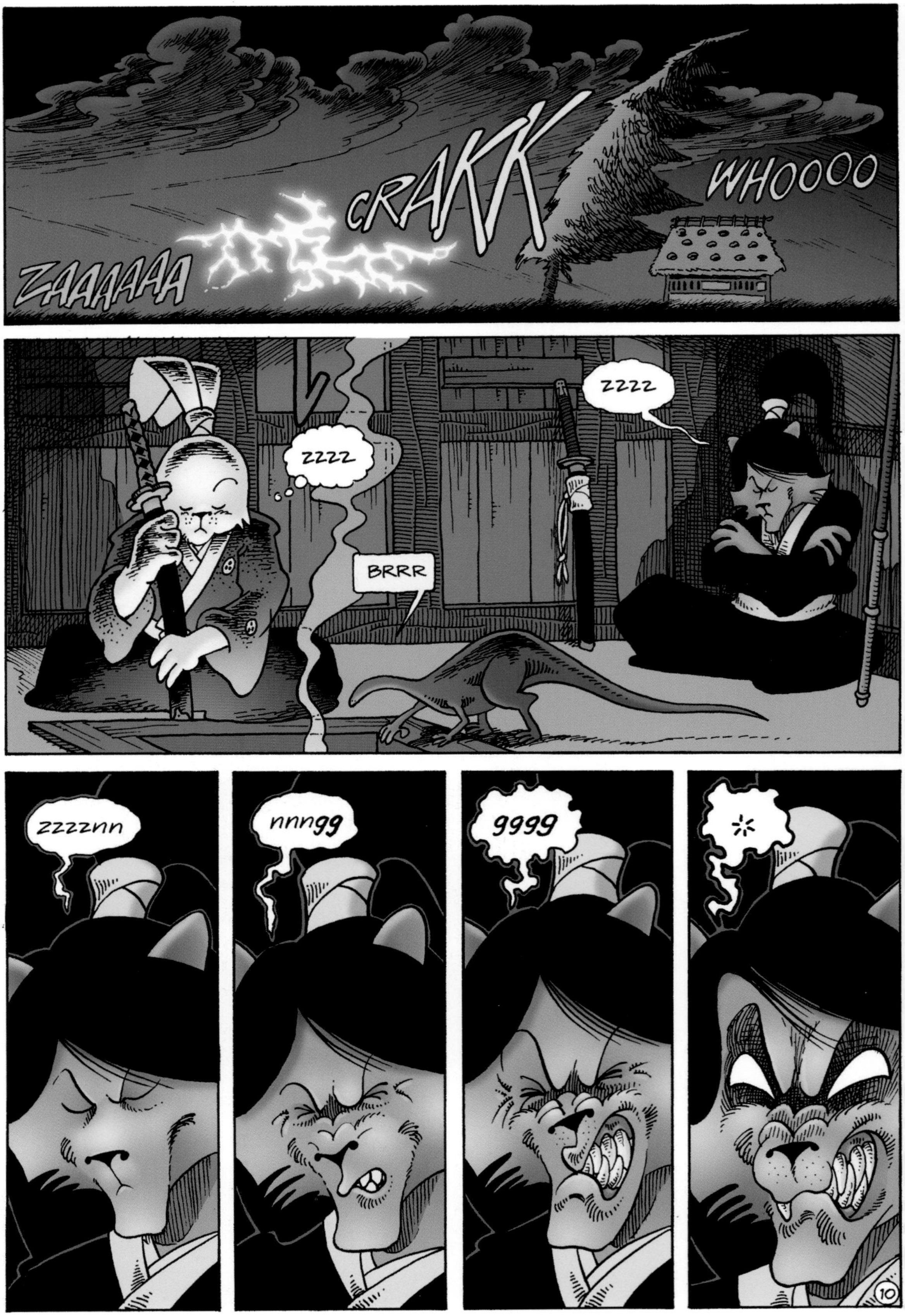
ZAAAAAA
CRAKK
WHOOOO
ZZZZ
ZZZZ
BRRR
zzzznn
nnngg
gggg
10

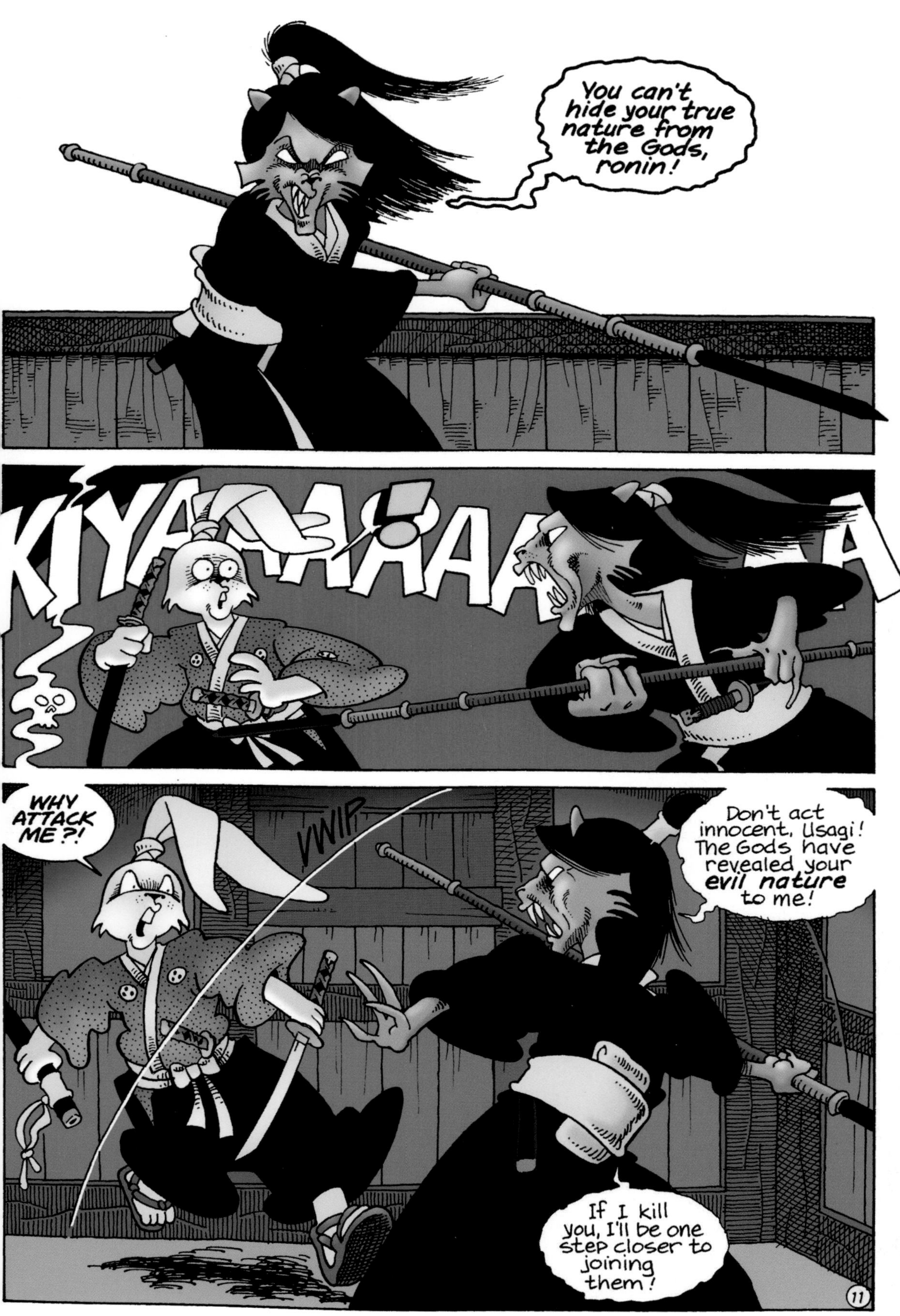
You can't hide your true nature from the Gods, ronin!
KIYAAAAAAAAA
WHY ATTACK ME?!
VWIP
Don't act innocent, Usagi! The Gods have revealed your **evil nature** to me!
If I kill you, I'll be one step closer to joining them!
11

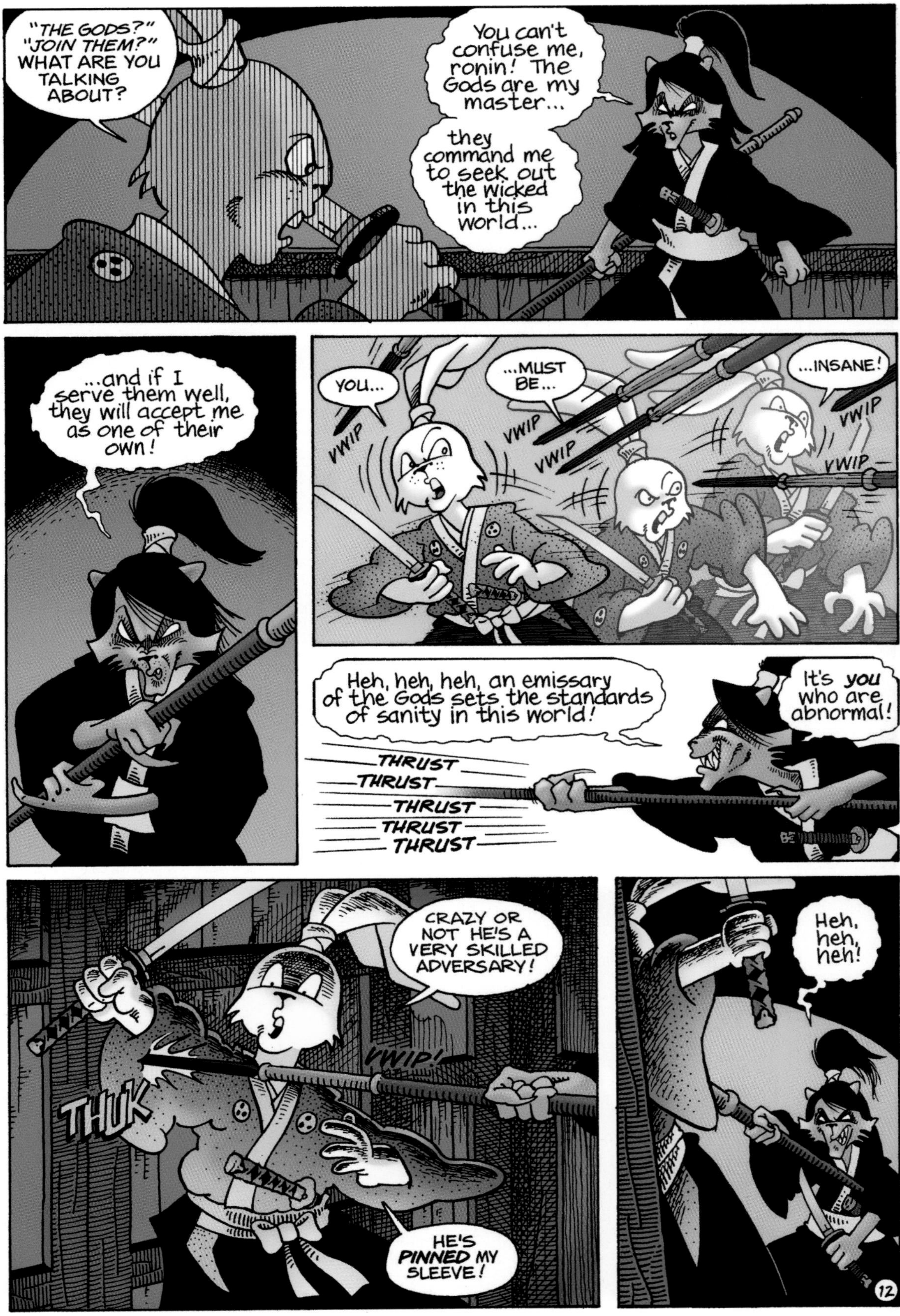
"THE GODS?" "JOIN THEM?" WHAT ARE YOU TALKING ABOUT?
You can't confuse me, ronin! The Gods are my master...
they command me to seek out the wicked in this world...
...and if I serve them well, they will accept me as one of their own!
YOU...
VWIP
...MUST BE...
VWIP
VWIP
...INSANE!
VWIP
VWIP
Heh, heh, heh, an emissary of the Gods sets the standards of sanity in this world!
It's you who are abnormal!
THRUST
THRUST
THRUST
THRUST
THRUST
CRAZY OR NOT HE'S A VERY SKILLED ADVERSARY!
VWIP!
THUK
HE'S PINNED MY SLEEVE!
Heh, heh, heh!
12

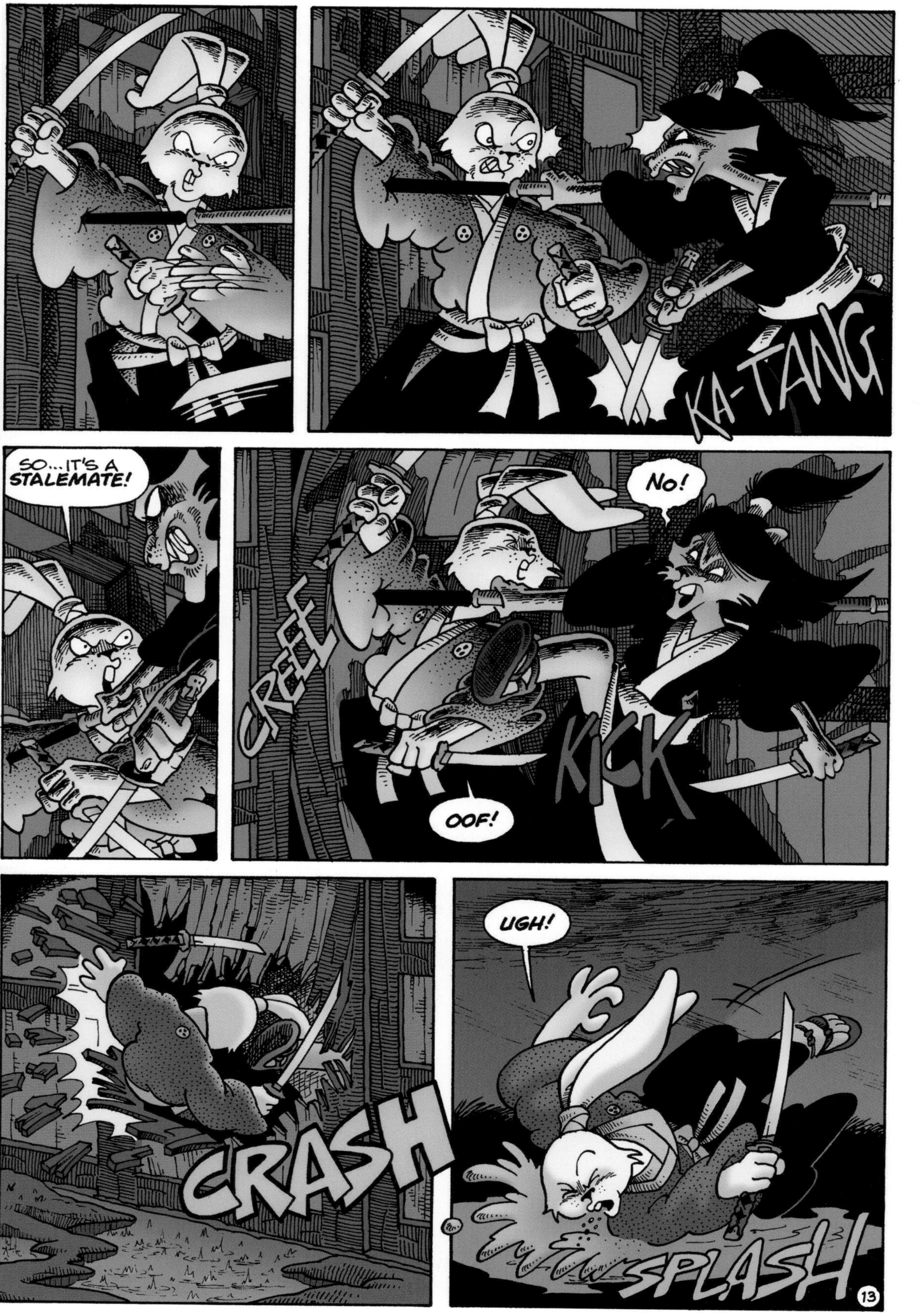
KA-TANG
SO...IT'S A STALEMATE!
No!
CREEE
KICK
OOF!
CRASH
UGH!
SPLASH
13

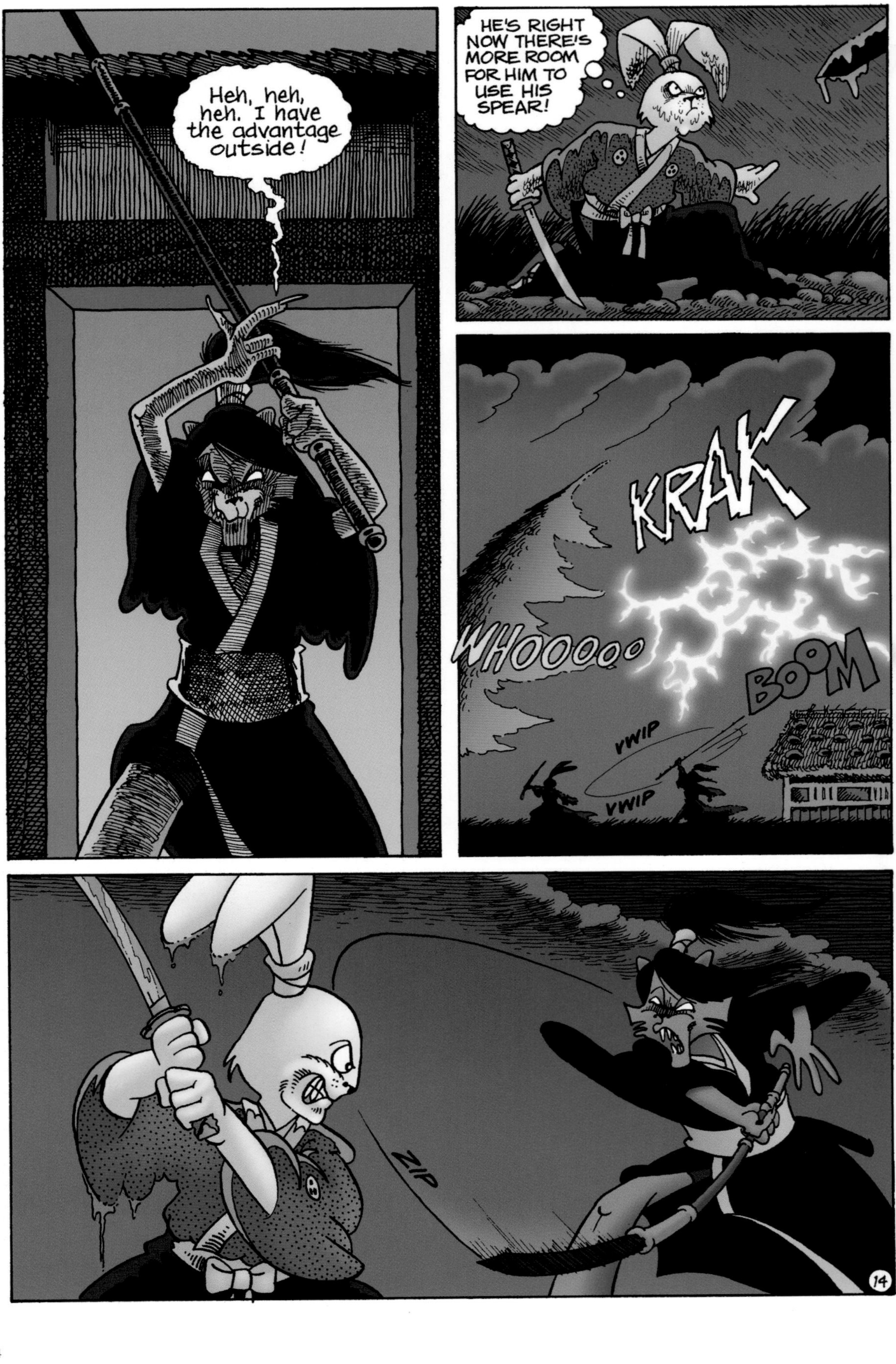

Heh, heh, heh. I have the advantage outside!
HE'S RIGHT NOW THERE'S MORE ROOM FOR HIM TO USE HIS SPEAR!
KRAK
WHOOOOOO
BOOM
VWIP
VWIP
ZIP
14

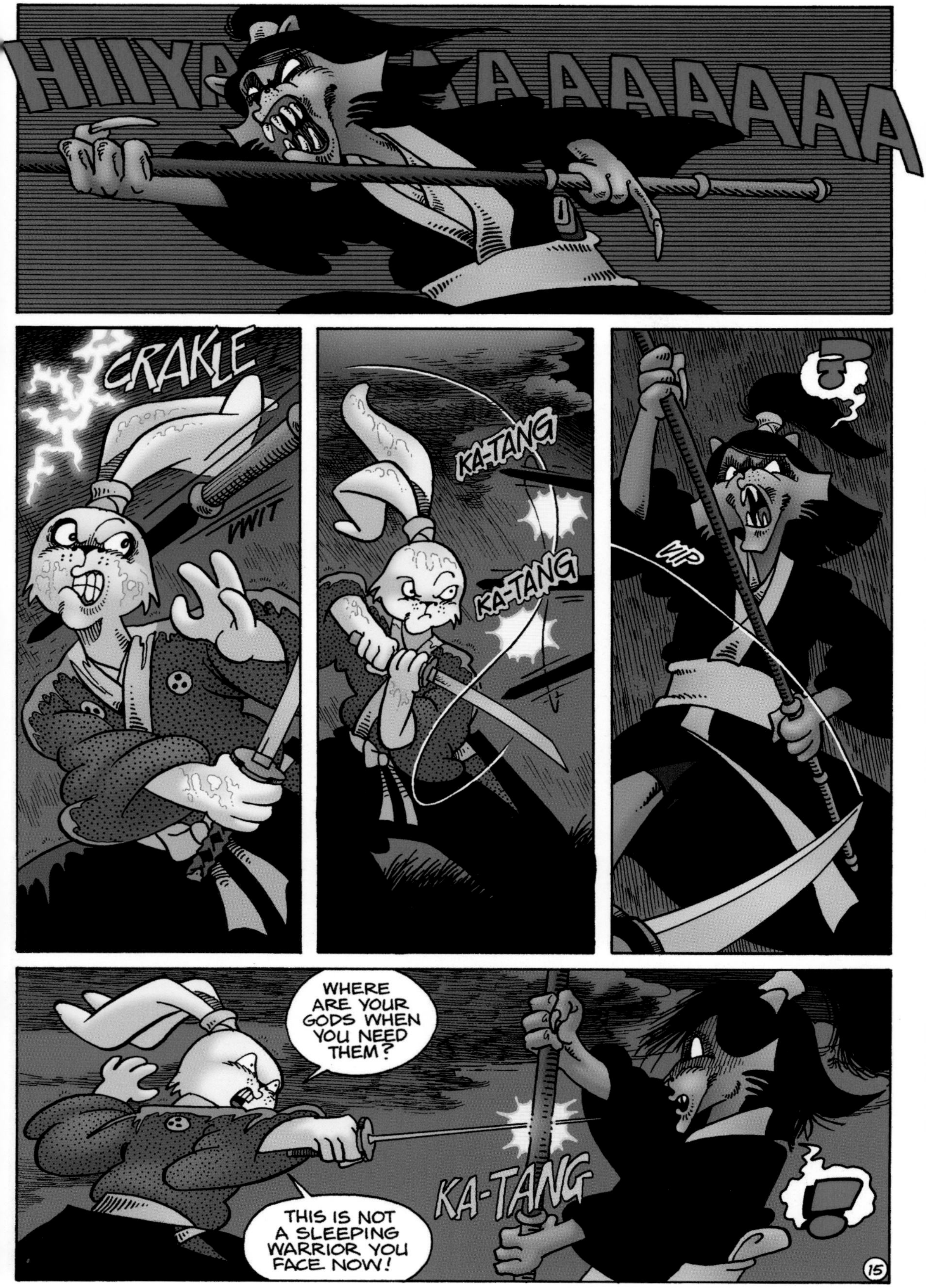
HIIYAAAAAAAAAA
CRAKLE
VWIT
KA-TANG
KA-TANG
VIP
?
WHERE ARE YOUR GODS WHEN YOU NEED THEM?
THIS IS NOT A SLEEPING WARRIOR YOU FACE NOW!
KA-TANG
!
15

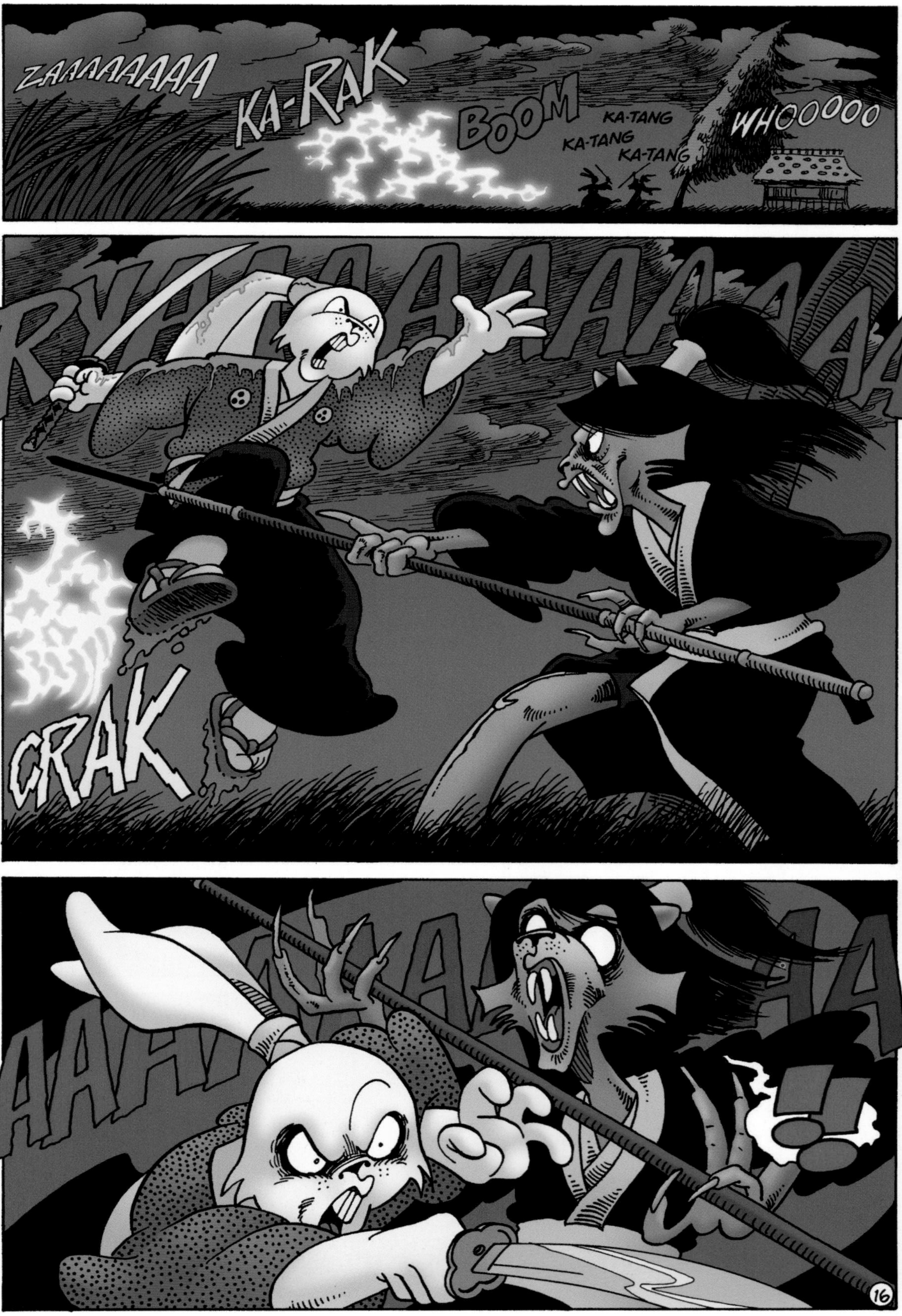
ZAAAAAAAA
KA-RAK
BOOM
KA-TANG
KA-TANG
KA-TANG
WHOOOOOO
RYAAAAAAAAAA
CRAK
AAAAAAAAAA
16

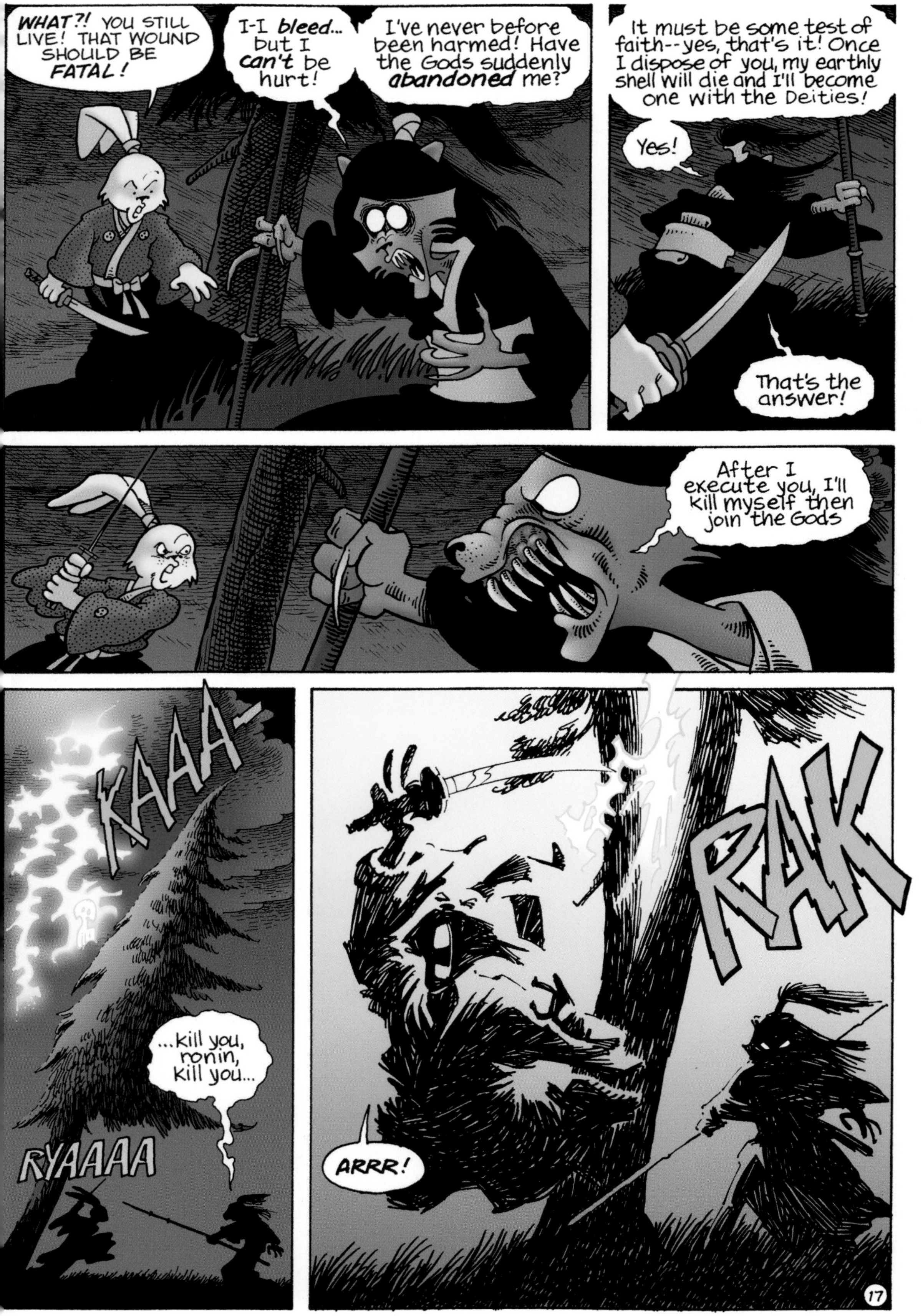
WHAT?! YOU STILL LIVE! THAT WOUND SHOULD BE FATAL!
I-I bleed... but I can't be hurt!
I've never before been harmed! Have the Gods suddenly abandoned me?
It must be some test of faith--yes, that's it! Once I dispose of you, my earthly shell will die and I'll become one with the Deities!
Yes!
That's the answer!
After I execute you, I'll kill myself then join the Gods
KAAA-
...kill you, ronin, kill you...
RYAAAA
RAK
ARRR!
17

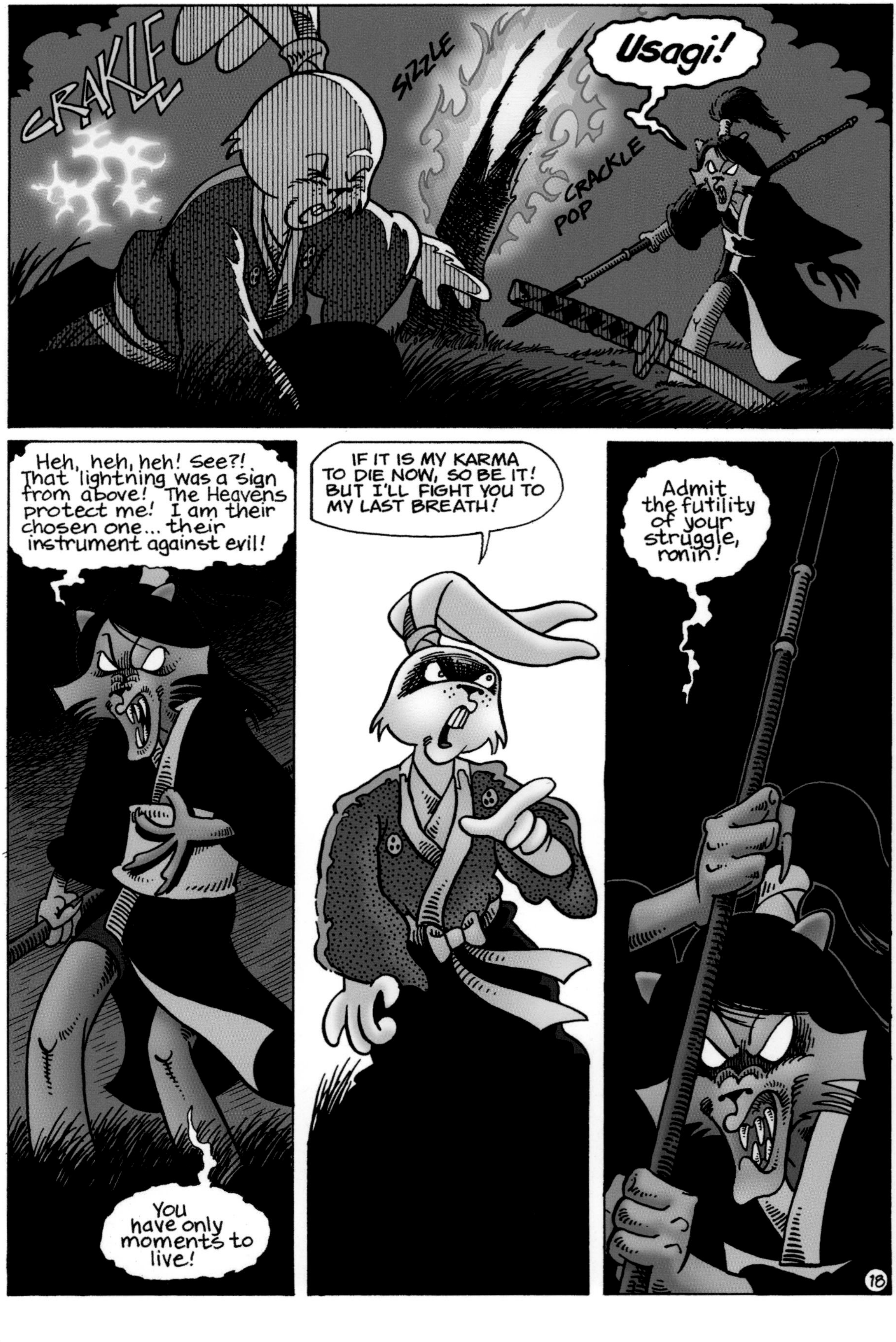
CRAKLE
SIZZLE
Usagi!
CRACKLE
POP
Heh, heh, heh! See?! That lightning was a sign from above! The Heavens protect me! I am their chosen one... their instrument against evil!
You have only moments to live!
IF IT IS MY KARMA TO DIE NOW, SO BE IT! BUT I'LL FIGHT YOU TO MY LAST BREATH!
Admit the futility of your struggle, ronin!
18

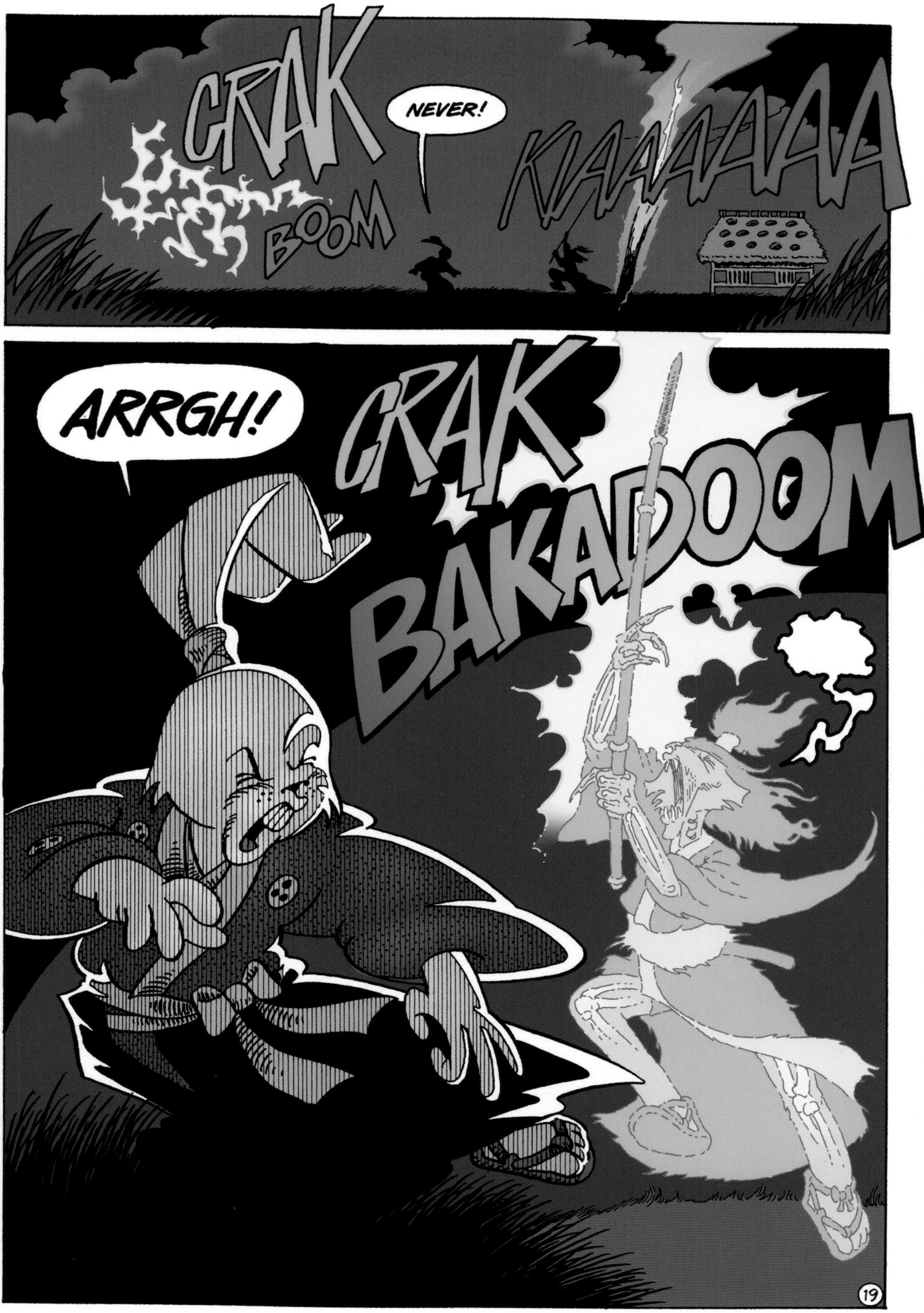
CRAK
BOOM
NEVER!
KIAAAAAAAA
ARRGH!
CRAK
BAKADOOM
19

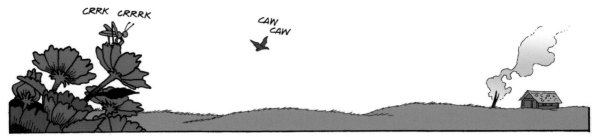

CRRK CRRRK

CAW CAW

CAW CAW

OOH... I'M ALIVE...

...SORT OF...

OWW... MY HEAD.

I CAN'T BELIEVE IT...

...ALMOST STRUCK BY LIGHTNING *TWICE* IN ONE NIGHT!

WHAT ABOUT JEI?

HE-HE'S *GONE*... THE LIGHTNING COMPLETELY *DESTROYED* HIM...

...OR WAS HE *REALLY* AN EMISSARY OF THE GODS NOW GONE TO JOIN THEM?

CAW CAW

I GUESS I'LL NEVER KNOW.

end.

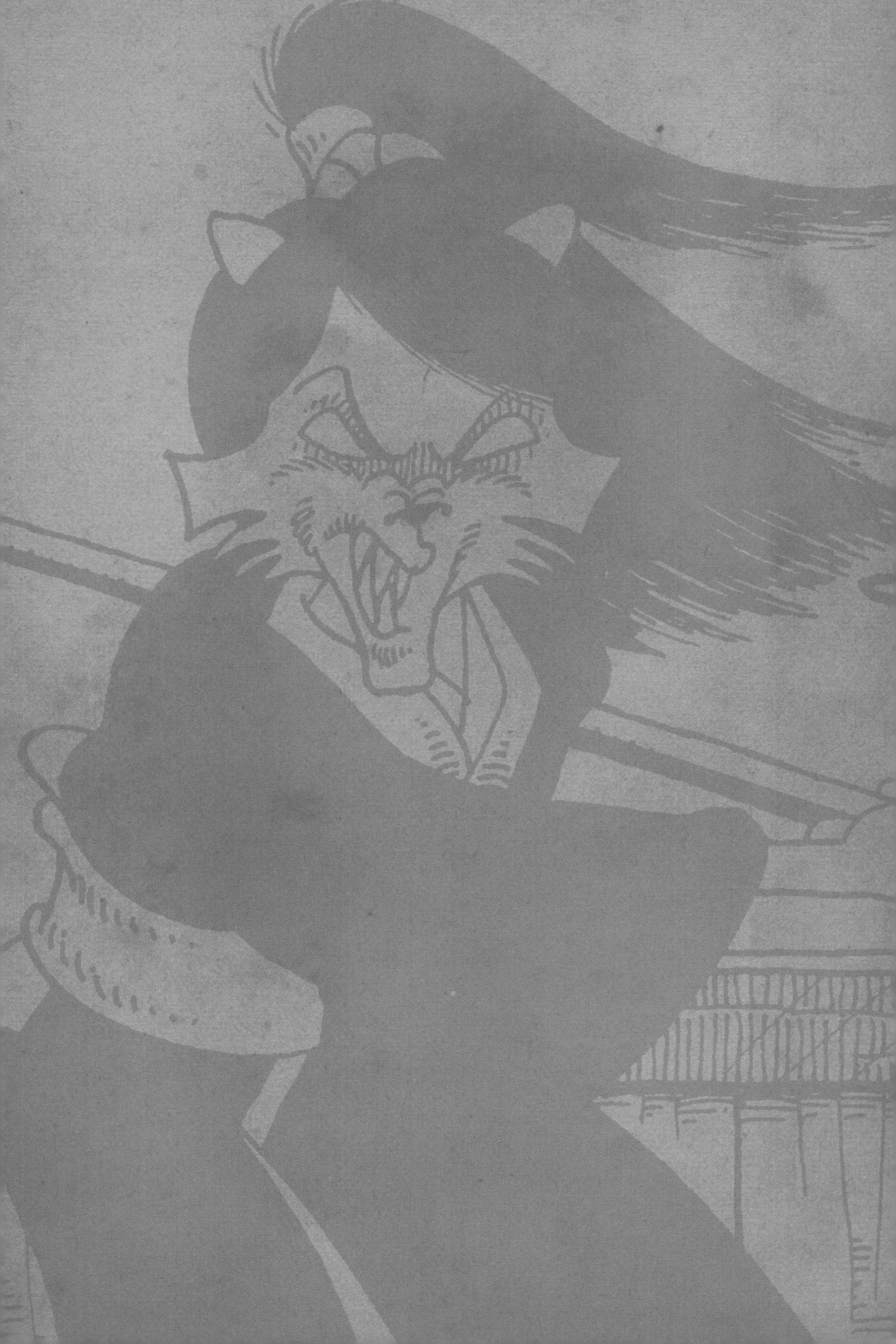

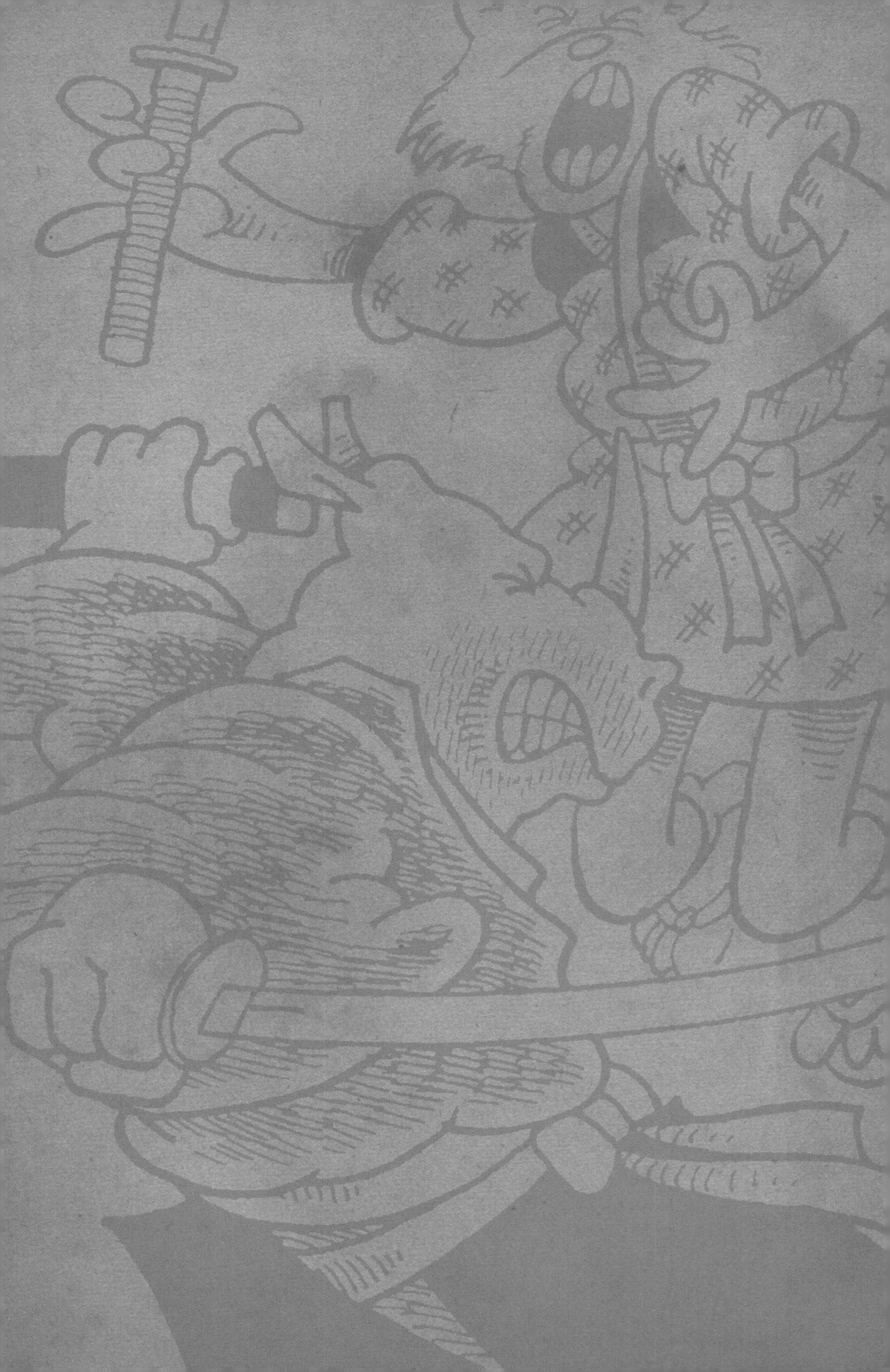

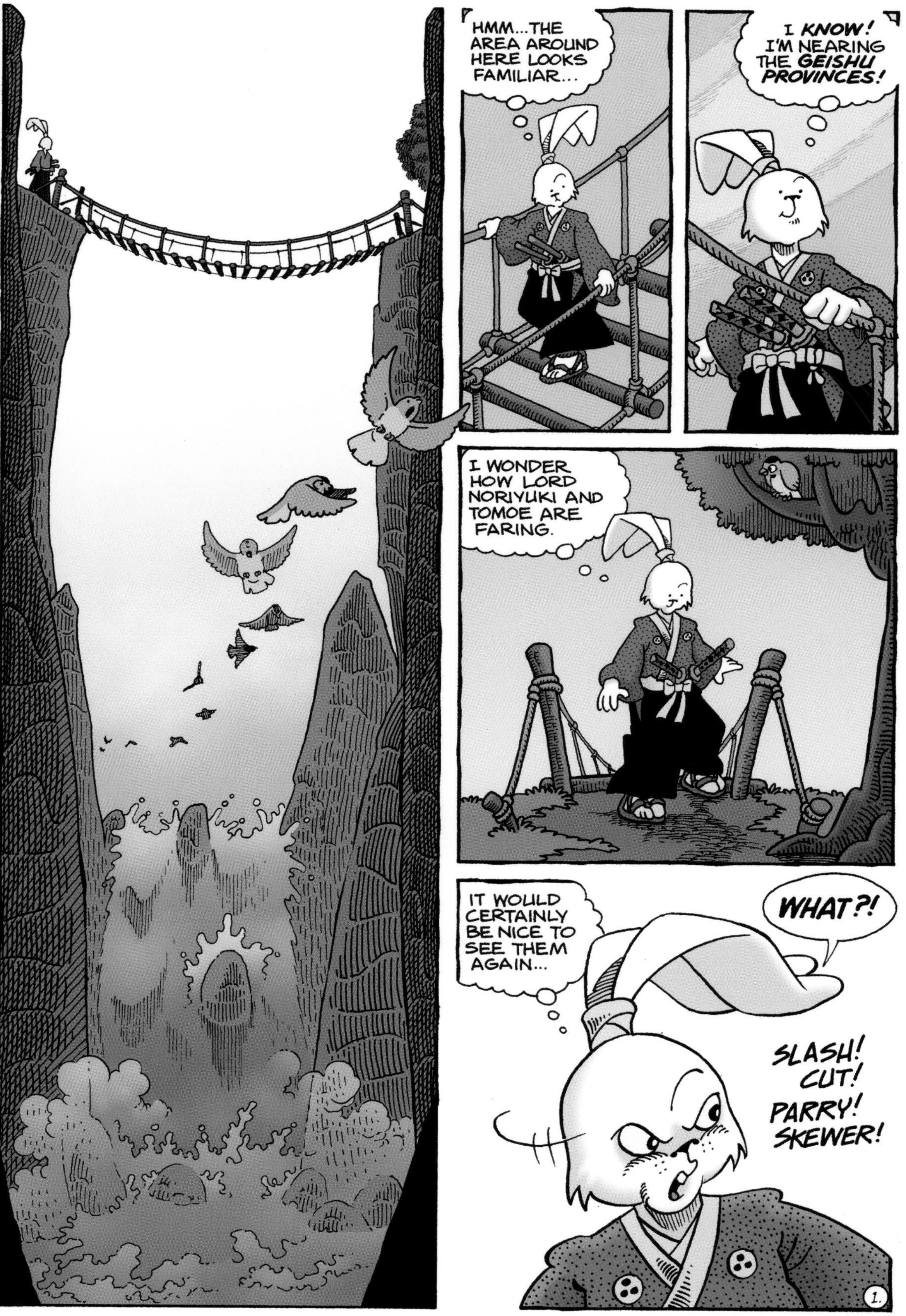
HMM...THE AREA AROUND HERE LOOKS FAMILIAR...
I KNOW! I'M NEARING THE GEISHU PROVINCES!
I WONDER HOW LORD NORIYUKI AND TOMOE ARE FARING.
IT WOULD CERTAINLY BE NICE TO SEE THEM AGAIN...
WHAT?!
SLASH! CUT! PARRY! SKEWER!
1.

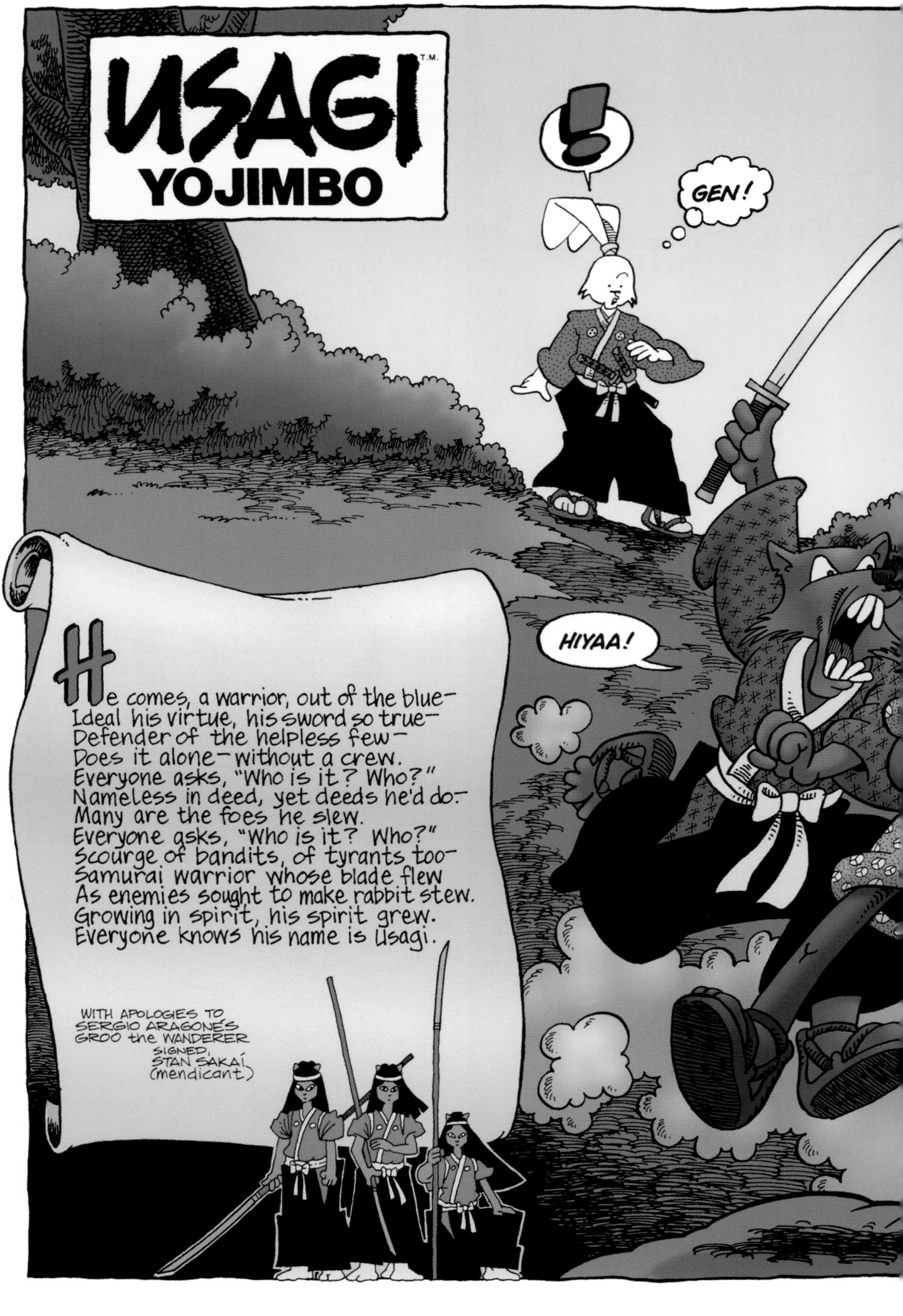
USAGI YOJIMBO T.M.
!
GEN!
HIYAA!
He comes, a warrior, out of the blue-
Ideal his virtue, his sword so true-
Defender of the helpless few-
Does it alone-without a crew.
Everyone asks, "Who is it? Who?"
Nameless in deed, yet deeds he'd do-
Many are the foes he slew.
Everyone asks, "Who is it? Who?"
Scourge of bandits, of tyrants too-
Samurai warrior whose blade flew
As enemies sought to make rabbit stew.
Growing in spirit, his spirit grew.
Everyone knows his name is Usagi.
WITH APOLOGIES TO
SERGIO ARAGONÉS
GROO the WANDERER
SIGNED,
STAN SAKAI
(mendicant)

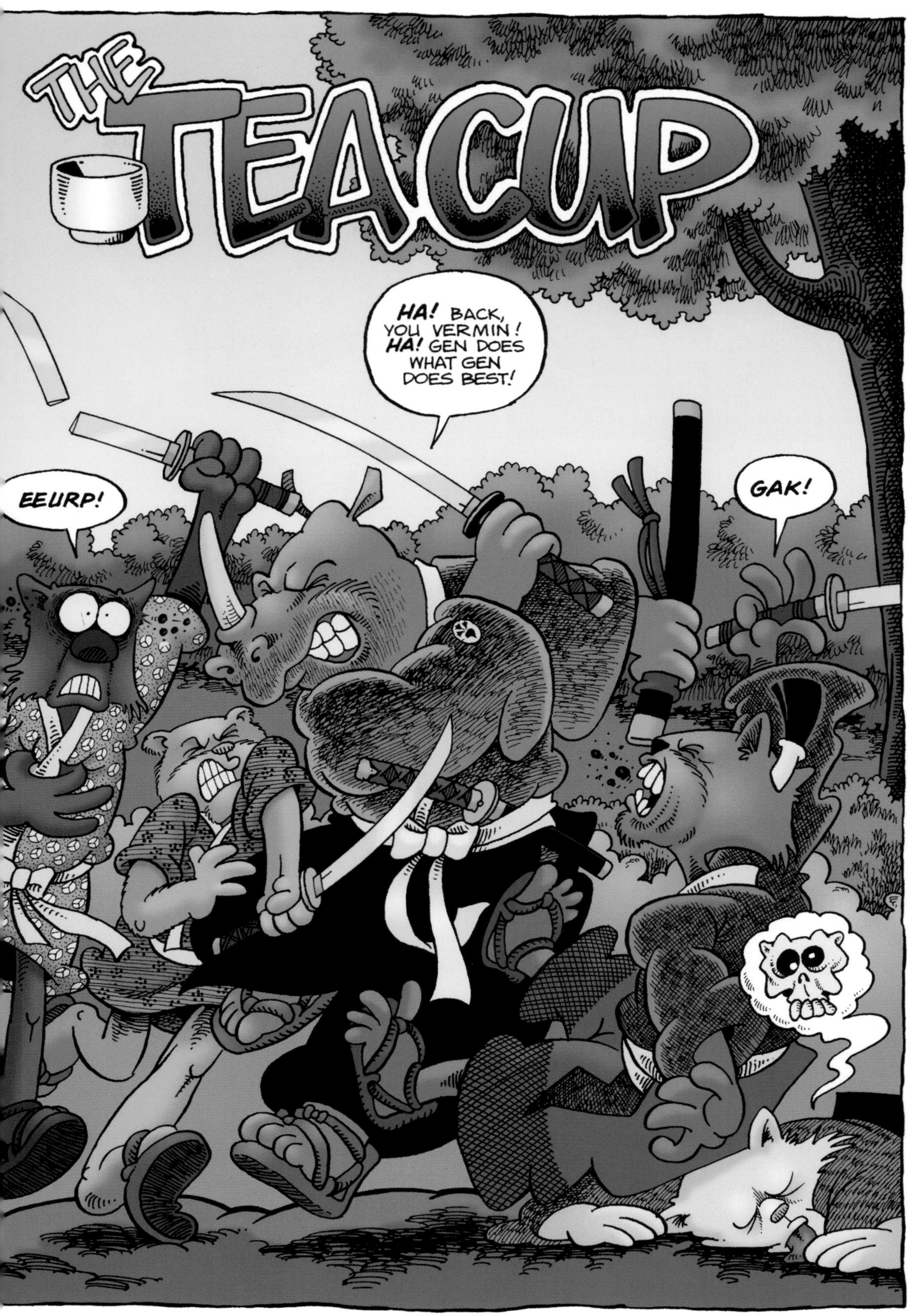
THE TEACUP
HA! BACK, YOU VERMIN! HA! GEN DOES WHAT GEN DOES BEST!
EEURP!
GAK!

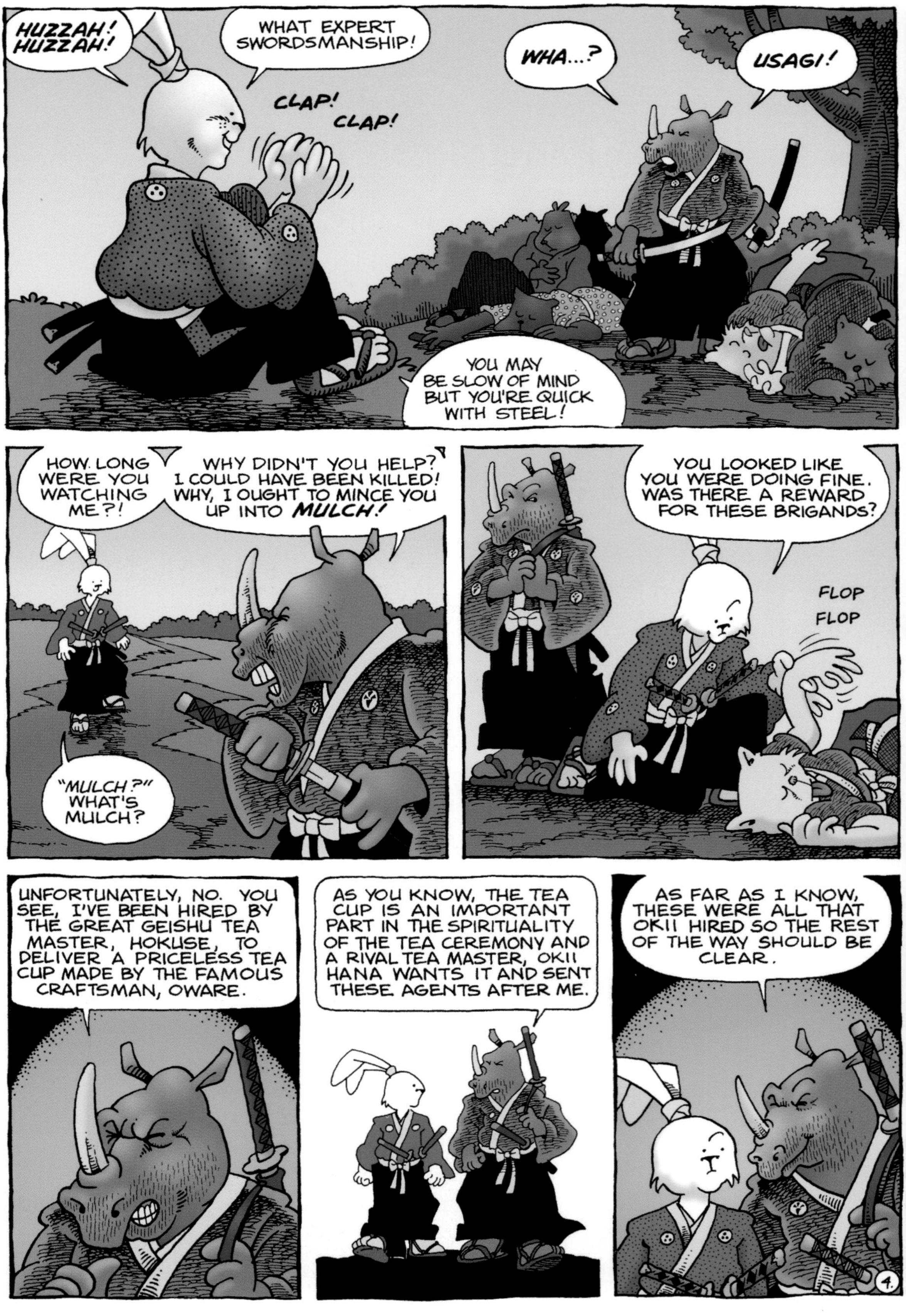
HUZZAH! HUZZAH!
WHAT EXPERT SWORDSMANSHIP!
CLAP! CLAP!
WHA...?
USAGI!
YOU MAY BE SLOW OF MIND BUT YOU'RE QUICK WITH STEEL!
HOW LONG WERE YOU WATCHING ME?!
WHY DIDN'T YOU HELP? I COULD HAVE BEEN KILLED! WHY, I OUGHT TO MINCE YOU UP INTO MULCH!
"MULCH?" WHAT'S MULCH?
YOU LOOKED LIKE YOU WERE DOING FINE. WAS THERE A REWARD FOR THESE BRIGANDS?
FLOP FLOP
UNFORTUNATELY, NO. YOU SEE, I'VE BEEN HIRED BY THE GREAT GEISHU TEA MASTER, HOKUSE, TO DELIVER A PRICELESS TEA CUP MADE BY THE FAMOUS CRAFTSMAN, OWARE.
AS YOU KNOW, THE TEA CUP IS AN IMPORTANT PART IN THE SPIRITUALITY OF THE TEA CEREMONY AND A RIVAL TEA MASTER, OKII HANA WANTS IT AND SENT THESE AGENTS AFTER ME.
AS FAR AS I KNOW, THESE WERE ALL THAT OKII HIRED SO THE REST OF THE WAY SHOULD BE CLEAR.
4.

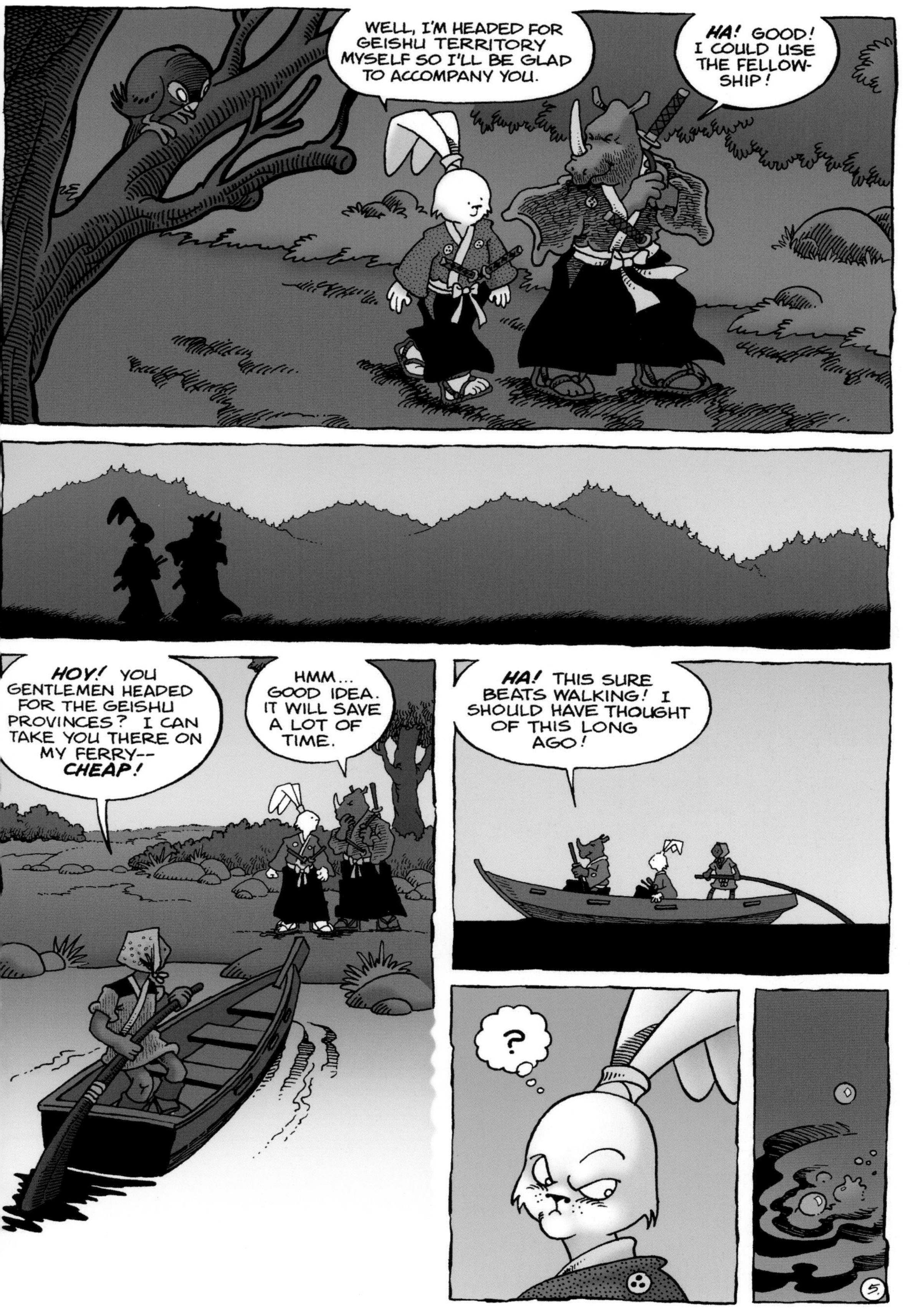
WELL, I'M HEADED FOR GEISHU TERRITORY MYSELF SO I'LL BE GLAD TO ACCOMPANY YOU.
HA! GOOD! I COULD USE THE FELLOW-SHIP!
HOY! YOU GENTLEMEN HEADED FOR THE GEISHU PROVINCES? I CAN TAKE YOU THERE ON MY FERRY-- CHEAP!
HMM... GOOD IDEA. IT WILL SAVE A LOT OF TIME.
HA! THIS SURE BEATS WALKING! I SHOULD HAVE THOUGHT OF THIS LONG AGO!
?
5.

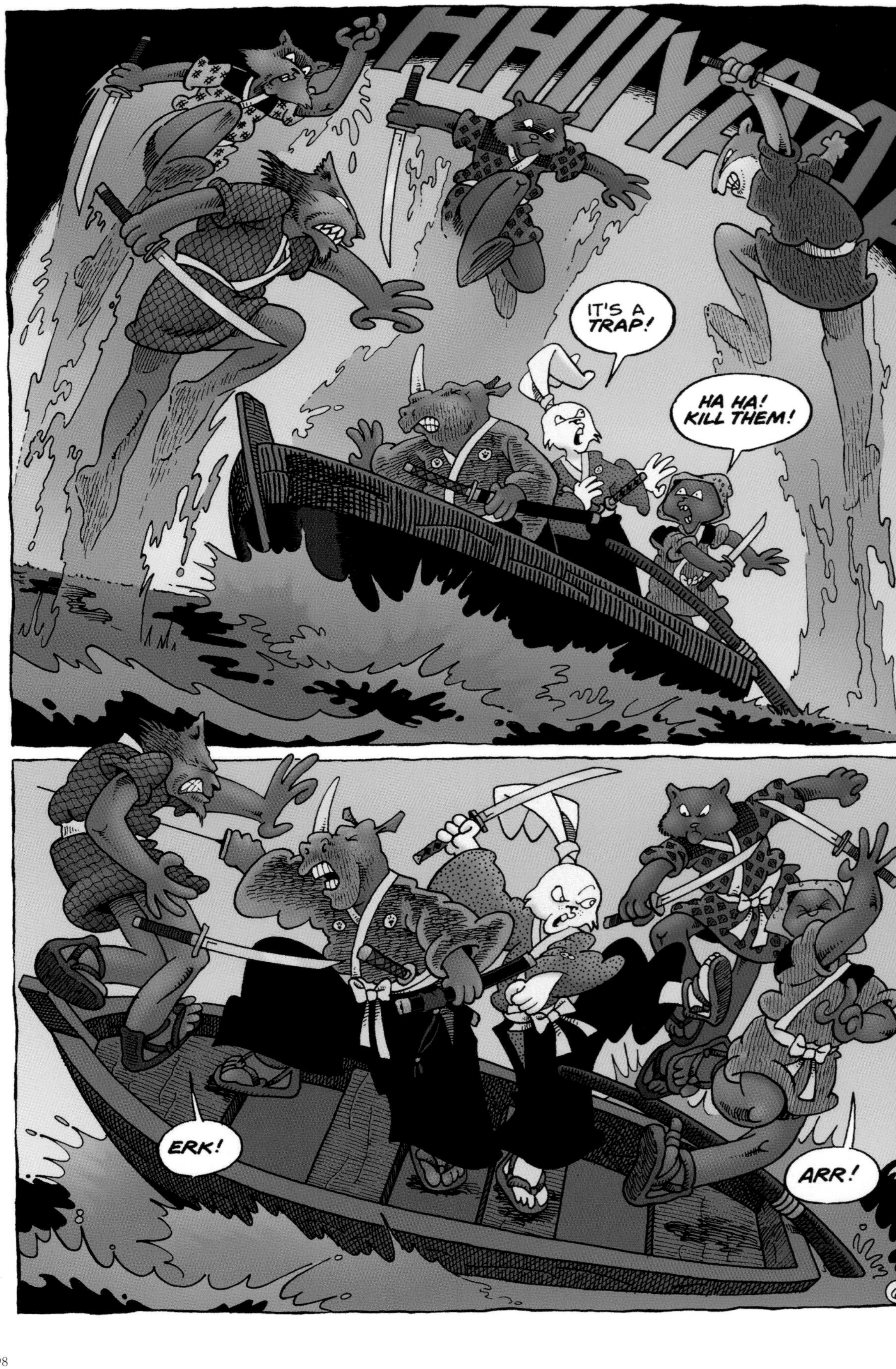
HHIIYAA
IT'S A TRAP!
HA HA! KILL THEM!
ERK!
ARR!
6

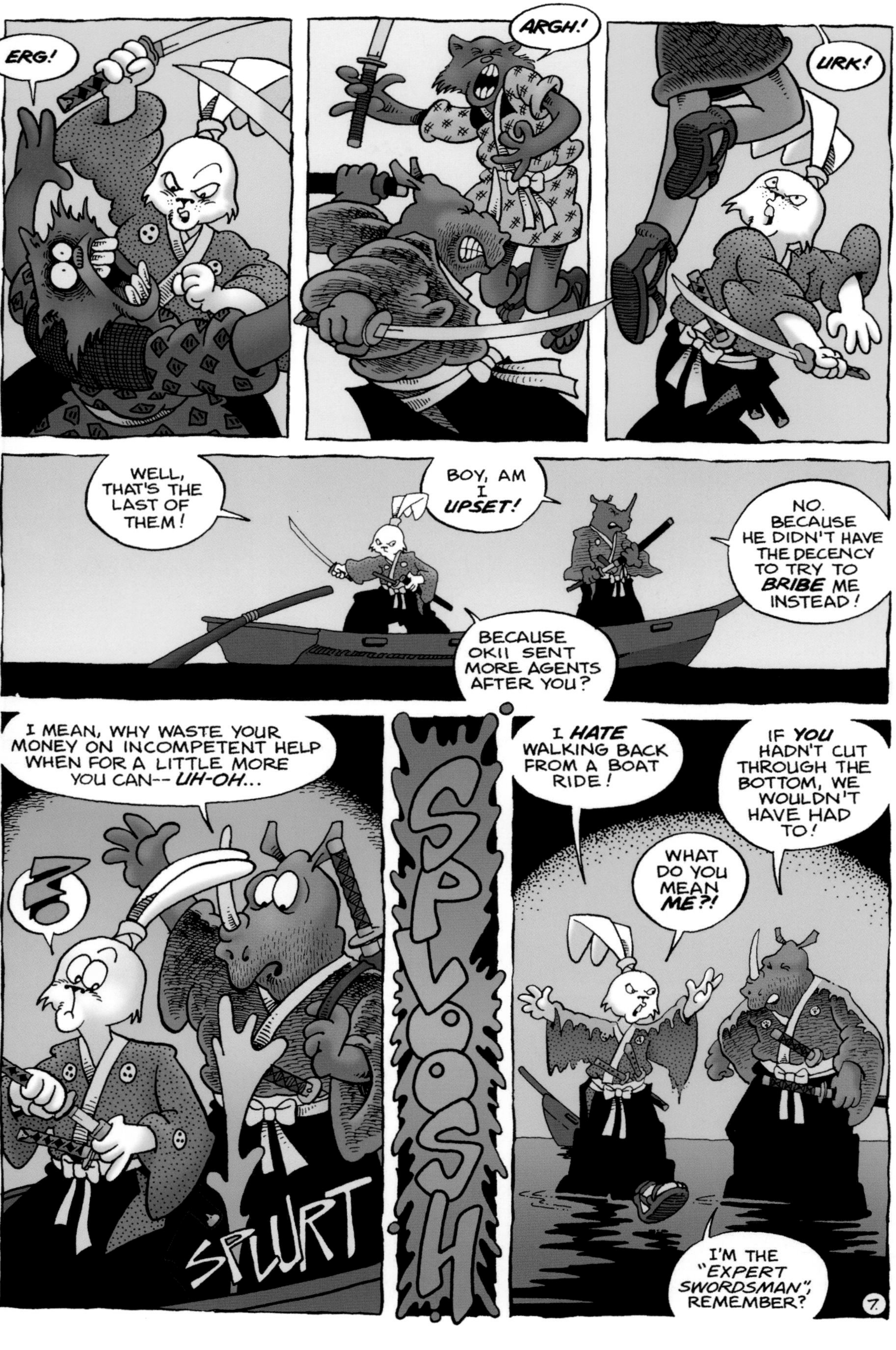
ERG!
ARGH!
URK!
WELL, THAT'S THE LAST OF THEM!
BOY, AM I UPSET!
BECAUSE OKII SENT MORE AGENTS AFTER YOU?
NO. BECAUSE HE DIDN'T HAVE THE DECENCY TO TRY TO BRIBE ME INSTEAD!
I MEAN, WHY WASTE YOUR MONEY ON INCOMPETENT HELP WHEN FOR A LITTLE MORE YOU CAN-- UH-OH...
SPLURT
SPLOOSH
I HATE WALKING BACK FROM A BOAT RIDE!
IF YOU HADN'T CUT THROUGH THE BOTTOM, WE WOULDN'T HAVE HAD TO!
WHAT DO YOU MEAN ME?!
I'M THE "EXPERT SWORDSMAN", REMEMBER?
7.

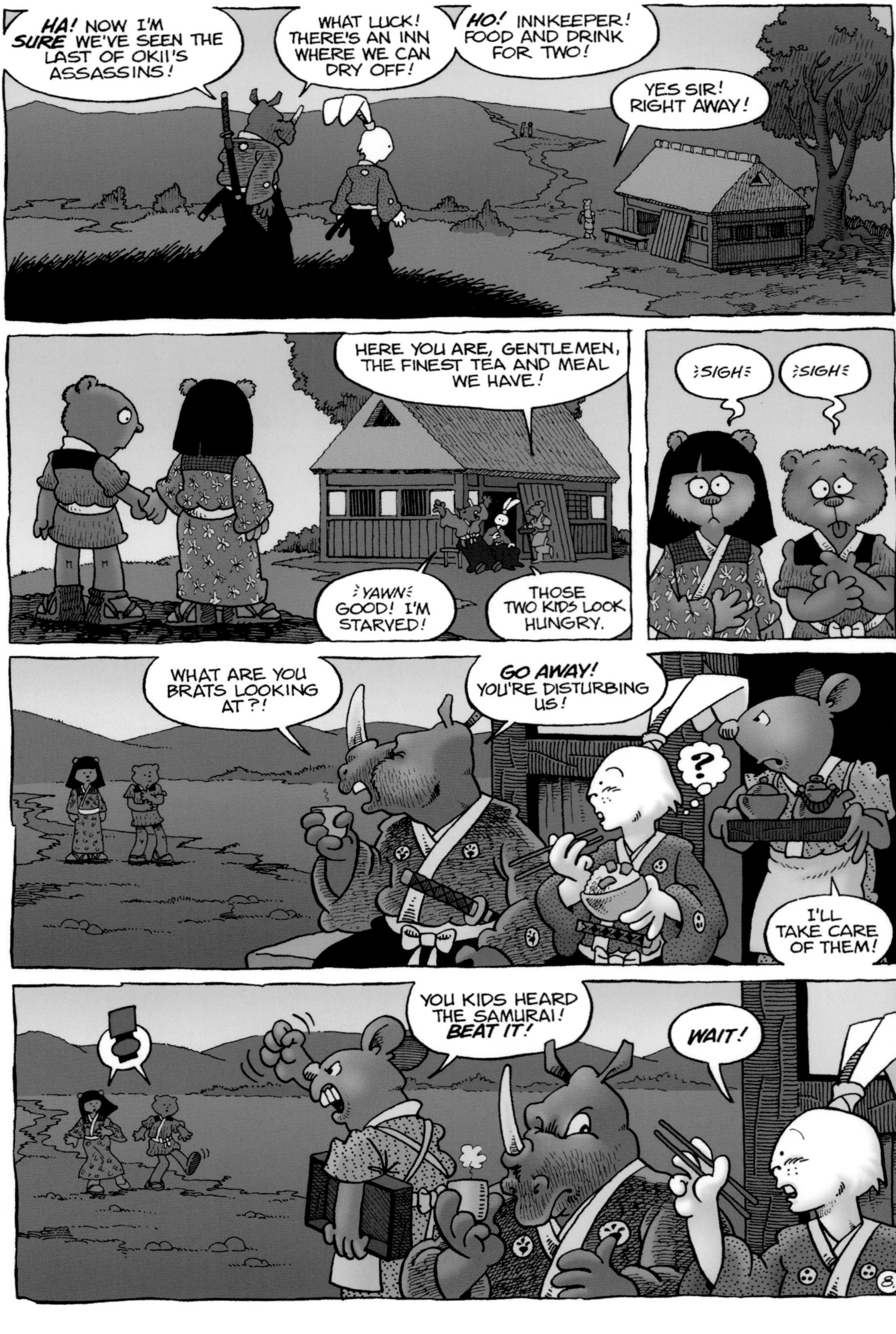
HA! NOW I'M SURE WE'VE SEEN THE LAST OF OKII'S ASSASSINS!
WHAT LUCK! THERE'S AN INN WHERE WE CAN DRY OFF!
HO! INNKEEPER! FOOD AND DRINK FOR TWO!
YES SIR! RIGHT AWAY!
HERE YOU ARE, GENTLEMEN, THE FINEST TEA AND MEAL WE HAVE!
YAWN GOOD! I'M STARVED!
THOSE TWO KIDS LOOK HUNGRY.
SIGH
SIGH
WHAT ARE YOU BRATS LOOKING AT?!
GO AWAY! YOU'RE DISTURBING US!
?
I'LL TAKE CARE OF THEM!
YOU KIDS HEARD THE SAMURAI! BEAT IT!
WAIT!
8.

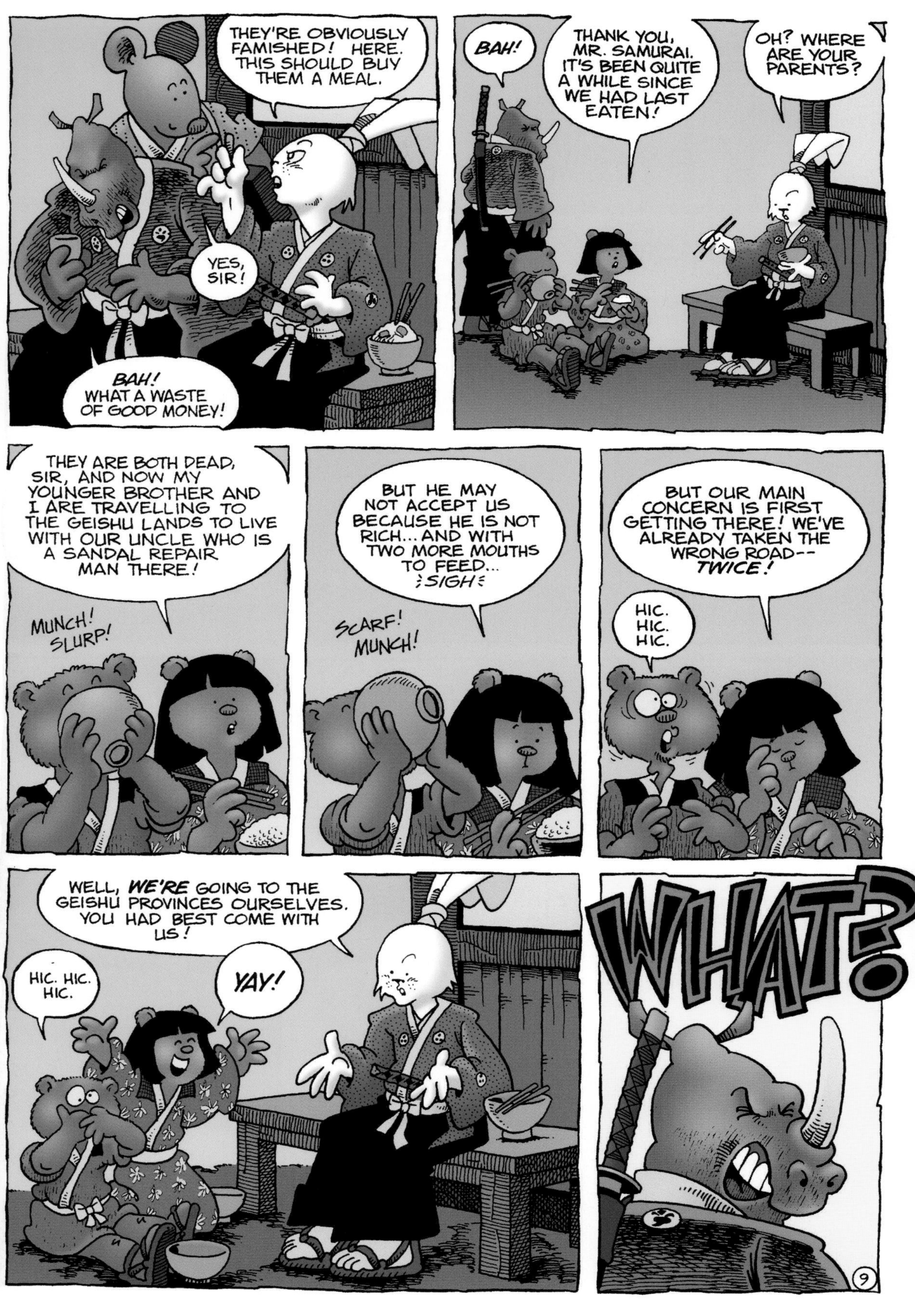
THEY'RE OBVIOUSLY FAMISHED! HERE. THIS SHOULD BUY THEM A MEAL.
YES, SIR!
BAH! WHAT A WASTE OF GOOD MONEY!
BAH!
THANK YOU, MR. SAMURAI. IT'S BEEN QUITE A WHILE SINCE WE HAD LAST EATEN!
OH? WHERE ARE YOUR PARENTS?
THEY ARE BOTH DEAD, SIR, AND NOW MY YOUNGER BROTHER AND I ARE TRAVELLING TO THE GEISHU LANDS TO LIVE WITH OUR UNCLE WHO IS A SANDAL REPAIR MAN THERE!
MUNCH! SLURP!
BUT HE MAY NOT ACCEPT US BECAUSE HE IS NOT RICH... AND WITH TWO MORE MOUTHS TO FEED... SIGH
SCARF! MUNCH!
BUT OUR MAIN CONCERN IS FIRST GETTING THERE! WE'VE ALREADY TAKEN THE WRONG ROAD-- TWICE!
HIC. HIC. HIC.
WELL, WE'RE GOING TO THE GEISHU PROVINCES OURSELVES. YOU HAD BEST COME WITH US!
HIC. HIC. HIC.
YAY!
WHAT?
9

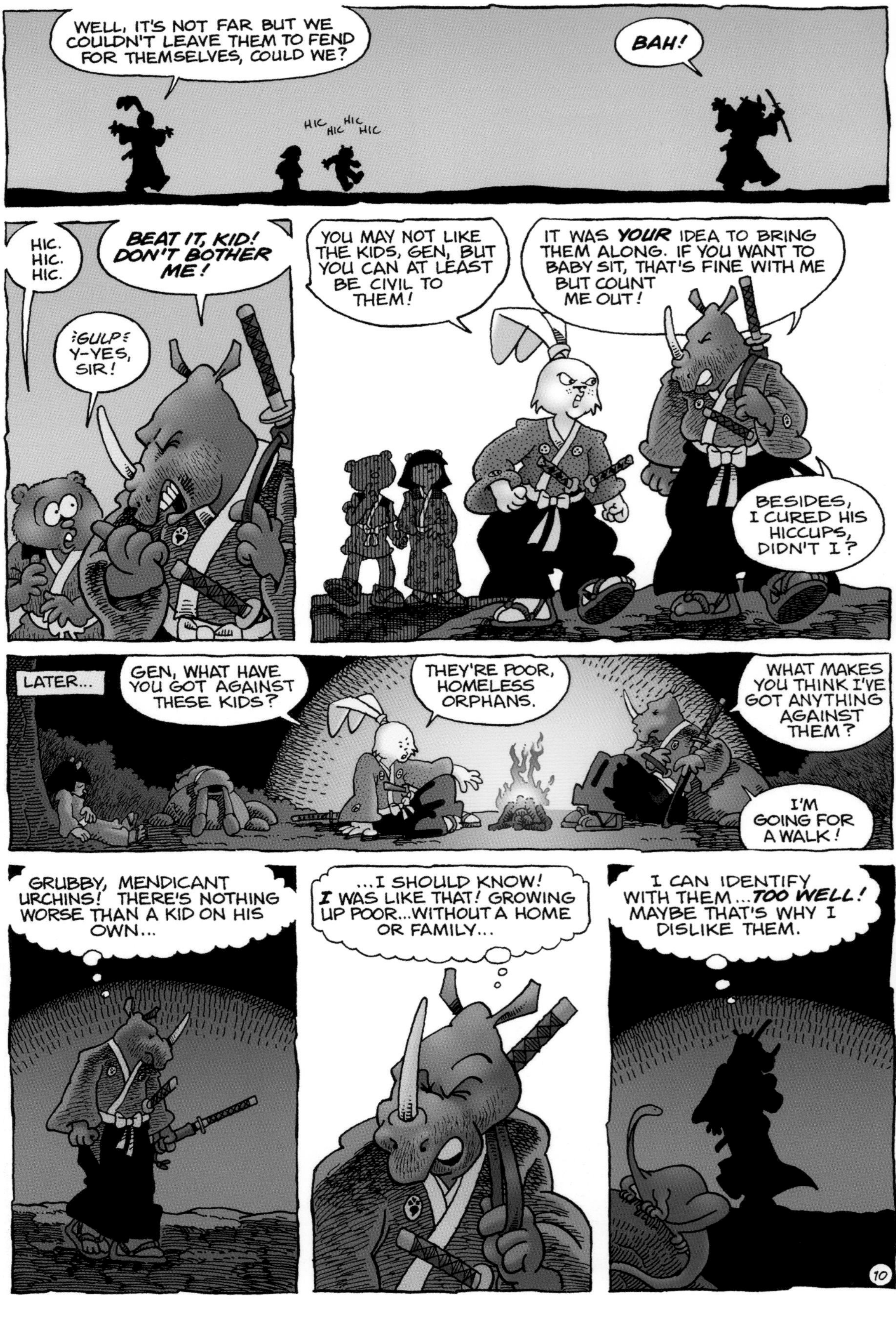
WELL, IT'S NOT FAR BUT WE COULDN'T LEAVE THEM TO FEND FOR THEMSELVES, COULD WE?
HIC HIC HIC HIC
BAH!
HIC. HIC. HIC.
BEAT IT, KID! DON'T BOTHER ME!
GULP Y-YES, SIR!
YOU MAY NOT LIKE THE KIDS, GEN, BUT YOU CAN AT LEAST BE CIVIL TO THEM!
IT WAS YOUR IDEA TO BRING THEM ALONG. IF YOU WANT TO BABY SIT, THAT'S FINE WITH ME BUT COUNT ME OUT!
BESIDES, I CURED HIS HICCUPS, DIDN'T I?
LATER...
GEN, WHAT HAVE YOU GOT AGAINST THESE KIDS?
THEY'RE POOR, HOMELESS ORPHANS.
WHAT MAKES YOU THINK I'VE GOT ANYTHING AGAINST THEM?
I'M GOING FOR A WALK!
GRUBBY, MENDICANT URCHINS! THERE'S NOTHING WORSE THAN A KID ON HIS OWN...
...I SHOULD KNOW! I WAS LIKE THAT! GROWING UP POOR...WITHOUT A HOME OR FAMILY...
I CAN IDENTIFY WITH THEM...TOO WELL! MAYBE THAT'S WHY I DISLIKE THEM.
10

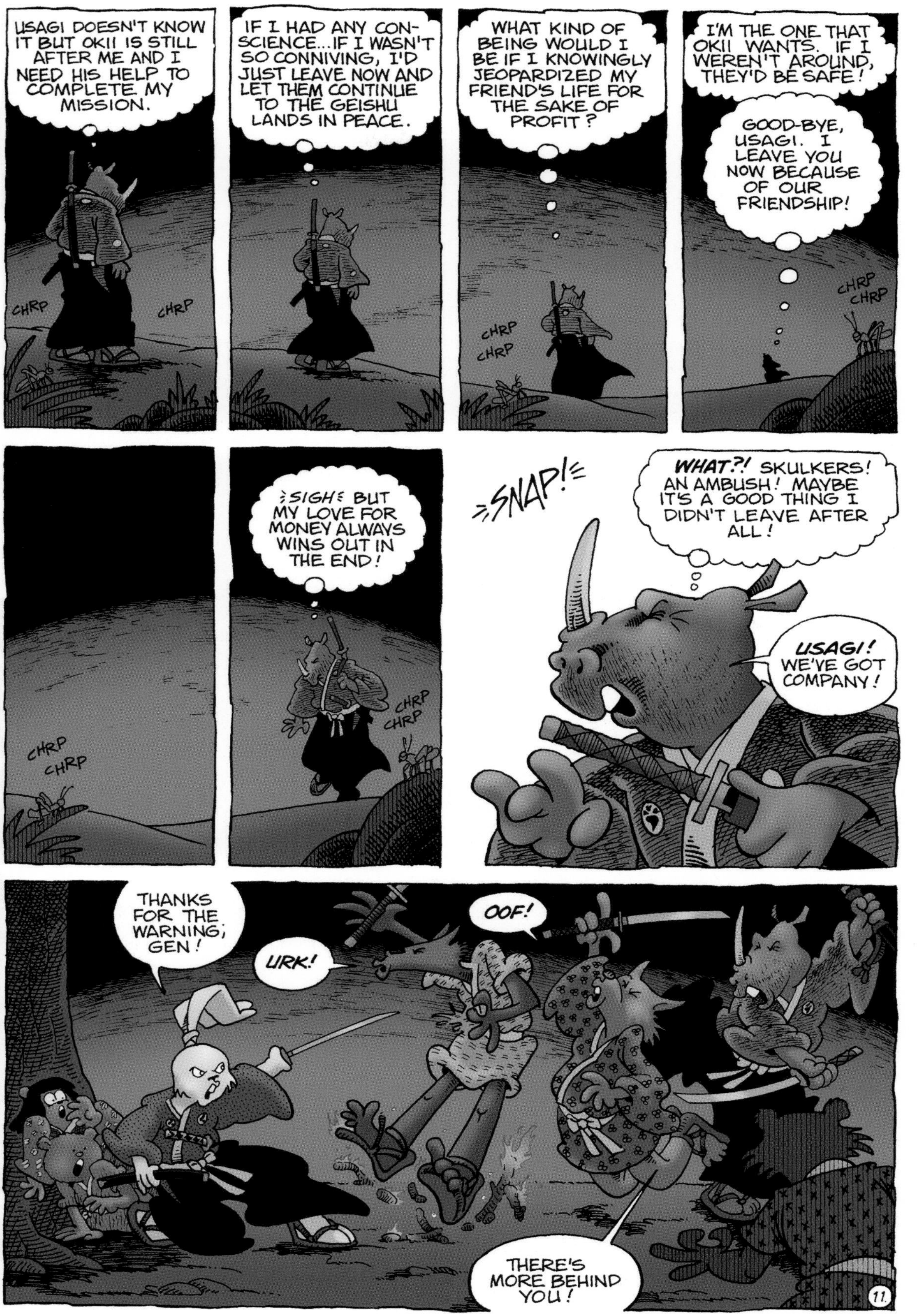
USAGI DOESN'T KNOW IT BUT OKII IS STILL AFTER ME AND I NEED HIS HELP TO COMPLETE MY MISSION.
CHRP
CHRP
IF I HAD ANY CONSCIENCE...IF I WASN'T SO CONNIVING, I'D JUST LEAVE NOW AND LET THEM CONTINUE TO THE GEISHU LANDS IN PEACE.
WHAT KIND OF BEING WOULD I BE IF I KNOWINGLY JEOPARDIZED MY FRIEND'S LIFE FOR THE SAKE OF PROFIT?
CHRP
CHRP
I'M THE ONE THAT OKII WANTS. IF I WEREN'T AROUND, THEY'D BE SAFE!
GOOD-BYE, USAGI. I LEAVE YOU NOW BECAUSE OF OUR FRIENDSHIP!
CHRP
CHRP
CHRP
CHRP
SIGH BUT MY LOVE FOR MONEY ALWAYS WINS OUT IN THE END!
CHRP
CHRP
SNAP!
WHAT?! SKULKERS! AN AMBUSH! MAYBE IT'S A GOOD THING I DIDN'T LEAVE AFTER ALL!
USAGI! WE'VE GOT COMPANY!
THANKS FOR THE WARNING, GEN!
URK!
OOF!
THERE'S MORE BEHIND YOU!
11

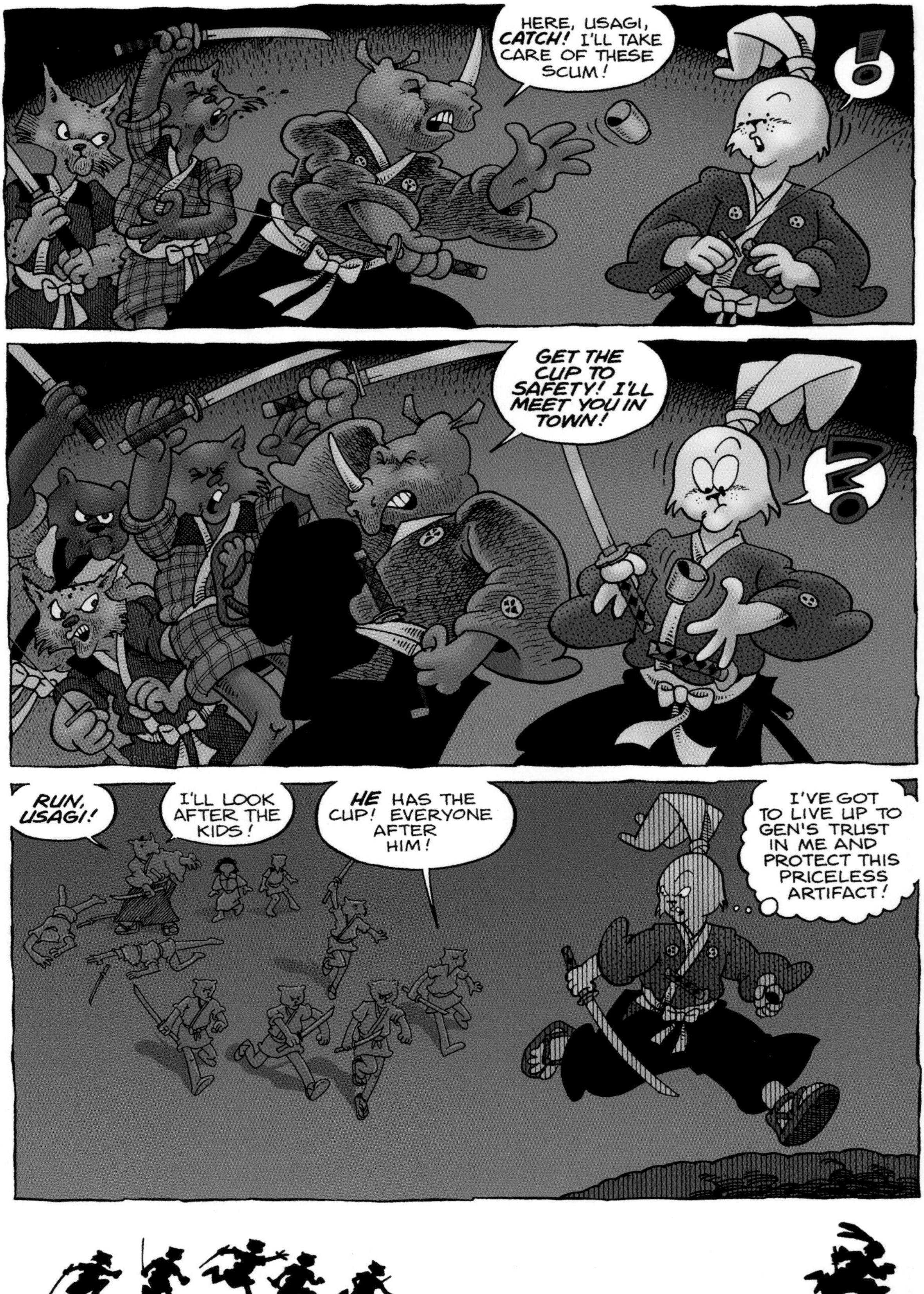
HERE, USAGI, CATCH! I'LL TAKE CARE OF THESE SCUM!
!
GET THE CUP TO SAFETY! I'LL MEET YOU IN TOWN!
?
RUN, USAGI!
I'LL LOOK AFTER THE KIDS!
HE HAS THE CUP! EVERYONE AFTER HIM!
I'VE GOT TO LIVE UP TO GEN'S TRUST IN ME AND PROTECT THIS PRICELESS ARTIFACT!

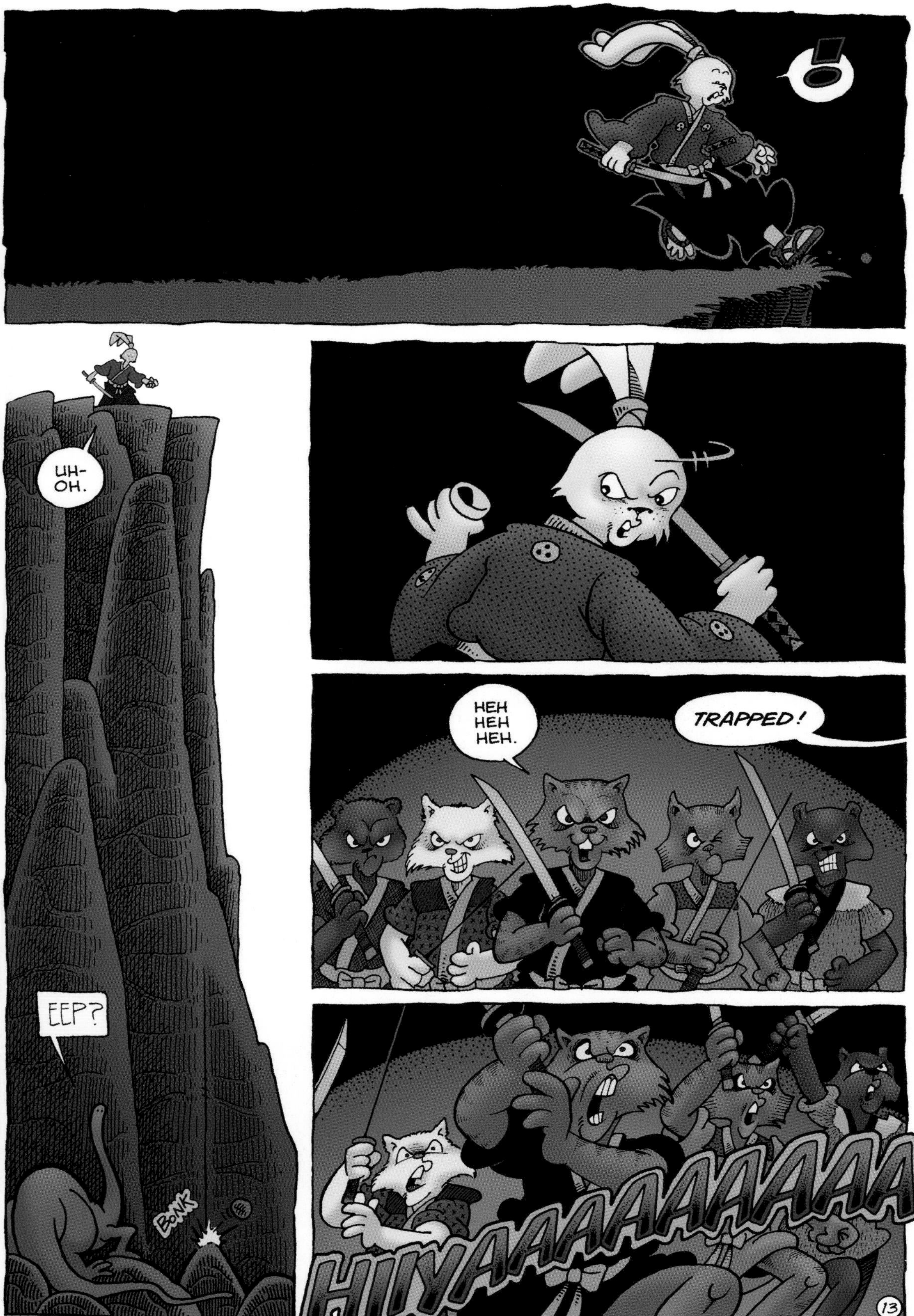
!
UH-OH.
EEP?
BONK
HEH HEH HEH.
TRAPPED!
HIYAAAAAAAAAAAA
13

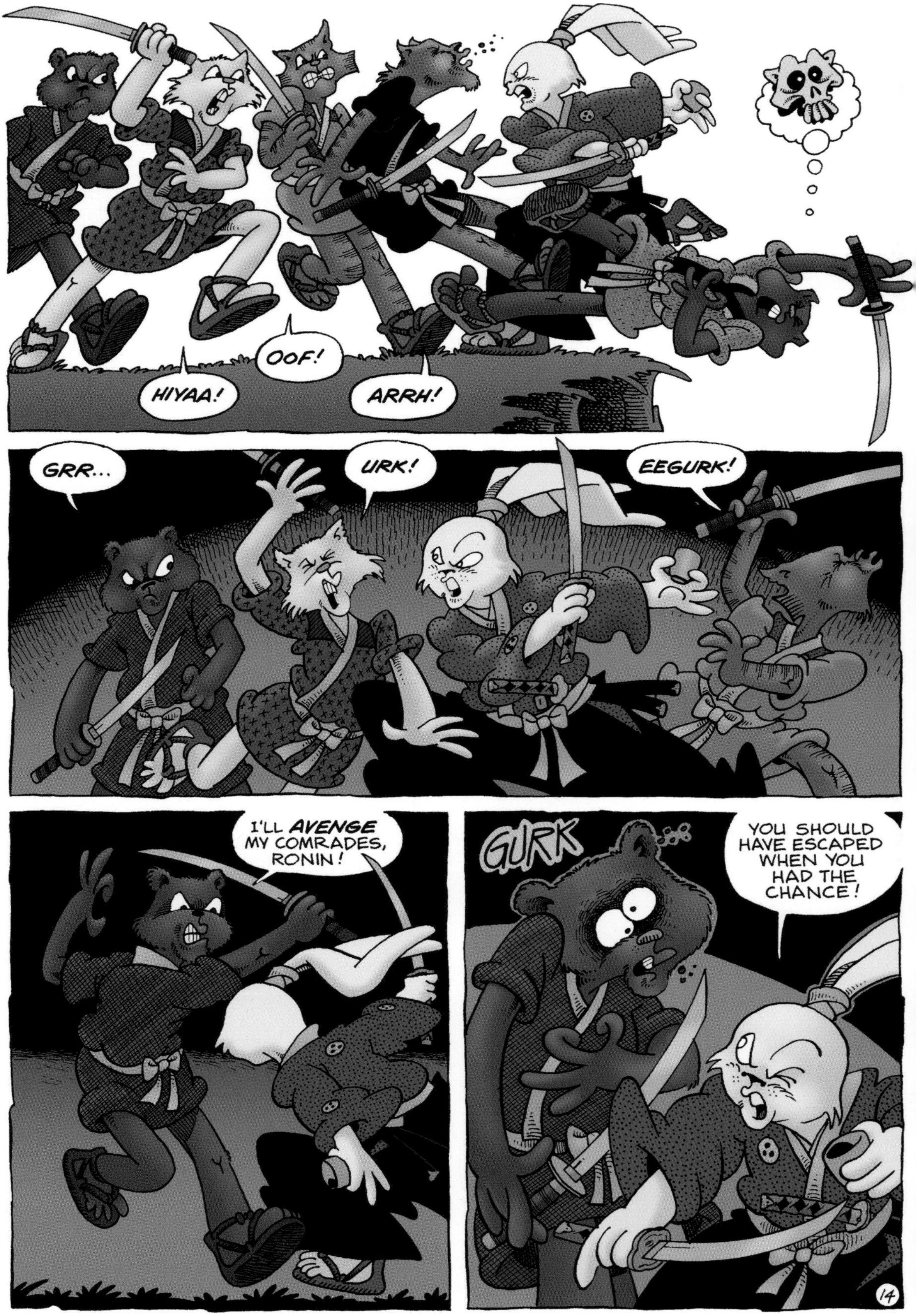
HIYAA!
OOF!
ARRH!
GRR...
URK!
EEGURK!
I'LL AVENGE MY COMRADES, RONIN!
GURK
YOU SHOULD HAVE ESCAPED WHEN YOU HAD THE CHANCE!
14

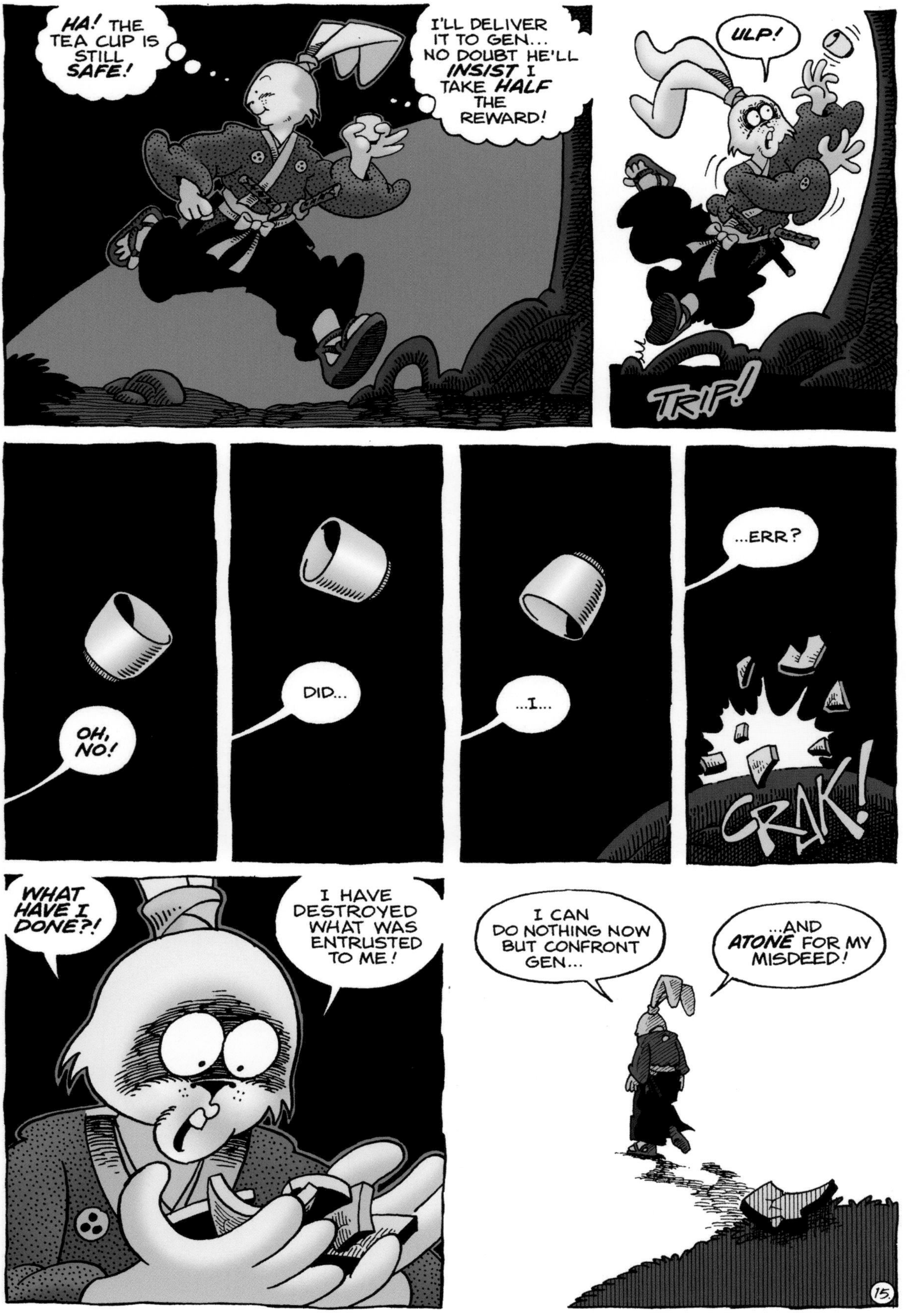
HA! THE TEA CUP IS STILL SAFE!
I'LL DELIVER IT TO GEN... NO DOUBT HE'LL INSIST I TAKE HALF THE REWARD!
ULP!
TRIP!
OH, NO!
DID...
...I...
...ERR?
CRAK!
WHAT HAVE I DONE?!
I HAVE DESTROYED WHAT WAS ENTRUSTED TO ME!
I CAN DO NOTHING NOW BUT CONFRONT GEN...
...AND ATONE FOR MY MISDEED!
15.

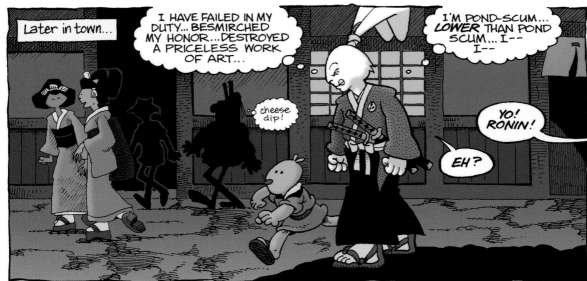

Later in town...

I HAVE FAILED IN MY DUTY... BESMIRCHED MY HONOR...DESTROYED A PRICELESS WORK OF ART...

cheese dip!

I'M POND-SCUM... *LOWER* THAN POND SCUM... I-- I--

YO! RONIN!

EH?

HA! THERE YOU ARE, USAGI! I'VE BEEN LOOKING ALL OVER TOWN FOR YOU!

GEN!

FORGIVE ME! I-I *FAILED* YOU! THE TEA CUP IS... IS *SHATTERED!*

"TEA CUP?" ⌐HEE HEE CHORTLE⌐ HA HA HA!

WHY DO YOU LAUGH?

THAT WAS JUST A CUP I TOOK FROM THAT ROADSIDE INN!

WORTHLESS... AS ANY FOOL COULD PLAINLY SEE!

WHAT?! YOU MEAN I WAS AGONIZING OVER A PIECE OF *JUNK?*

WHY, I OUGHT TO *MINCE* YOU INTO *MULCH!*

WHAT'S "MULCH?"

16

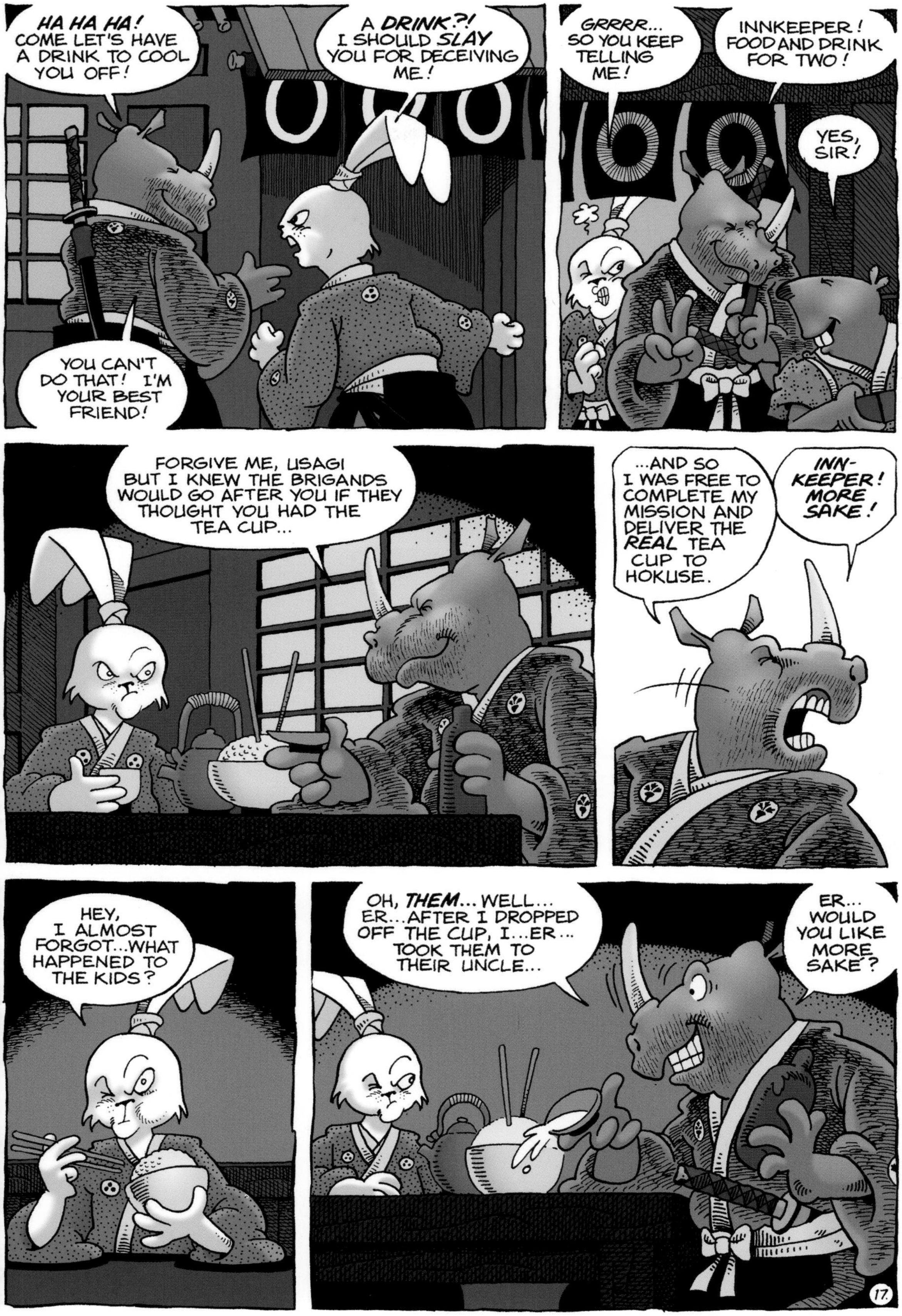
HA HA HA! COME LET'S HAVE A DRINK TO COOL YOU OFF!
A DRINK?! I SHOULD SLAY YOU FOR DECEIVING ME!
YOU CAN'T DO THAT! I'M YOUR BEST FRIEND!
GRRRR... SO YOU KEEP TELLING ME!
INNKEEPER! FOOD AND DRINK FOR TWO!
YES, SIR!
FORGIVE ME, USAGI BUT I KNEW THE BRIGANDS WOULD GO AFTER YOU IF THEY THOUGHT YOU HAD THE TEA CUP...
...AND SO I WAS FREE TO COMPLETE MY MISSION AND DELIVER THE REAL TEA CUP TO HOKUSE.
INN-KEEPER! MORE SAKE!
HEY, I ALMOST FORGOT...WHAT HAPPENED TO THE KIDS?
OH, THEM...WELL... ER...AFTER I DROPPED OFF THE CUP, I...ER... TOOK THEM TO THEIR UNCLE...
ER... WOULD YOU LIKE MORE SAKE?
17.

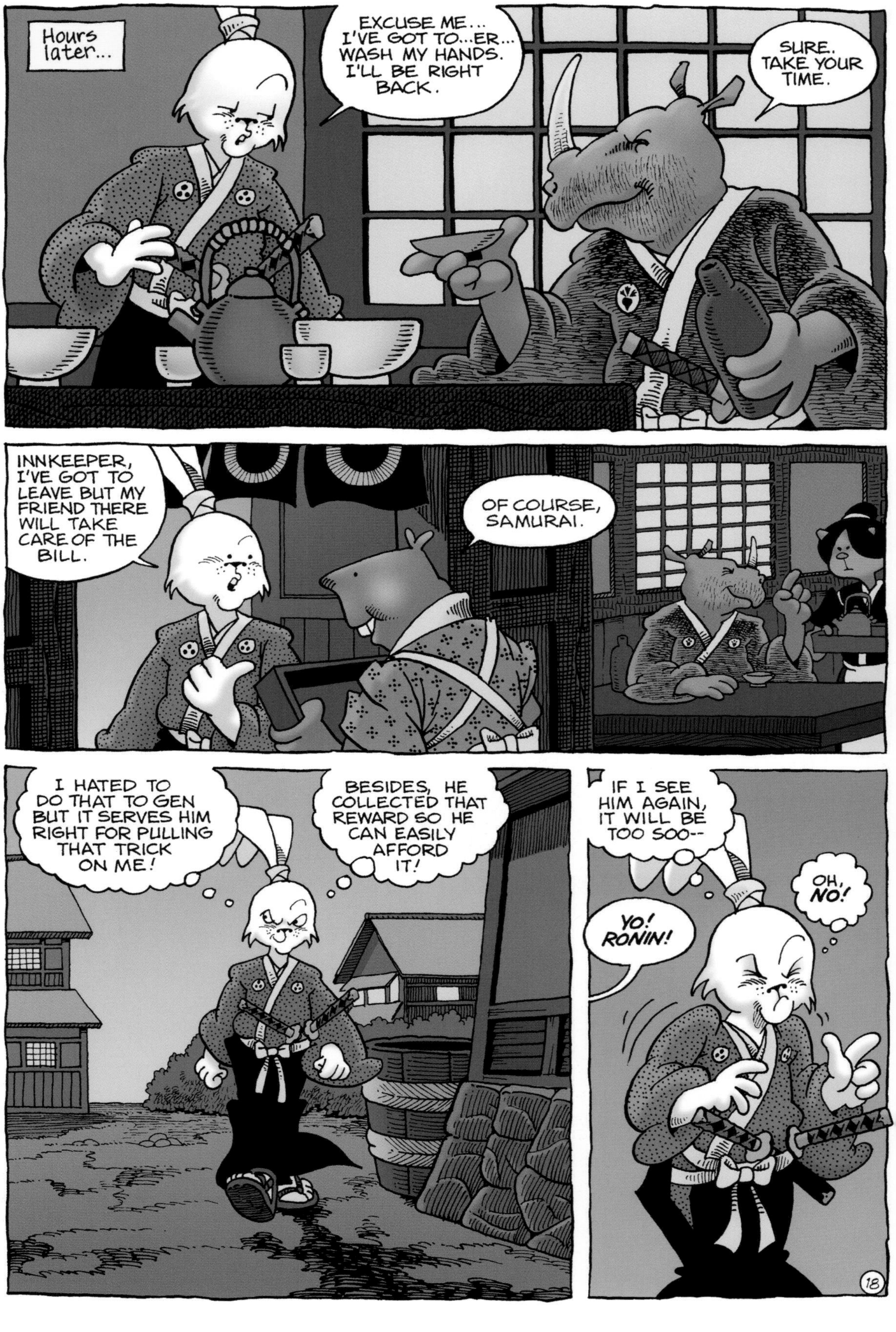
Hours later...
EXCUSE ME... I'VE GOT TO...ER... WASH MY HANDS. I'LL BE RIGHT BACK.
SURE. TAKE YOUR TIME.
INNKEEPER, I'VE GOT TO LEAVE BUT MY FRIEND THERE WILL TAKE CARE OF THE BILL.
OF COURSE, SAMURAI.
I HATED TO DO THAT TO GEN BUT IT SERVES HIM RIGHT FOR PULLING THAT TRICK ON ME!
BESIDES, HE COLLECTED THAT REWARD SO HE CAN EASILY AFFORD IT!
IF I SEE HIM AGAIN, IT WILL BE TOO SOO--
YO! RONIN!
OH, NO!
18

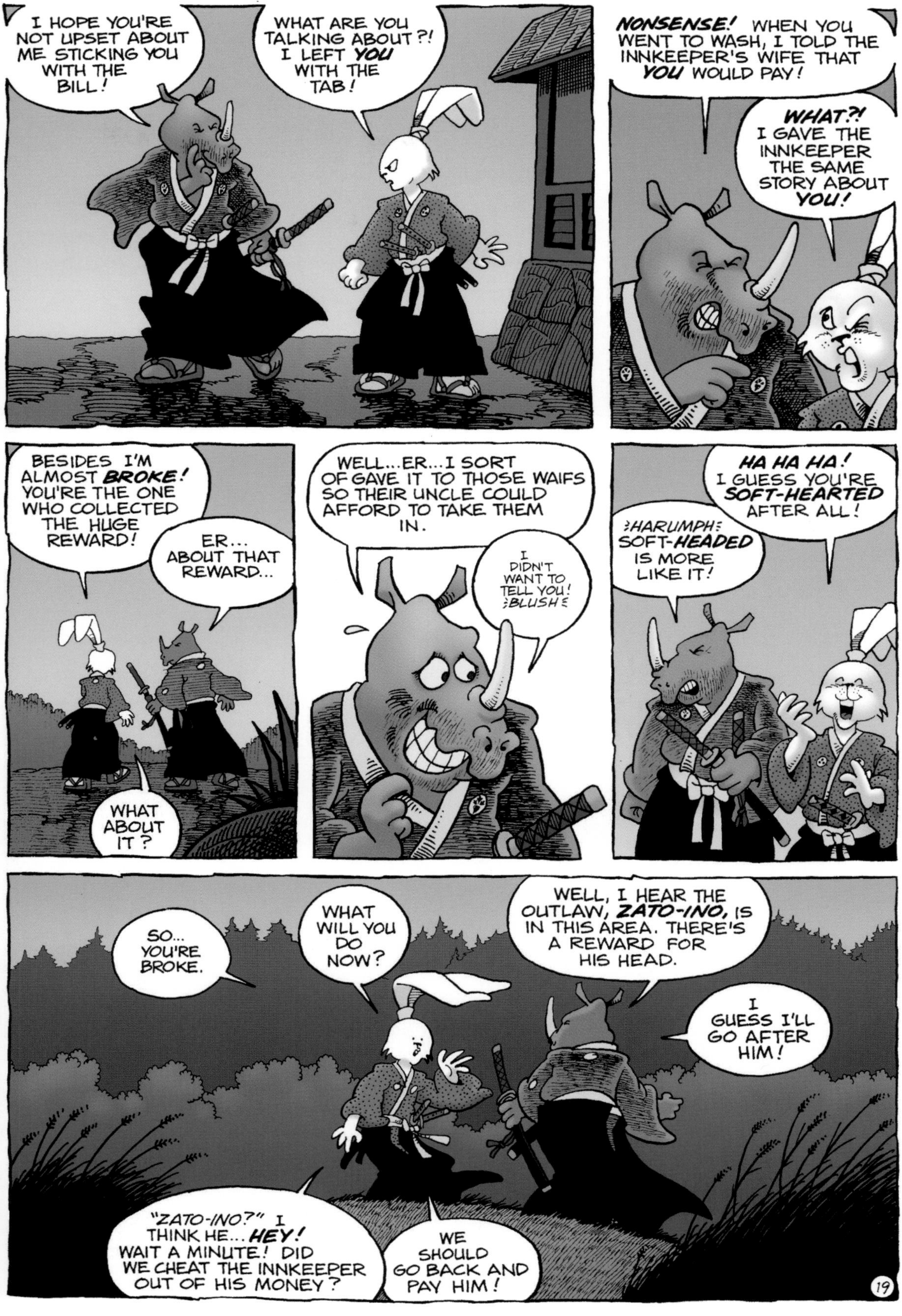
I HOPE YOU'RE NOT UPSET ABOUT ME STICKING YOU WITH THE BILL!
WHAT ARE YOU TALKING ABOUT?! I LEFT YOU WITH THE TAB!
NONSENSE! WHEN YOU WENT TO WASH, I TOLD THE INNKEEPER'S WIFE THAT YOU WOULD PAY!
WHAT?! I GAVE THE INNKEEPER THE SAME STORY ABOUT YOU!
BESIDES I'M ALMOST BROKE! YOU'RE THE ONE WHO COLLECTED THE HUGE REWARD!
ER... ABOUT THAT REWARD...
WHAT ABOUT IT?
WELL... ER... I SORT OF GAVE IT TO THOSE WAIFS SO THEIR UNCLE COULD AFFORD TO TAKE THEM IN.
I DIDN'T WANT TO TELL YOU! ⸗BLUSH⸗
HA HA HA! I GUESS YOU'RE SOFT-HEARTED AFTER ALL!
⸗HARUMPH⸗ SOFT-HEADED IS MORE LIKE IT!
SO... YOU'RE BROKE.
WHAT WILL YOU DO NOW?
WELL, I HEAR THE OUTLAW, ZATO-INO, IS IN THIS AREA. THERE'S A REWARD FOR HIS HEAD.
I GUESS I'LL GO AFTER HIM!
"ZATO-INO?" I THINK HE... HEY! WAIT A MINUTE! DID WE CHEAT THE INNKEEPER OUT OF HIS MONEY?
WE SHOULD GO BACK AND PAY HIM!
19

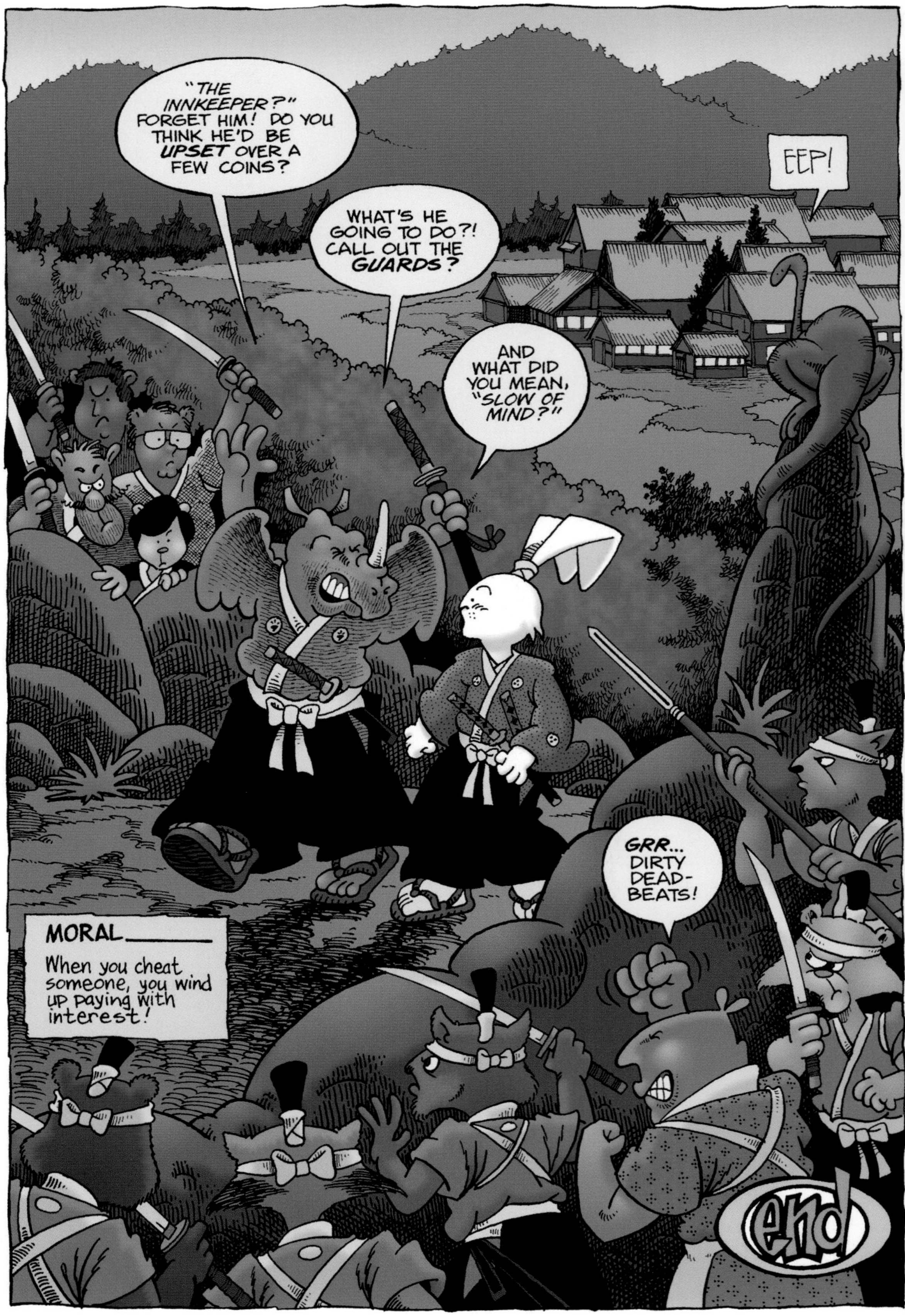
"THE INNKEEPER?" FORGET HIM! DO YOU THINK HE'D BE UPSET OVER A FEW COINS?
WHAT'S HE GOING TO DO?! CALL OUT THE GUARDS?
AND WHAT DID YOU MEAN, "SLOW OF MIND?"
EEP!
GRR... DIRTY DEAD-BEATS!
MORAL
When you cheat someone, you wind up paying with interest!
end

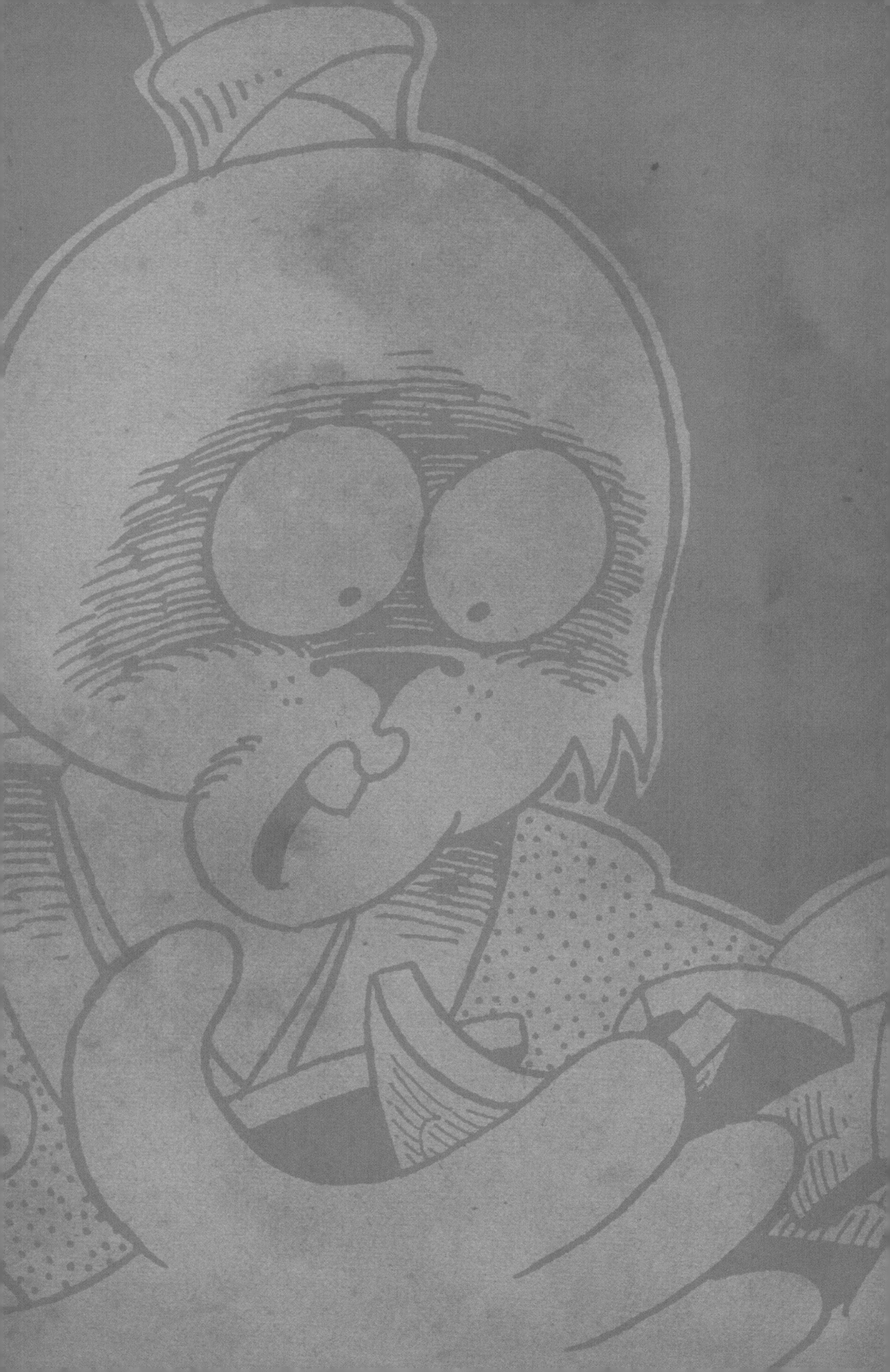

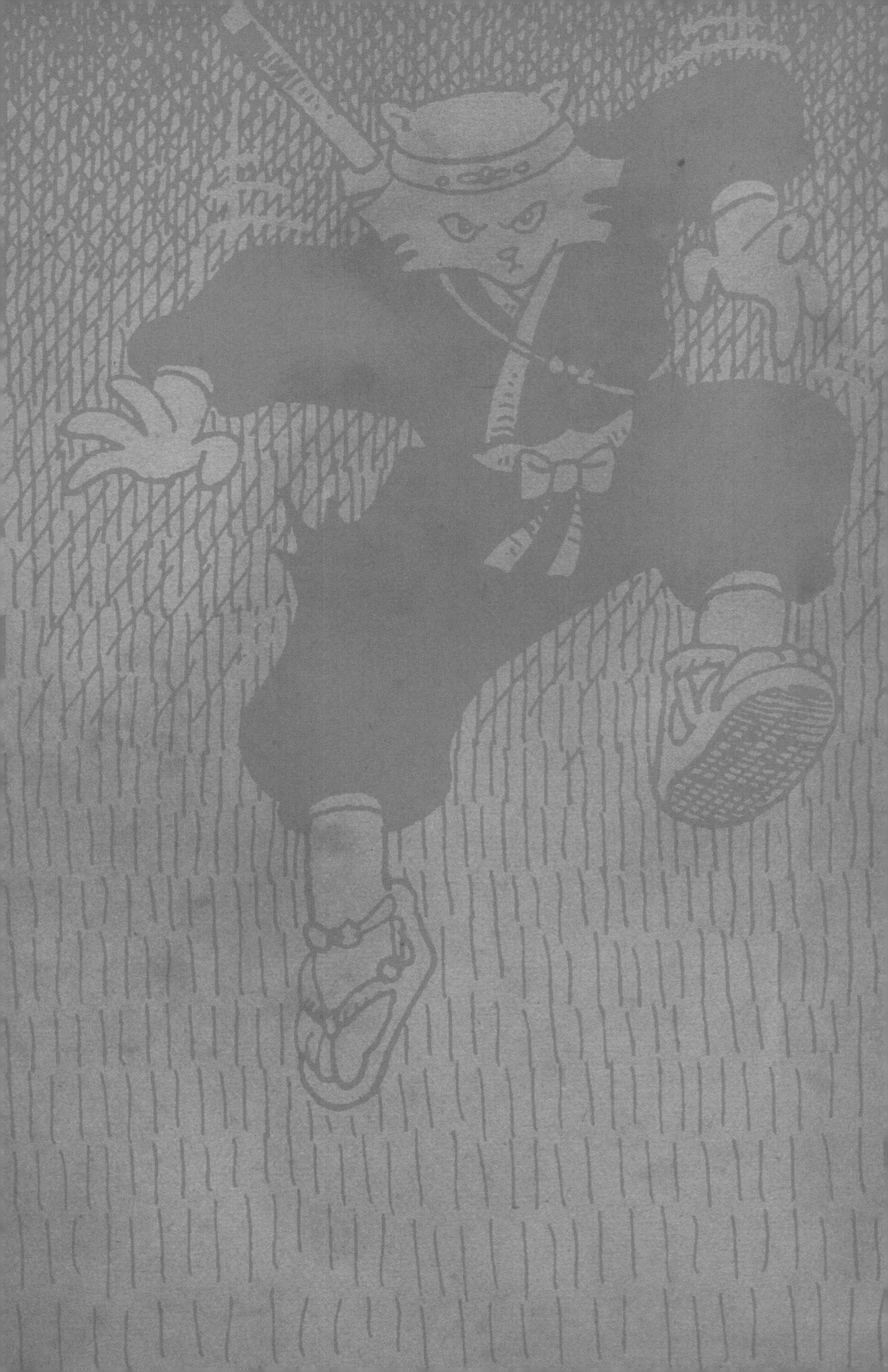

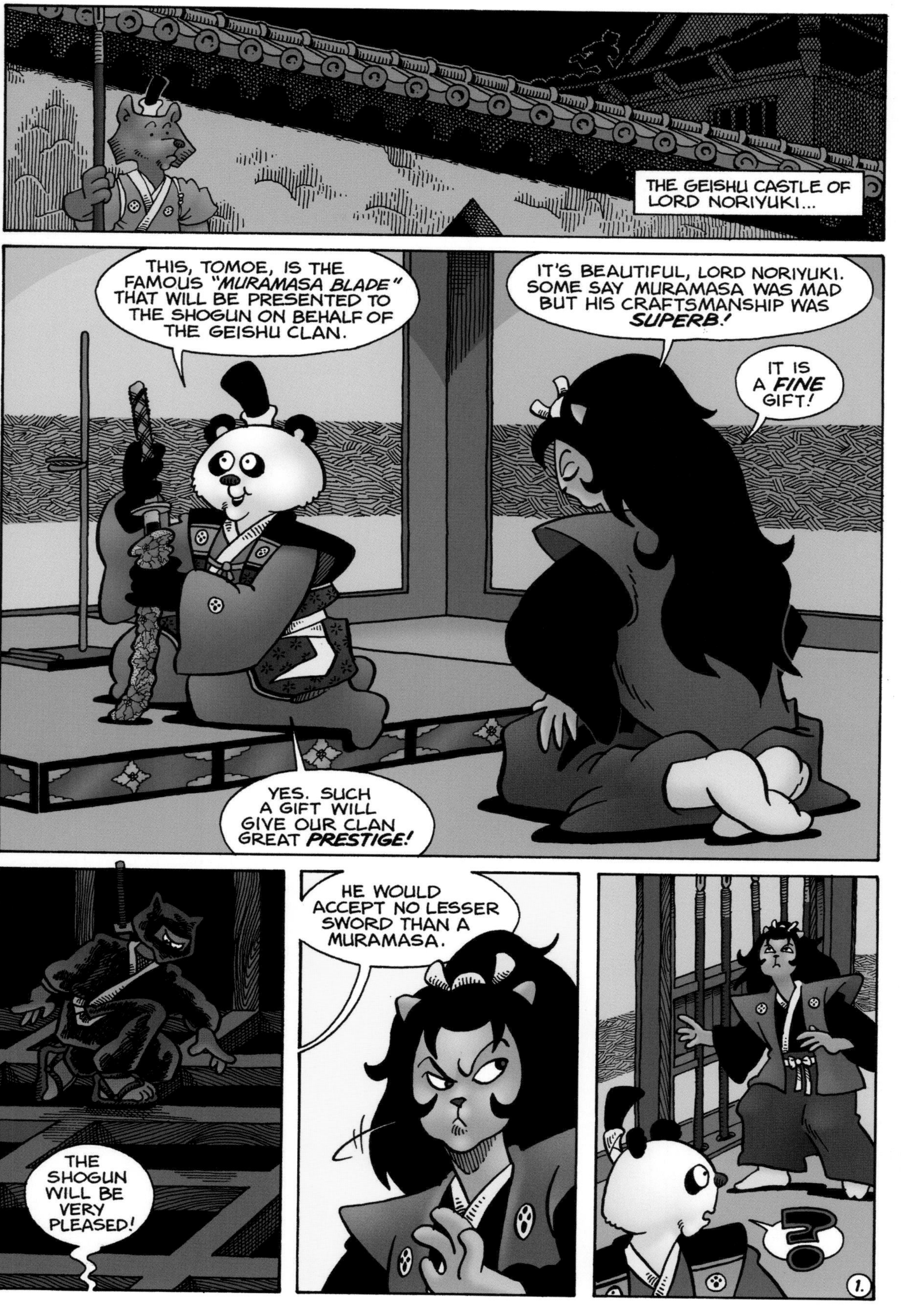
THE GEISHU CASTLE OF LORD NORIYUKI...
THIS, TOMOE, IS THE FAMOUS "MURAMASA BLADE" THAT WILL BE PRESENTED TO THE SHOGUN ON BEHALF OF THE GEISHU CLAN.
IT'S BEAUTIFUL, LORD NORIYUKI. SOME SAY MURAMASA WAS MAD BUT HIS CRAFTSMANSHIP WAS SUPERB!
IT IS A FINE GIFT!
YES. SUCH A GIFT WILL GIVE OUR CLAN GREAT PRESTIGE!
THE SHOGUN WILL BE VERY PLEASED!
HE WOULD ACCEPT NO LESSER SWORD THAN A MURAMASA.
?
1.

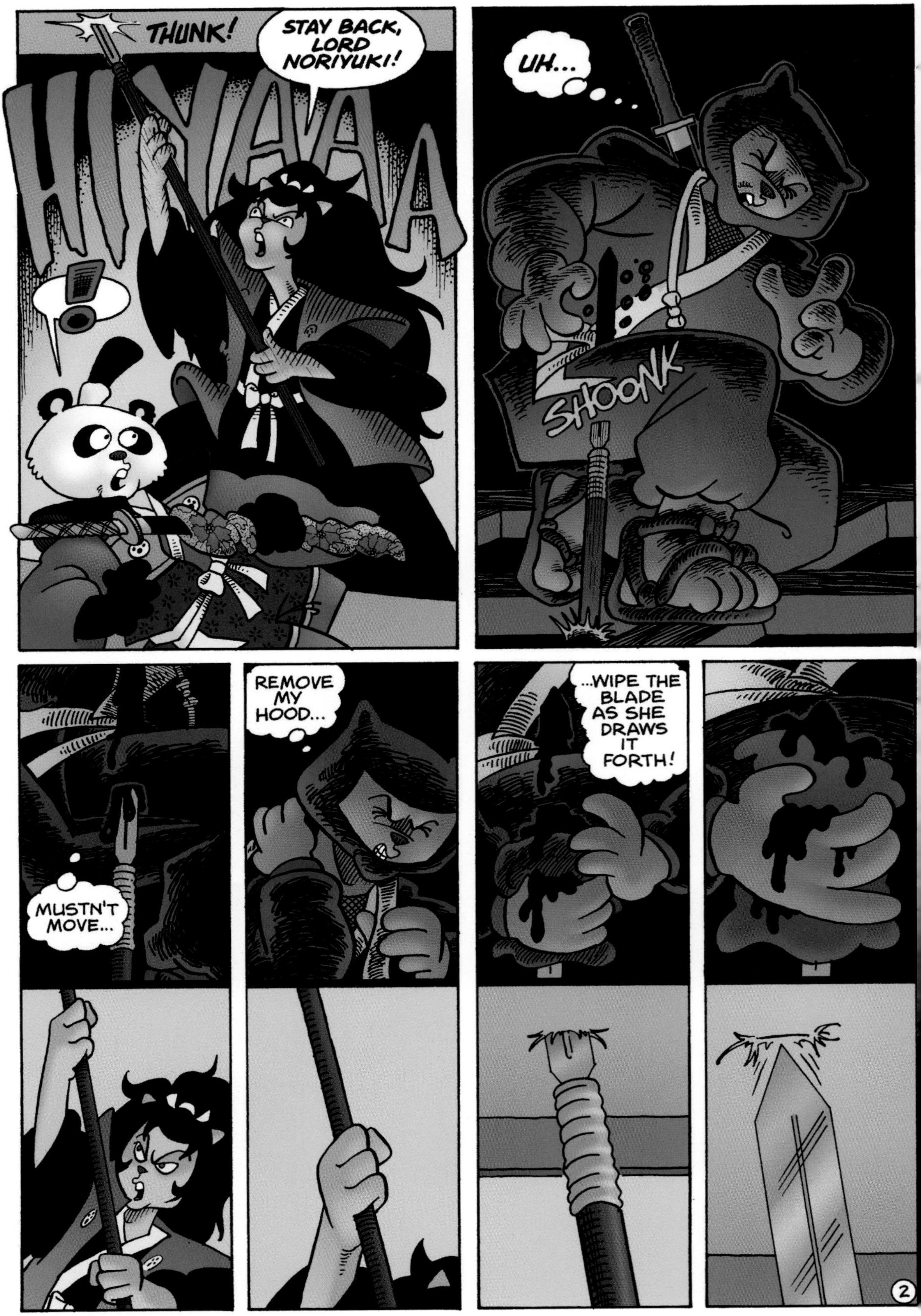
THUNK!
STAY BACK, LORD NORIYUKI!
HIYAAAA
!
UH...
SHOONK
MUSTN'T MOVE...
REMOVE MY HOOD...
...WIPE THE BLADE AS SHE DRAWS IT FORTH!
2

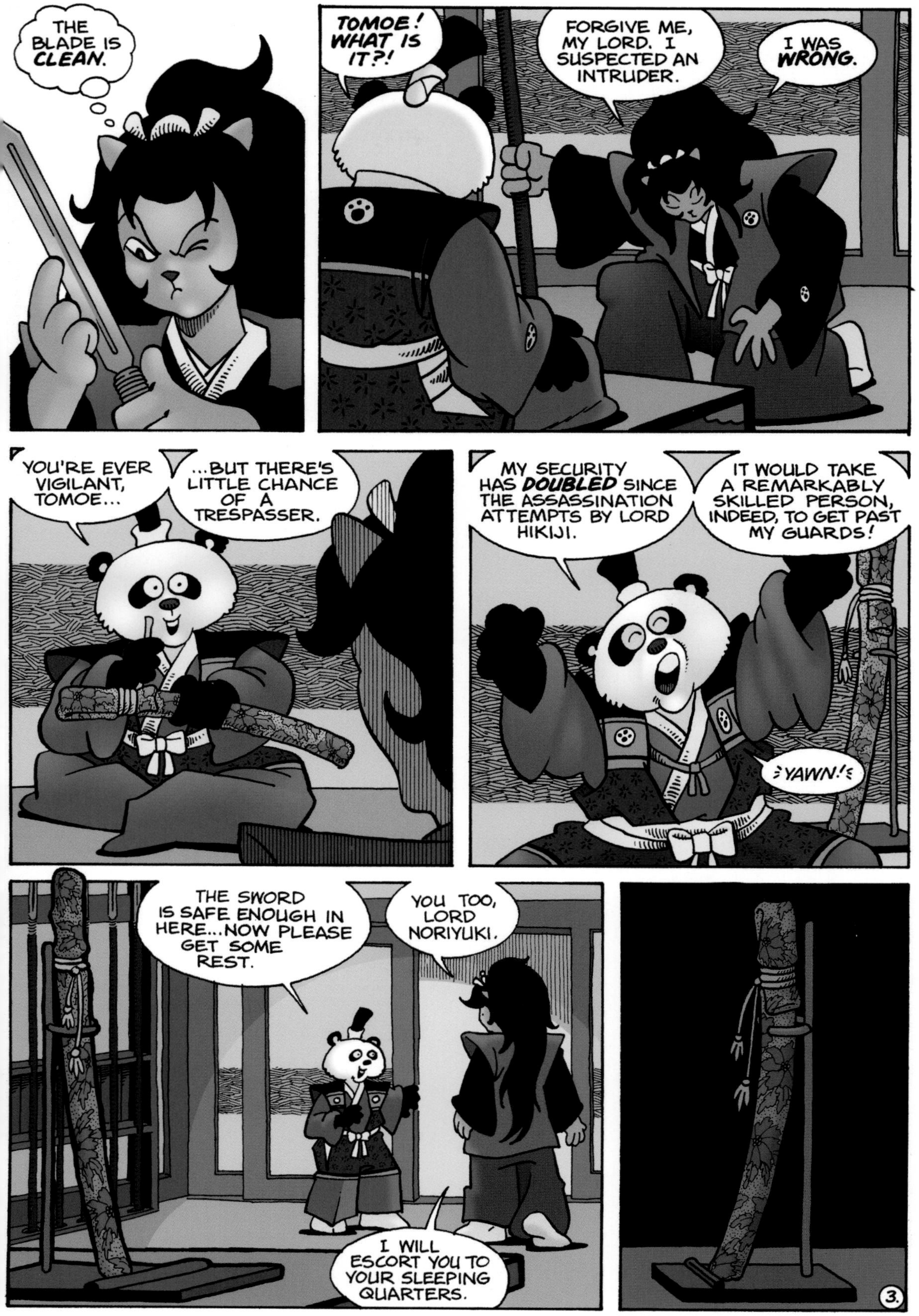
THE BLADE IS CLEAN.
TOMOE! WHAT IS IT?!
FORGIVE ME, MY LORD. I SUSPECTED AN INTRUDER.
I WAS WRONG.
YOU'RE EVER VIGILANT, TOMOE...
...BUT THERE'S LITTLE CHANCE OF A TRESPASSER.
MY SECURITY HAS DOUBLED SINCE THE ASSASSINATION ATTEMPTS BY LORD HIKIJI.
IT WOULD TAKE A REMARKABLY SKILLED PERSON, INDEED, TO GET PAST MY GUARDS!
YAWN!
THE SWORD IS SAFE ENOUGH IN HERE...NOW PLEASE GET SOME REST.
YOU TOO, LORD NORIYUKI.
I WILL ESCORT YOU TO YOUR SLEEPING QUARTERS.
3.

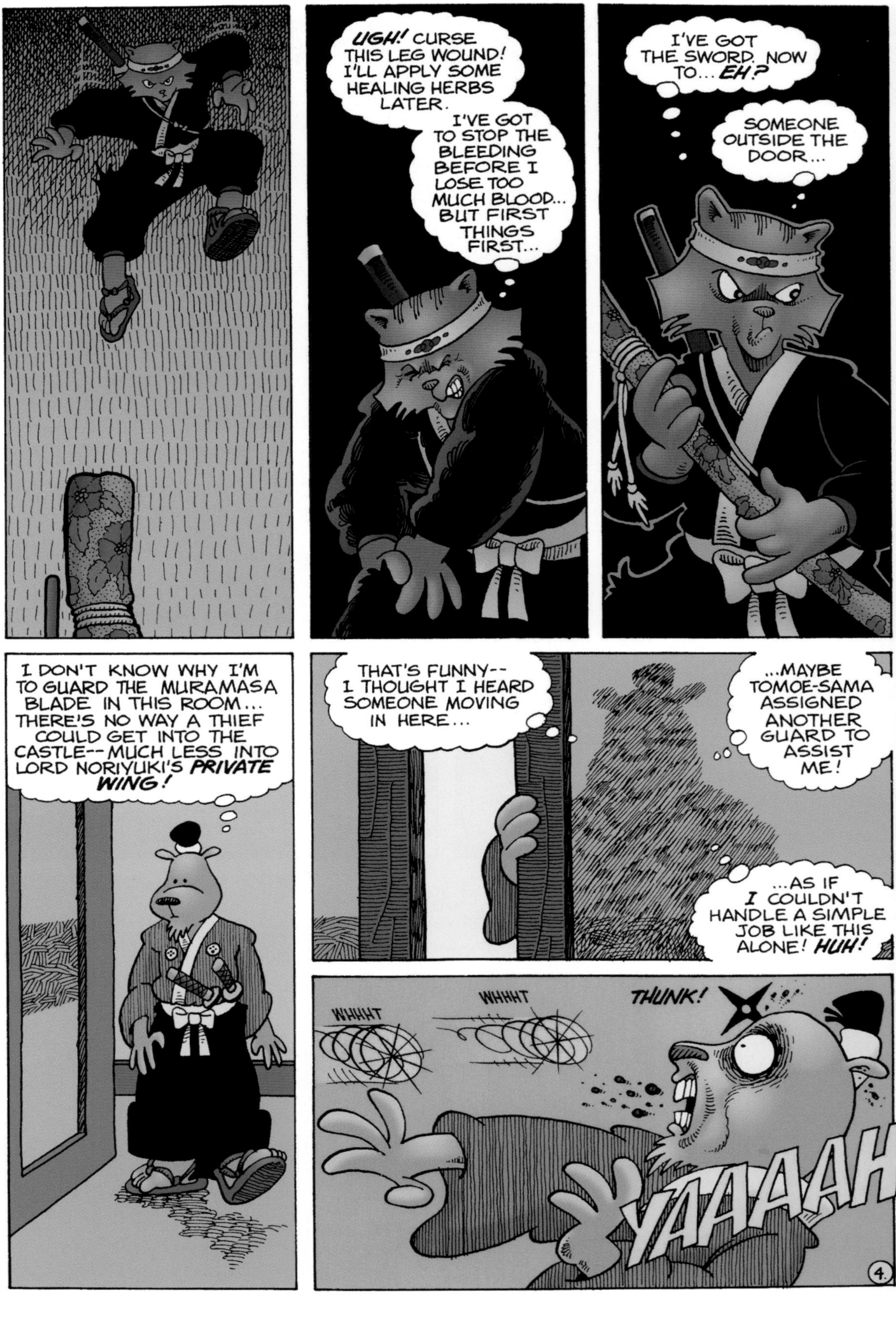
UGH! CURSE THIS LEG WOUND! I'LL APPLY SOME HEALING HERBS LATER.
I'VE GOT TO STOP THE BLEEDING BEFORE I LOSE TOO MUCH BLOOD... BUT FIRST THINGS FIRST...
I'VE GOT THE SWORD. NOW TO... EH?
SOMEONE OUTSIDE THE DOOR...
I DON'T KNOW WHY I'M TO GUARD THE MURAMASA BLADE IN THIS ROOM... THERE'S NO WAY A THIEF COULD GET INTO THE CASTLE--MUCH LESS INTO LORD NORIYUKI'S PRIVATE WING!
THAT'S FUNNY-- I THOUGHT I HEARD SOMEONE MOVING IN HERE...
...MAYBE TOMOE-SAMA ASSIGNED ANOTHER GUARD TO ASSIST ME!
...AS IF I COULDN'T HANDLE A SIMPLE JOB LIKE THIS ALONE! HUH!
WHHHT
WHHHT
THUNK!
YAAAAAH
4.

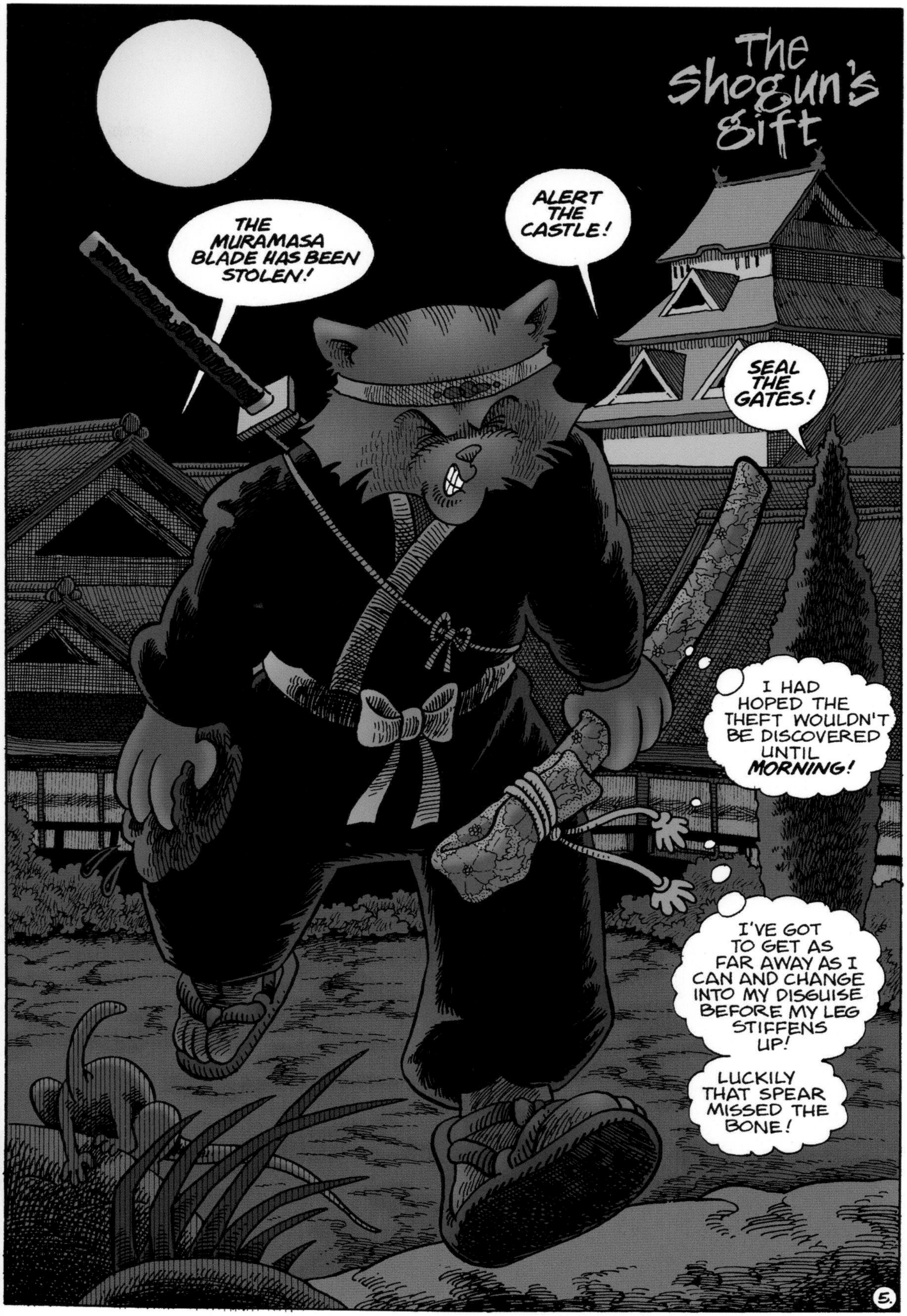
The Shogun's gift
THE MURAMASA BLADE HAS BEEN STOLEN!
ALERT THE CASTLE!
SEAL THE GATES!
I HAD HOPED THE THEFT WOULDN'T BE DISCOVERED UNTIL MORNING!
I'VE GOT TO GET AS FAR AWAY AS I CAN AND CHANGE INTO MY DISGUISE BEFORE MY LEG STIFFENS UP!
LUCKILY THAT SPEAR MISSED THE BONE!
5.

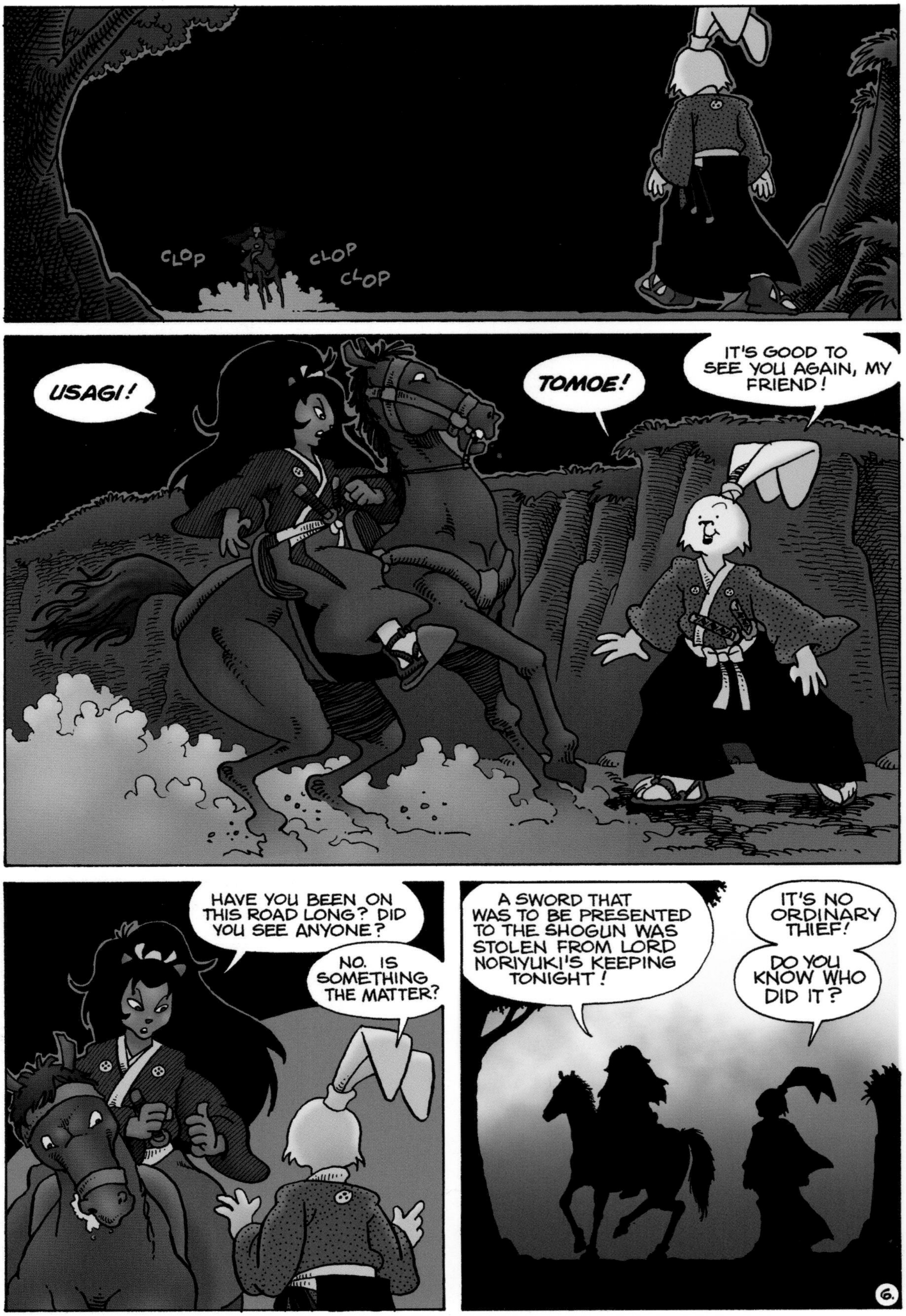
CLOP
CLOP
CLOP
USAGI!
TOMOE!
IT'S GOOD TO SEE YOU AGAIN, MY FRIEND!
HAVE YOU BEEN ON THIS ROAD LONG? DID YOU SEE ANYONE?
NO. IS SOMETHING THE MATTER?
A SWORD THAT WAS TO BE PRESENTED TO THE SHOGUN WAS STOLEN FROM LORD NORIYUKI'S KEEPING TONIGHT!
IT'S NO ORDINARY THIEF!
DO YOU KNOW WHO DID IT?
6.

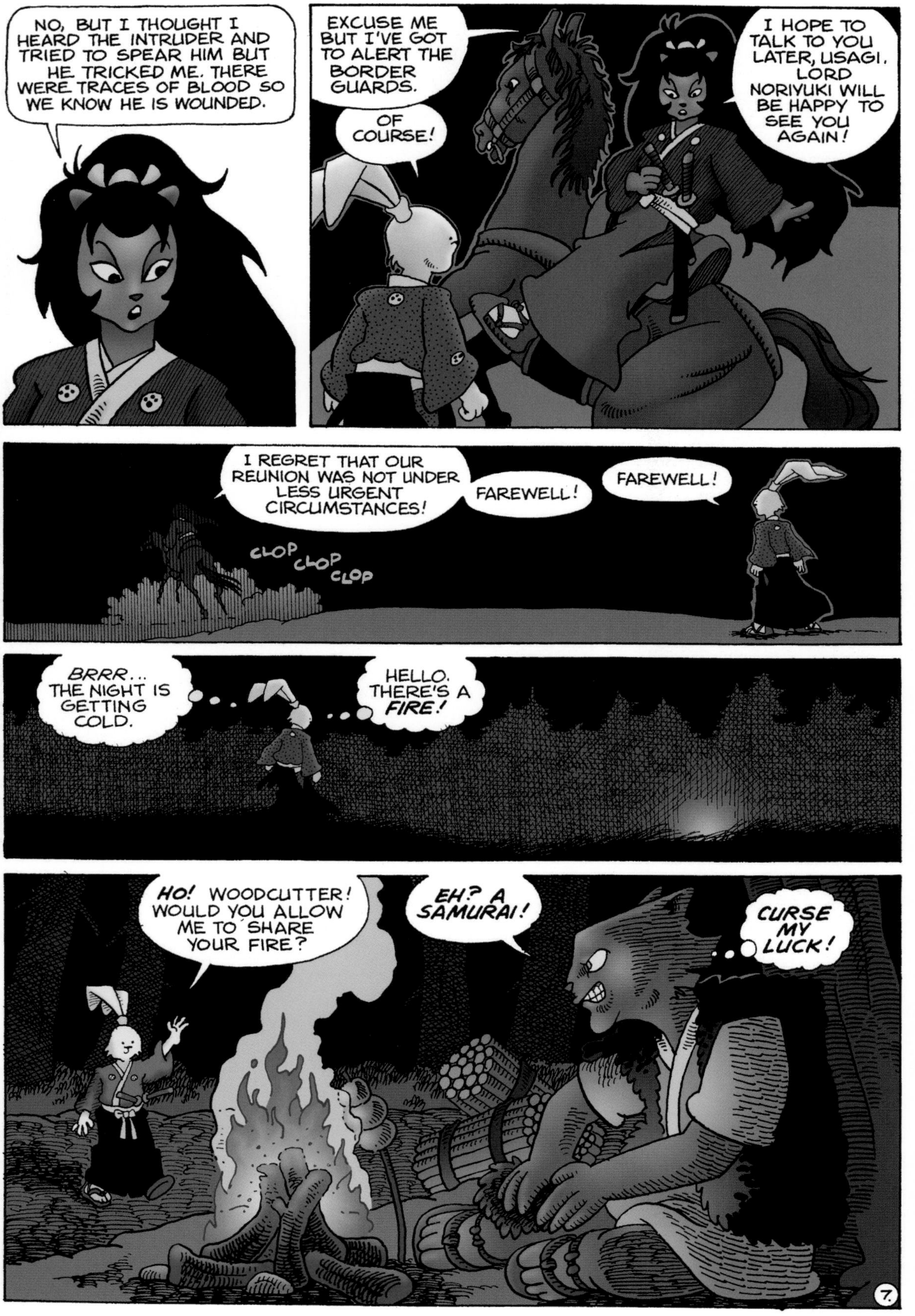
NO, BUT I THOUGHT I HEARD THE INTRUDER AND TRIED TO SPEAR HIM BUT HE TRICKED ME. THERE WERE TRACES OF BLOOD SO WE KNOW HE IS WOUNDED.
EXCUSE ME BUT I'VE GOT TO ALERT THE BORDER GUARDS.
OF COURSE!
I HOPE TO TALK TO YOU LATER, USAGI. LORD NORIYUKI WILL BE HAPPY TO SEE YOU AGAIN!
I REGRET THAT OUR REUNION WAS NOT UNDER LESS URGENT CIRCUMSTANCES!
FAREWELL!
FAREWELL!
CLOP CLOP CLOP
BRRR... THE NIGHT IS GETTING COLD.
HELLO. THERE'S A *FIRE!*
HO! WOODCUTTER! WOULD YOU ALLOW ME TO SHARE YOUR FIRE?
EH? A SAMURAI!
CURSE MY LUCK!
7.

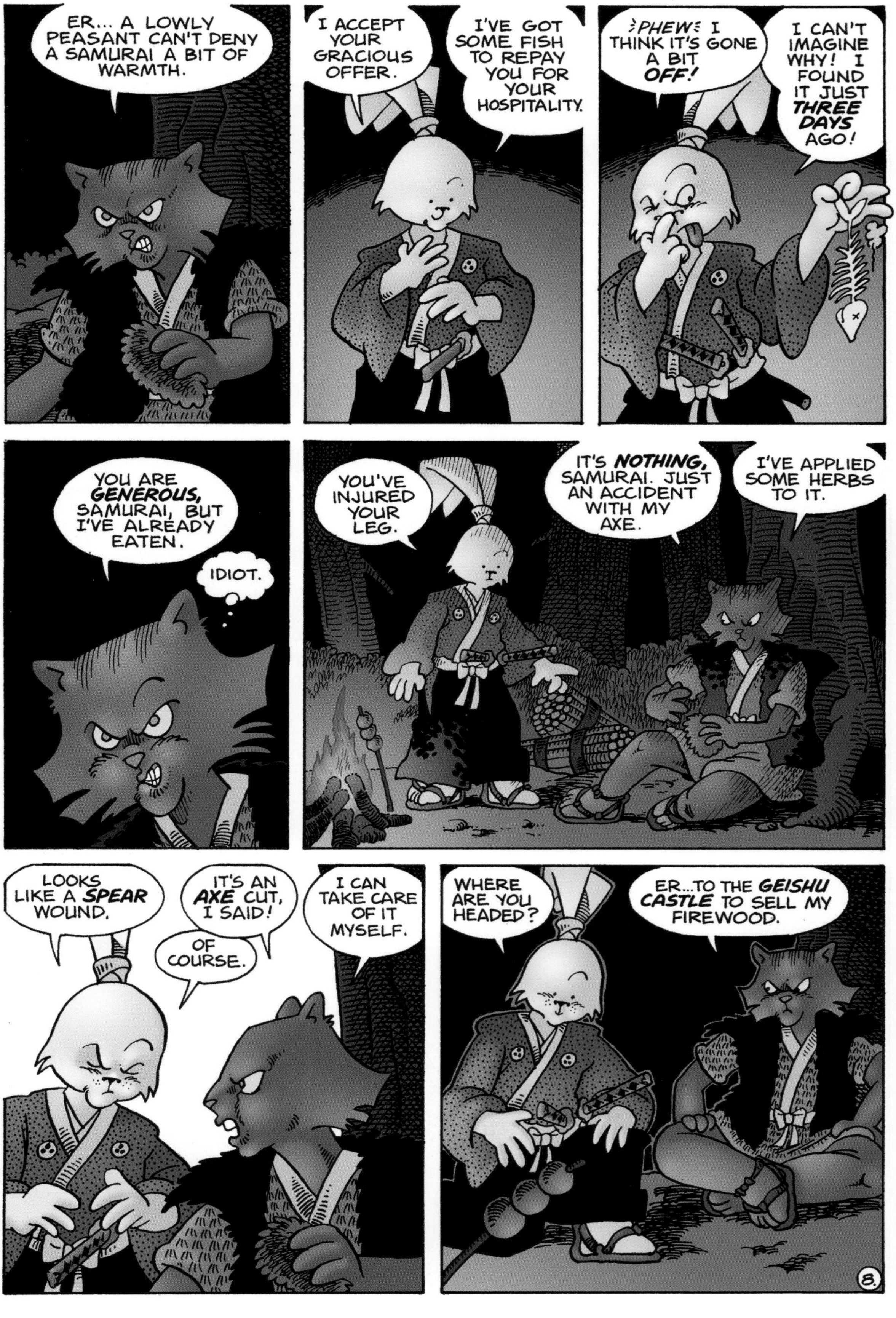
ER... A LOWLY PEASANT CAN'T DENY A SAMURAI A BIT OF WARMTH.
I ACCEPT YOUR GRACIOUS OFFER.
I'VE GOT SOME FISH TO REPAY YOU FOR YOUR HOSPITALITY.
PHEW! I THINK IT'S GONE A BIT **OFF!**
I CAN'T IMAGINE WHY! I FOUND IT JUST **THREE DAYS** AGO!
YOU ARE **GENEROUS,** SAMURAI, BUT I'VE ALREADY EATEN.
IDIOT.
YOU'VE INJURED YOUR LEG.
IT'S **NOTHING,** SAMURAI. JUST AN ACCIDENT WITH MY AXE.
I'VE APPLIED SOME HERBS TO IT.
LOOKS LIKE A **SPEAR** WOUND.
IT'S AN **AXE** CUT, I SAID!
OF COURSE.
I CAN TAKE CARE OF IT MYSELF.
WHERE ARE YOU HEADED?
ER...TO THE **GEISHU CASTLE** TO SELL MY FIREWOOD.
8.

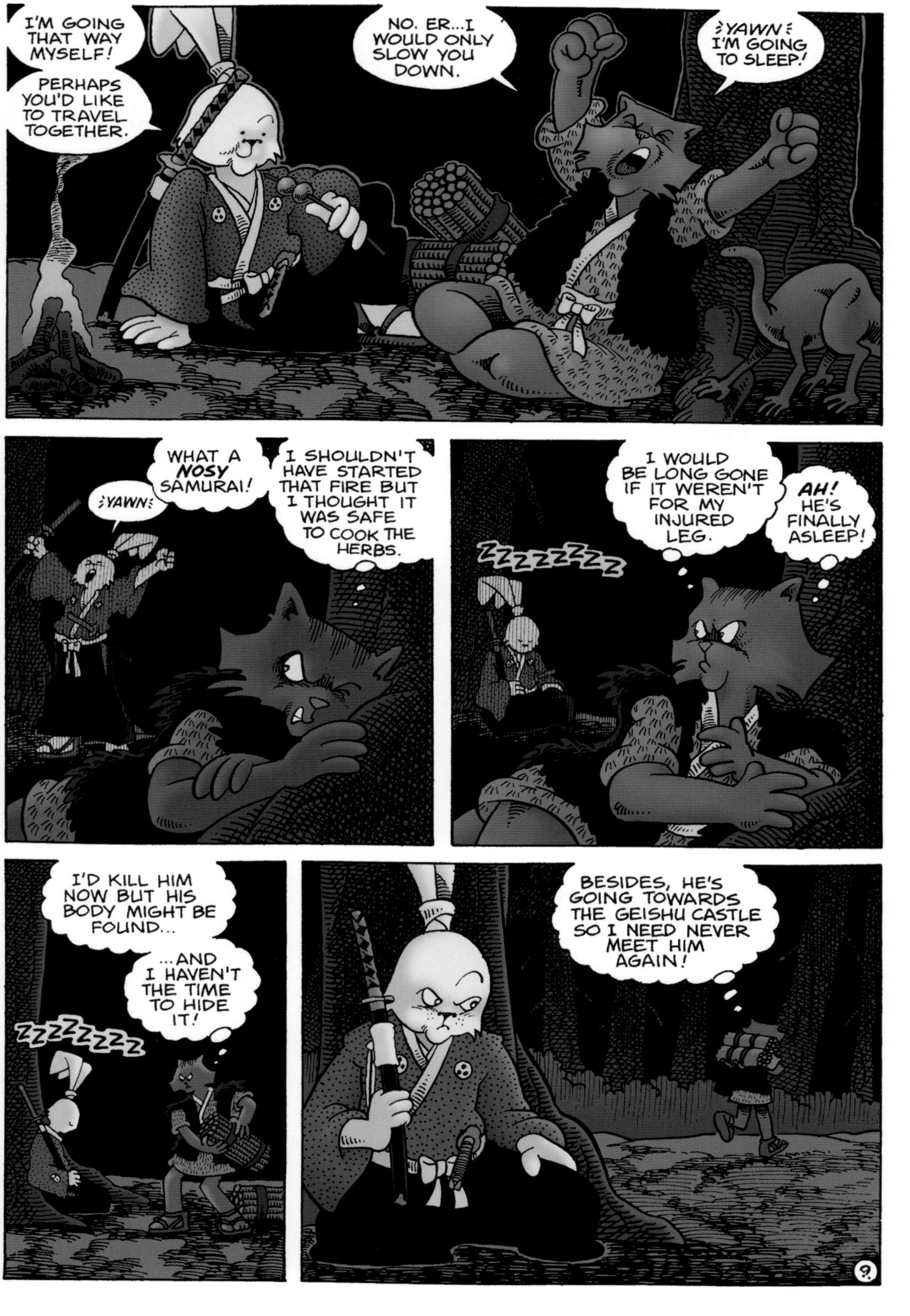
I'M GOING THAT WAY MYSELF!
PERHAPS YOU'D LIKE TO TRAVEL TOGETHER.
NO. ER...I WOULD ONLY SLOW YOU DOWN.
YAWN
I'M GOING TO SLEEP!
YAWN
WHAT A NOSY SAMURAI!
I SHOULDN'T HAVE STARTED THAT FIRE BUT I THOUGHT IT WAS SAFE TO COOK THE HERBS.
ZZZZZZZZ
I WOULD BE LONG GONE IF IT WEREN'T FOR MY INJURED LEG.
AH! HE'S FINALLY ASLEEP!
I'D KILL HIM NOW BUT HIS BODY MIGHT BE FOUND...
...AND I HAVEN'T THE TIME TO HIDE IT!
ZZZZZZZZ
BESIDES, HE'S GOING TOWARDS THE GEISHU CASTLE SO I NEED NEVER MEET HIM AGAIN!

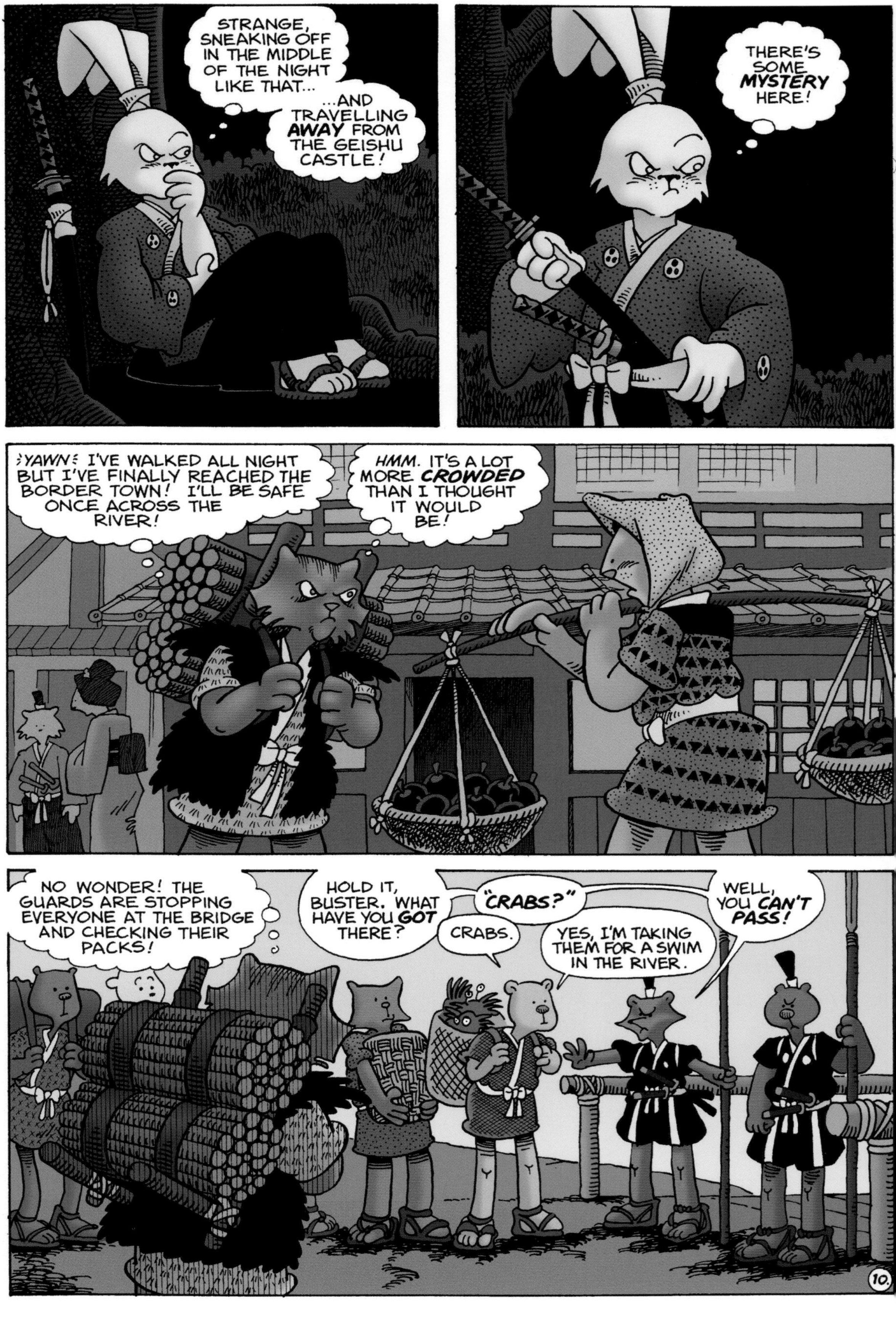
STRANGE, SNEAKING OFF IN THE MIDDLE OF THE NIGHT LIKE THAT...
...AND TRAVELLING AWAY FROM THE GEISHU CASTLE!
THERE'S SOME MYSTERY HERE!
YAWN I'VE WALKED ALL NIGHT BUT I'VE FINALLY REACHED THE BORDER TOWN! I'LL BE SAFE ONCE ACROSS THE RIVER!
HMM. IT'S A LOT MORE CROWDED THAN I THOUGHT IT WOULD BE!
NO WONDER! THE GUARDS ARE STOPPING EVERYONE AT THE BRIDGE AND CHECKING THEIR PACKS!
HOLD IT, BUSTER. WHAT HAVE YOU GOT THERE?
CRABS.
"CRABS?"
YES, I'M TAKING THEM FOR A SWIM IN THE RIVER.
WELL, YOU CAN'T PASS!
10.

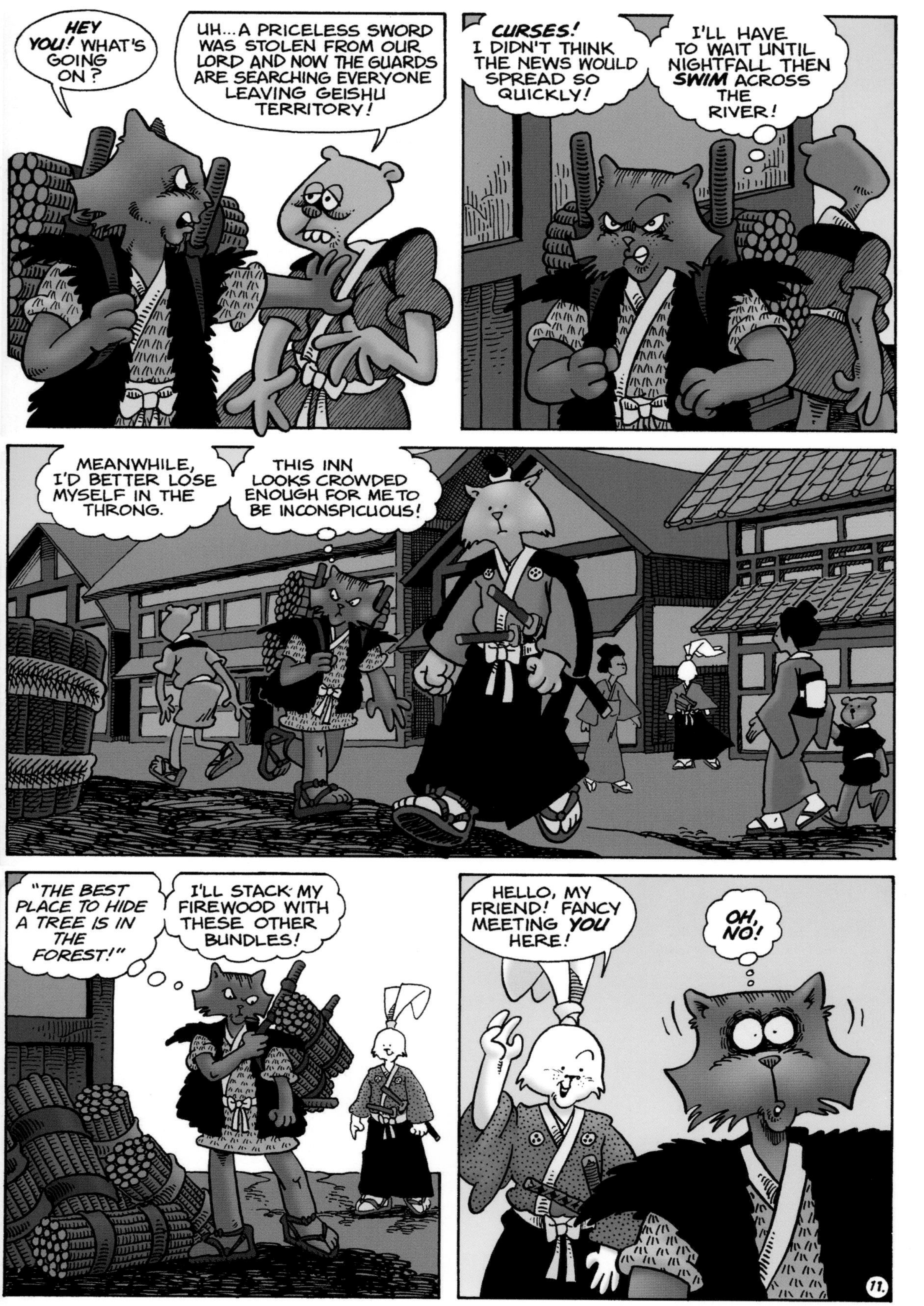
HEY YOU! WHAT'S GOING ON?
UH...A PRICELESS SWORD WAS STOLEN FROM OUR LORD AND NOW THE GUARDS ARE SEARCHING EVERYONE LEAVING GEISHU TERRITORY!
CURSES! I DIDN'T THINK THE NEWS WOULD SPREAD SO QUICKLY!
I'LL HAVE TO WAIT UNTIL NIGHTFALL THEN SWIM ACROSS THE RIVER!
MEANWHILE, I'D BETTER LOSE MYSELF IN THE THRONG.
THIS INN LOOKS CROWDED ENOUGH FOR ME TO BE INCONSPICUOUS!
"THE BEST PLACE TO HIDE A TREE IS IN THE FOREST!"
I'LL STACK MY FIREWOOD WITH THESE OTHER BUNDLES!
HELLO, MY FRIEND! FANCY MEETING YOU HERE!
OH, NO!
11.

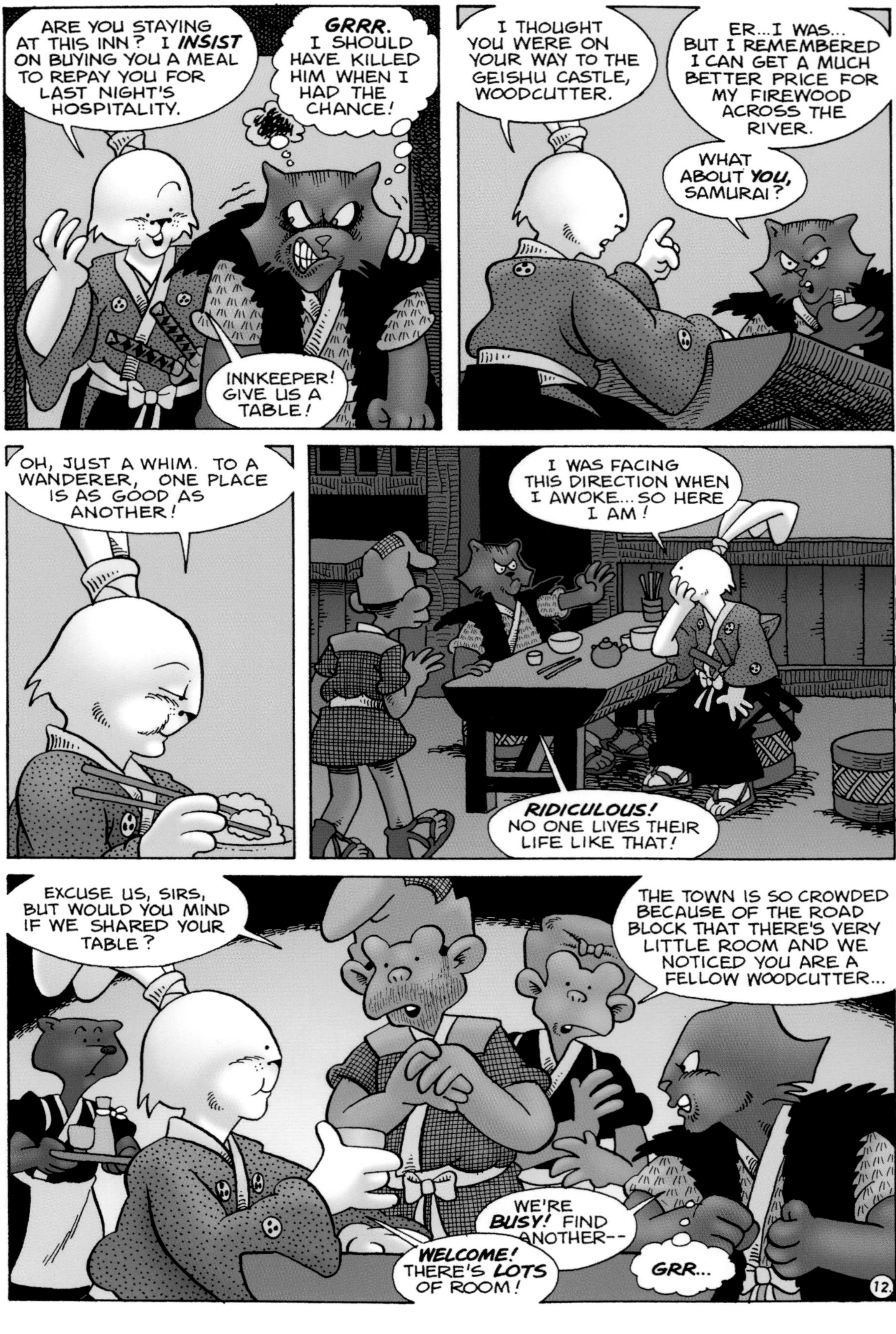

ARE YOU STAYING AT THIS INN? I *INSIST* ON BUYING YOU A MEAL TO REPAY YOU FOR LAST NIGHT'S HOSPITALITY.
GRRR. I SHOULD HAVE KILLED HIM WHEN I HAD THE CHANCE!
INNKEEPER! GIVE US A TABLE!
I THOUGHT YOU WERE ON YOUR WAY TO THE GEISHU CASTLE, WOODCUTTER.
ER...I WAS... BUT I REMEMBERED I CAN GET A MUCH BETTER PRICE FOR MY FIREWOOD ACROSS THE RIVER.
WHAT ABOUT *YOU,* SAMURAI?
OH, JUST A WHIM. TO A WANDERER, ONE PLACE IS AS GOOD AS ANOTHER!
I WAS FACING THIS DIRECTION WHEN I AWOKE... SO HERE I AM!
RIDICULOUS! NO ONE LIVES THEIR LIFE LIKE THAT!
EXCUSE US, SIRS, BUT WOULD YOU MIND IF WE SHARED YOUR TABLE?
THE TOWN IS SO CROWDED BECAUSE OF THE ROAD BLOCK THAT THERE'S VERY LITTLE ROOM AND WE NOTICED YOU ARE A FELLOW WOODCUTTER...
WE'RE *BUSY!* FIND ANOTHER--
WELCOME! THERE'S *LOTS* OF ROOM!
GRR...
12.

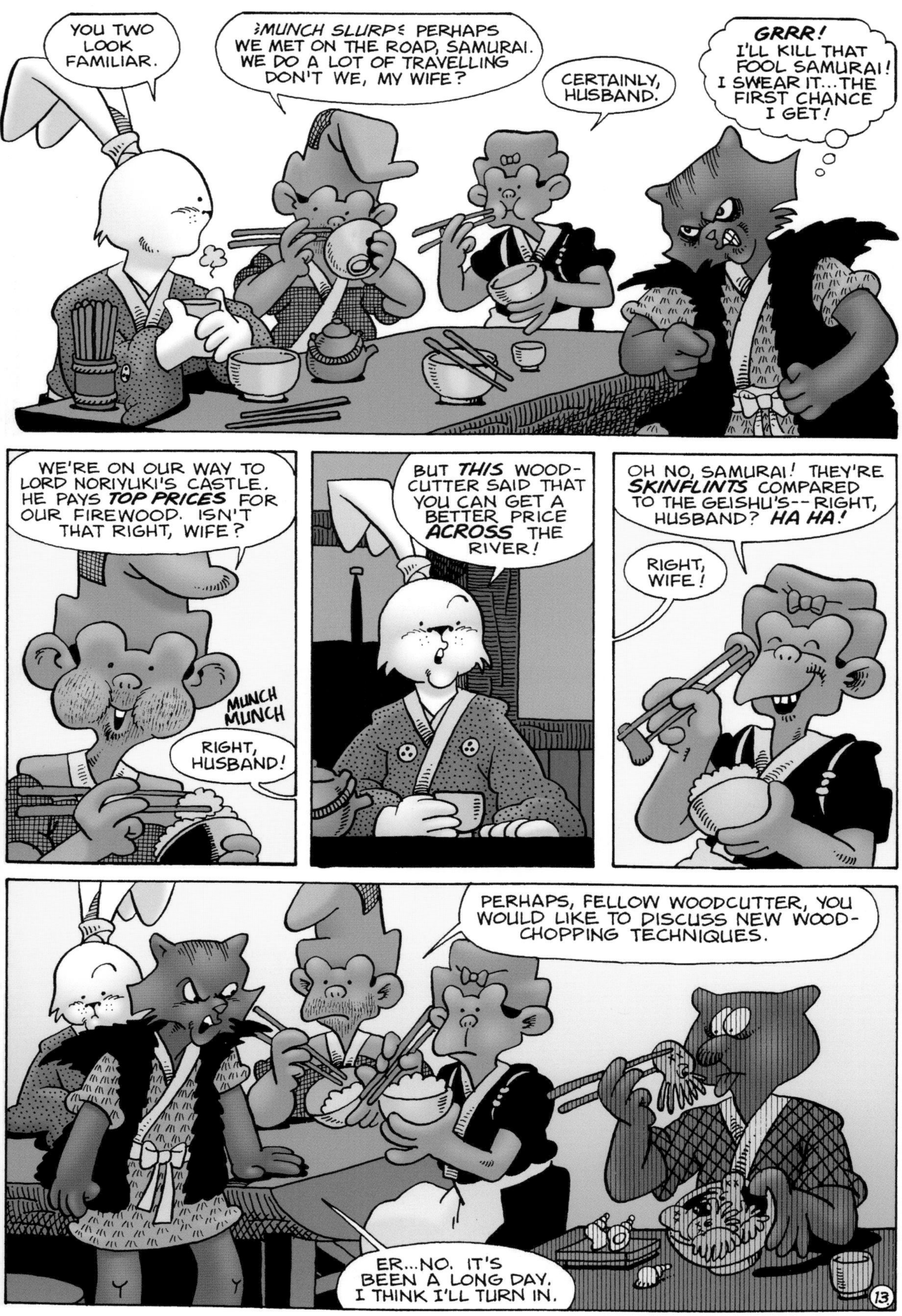
YOU TWO LOOK FAMILIAR.
¿MUNCH SLURP¿ PERHAPS WE MET ON THE ROAD, SAMURAI. WE DO A LOT OF TRAVELLING DON'T WE, MY WIFE?
CERTAINLY, HUSBAND.
GRRR! I'LL KILL THAT FOOL SAMURAI! I SWEAR IT... THE FIRST CHANCE I GET!
WE'RE ON OUR WAY TO LORD NORIYUKI'S CASTLE. HE PAYS TOP PRICES FOR OUR FIREWOOD. ISN'T THAT RIGHT, WIFE?
MUNCH MUNCH
RIGHT, HUSBAND!
BUT THIS WOOD-CUTTER SAID THAT YOU CAN GET A BETTER PRICE ACROSS THE RIVER!
OH NO, SAMURAI! THEY'RE SKINFLINTS COMPARED TO THE GEISHU'S-- RIGHT, HUSBAND? HA HA!
RIGHT, WIFE!
PERHAPS, FELLOW WOODCUTTER, YOU WOULD LIKE TO DISCUSS NEW WOOD-CHOPPING TECHNIQUES.
ER...NO. IT'S BEEN A LONG DAY. I THINK I'LL TURN IN.
13

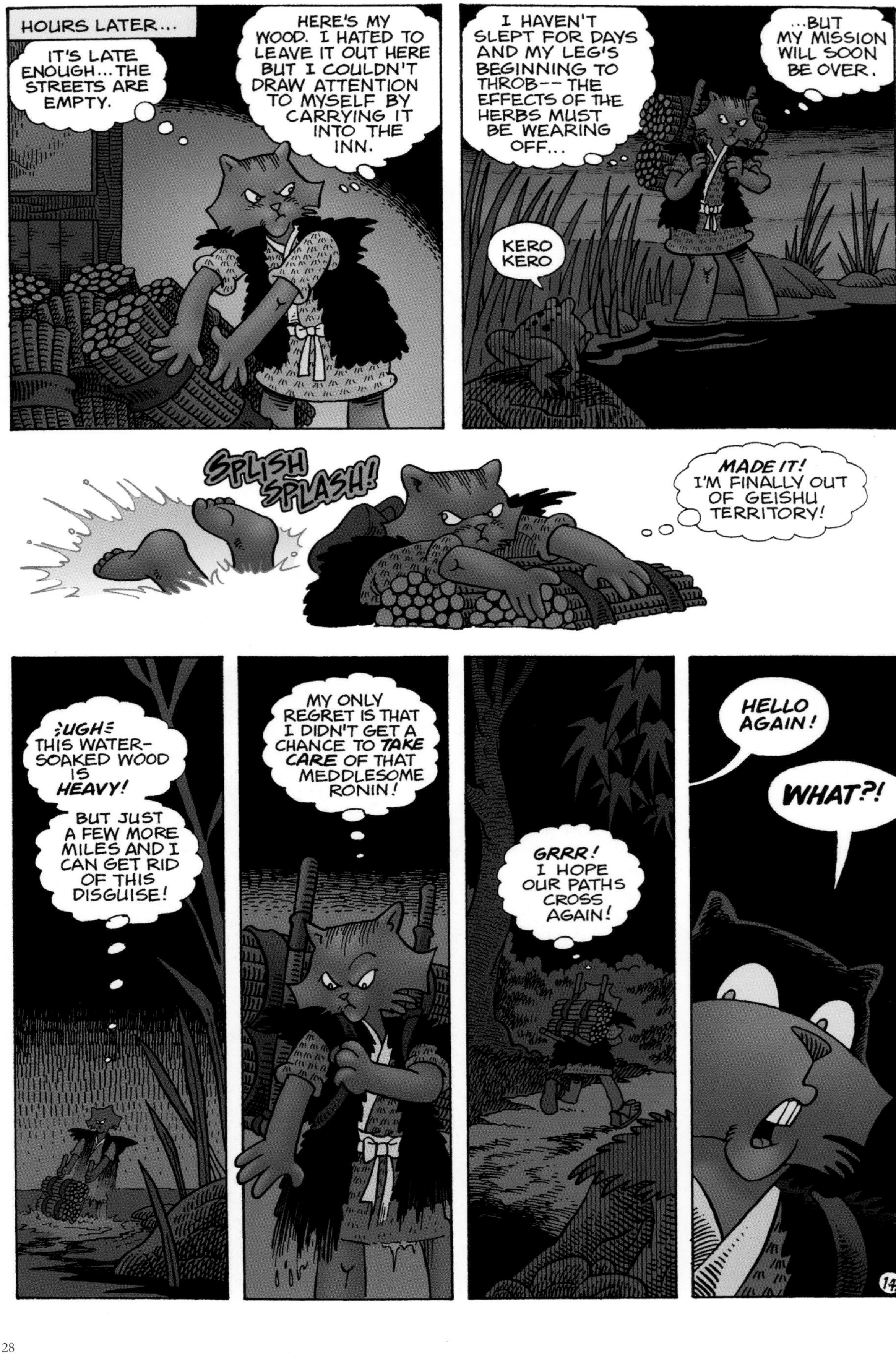

HOURS LATER...
IT'S LATE ENOUGH...THE STREETS ARE EMPTY.
HERE'S MY WOOD. I HATED TO LEAVE IT OUT HERE BUT I COULDN'T DRAW ATTENTION TO MYSELF BY CARRYING IT INTO THE INN.
I HAVEN'T SLEPT FOR DAYS AND MY LEG'S BEGINNING TO THROB-- THE EFFECTS OF THE HERBS MUST BE WEARING OFF...
...BUT MY MISSION WILL SOON BE OVER.
KERO KERO
SPLISH SPLASH!
MADE IT! I'M FINALLY OUT OF GEISHU TERRITORY!
UGH THIS WATER-SOAKED WOOD IS HEAVY!
BUT JUST A FEW MORE MILES AND I CAN GET RID OF THIS DISGUISE!
MY ONLY REGRET IS THAT I DIDN'T GET A CHANCE TO TAKE CARE OF THAT MEDDLESOME RONIN!
GRRR! I HOPE OUR PATHS CROSS AGAIN!
HELLO AGAIN!
WHAT?!
14.

YOU!

YES, I WAS RESTLESS SO I DECIDED TO LEAVE THE INN EARLY.

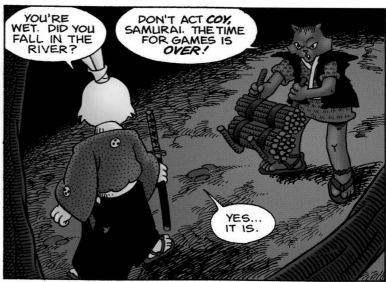

YOU'RE WET. DID YOU FALL IN THE RIVER?

DON'T ACT *COY*, SAMURAI. THE TIME FOR GAMES IS *OVER!*

YES... IT IS.

CLICK!

I AM *SHINGEN* OF THE NEKO NINJA CLAN... YOU ARE A *DEAD MAN!*

CLICK!

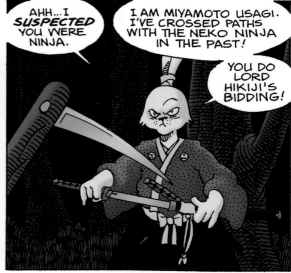

AHH... I *SUSPECTED* YOU WERE NINJA.

I AM MIYAMOTO USAGI. I'VE CROSSED PATHS WITH THE NEKO NINJA IN THE PAST!

YOU DO LORD HIKIJI'S BIDDING!

YES. HE WANTED THE GEISHU TO LOSE FACE SO HE DIRECTED ME TO STEAL THE MURAMASA SWORD-- THEIR GIFT TO THE SHOGUN.

BUT YOU *AREN'T* A GEISHU RETAINER! WHY DO YOU INVOLVE YOURSELF?!

I GUESS I'M JUST A BUSY-BODY!

15

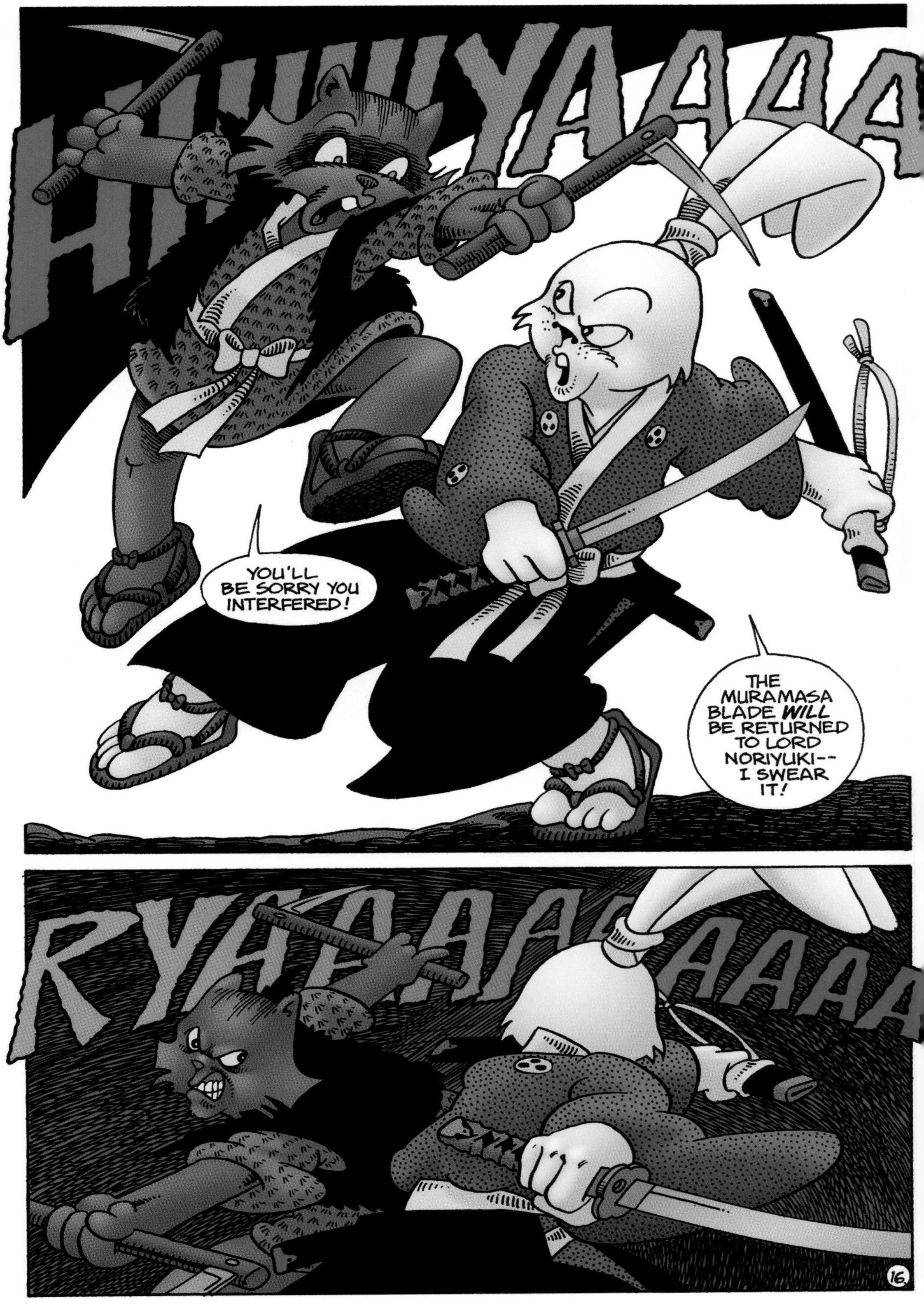
HIIIIIYAAAAA
YOU'LL BE SORRY YOU INTERFERED!
THE MURAMASA BLADE WILL BE RETURNED TO LORD NORIYUKI-- I SWEAR IT!
RYAAAAAAAAAA
16

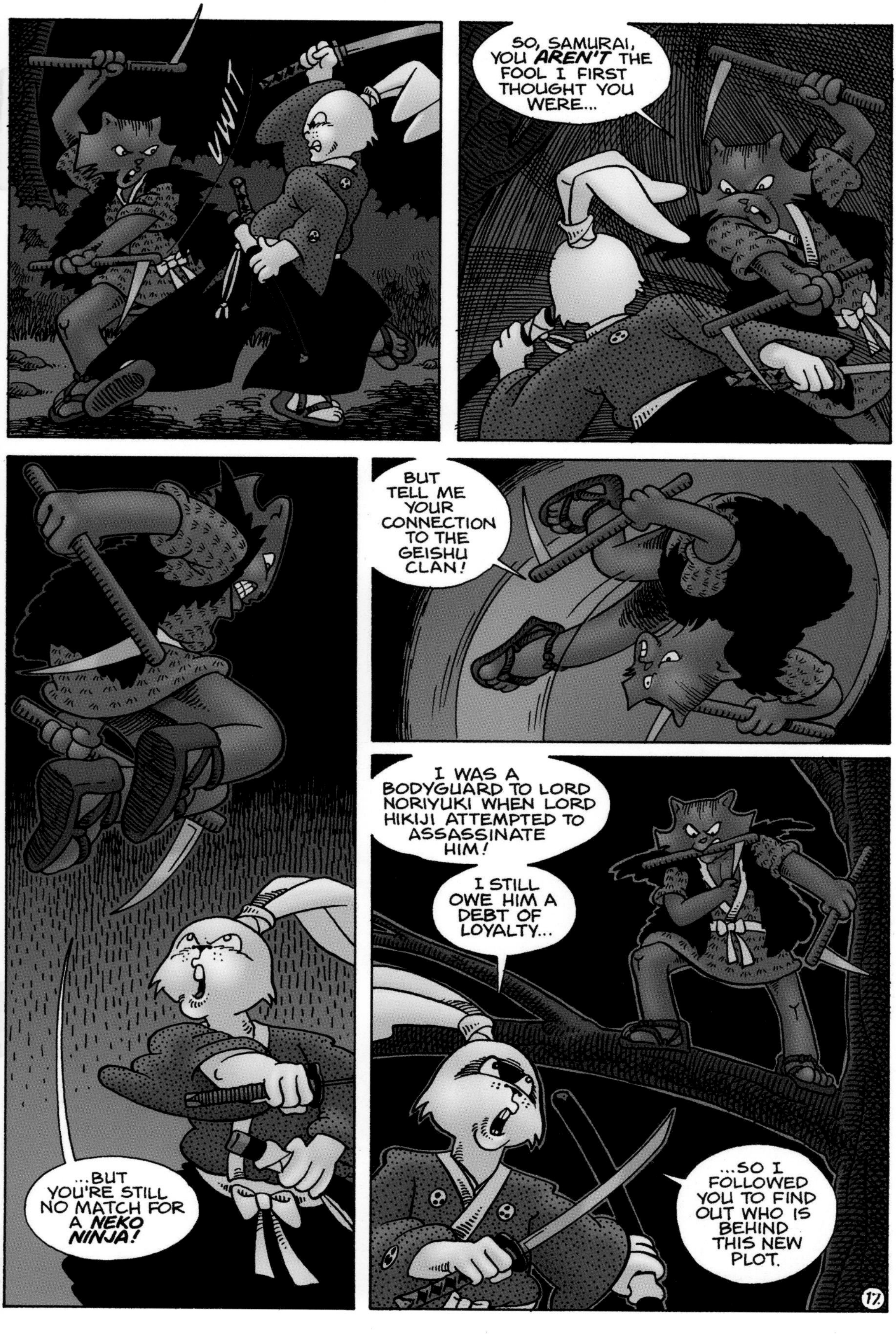
UWIT
SO, SAMURAI, YOU AREN'T THE FOOL I FIRST THOUGHT YOU WERE...
BUT TELL ME YOUR CONNECTION TO THE GEISHU CLAN!
...BUT YOU'RE STILL NO MATCH FOR A NEKO NINJA!
I WAS A BODYGUARD TO LORD NORIYUKI WHEN LORD HIKIJI ATTEMPTED TO ASSASSINATE HIM!
I STILL OWE HIM A DEBT OF LOYALTY...
...SO I FOLLOWED YOU TO FIND OUT WHO IS BEHIND THIS NEW PLOT.
17

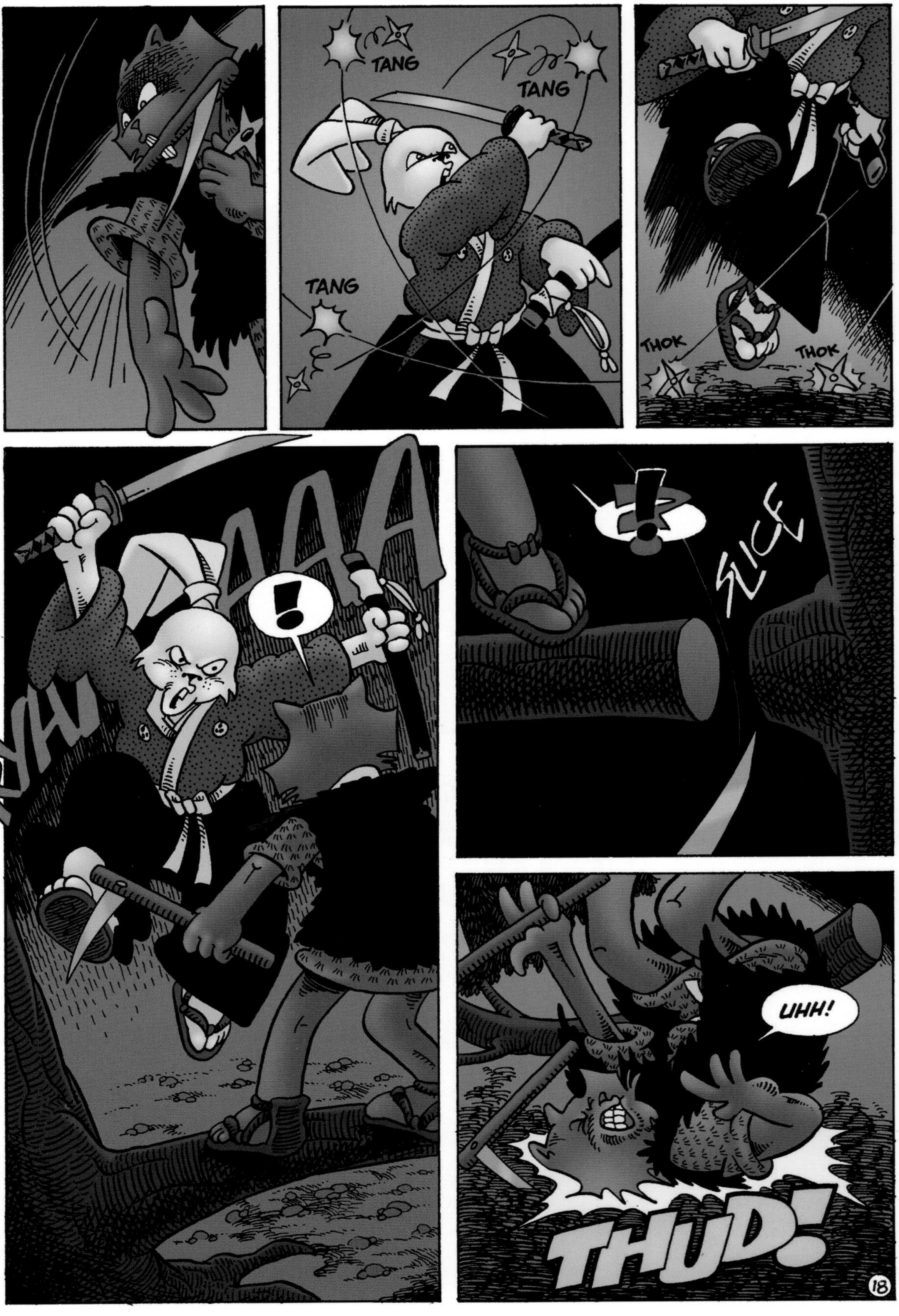
TANG
TANG
TANG
THOK
THOK
RYAAAAA
!
!
SLICE
UHH!
THUD!
18

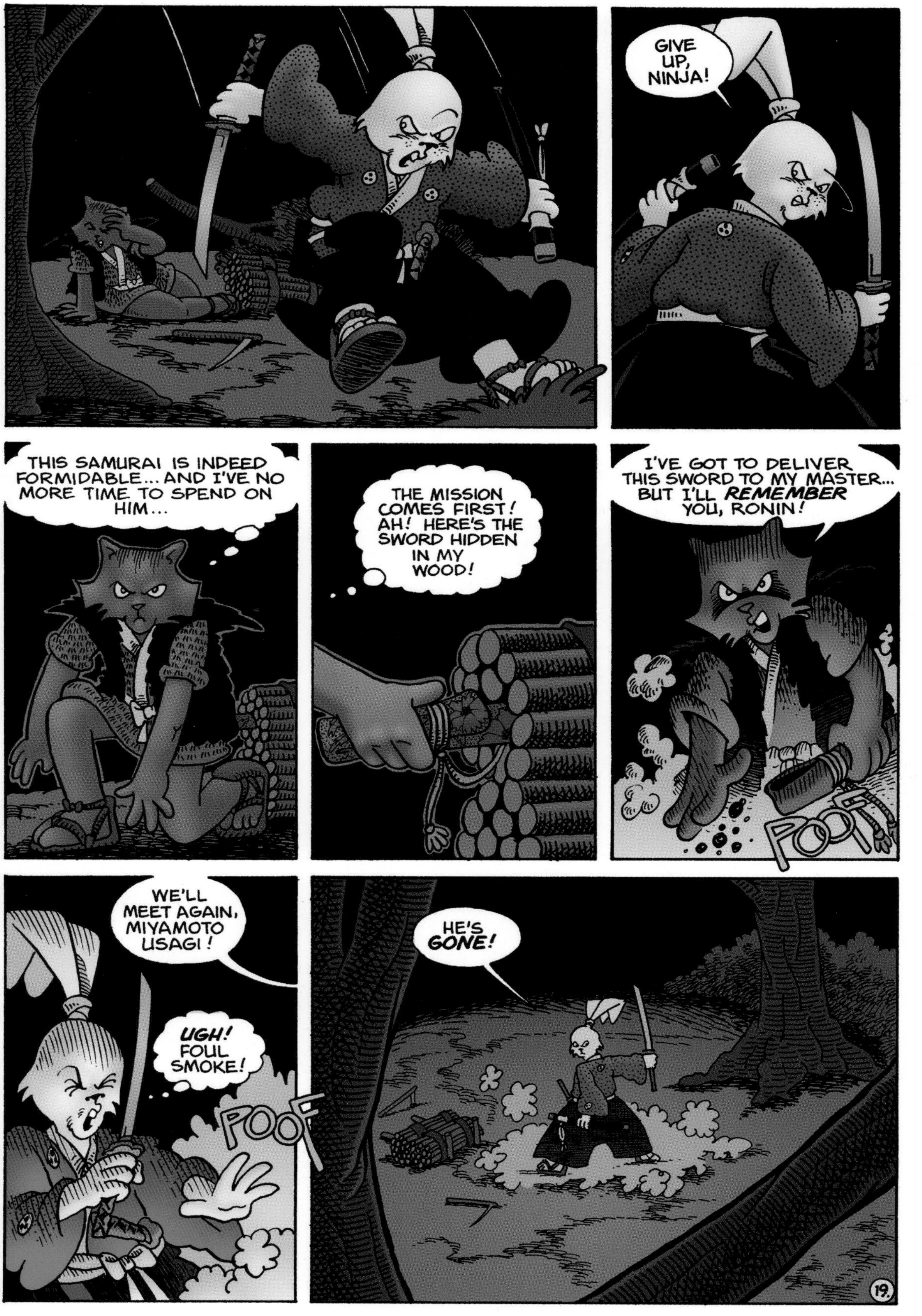
GIVE UP, NINJA!
THIS SAMURAI IS INDEED FORMIDABLE... AND I'VE NO MORE TIME TO SPEND ON HIM...
THE MISSION COMES FIRST! AH! HERE'S THE SWORD HIDDEN IN MY WOOD!
I'VE GOT TO DELIVER THIS SWORD TO MY MASTER... BUT I'LL *REMEMBER* YOU, RONIN!
POOF
WE'LL MEET AGAIN, MIYAMOTO USAGI!
UGH! FOUL SMOKE!
POOF
HE'S *GONE!*
19.

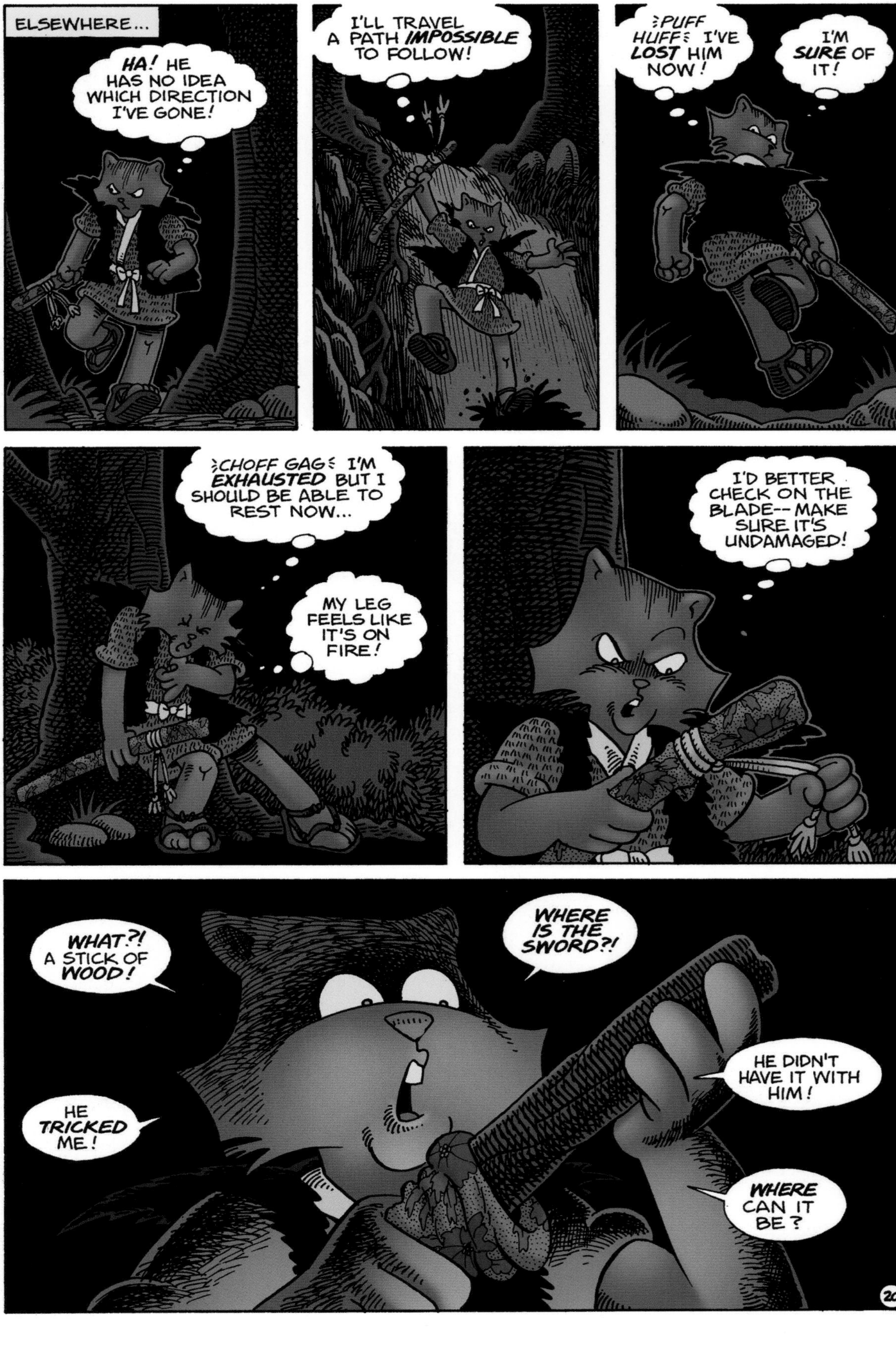
ELSEWHERE...
HA! HE HAS NO IDEA WHICH DIRECTION I'VE GONE!
I'LL TRAVEL A PATH IMPOSSIBLE TO FOLLOW!
PUFF HUFF I'VE LOST HIM NOW!
I'M SURE OF IT!
CHOFF GAG I'M EXHAUSTED BUT I SHOULD BE ABLE TO REST NOW...
MY LEG FEELS LIKE IT'S ON FIRE!
I'D BETTER CHECK ON THE BLADE-- MAKE SURE IT'S UNDAMAGED!
WHAT?! A STICK OF WOOD!
WHERE IS THE SWORD?!
HE DIDN'T HAVE IT WITH HIM!
HE TRICKED ME!
WHERE CAN IT BE?
20.

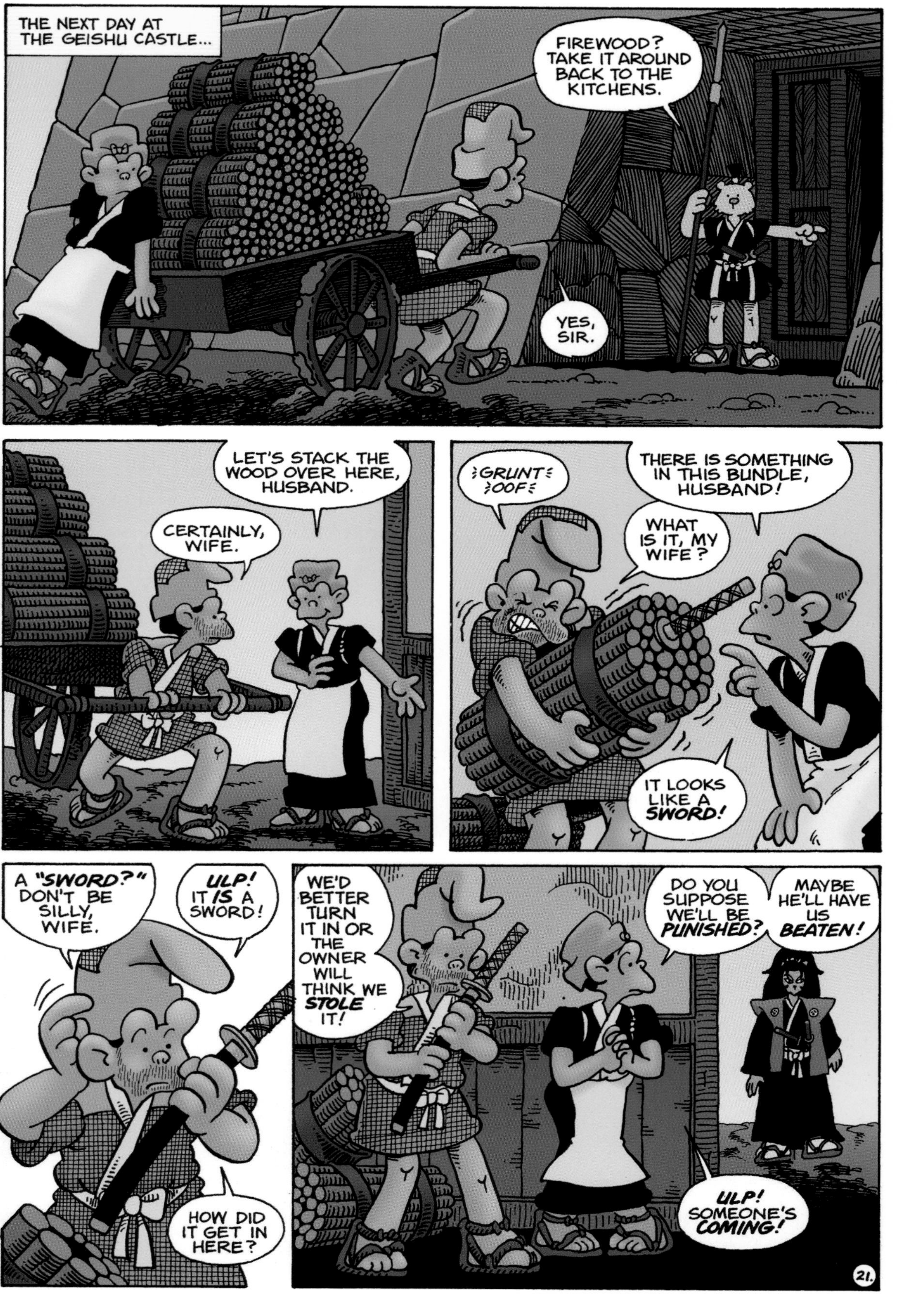
THE NEXT DAY AT THE GEISHU CASTLE...
FIREWOOD? TAKE IT AROUND BACK TO THE KITCHENS.
YES, SIR.
LET'S STACK THE WOOD OVER HERE, HUSBAND.
CERTAINLY, WIFE.
GRUNT OOF
THERE IS SOMETHING IN THIS BUNDLE, HUSBAND!
WHAT IS IT, MY WIFE?
IT LOOKS LIKE A SWORD!
A "SWORD?" DON'T BE SILLY, WIFE.
ULP! IT IS A SWORD!
HOW DID IT GET IN HERE?
WE'D BETTER TURN IT IN OR THE OWNER WILL THINK WE STOLE IT!
DO YOU SUPPOSE WE'LL BE PUNISHED?
MAYBE HE'LL HAVE US BEATEN!
ULP! SOMEONE'S COMING!
21.

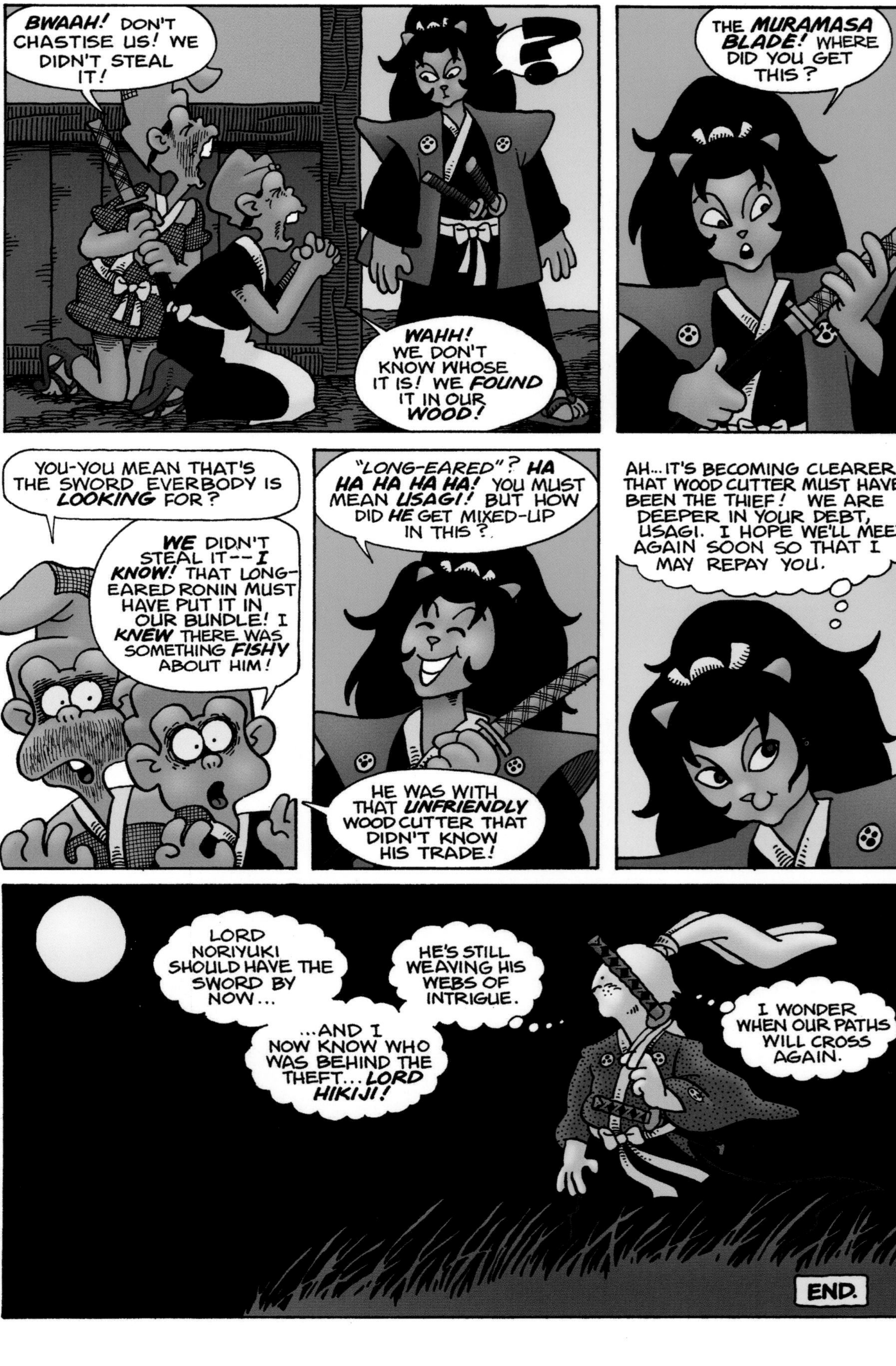

BWAAH! DON'T CHASTISE US! WE DIDN'T STEAL IT!
?
WAHH! WE DON'T KNOW WHOSE IT IS! WE FOUND IT IN OUR WOOD!
THE MURAMASA BLADE! WHERE DID YOU GET THIS?
YOU-YOU MEAN THAT'S THE SWORD EVERBODY IS LOOKING FOR?
WE DIDN'T STEAL IT-- I KNOW! THAT LONG-EARED RONIN MUST HAVE PUT IT IN OUR BUNDLE! I KNEW THERE WAS SOMETHING FISHY ABOUT HIM!
"LONG-EARED"? HA HA HA HA HA! YOU MUST MEAN USAGI! BUT HOW DID HE GET MIXED-UP IN THIS?
HE WAS WITH THAT UNFRIENDLY WOOD CUTTER THAT DIDN'T KNOW HIS TRADE!
AH... IT'S BECOMING CLEARER. THAT WOOD CUTTER MUST HAVE BEEN THE THIEF! WE ARE DEEPER IN YOUR DEBT, USAGI. I HOPE WE'LL MEET AGAIN SOON SO THAT I MAY REPAY YOU.
LORD NORIYUKI SHOULD HAVE THE SWORD BY NOW...
...AND I NOW KNOW WHO WAS BEHIND THE THEFT... LORD HIKIJI!
HE'S STILL WEAVING HIS WEBS OF INTRIGUE.
I WONDER WHEN OUR PATHS WILL CROSS AGAIN.
END.

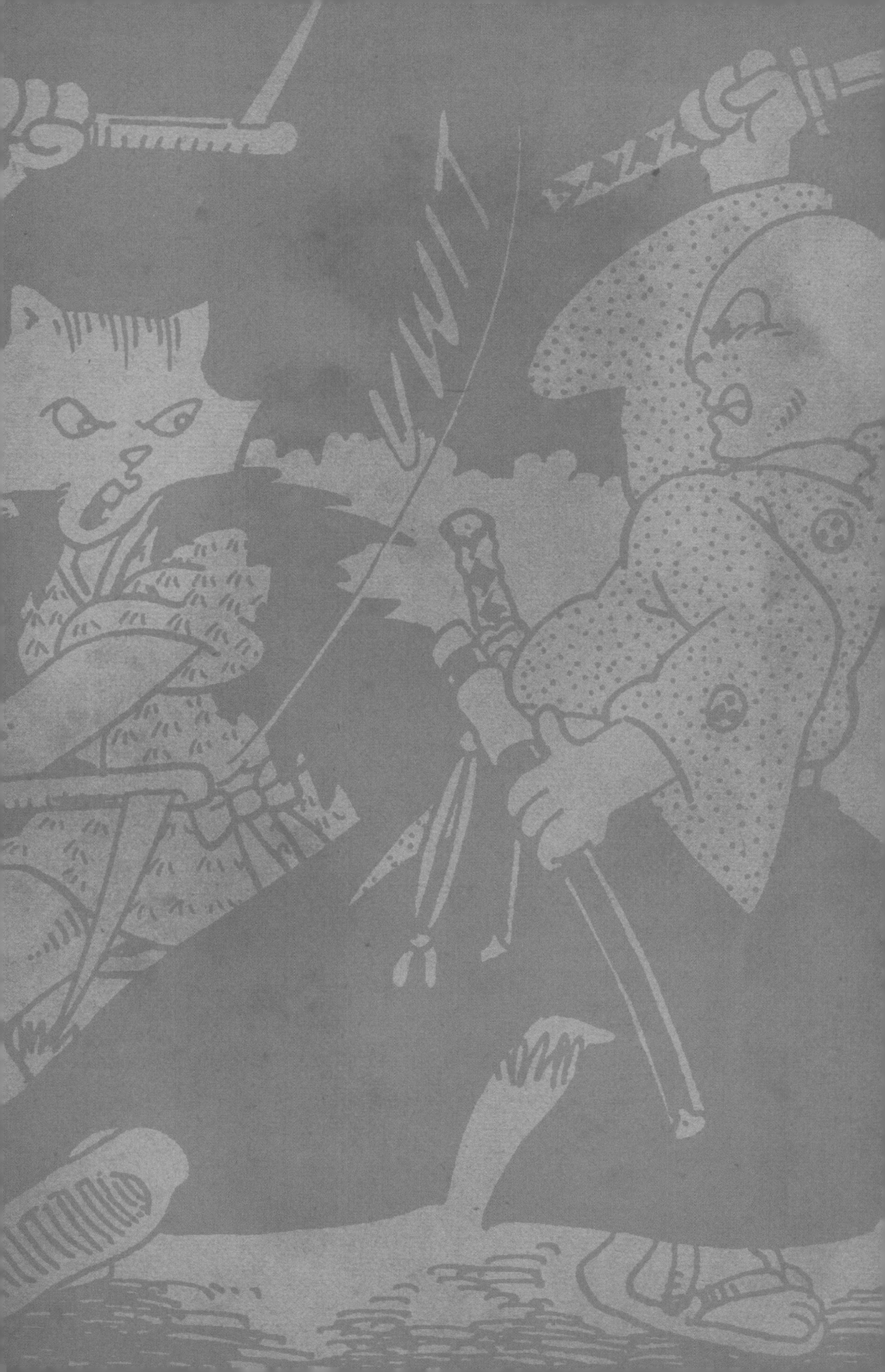

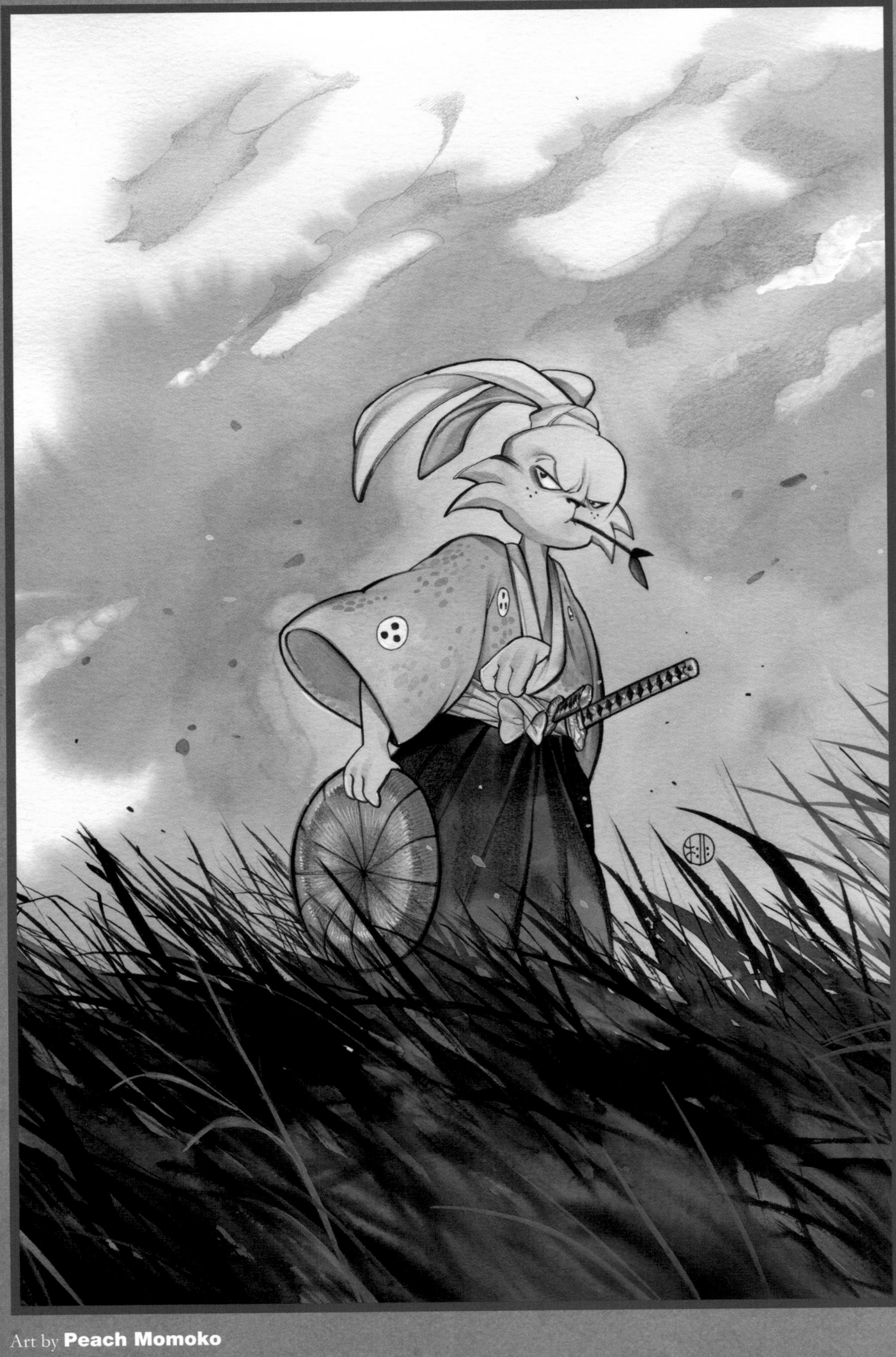

Art by **Peach Momoko**

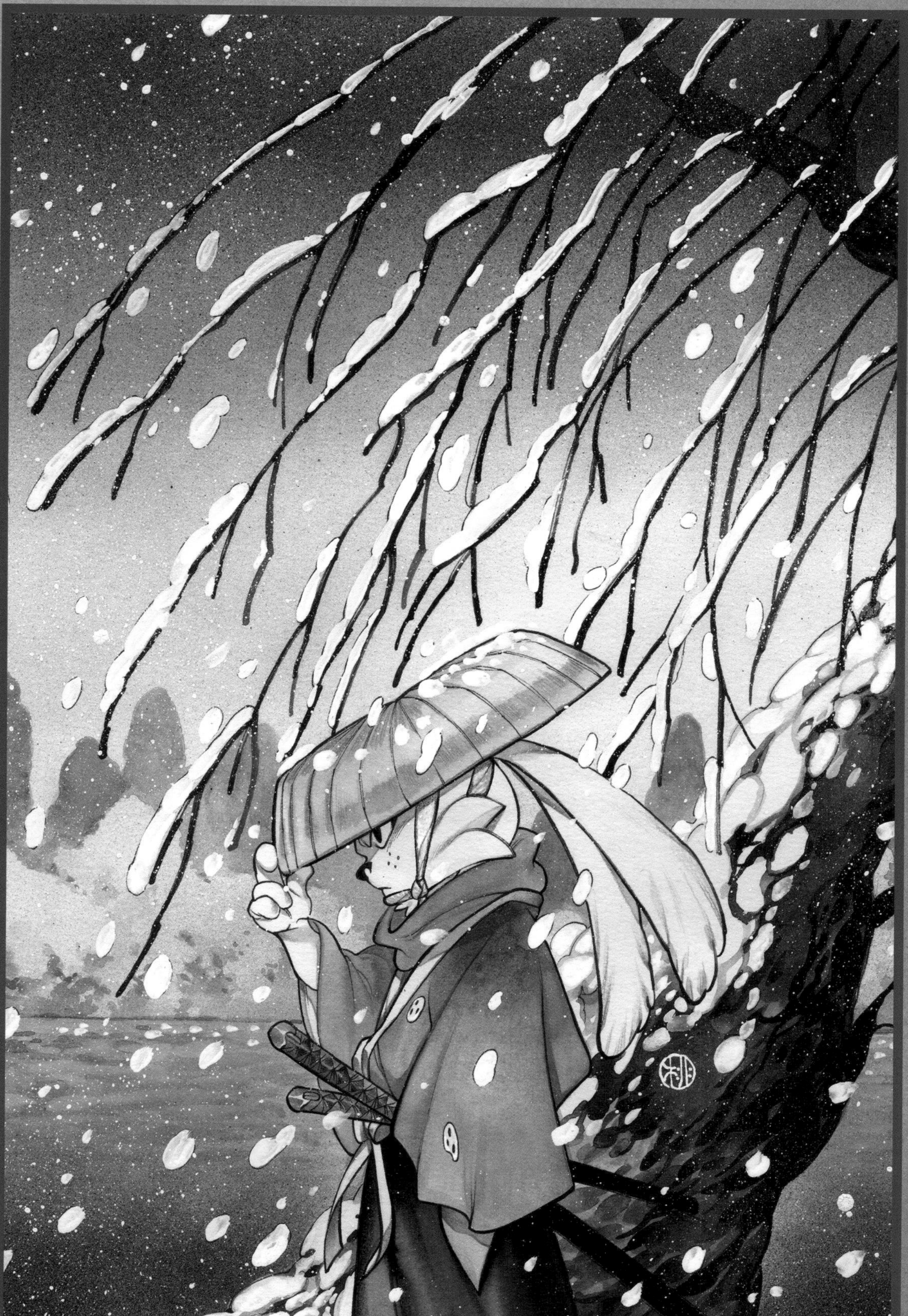

Art by **Peach Momoko**

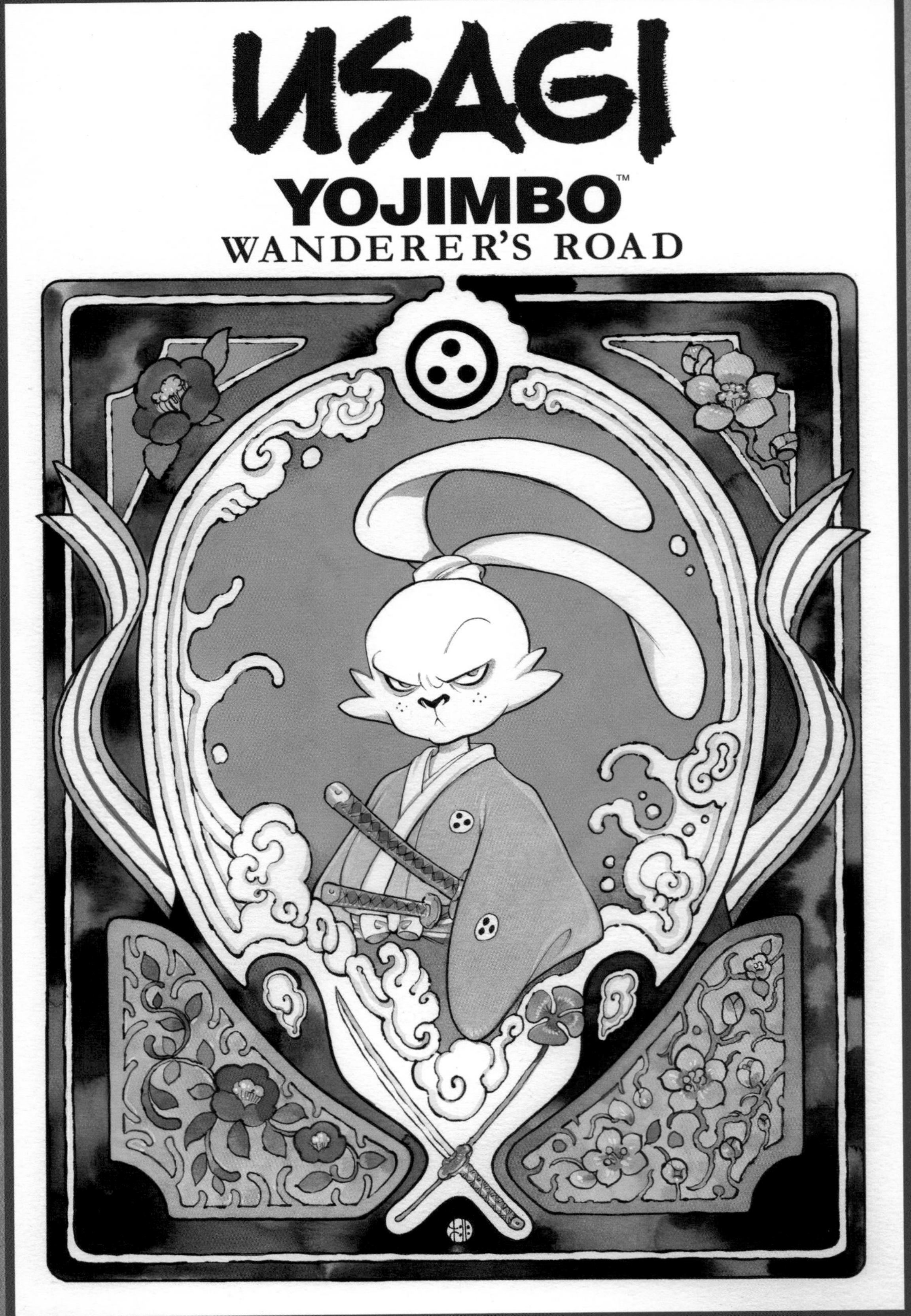
USAGI
YOJIMBO™
WANDERER'S ROAD

Art by **Peach Momoko**

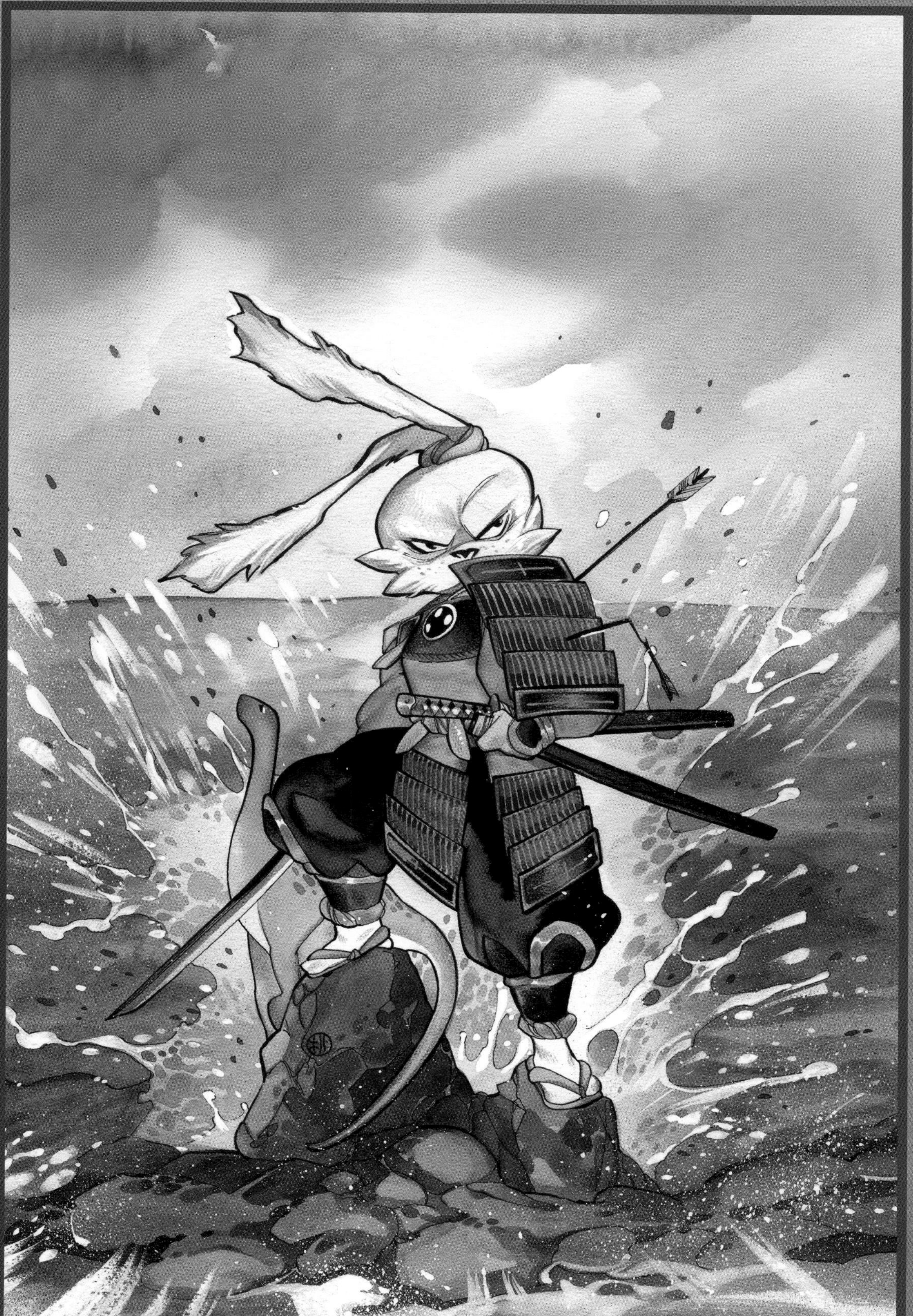

Art by **Peach Momoko**

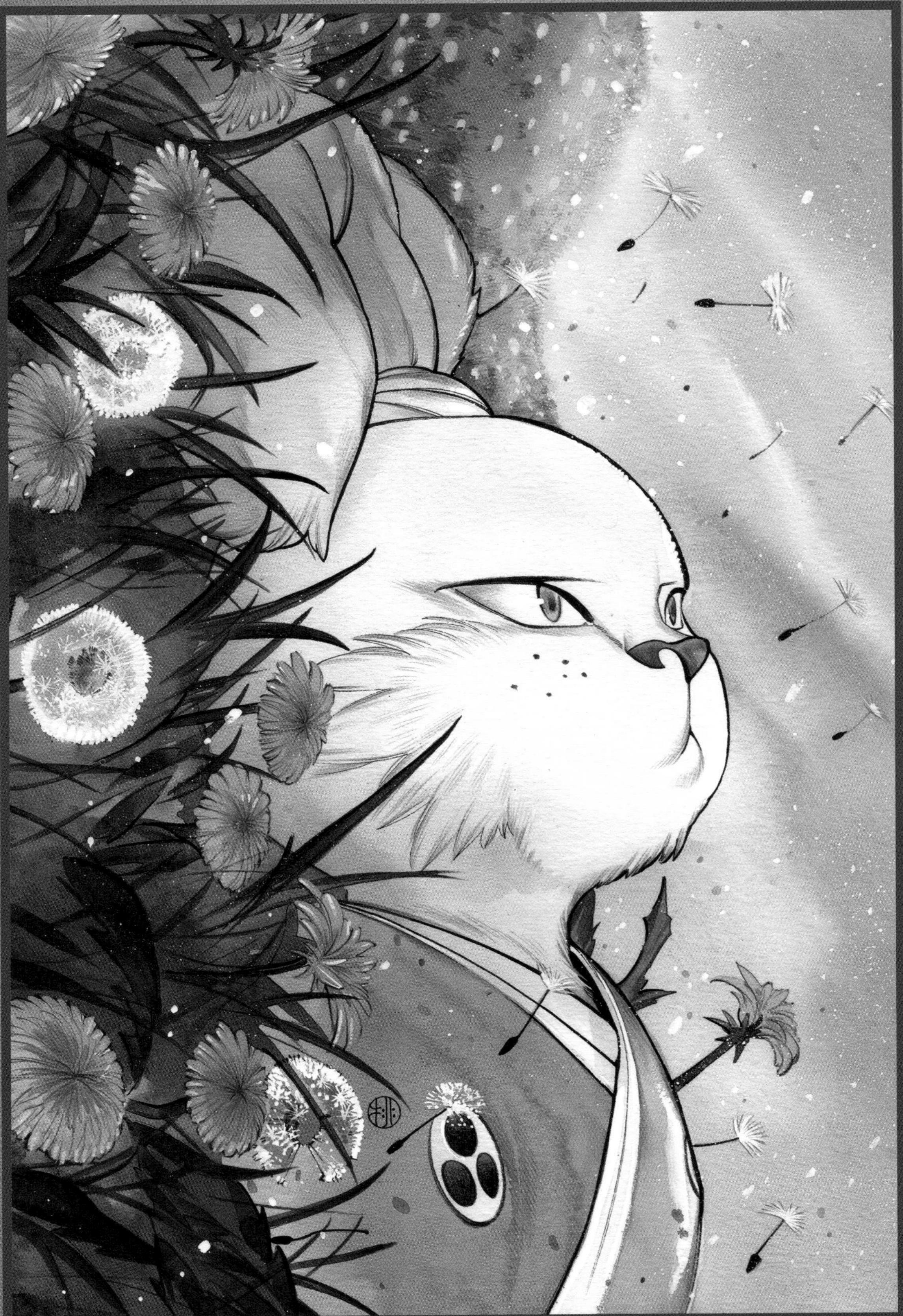

Art by **Peach Momoko**

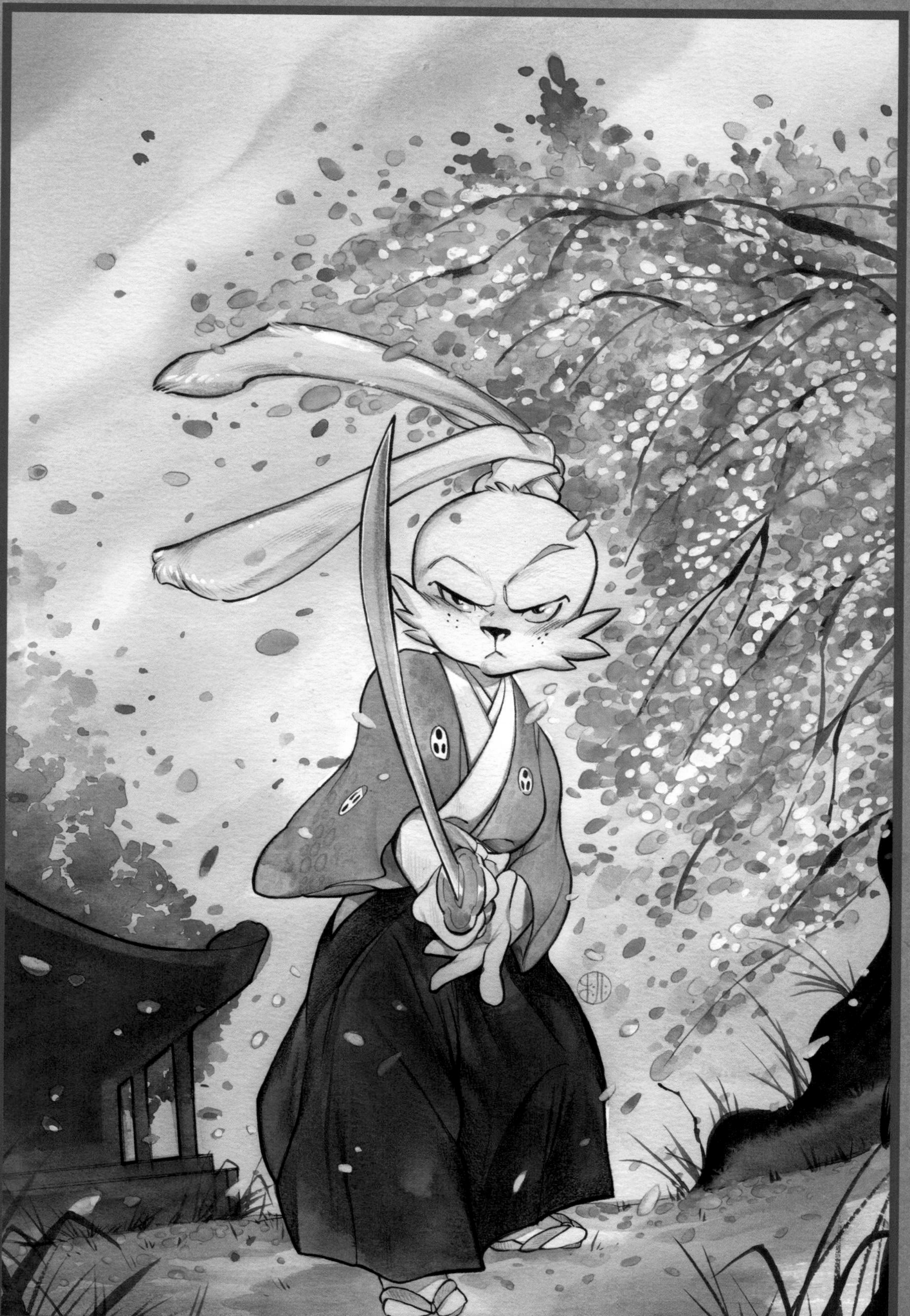

Art by **Peach Momoko**

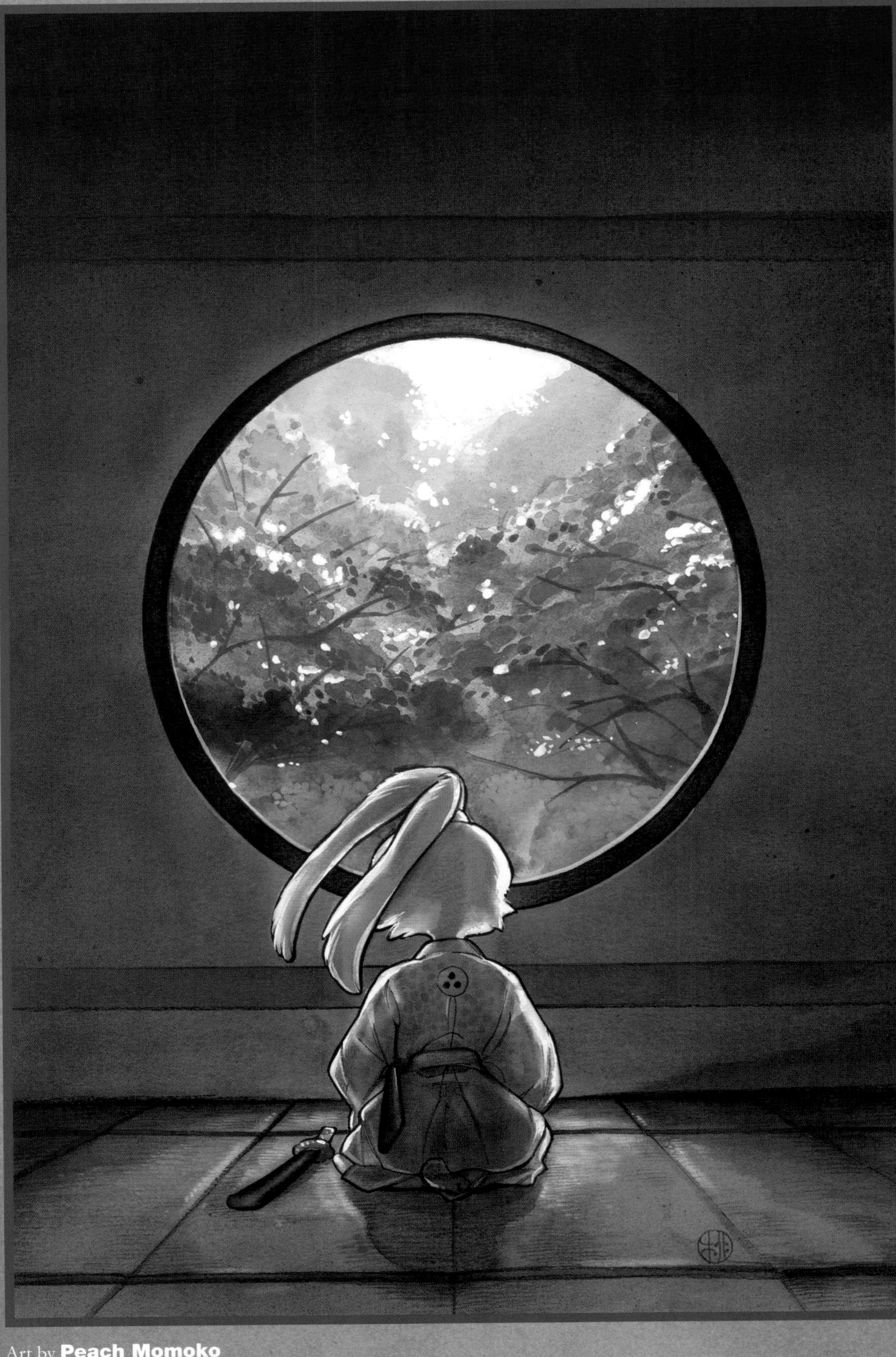

Art by **Peach Momoko**

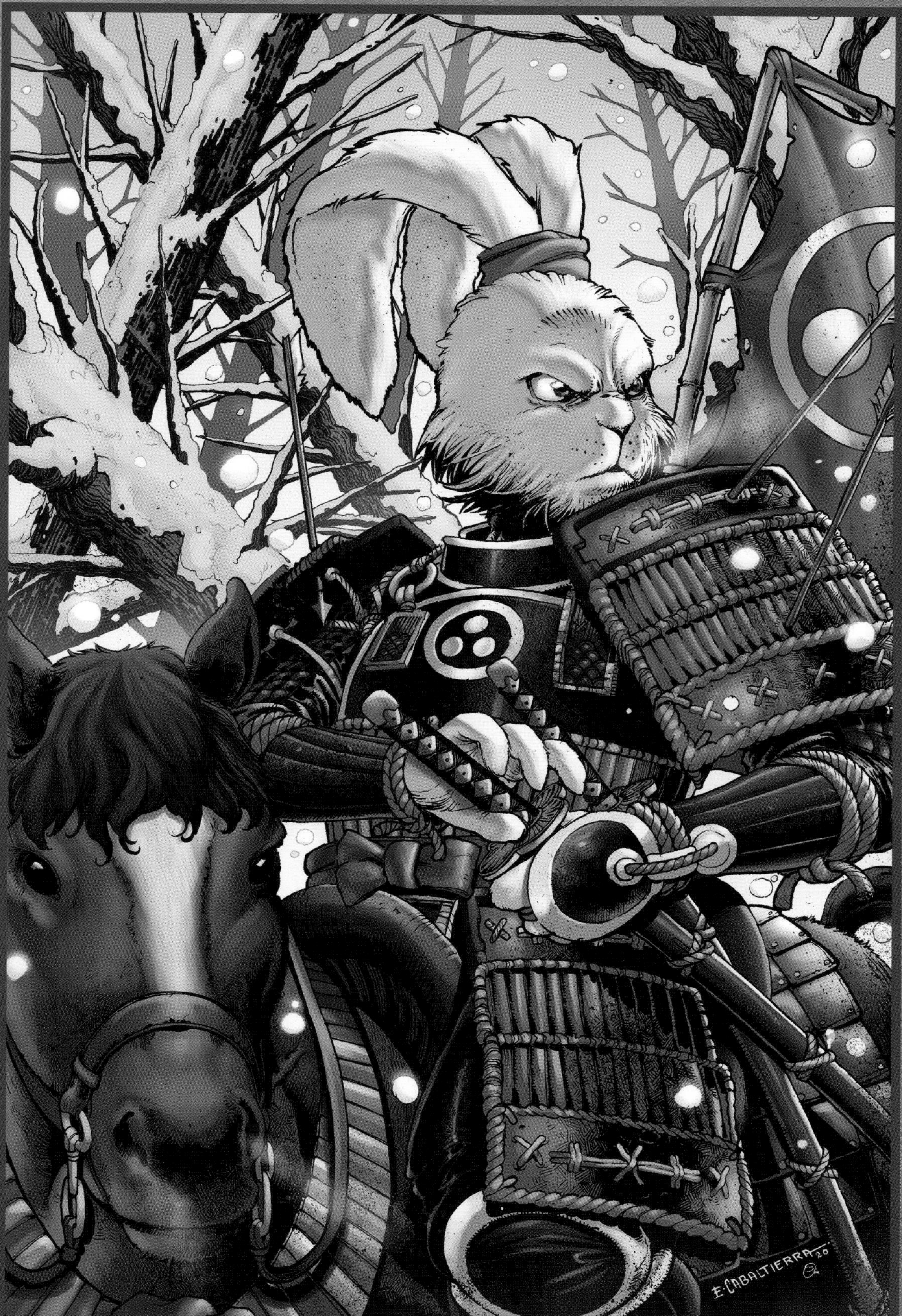
E. CABALTIERRA '20

Art by **Emil Cabaltierra**

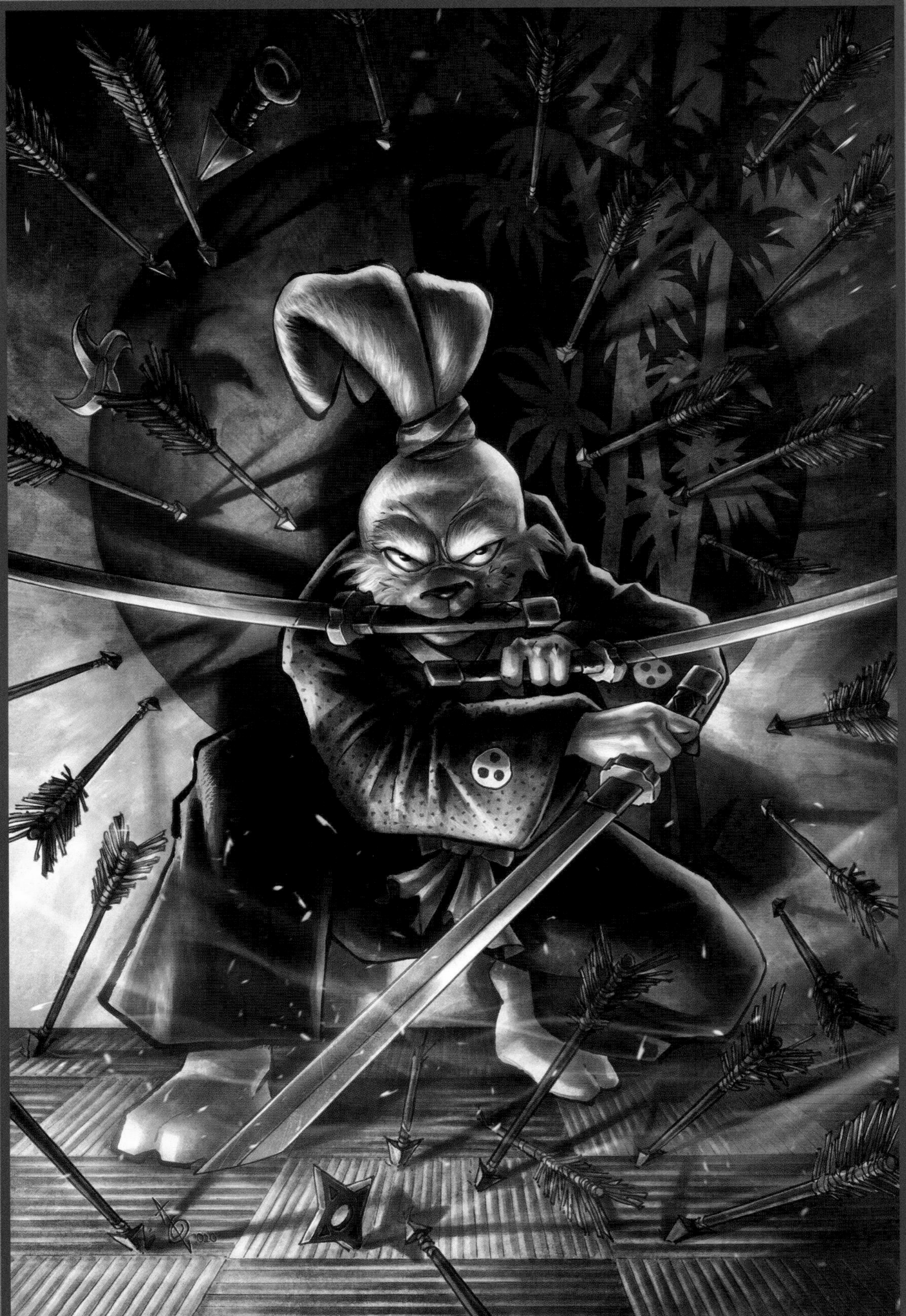

Art by **Alan Quah**

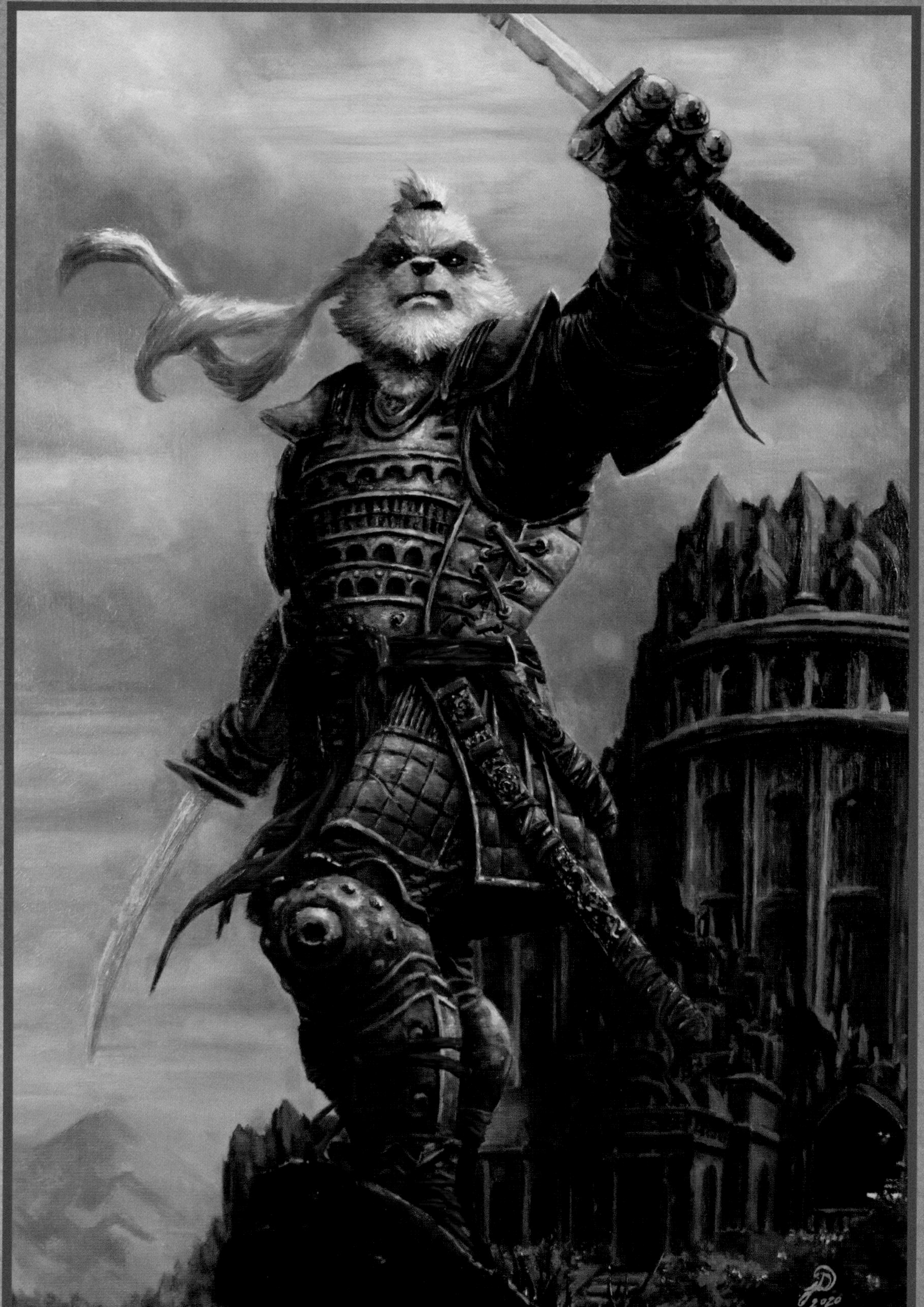

Art by **Johnny Desjardins**

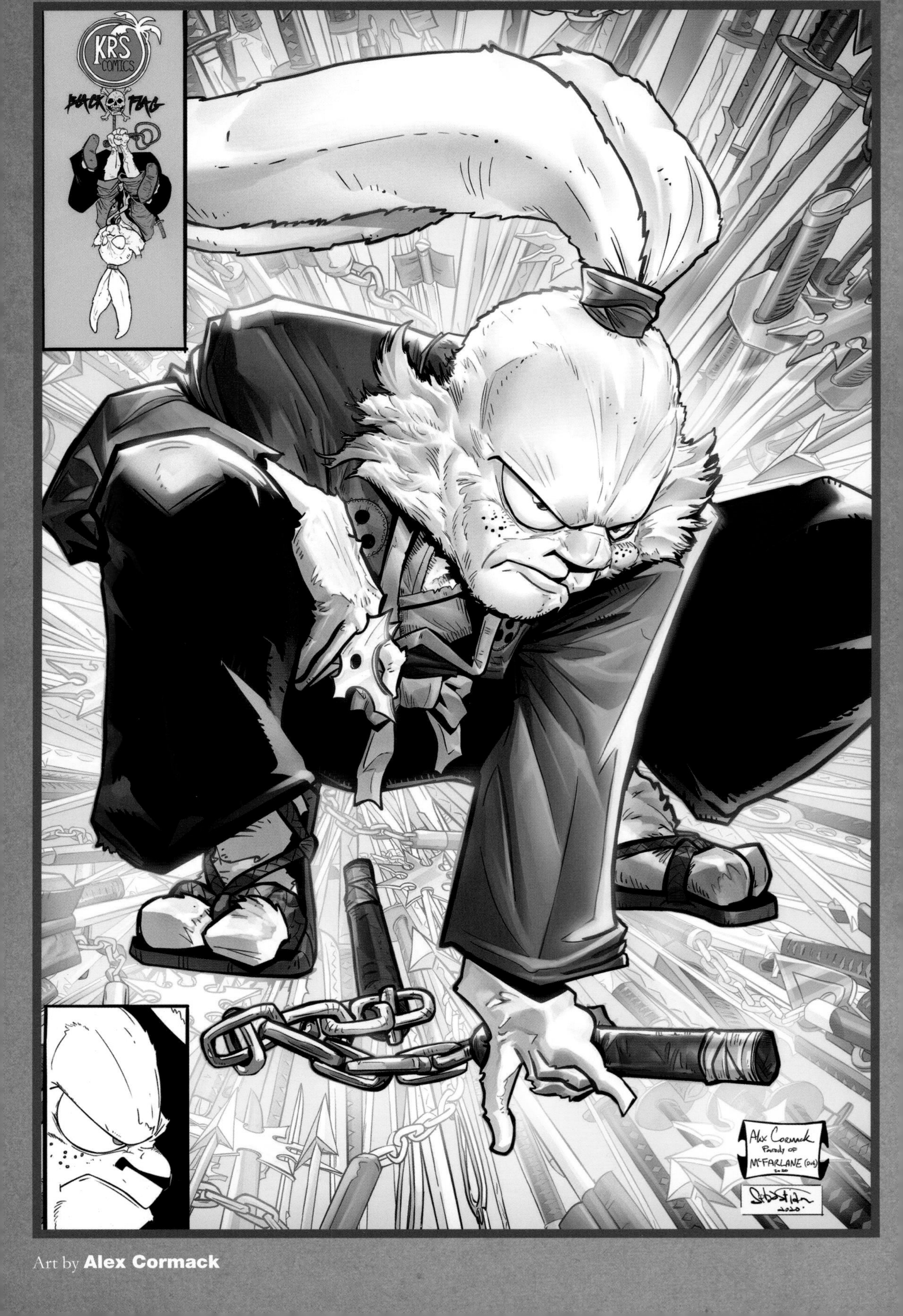
KRS COMICS
BLACK FLAG
Alex Cormack
Parody of
McFARLANE

Art by **Alex Cormack**

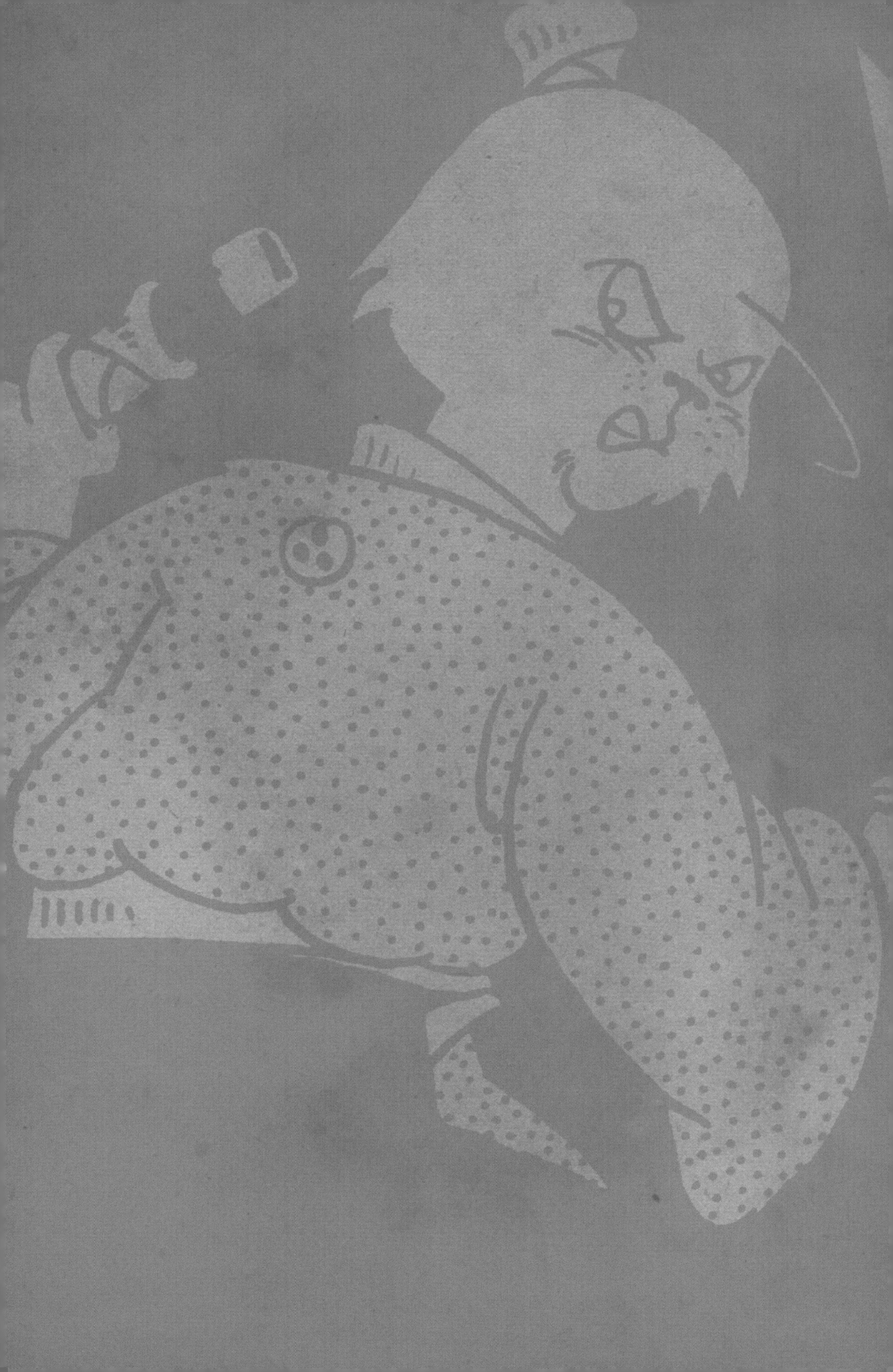

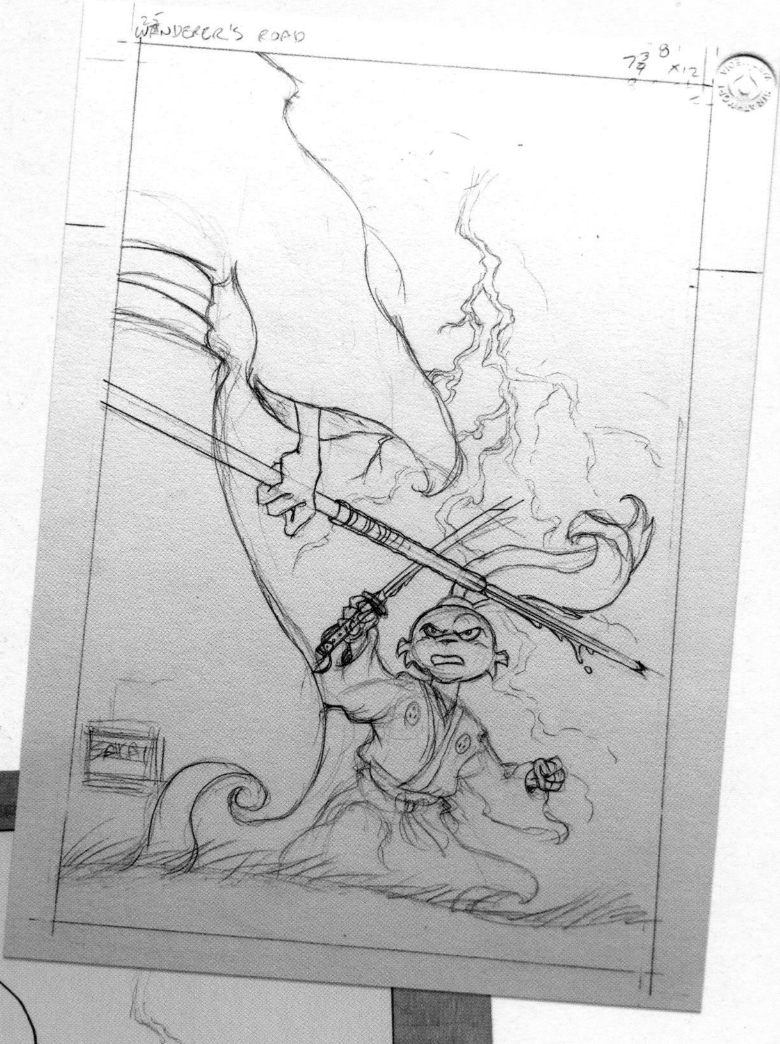
WANDERER'S ROAD
SAKAI

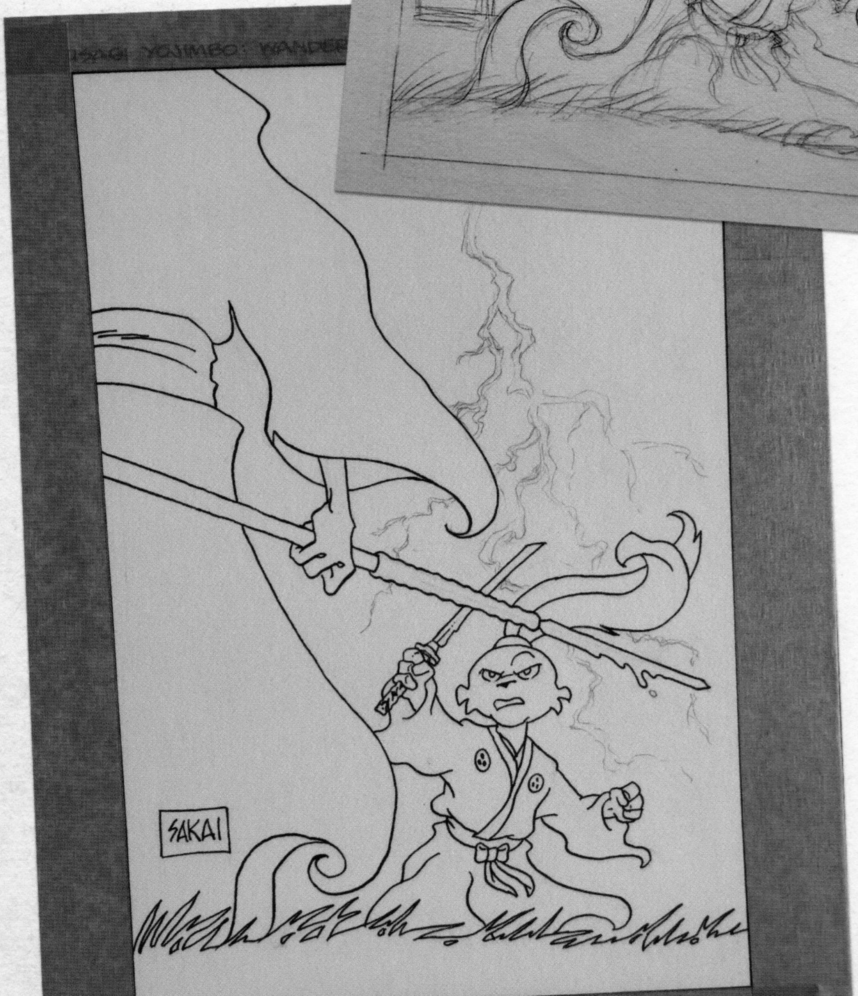
SAKAI

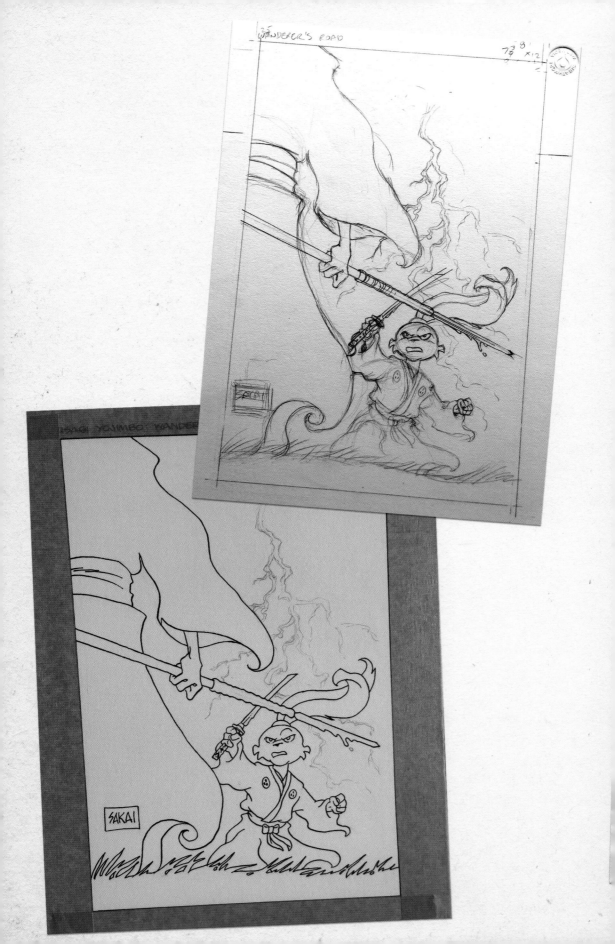

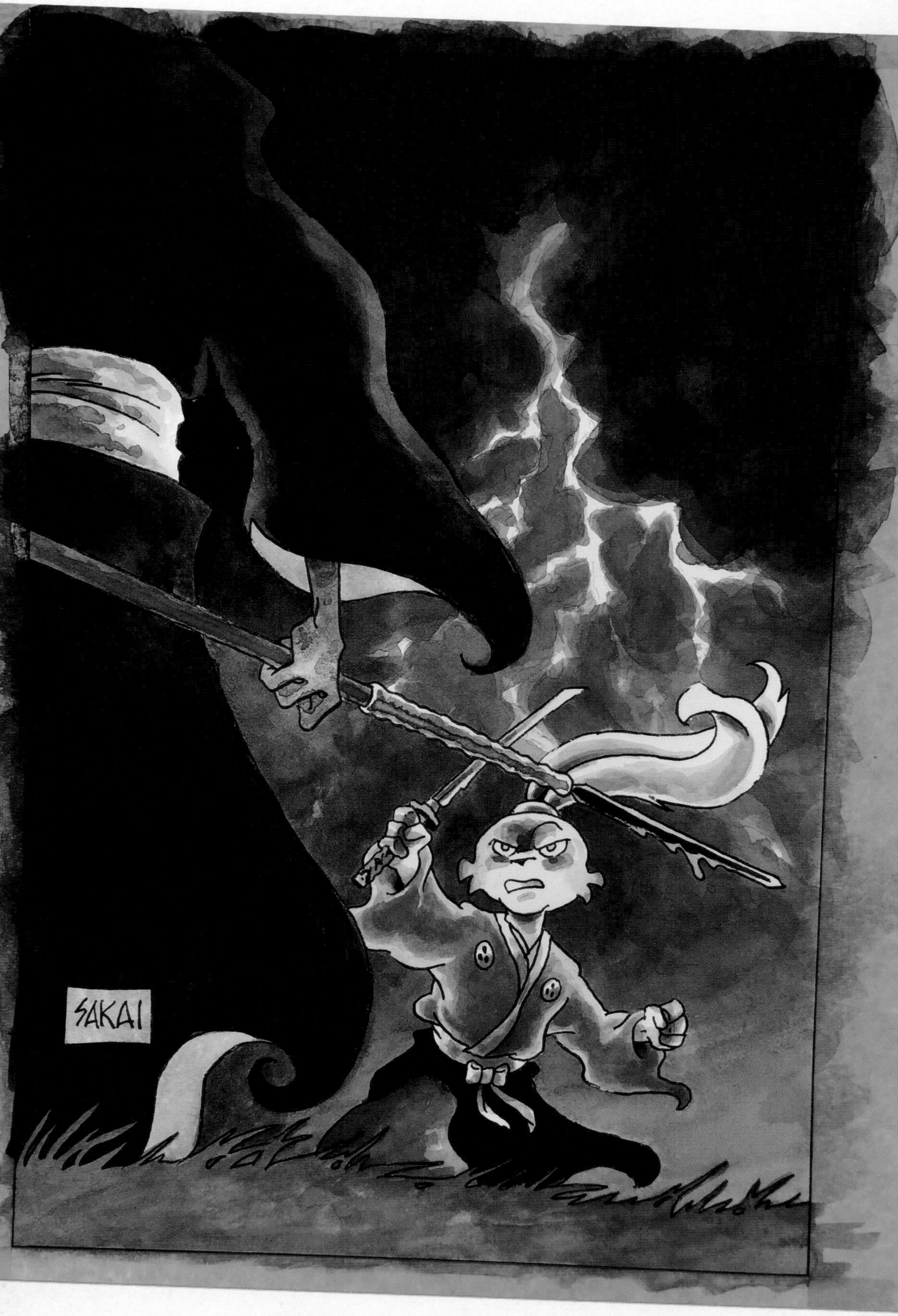
SAKAI

Overlooking Budapest, Hungary   Photo by Emi Fujii Photography

Stan Sakai was born in Kyoto, Japan, grew up in Hawaii, and now lives in California with his wife, Julie. He has two children, Hannah and Matthew, and two stepchildren, Daniel and Emi. Stan received a fine arts degree from the University of Hawaii and furthered his studies at the Art Center College of Design in Pasadena, California.

Stan's creation *Usagi Yojimbo* first appeared in the comic book *Albedo Anthropomorphics* #2 in 1984. Since then, Usagi has been on television as a guest of the Teenage Mutant Ninja Turtles and has been made into toys, seen on clothing, and his stories have been collected in more than three dozen graphic novels and translated into 16 languages.

Stan is the recipient of a Parents' Choice Award, an Inkpot Award, an American Library Association Award, two Harvey Awards, five Spanish Haxturs, eight Will Eisner Awards and two National Cartoonists Society Silver Reubens. In 2011 Stan received the Cultural Ambassador Award from the Japanese American National Museum for spreading Japanese history and culture through his stories. Stan was awarded the inaugural Joe Kubert Excellence in Storytelling Award in 2018 and was inducted into the Will Eisner Hall of Fame in 2020. Stan, in partnership with Gaumont USA, is currently developing an Usagi animated series for Netflix.